T0367429

Wealth and Privilege

by
Jeanette Watts

AuthorHouse™ LLC
1663 Liberty Drive
Bloomington, IN 47403
www.authorhouse.com
Phone: 1-800-839-8640

Published by AuthorHouse 05/13/2014

ISBN: 978-1-4969-0400-3 (sc)
ISBN: 978-1-4969-0399-0 (e)

This book is printed on acid-free paper.

To Adriann, without whom this book never would have been started. And to Leah, without whom this book would never, ever have gotten finished.

Chapter 1

Irritating his mother wasn't specifically Thomas' favorite hobby. She did, however, seem to excel at providing him with opportunities to do so. He didn't have to try very hard. His very existence was an obvious irritant to her. It wasn't because of who he was—Thomas knew perfectly well it was all about what he wasn't.

He wasn't everything his older brother Benjamin had been; quick and clever and charming and talkative. The entire Baldwin family—especially his mother, Eugenia Baldwin, aspiring family matriarch and his most verbal critic—admitted that Thomas was the much more handsome of the two. Then everyone shrugged. Pretty is as pretty does.

Thomas had to agree on that point. He gladly would have traded his bright blue eyes and much-admired dark hair for the ability to know what to say to people.

He stood at the entrance to the ballroom in his parents' house, surrounded by giggling girls all wishing him a happy birthday with their dance cards not-so-subtly dangling from their wrists. Trying to smile, he offered his hand to accept the little pencils and sign the blasted things.

It wasn't that he disliked dancing, really. He just loathed having to go through the process of begging for dances, and inflicting himself on the expectant young ladies who smiled sweetly and patiently at him. He wasn't a bad dancer, but he wasn't a brilliant one, either. And hanging over him like a cloud was that dreaded requirement to make small talk. He could see his mother glaring at him from the chair where she was holding court on the far side of the hallway. He hadn't said anything for a while, as a fresh batch of young women wished him a happy birthday and smiled up at him while he signed his name. With a mental sigh, he searched for something to say.

"So, am I supposed to make more mature small talk, now that I'm a quarter century old?"

He almost flinched as the cluster burst into peals of merriment, entirely out of proportion for such a lame little joke. But no doubt it was very much in keeping with the instructions each girl received from her mama before leaving for his birthday dance. "Now, sweetheart, I know he bores you, but the Baldwin family is worth a fortune. Smile for him. Laugh at his jokes. Make a good impression, for goodness' sake."

He should feel a sense of comradeship; after all, his mother had delivered a similar lecture to him. "Now, Thomas, please try and be charming tonight. No slipping off to avoid signing dance cards. It's your birthday party. Smile. Say something. Make a good impression, for goodness' sake."

But when he looked into their eyes, he never found a kindred spirit looking back. He saw a sort of demure ambition that made him want to run and hide. Unfortunately, that wasn't a viable option. He suffered through each glance, and felt himself slowly suffocating.

It was a typical Baldwin family function. Aunt Eleanor had arrived first, her daughters Ella and Margaret in tow, determined to undermine the placement of every piece of greenery the servants had placed without her express approval. For some mysterious reason, his mother followed behind, drinking in their every word. Thomas' favorite cousin Edgar also came early, since of course he wanted to have a few words with the musicians before the dancing started. He was outgoing, fun-loving, charming (just like Ben had been), and the natural leader for the dancing party games that would replace the regular dancing after midnight supper. He kept such a collection of Germans in his head, he was eagerly invited to parties all over Pittsburgh. Then the rest of the family and friends started arriving. Quiet Uncle Alfred and Aunt Rebecca came with their four stoic sons, Albert, Osric, Stefen, and Peter, followed by a merry party led by Edgar's always gay siblings, Lily and John.

Old friends of the family, the Masons (with their dark-haired daughter Janey), were followed by business friends of his father's, the Burkes and the Thompsons (with their marriage-aged daughters, Meredith and Elsie). Thomas was glad to see the Garretts brought along Grandma Lizzie, who declared years ago that if she were fifty years younger she would've married him. She always claimed the first polka. But they also brought slender nineteen-year-old Rose, whose brown eyes always seemed to be telegraphing to Thomas that she shared her grandmother's intentions—and not for a polka.

The flow of people became a flood. He thought he caught a glimpse of the Mellon boys, which meant his father must be thinking about getting a loan for something. His mother didn't like Mrs. Mellon, so they were only invited to parties when his father specifically wanted something.

Coats and overshoes came off and went away. Ladies disappeared to primp, and returned. Then the ball cards appeared for the ritual torture of single men and ladies, and the mothers of single men, of course.

Eventually, the ball cards were signed, Edgar gave Thomas a significant eyebrow, and the birthday boy led his guests into the ballroom. Thomas danced the first waltz with his mother, the first polka with Grandma Lizzie. Then began the parade of quadrilles, gallops, waltzes and schottisches, which Thomas dutifully danced with every single lady in the room. He found himself wondering if the Prince Charming in the children's fairy tale felt as much like a prize bull as he did.

****

It was blessedly quiet in the conservatory. If Thomas listened very hard, he could hear the orchestra playing a lively polka. His head ached mildly and his ears were ringing from the incessant giggling of his various feminine partners. Just once, he thought, he wanted to hear a woman laugh. A deep, hearty, belly laugh. He'd marry a woman if he could stand the way she laughed.

As if on cue, his mother appeared in the doorway of the conservatory. "Thomas? I told you, no running off to hide tonight. You're the host, for goodness' sake. What are you doing here?"

"I had to get away for a moment, Mother," he said, trying not to sound petulant. "My head aches something awful."

"Don't talk to me about headaches, boy," his mother answered sharply. "You're giving me quite a headache right now."

Thomas managed a small smile. "I'm sure I am, Mother. Please don't lecture me about my manners. I had to sneak out. Otherwise, that flock of girls would have wanted to come along to comfort me, and I wouldn't get any quiet."

Eugenia saw her opportunity. "Well, if you'd only pick one of the crowd that's been hovering around you, then you could have one companion to comfort you."

Thomas groaned. "Mother . . ."

Eugenia interrupted, "Don't 'Mother' me. Honestly, I do wish you could be just a little more like your brother."

Benjamin had been six years older than Thomas, and was seventeen when Southern rebels fired on Fort Sumter. Ben impatiently followed the Rebellion for a year, while both parents loudly and frequently forbade his enlistment. But when the call went out seeking men of good character for a volunteer cavalry, it was more than Ben could stand. His parents were horrified, and livid—for a month, until Ben's unit was called out of drill practice and sent to Antietam. Ben became a hero in the field—and became a hero again when he died someplace in Tennessee called Stone River.

His mother had worshipped her firstborn son thoroughly enough while he was alive. He was completely sanctified in the twelve years and two months since his death. So much so, Thomas had trouble separating the facts of the brother he remembered from the fiction his mother created.

"Benjamin never had so many girls following him around as you have—you've always been the handsome one—but at least he could talk to them. Somehow, he got all the charm, you got all the looks."

Thomas had been hearing that particular phrase as long as he could remember. Sometimes he entertained himself wondering what clever answers Ben would have given their mother. "So you're saying I'm as ugly as an old shoe, eh, Mum? You've wounded me!" Ben could—and did—say anything to their mother, and she would only smile. Thomas could say the same things, and usually got a sigh and a frown instead. He wished he could have been blessed with the charm, instead of the looks.

"I'm not Benjamin, mother. And if he were standing here with us, he'd roll his eyes and say 'Thank goodness for that!'"

His mother wasn't listening. She'd passed on from one of her favorite subjects—comparing him to his brother—to her other favorite subject—complaining about his father. "I told your father that compared to Benjamin you were backward. But he couldn't seem to find any time to help me raise his children. I had to try to bring you up all by myself." Thomas wisely held his tongue.

"You'd think I was a widow, for all the help I got with you. Fathers are supposed to teach their sons how to talk to women. All your father can teach you is business." The combative gleam in her face told Thomas she was coming full circle; he was about to become the recipient of her ire once again. "But you're not trying, Thomas," she frowned at him, a puzzled look twisting her face. "Maybe I've taught you how to treat girls too well. I don't fault you for being a gentleman, but maybe you're being too much of a gentleman."

Thomas was amused by his mother's attempt to analyze his failure to secure one of the pretty brainless creatures who'd been pursuing him all evening. It never occurred to her that he just didn't like them.

"Too much of a gentleman? For most of my life, Mother, you've been drilling it into my head how to be a complete and proper gentleman."

"Well, at least be enough of a cad to let a girl know that you like her!" his mother snapped impatiently. "I don't care how you do it—but it's about time you did! Just what do you suppose will come of the Baldwin name if you don't keep the family going?"

Thomas smiled a small, ironic smile and did some quick mental arithmetic. "Assuming Aunt Mary and Aunt Rebecca don't have any more children? Well, even if I leave no offspring, there are three more Baldwin males in my generation, and two of them are already married. Then Father's cousins Henry and Margaret have two boys. So that's five other Baldwins in the city of Pittsburgh alone. Henry has brothers, too, doesn't he? Relatives in Cincinnati? The Baldwin name is in no danger of extinction. As to our little branch and our little empire, well, after we're all dead the surviving Baldwins can fight over it. Or none of them will want it, and they'll put all of it up on the auction block."

Eugenia stared at her son with confusion while he assessed the family tree, then she dismissed him with a wave of her gloved and bejeweled hand. "Rubbish," she snorted. "Olympic Ironworks up for auction? Bah!" Not willing to be sidetracked, she returned to the subject. "Thomas, there are fifteen girls on that dance floor who would be perfectly suitable additions to the family. What exactly are you looking for?"

Thomas gazed steadily at his mother. "Before I answer that, would you tell me just what makes those particular fifteen suitable?"

His question flustered Eugenia. "Why, they're all pretty girls," she stammered. "Victoria's the heiress to a fortune in coal fields, Yvette's from one of the oldest families in the city."

"So, then the criteria are beauty, money and family? Does it have to be all three, or merely one or two of them? If I find a beautiful serving maid, will that do? What if she's homely, but rich? What if she's beautiful, but dreadfully poor, but she comes from an old family? British royalty, maybe? I understand a lot of the nobility are frightfully poor and looking for rich Americans to support them. Maybe that's what I'm doing wrong. I should be in London, wooing a Duke's daughter. Maybe a Duke's daughter would be the only woman who could compare with my formidable mother." Thomas reached over and picked an orchid, presenting it to her with a kiss on the cheek.

Eugenia looked down at the flower, then up at her son, and sighed. "I don't understand you, Thomas. You're nothing like your brother was. Every time you open your mouth I have trouble believing that you're my flesh and blood."

"Biologically speaking, Mother, you had to be there when I was born . . ."

That was a mistake. The reprimand came sharply back into Eugenia's voice. "I also have trouble believing my son can speak in such a crude manner to any woman—even his own mother," she said sharply. "Is that how you keep young ladies at bay? With that—that frank language?"

"Now, Mother," Thomas reasoned, "do any of those young ladies seem to be at bay? They're all over me like bloodhounds at a foxhunt."

Eugenia frowned at him. "You've never been on a foxhunt."

"I'm using my imagination, Mother."

Eugenia was blessed with very little imagination, and did not care for his. Nor did she take kindly to this latest turn in the conversation. She knew, dimly, that she did not argue logically, and that somehow she did not fare well in any argument with her son. She was, however, enough of a tactician to realize that escaping with the last word was an acceptable substitute for victory. "I'm heading back to the party now. I expect you to follow me. And if you don't choose a fiancée soon, keep in mind that I will choose one for you." With her head high, she turned her back, and left the room in a dignified swish of taffeta.

Threats. Every time he argued with his mother, she ended the argument by delivering a threat, then leaving the room. Angry, he wanted to break something. But the hothouse didn't have much to offer besides plants. Plopping down on a bench, he scooped up a handful of tiny decorative stones and hurled them one by one into the decorative pool in the center of the conservatory. Then he hurled the rest at the wall of palms which obliterated the view of the rest of the greenhouse.

A startled cry of pain arose from the direction of the palms.

In confusion, Thomas stood up and stared at the palm leaves. "Hello?"

A pained but amused voice rose from behind the curtain of fronds. "The breeding of money has always been ugly. I didn't realize it had also become dangerous."

Thomas jumped forward and parted the curtain of palm fronds. Standing in the middle of the path was a woman, dressed in dark red, holding her handkerchief to a small cut on her face. Thomas could see that several of the stones he'd thrown had lodged in the ruffles of her overskirt.

"What are you doing back here?" Thomas stammered.

The woman smiled ruefully. "Mostly demonstrating my boundless talent for bad timing. I was hoping to find someplace quiet for a moment. I had no idea I was merely the advance guard before your tête-à-tête with your mother and—"she surveyed the red spots on her handkerchief with a deep chuckle, "directly in the line of fire."

Thomas flushed. "I'm terribly sorry. I—thought I was alone."

"Of course you did," the woman answered. "Your family throws magnificent parties, and only those of us with no manners whatsoever would dream of sneaking away in the midst of such gaiety. Well," she amended with an amused twist to her mouth, "that is, I'm sure others sneak off, but not alone."

Thomas sighed despondently and sank back onto his bench. "It always comes back to mating rituals, doesn't it?"

"Usually." The woman eyed him with impartial curiosity for a moment, then with a great rustling of red silk settled herself on the bench beside him. "So is it marriage you object to? Or the specifics of mating? I've known people who've objected to one, and I've known people who've objected to the other."

Thomas toyed with a palm frond. "Oh, it's neither one. It's just . . . ." He stopped. He could feel his face getting warm, and suddenly he could not look in her direction.

She laughed; a warm, rich, deep laugh. Thomas remembered his recent longing for a female who didn't giggle. His heart beat a little faster, and he looked studiously at the palm he was now shredding into thin strands.

"No, I don't suppose this conversation falls on your mother's list of acceptable topics to discuss at social gatherings."

Thomas looked up at her in surprise. "How did you know . . ." In looking up, he fell straight into a pair of warm, black eyes that seemed to see all the way through him. Further disarmed, he dropped his gaze again.

"My mother gave me the same list," she answered, laughing again. It was a deep, musical sound. Warm and rich. Thomas listened, transfixed. He'd read descriptions comparing a laugh to honey, but he'd never heard such a sound before. Until now.

Unaware of his musings, she continued, "I've spent delicious and scandalous years since I received that list, trying to break every rule on it."

Thomas stared at his companion, too fascinated to be embarrassed. The face looking back at him was an open, honest face. Her black eyes twinkled with good humor. A full, moist set of lips curved in a confident, almost conspiratorial smile. She was dressed entirely in a deep claret red. Ruby earrings drew the eye downwards to a ruby necklace on a long, graceful neck. Her shapely shoulders were framed by the top edge of her black-shot red taffeta bodice. Her dark hair sparkled from the red-jeweled pins keeping an elaborate pile of curls in place.

She exuded wealth—she also exuded an intelligence and independence that made her seem appealingly exotic to Thomas.

She smiled, and his eyes were drawn to the frank sensuality in her smile. "Well?" she asked, bringing him out of his scrutiny.

"Well what?" he asked, unsure of how to answer her question.

"You've studied me pretty thoroughly. What conclusions have you reached?"

Thomas blushed. She laughed. "Do you always embarrass this easily? She asked.

"No. I mean, yes. I mean," Thomas stammered.

"Well, which is it?"

Thomas returned her direct gaze. "Do you know that you're a very disconcerting person?"

His guest nodded agreeably. "Yes, I am," she admitted easily. "Which is very rude of me, I'm sure."

"Oh, no," Thomas hastened to dissemble. "Certainly not."

Her eyes twinkled. "You're only saying that because it's polite," she pointed out. "But isn't it also rude to contradict people? Besides, it's not honest. Why isn't honesty considered polite?"

At ease again, Thomas laughed. "You win. You're terribly rude. And you've got the oddest way of looking at things."

"There, wasn't that refreshing? You just said exactly what you were thinking, without censoring yourself. I bet it's been a very long while since you've done that."

"Well, I certainly hadn't said a single honest thing all night, until I came in here," he smiled.

His smile faded away, however, at the sound of giggling voices approaching from the hallway.

"It sounds like you're not done with censorship for the night," his guest observed.

Four girls burst loudly into the conservatory. "Thomas!?" They squealed merrily, then their gazes turned hostile as they saw his companion. "Your mama sent us to find you and bring you back to the party."

Stiffly, Thomas stood up, then glanced down inquisitively at the enigmatic woman in red. She smiled up at him.

"Thank you so much for escorting me to your conservatory," she lied calmly. "I'm sure I'll feel better once I've sat for a little while. I do hope your guests will forgive me for imposing on their dance partner." She turned a warm, yet somehow condescending smile upon the gaggle of girls standing in a clutch around Thomas, each maneuvering to be touching him in some fashion.

Her look subdued the noisy little crowd. Collectively, they dropped their eyes. "Of course," "Sorry you're not feeling well," they murmured, gloved fingers still locked onto Thomas.

He looked at the woman on the bench almost imploringly. "If there's nothing else I can do for you, then?"

She smiled up at him, and he detected subtle mischief in her face. "It would be rude of me to keep you from such delightful company," she answered.

He opened his mouth, and closed it again, unable to think of anything he could say in answer. Hoping his eyes could convey his respect, he bowed to her, then allowed the gaggle of young ladies to drag him away.

The foursome could barely contain their curiosity until they were out of earshot.

"What were you doing with her?" Elsie Thompson asked, appalled.

Confounded by the question, Thomas responded, "The lady had a headache. I showed her to the conservatory so she could sit where it was quiet for a while."

"Well, I can imagine why that sort would have a headache," Meredith Burke sniffed. "Reading too many books, I suppose."

"Mama says she's no lady." Janey Mason chimed in.

"What kind of a lady would actually attend that college in Waynesburg?" Rose Garrett sneered. Thomas wondered to himself if it was ladylike to sneer. He assumed not.

"Attend, nothing," Elsie Thompson added importantly. "I hear she has a degree from there!"

"So tell me," he asked as casually as he could, "who is this woman you say is no lady because she has an advanced education?"

"Why, don't you know," Rose Garrett gasped, "That's Regina Waring. *The* Mrs. Waring!"

Regina Waring. *The* Mrs. Waring. Of course Thomas had heard of her. Everyone in Pittsburgh, Allegheny, and, heck, all of Allegheny County had heard of her. Perhaps the entire industrialized world knew who she was. Wife of the eccentric Henry Thorougood

Waring, who swore proudly, frequently, and publicly that no one, man or woman, in any country, could compete with his wife's business acumen.

While fashionable women whispered in their parlors about Regina's unseemly—no, unwomanly—behavior, Regina was welcomed behind the closed doors of board rooms where powerful men made deals—and made money.

Together, the Warings had turned Henry's father's flour mill into an industrial empire. Opportunity was everywhere in Pittsburgh, at least for good businessmen with something to sell. With the country expanding westward and the railroads spreading fast, the demand for goods like flour was large. So were the profits of those who could meet those demands. The Warings had turned those profits back into more flour mills, into an immense glassworks along the southern bank of the Monongahela River, and into copperworks somewhere close to Johnstown, east of Pittsburgh up in the Laurel Highlands.

The Warings, Thomas reflected, made their fortunes the same way his own father had. Except that Thomas' mother made party arrangements, not business deals. Thomas was intrigued, and crushed. He had just fallen in love at first sight with a married woman!

Thomas' mind had run out of useful information about the dashing Regina Waring by the time his escorts finished dragging him back to the ballroom. Absentmindedly, he danced with each of the young ladies in turn, leaving the other three to put their heads together and whisper.

He was dancing the York with little blonde Meredith Burke when he saw his lady in red enter the room.

Upon second viewing, he concluded she was the most stunning creature he'd ever seen. Her dark red contrasted sharply against the pale, gay swirls of color standing in clusters near the door. She was neither the tallest nor the shortest woman present, but she carried herself with an elegance every other female in the room was lacking.

His eyes couldn't memorize the sight of her fast enough. The red dress flattered her figure most emphatically. The long, curved lines of her bodice advertised a tiny waist, calling an enticing invitation to masculine hands. Her skirts tumbled to the floor in playful waves, tucked here, billowing there.

An irritated cough called his mind back onto the dance floor. Meredith was regarding him indignantly, as they silently went through the motions of the dance. Thomas leaped on the opportunity she had just afforded him.

"You're not altogether well tonight!" he exclaimed solicitously. "How thoughtless of me to keep you out here. We can finish this dance another time. Let me fetch you a glass of water for that cough." Deftly, overriding her protests with his own protests of concern, he maneuvered his partner to the corner where the other three had their heads together, and deposited a now very indignant Meredith among her friends. Excusing himself, he dashed to the door.

He reached the stairs, and stopped to watch in fascination as Regina descended. There was an animal grace about the way she moved, a thinly veiled power; and in her smile, a frank sensuality Thomas found mesmerizing.

He wasn't the only one. Thomas was astonished to recognize the members of the small male crowd that stopped her halfway down the stairs; George Westinghouse, the enthusiastic genius inventor of the air brake; Tom Carnegie, who was building a steel mill up the Monongahela in McKeesport for his brother Andrew; Jacob Vandergrift, the local oil and gas king, and, of all people, his own father!

Thomas couldn't believe his ears as the foursome all clamored for a dance. He could pick out his father's voice, claiming, "Since Henry couldn't join us tonight, you'll have to let me fill in for him!"

"Oh, no!" Three other voices rose as one, then broke into separate protestations as each man pressed his claim upon her.

Thomas stood, rooted to the spot, as the group resumed their descent, each of the four gentlemen insisting on the next dance.

Richard Baldwin rarely took any notice of his only surviving son, who was his ever-present shadow in all affairs regarding the running of the family empire. But even he couldn't miss the sight of Thomas, standing bug-eyed at the bottom of the stairs. "Thomas!

Come meet the most beautiful capitalist in America." Richard grinned foolishly at the lady. "Thomas, this is the incomparable Regina Waring. Regina, this is my boy Thomas."

Boy? Thomas was thrown by his father's term. It made him feel backwards—more specifically, like he was twelve years old.

Regina smiled at him, holding out a slender black-gloved hand. "We've met already. Your son had—lost something." Thomas caught that twinkle of humor in her eyes. "Have you found it again?"

"Yes, thank you." Thomas responded, understanding her veiled reference to his temper, and looking desperately for something clever to say. "I believe I have," was all that he could think of.

The two looked at each other for a brief second. Detecting that there was nothing more to say, Richard jumped in, thinking to cover for his awkward son.

"Excuse us, Thomas," he said, taking Regina's hand from where it still lay in Thomas' grasp. "I'm *determined* this lady has the next dance with me!"

Thomas didn't hear the friendly protest of his father's friends. Already, the clever phrases it was too late to say came bubbling to his lips; "Why, yes, it was kind of you to help me look for it." "I couldn't help overhearing that you are missing your usual escort tonight. Rather than start a war among these fine gentlemen, may I fill in?"

He looked after the departing group, and watched as Regina and Tom Carnegie separated from the rest and joined the dancers. Married. The most musical laugh he'd ever heard, and she was already married. His father was already better acquainted with her than he could ever hope to be.

As Thomas stared after his muse in red, a conference was taking place halfway across the ballroom. Frustrated and angry at Thomas' desertion, Meredith Burke sought out her mother.

"Mother! Janey, Rose, Elsie and I found Thomas alone in the conservatory with Mrs. Waring. And now, he won't even look at us! He abandoned me in the middle of a dance so he could stand and *stare* at her. Look!" She pointed him out, halfway up the stairs, gazing dumbfounded into the crowd of dancers. "He's still standing there staring at her!"

Marjorie Burke was a practical woman. She was the daughter of a barge driver and a laundress, who married a man with a little money and a lot of drive. Her ambition in life was to marry all her children off to families wealthier than their own. Meredith was the last of four; she'd succeeded with the first three. Marjorie was not about to lose sight of her goal now. Thomas was the choicest bachelor any of her daughters had gotten close to.

She followed her daughter's gaze to where Thomas stood, rooted to the ground as he watched the ever-dazzling Mrs. Waring whirling about in the arms of a carefully attentive A.W. Mellon. Mrs. Burke's figure stiffened in dislike. It was bad enough that woman turned the heads of every married man in the city. Now she was keeping the unmarried men from paying their attentions to the marriageable girls in the room!

"Well, my girl," Mrs. Burke said briskly to her daughter, "It looks like it's going to take some rather drastic measures if we're going to pry one more victim from Mrs. Waring's lovely fingertips. I have a very melodramatic idea," she said, firmly taking her daughter's arm and guiding her outside on the terrace for a brief lecture in the icy February air, where no one would be apt to overhear them.

Even by Baldwin family standards, the midnight supper was a grand affair. The buffet table supported just about every type of meat that could be roasted, every vegetable available in February, and a large selection of aromatic potato dishes. There were multiple cakes to celebrate the occasion: layered cream cakes, apple-filled spice cakes, and an almond sponge cake—since the cook knew that it was Thomas' favorite. Thomas could guess at the reason for such an exuberant menu—since it was his 25th birthday, he was now of that ideally suitable age for marrying. His mother was celebrating the fact.

Usually the older people left after dinner, as the young people returned to the ballroom for the cotillions. Tonight, for whatever reason, several seemed to linger over coffee, or even come back to the ballroom to watch the party games.

Of all nights to have an audience. Since it was his birthday, he had more than his usual share of favors. His cousin Edgar selected him over and over again, while the ladies also made a special point of singling him out for attention. His lapel sprouted gaily with decorative pins, a paper foolscap ended up on his head, and multiple watch chains dangled from his pockets as he was chosen over and over again to lead the various games in waltz or polka time. He laughed dutifully when it was his turn to catch a waltzing couple with his knees tied together, and tried to present the fans, hair combs, rings and pins his mother had collected for ladies' favors with something like gallantry.

His composure fell to pieces, however, during the shawl game. Two gentlemen held up a massive black shawl, and the ladies put out a hand for the men to select anonymously. When the shawl dropped, Thomas was looking into the merry face of Regina Waring.

"I . . . hello!" Thomas spluttered in surprise.

Regina laughed at his surprise, then held up her arms, waiting for him to collect her waist and begin waltzing. "I'm sorry—I'm disconcerting you again. I hope you're not too disappointed getting stuck with an old married lady. Everyone's having so much fun, I couldn't resist the urge to join in."

Embarrassment battled against a desperate need to redistinguish himself after his poor showing in front of his father. Encouraged by her unexpected appearance, he blurted out honestly, "I'm not disappointed at all! I didn't think I'd *ever* get a chance to dance with you!"

Regina smiled. "The gentlemen have been a little over-zealous in making sure I'm not moping while Henry's gone," she acknowledged.

Thomas was glad people couldn't read minds. He didn't want her to see the black stab of jealousy that shot through him at her reference to her husband. "How long will he be gone?" he asked as casually as he could.

"Hard to say—a few more weeks, at least," she answered. "He's in Chicago negotiating with our suppliers, which can take a while. I have to stay here to oversee some rather drastic changes we're making at the Glassworks."

Thomas was intrigued by the partnership. "Divide and conquer, huh?" He was sorry as soon as he said it. What a stupid thing to say! They're not dividing a united enemy, they're dividing themselves to conquer different 'enemies.'

But Regina just smiled her warm, easy smile. "That's frequently the best strategy. We can be in two places at once. Although sometimes that doesn't seem to be enough!"

Just as the conversation seemed in danger of lagging, the music ended. Thomas offered his arm to escort Regina to a chair, but she requested, "Why don't you deposit me by the door? I'll slip out while he's starting the next game. I snuck in to try and get a dance with you—since I succeeded on the first try, I shall now retire with full honors."

Thomas' heart sprouted wings. She'd joined the game specifically to dance with *him*! He stopped at the door as she requested, bent over her hand and bade her good night, then watched her graceful dark figure slip between the onlookers. He was vaguely aware that he must have a very goofy grin on his face. His eyes drifted, unseeing, over the amused faces of the adults crowded in the door. He was jolted out of his euphoria, however, when he found himself staring into the eyes of Mrs. Burke.

Meredith's mother's eyes were boring into him, with a cold look that was somehow different than the disapproving glare he was used to receiving from his Aunt Eleanor or his mother. Just as he was wondering why on earth she was looking at him like that, his cousin's voice summoned him from across the ballroom. "Thomas! Oh, birthday boy, would you come here, please?" Shrugging off Mrs. Burke's odd expression, he turned to rejoin the games.

Finally it was over. A long train of guests retrieved their cloaks and departed in a parade of carriages, clattering gaily down the cobblestone drive. As the bleary-eyed guests were going home, the musicians were packing up their instruments, and the sleepy-eyed maids were just starting their day, cleaning up after the night's festivities.

Thomas' ears still rang with the giggles of departing young ladies, all insisting on saluting his cheek with chaste birthday kisses.

"We behaved with a sense of decorum when we were that age," Aunt Eleanor observed with her usual disapproving frown.

Thomas was used to her disapproving frowns. "I'm sure you did, Auntie," he answered politely, offering his arm to escort her to her waiting carriage.

Having deposited his disagreeable aunt in her carriage, Thomas had an intense desire to be alone. Glancing swiftly around the foyer, peopled only by the few lingering guests, he slipped down the hallway, unaware that one last pair of feminine eyes observed his escape.

He did not hear the faint whisper of pale blue velvet, but he turned at the sound of the heavy music room door turning on its massive hinges.

"Mr. Baldwin?" He saw Meredith Burke's merry face peeking at him from behind the door. Giggling and blushing furiously, she was beckoning at him with a small gloved finger. "Come *here*," she reached around the door, and tugged on his hand. "I've got a secret to tell you," she giggled, and pulled harder.

Remembering one last time his mother's admonition to "at least try to be sociable," Thomas allowed the petite blonde to pull him into the music room.

Meredith turned in the middle of the room, where the glow from the gas lamp fell directly on her golden curls and bare shoulders, and looked at him with soft blue eyes. "You know, it's impossible to get any time alone with you," she murmured softly.

Thomas freed his hand, and wandered among the instruments until he'd managed to put a harp between himself and the moon-eyed damsel. He'd seen that same look in many a feminine eye tonight. The look of a hunter appraising a deer before raising a weapon to make the kill. "No one gets to spend any real time talking at a party like this," he pointed out, running an idle hand over the harp strings. "Either one is too busy dancing, or too busy trying to talk to everyone. As a host, I have to see to all of my guests. Which means I really get to see none of my guests."

Meredith pouted and circumnavigated the harp in a slithering of sky blue velvet train. "You neglected all your guests tonight," she accused him. "Everybody noticed it. The only person you made time for was that Waring woman. Everyone was scandalized. She's got loads of money, of course. But you're wasting your time on her."

Thomas didn't want to hear Meredith talking about the fascinating friend he'd made among the palms. He could hear the malice in Meredith's voice, which seemed to sully the fineness, the strength of character he'd glimpsed during his conversation with "that Waring woman." He sat down on the piano stool and abruptly changed the subject. "So what's this secret you wanted to tell me?"

The predatory gleam shone more brightly in pale blue eyes as she glided toward him. She giggled again—the sound grated across his ears. "My secret is that I'm in love with you, Thomas. The whispers about you and that woman were more than I could bear, when I love you with all my heart and soul." Deliberately, her hands went to her bodice. She swiftly unfastened the buttons, and parted the edges, displaying her breasts above her ivory corset. "If you want someone to shock you, let me shock you," she whispered, reaching forward and taking his hand.

She placed his hand on her bared breast, round and glowing in the candlelight. "Christmas!" he gasped, standing up and inadvertently knocking over the piano stool. She pressed up against him, both her hands now clutching his hand against her naked breast. He could see the other breast against their hands, pushed high by the confines of her corset, the rosy nipple erect.

Distracted by the sight, he didn't hear the door until the heavy hinge was in full motion. It swung open to reveal three silent spectators—Meredith's parents, and his mother. Thomas froze, his hand still wrapped around one bare breast.

"Well," he heard his mother say, as if she were much farther away than across the room, "it looks like you have been showing some interest in one of your guests, after all."

"It looks like," Meredith's father declared sternly, "we have wedding arrangements to make."

Thomas looked down in time to catch the triumphant look that passed between Meredith and her mother.

Chapter 2

Pittsburgh was an industrial city—compared to New York or Chicago, there were few diversions. A wedding, especially a socially visible one, was bound to generate excitement.

Thomas' engagement to Meredith was announced the week after she cornered him in the music room. The first engagement dinner was two days after that, another engagement party a few days later.

His father, Richard Baldwin, was a pillar of the industrial world of Pittsburgh. Meredith's father Warren was a well-established brewer and liked by most of the city. The celebrations were many and merry, as thc two fathers proudly accepted the luncheons, theatre parties, dinners, and suppers thrown on behalf of the engaged couple.

Thomas was painfully aware that the entire city was gleefully whispering about the sudden engagement, even though none of it was supposed to be public knowledge. To combat the gossip, Meredith and her mother set a wedding date the proper three months forward, and tossed their blonde heads at the friends and family members who warned them, "Marry in May, and rue the day."

"Well, it's silly to try to rush plans just to get married in April, and no one believes in long engagements," Meredith would echo her mother's lofty pragmatism. At least Thomas could appreciate his fiancée's lack of superstition, although he suspected it arose from a lack of imagination, rather than common sense. Although no one could argue that she (or her mother) had found an imaginative way to get engaged in the first place . . . .

The usual wedding trappings were conjured out of the usual resources. As the groom, Thomas had very little to do with the preparations. He merely heard about these matters while accompanying his fiancée to the next scheduled festivity. The groom, he deduced, played a role similar to that of the cake knife. Not an active participant, but rather a necessary prop.

A Worth dress was ordered from Paris, the cakes and flowers from nearby bakeries and florists, the bridesmaids and groomsmen chosen from the local family members. Thomas accepted his cousin Edgar's services when Edgar approached him, offering to stand in Benjamin's place.

"I know you would've wanted Ben with you on your wedding day. Not that a cousin's love can replace a brother's, but I think if he could haunt us, he'd be asking me to look out for you."

Thomas swallowed the lump in his throat. Yes, Ben would have looked out for him. If Ben were alive, he wondered, would he be getting married? If he'd told him what happened in the music room, would he have figured a way out of this mess?

Well, Ben wasn't alive. And Thomas couldn't tell Edgar the whole sordid story. "Thank you, Ed, I *do* need an attendant. I would be most obliged if you would fill in for Ben's duties."

He'd never thought much about his wedding day—but he'd supposed he would be standing at the altar in loving anticipation of the sight of his bride coming up the aisle toward him. Instead, on the fateful day, he was full of loathing. Loathing for the men who looked at him with pity, but offered no way to help him out of his plight. Loathing for the women who ignored him for three months as they fawned over Meredith, her new wardrobe, the wedding presents, and congratulated her on "her catch." And most especially, loathing for Meredith herself. After the tête-à-tête in the music room, their families had raised their collective eyebrows, stared at him, and pronounced, "Of course, they're getting married . . . . as soon as possible."

A curt note from Thomas to Meredith saying simply, "Name the day" was all the proposal he needed to make.

The two had sat side-by-side at each festivity thrown in their honor. Thomas attended dutifully if coolly upon his fiancée; danced with her a very proper one time at each dance they attended, stood beside her as she talked gaily to well-wishers, answered her questions with civility. The rules of etiquette, which dictated an engaged couple not show too much affection toward each other, meant he did not need to demonstrate anything he did not feel. Of course, now that it was woefully too late, society's rules provided a protective barrier; they were never alone together without a proper chaperone in attendance.

Mothers, aunts, and cousins were all happy to provide their services. Thomas suspected that, besides the usual glamour attached to associating with the bride and groom during this "most exciting and romantic" time, there was a more prurient motive. Everyone was watching and listening for some hint, some sign of past impropriety.

Thomas had too little interest in the bridal proceedings to give the family more to gossip about. He was grateful that social conventions provided a constant third party. Meredith would chatter away with that presence, leaving him to withdraw into himself, thinking of more pleasant things.

While the ladies talked of jewelry or styles of hairdressing, Thomas escaped to thoughts of sparkling rubies nestled into black curls piled in waves above a long and graceful neck. As he escorted Meredith and her gaggle of friends to the glovemakers, he saw the elegant motion of a black-gloved hand reaching out to him. As he waited outside the ladies' dressing area before providing escort to dinner, he saw the smooth curve of a red-clad waist, the sheen of embroidery over the curves of her breasts.

He had not seen Regina Waring since that night. His father thought the Warings were tending to their Johnstown affairs. But he managed to find out that they had responded in the affirmative to the wedding invitation, as had the rest of the industrial community of Pittsburgh.

Surreptitiously looking around as the ceremony started, Thomas could not spot Regina in the crowd. The First Presbyterian Church was filled; at least 500 faces watched him as he glumly looked back. Eyes moved from him to the rear entrance in anticipation. He tried, through sheer will, to conjure a shout coming from the back of the church announcing that Meredith had changed her mind, had jumped back into the carriage he had just handed her out of a scant half hour ago, and run away.

The organist began playing the Bridal March from Lohengrin. Well, so much for that idea. Meredith came up the aisle, to the satisfied sigh of the collected audience. Yes, she was certainly the stylish bride; her white Worth dress was covered in flounces and lace, her veil was as long as her train, the inevitable orange blossoms were in her hair. His grandmother's pearl necklace gleamed at her throat.

The thought of a white throat sent Thomas' eyes scanning the crowd again. He wondered what Regina Waring had worn as a bride.

The aisle of First Presbyterian was as long and grand as everything else about the Gothic building. But it was not long enough for Thomas. Meredith and her father reached the altar. Her father placed her hand in Reverend Scovel's, and disappeared to his seat. Reverend Scovel placed Meredith's hand in Thomas,' and the shock of her gloved hand on his jolted him out of the half-dreamlike trance of denial in which he'd been living.

Meredith looked triumphant. Well, why not? She'd just achieved what she wanted. He glanced back over his shoulder. Yes, his mother looked even happier. Actually—happy wasn't a strong enough word for her. She looked ecstatic.

Thomas' eyes roamed once more over the congregation. Why was everyone looking so happy at his upcoming misery?

There was no place to go but forward. Meredith's hand still in his, he turned and faced the altar.

The service was a painfully unhurried affair. He felt the hard floor under his feet. He could hear the pronunciation of each one of the minister's words, but his mind refused to connect them into sentences. His cousin Edgar handed him a ring. It was cold and smooth in his hand. He turned, repeated the words fed to him by the minister. The ring slid onto Meredith's third finger, rested next to the diamond-and-sapphire engagement ring his mother had picked out for him.

Then there was nothing more to be said. Meredith turned her face up to receive his kiss. He looked down into her upturned face, repulsed, feeling the eyes of the world staring at him. He had never kissed her, and he didn't want to, now! Reluctantly, he briefly touched his lips to her face, missing her lips.

He saw a flash of uncertainty cross Meredith's face. It was interrupted when Reverend Scovel delivered the customary kiss to the bride, and she turned away to smile brilliantly at the crowd.

Weddings focus on the bride, he thought as he walked up the aisle with his wife clutching his arm. So much so, that a man can get married to a woman who disgusts him—and not a soul will notice.

****

The receiving line in the Burkes' drawing room was endless. Thomas stood in a haze under the white floral bell next to Meredith, while streams of smiling faces floated past. Numbly, he smiled back, shook hands, said thank you.

Where did all these people come from? He couldn't possibly have this many relatives. But the cousins, aunts, great-uncles kept coming. Then her relatives. Then his mother's friends. There was a brief pause in the proceedings when Meredith was whisked away for some quick emergency repairs to drooping curls. As he waited for her to return, he idly realized that weddings were not for the benefit of the bride or groom (he made a mental snort at that), but for their parents. There were more of his father's business associates here than anyone associated with himself. Once again, he wondered where Regina Waring was.

As if summoned by his thoughts, a gloved hand lightly touched his arm.

"It was all over before you knew what hit you."

Thomas looked right into the compassionate depths of Regina Waring's black eyes.

"Are you all right?" she asked quietly, her voice much softer than the loud, happy clamor of voices, as guests enjoyed the refreshments and company of fellow guests. "Nothing broken, I hope."

Thomas felt his knees tremble. Of course—of all the human beings in the world, this one amazing woman could see through the merriment of the surroundings. This goddess actually took a look at the groom.

He covered her hand with his own as waves of gratitude washed over him. "Thank you for asking," he murmured, while his eyes drank in the sight of her.

She was an angel in emerald green. In a glance, he took in the saucy little hat perched above the piles of dark curls, the emerald dangling from a black velvet ribbon around her throat, the black lace lying against her skin above the emerald brocade of her basque.

As he stood staring at her, another body moved to stand beside her. Thomas looked up into the face of Henry Thorougood Waring. Mr. Waring was at least ten years his wife's senior, a giant that towered above every other male in Westmoreland County. Two sharp but kind eyes were measuring him up with a sympathetic air. He shook Thomas' hand with a grip so strong, it hurt. "So you're the young Baldwin my wife's been telling me about. I'm Henry Waring."

Thomas didn't want to like the man who was married to Regina Waring, but as he looked up into the honest, friendly face, he couldn't help himself. The man was instantly likeable. "Thomas Baldwin. Although I gather you already knew that. Thank you for coming to the wedding. I appreciate having some friends here, which is an odd thing to say, since we've only just met."

"We've both known your father for years, we're just glad to finally get to know you. Regina said you seemed like an old friend the moment she met you."

Regina laughed at her husband's honesty. "Henry," she rebuked him gently, even as Thomas asked, "She said that?"

Henry Waring shrugged unapologetically at his indiscreet admission, and grinned down at his wife. "Regina's never wrong about people." Thomas felt a jealous pang shoot through him at the pride in the older man's eyes, even as he felt terribly pleased to know what the fascinating Mrs. Waring had thought about their first meeting. "She filled me in on a few things. I'm sure we'll be seeing more of you, Baldwin."

Meredith returned to the place of honor, giving Thomas a quizzical look for receiving guests without her. Thomas presented Mr. and Mrs. Henry Waring to her.

"We just slipped in to keep Thomas company while you were away from your post," Regina excused their breach of decorum to the bride. Thomas could swear he heard a touch of irony in Mrs. Waring's voice as she told the bride, "You looked very, very happy up there."

Henry was obviously less given to subtlety than his wife. He perfunctorily kissed the bride on the cheek and observed, "Well, I see you got what you wanted, young lady."

Meredith flushed a little at Henry Waring's greeting, then turned a nervous glance up toward Thomas as the Warings moved away. Finding his eyes on her, she flushed a deeper shade, and smiled at him.

Not returning her smile, he turned a shoulder toward her, and offered his hand to the next guests in line.

As soon as the last person paid his respects, Thomas excused himself with the mission of bringing champagne for the bride and her mother. He had to get away from everyone for a moment—he felt he was going to strangle if he was pleasant to just one more person.

He never made it as far as the balcony. In the middle of the room, he caught sight of his father, deep in conversation with the Warings. Thomas stopped to watch.

From this distance, he had a full view of Regina. Once again, she stood apart by virtue of employing the cleverest dressmaker in town. Or did she simply have the most beautiful figure in town? A black underskirt trimmed in green melted from under a green overskirt trimmed in black. The excess drapery of bustle gracefully emphasized the slender waist. The black lace inserts over the green brocade drew the eye toward the uppermost curve of two lovely breasts—framing the emerald at her throat—which could not match the sparkle of her eyes.

All three faces in the conversation were alight with interest. Thomas was too far away to hear what they were saying. Talking business, no doubt. Only business could put that gleam in his father's eye. He watched with envy as the Warings looked at each other at the same moment, then looked back at his father and nodded together. They moved as a unit, and Thomas speculated that they probably thought as a unit, as well.

It only stood to reason. Naturally, such a perfect woman would make a perfect match.

He could see it was a perfect match. The way Henry's hand rested lightly along his wife's back, the expression on her face when she looked up at him; this pair was a rarity. They not only loved each other, they even *liked* each other.

"Thomas?" Meredith's voice broke his reverie. Some men had all the luck, he thought, turning to look into his wife's and mother-in-law's petulant faces.

"Mother and I are *waiting*," Meredith whined, with a pout that she probably thought was cute.

"So sorry," he said with a slight bow to both the offended parties. "Was just admiring the view. Your florist is really very talented," he dissembled quickly, with an appreciative nod at the rose-and-ivy trimmings which draped from every surface. "I'll be right back with those glasses," he promised, retreating.

The wedding breakfast was endless. He danced attendance upon Meredith, her mother, and his mother, ignored the ribbings of his older married cousins, escorted Meredith into the breakfast room and sat beside her through the meal, stood by while Meredith performed her first domestic duty cutting the wedding cake, then sat through toast after toast offered "to the happy couple."

"Do I look happy? Do I look even vaguely happy?" Thomas thought to himself resentfully. His eyes roamed the hall as the toasts finished and the guests resumed their seats. He looked for other married couples. His parents, Meredith's parents, and a few of their peers sat together at a table just to his right. The men were all talking at once. His father looked interested. His mother looked annoyed. Come to think of it, his mother usually looked annoyed when his father was talking. And his father usually looked bored when his mother was talking.

"Dear God," he realized with a start. "I've been dragged into a marriage just like my parents'!"

When the bride and her attendants retired for the ritual change out of her bridal finery, Thomas knew this was the last moment of solitude he might find for a very long time. Thomas stepped outside to admire the Burkes' rather extensively manicured gardens. Little paths meandered past blooming rose bushes, under charming trellises, and around bubbling fountains.

His heart stopped. There, in a little green nook, Regina Waring was sitting alone!

He turned around as nonchalantly as he could manage. He passed through the house, slipped past anyone who might attempt to stop him, procured a glass of punch and a glass of champagne, and got himself out into the garden without notice. He squinted anxiously when he made it outdoors. Yes! She was still on her bench and alone.

Aware that any number of onlookers could see him either from the house or the gardens, and of course the lady herself wouldn't know what to think if he broke into a run just to dash over and sit with her, he bent his concentration to not spilling the contents of either glass while he paced the endless distance out to her bench.

He had the entire journey to figure out what on earth he was going to say to her when he actually got there. By the time she looked up and saw him coming, he'd had time to rehearse the words over in his head a few times.

"What a recluse you are!" he called out with what he hoped was a charming laugh. "First our conservatory, now the gardens. Are you always in the habit of slipping off alone in the middle of a party?"

"Not usually," she smiled up at him. "Although you wouldn't know it—you've caught me twice now in odd circumstances. If it happens again, we'll both know it's a habit. It was so warm in there,

I just needed to step outside, and then the azaleas were so inviting. I suppose I should have told Mr. Waring where I am."

"I can find him if you'd like," Thomas offered gallantly, although fetching her husband was a deflating idea. "I saw you out here, and it looked like you were in need of one of these two glasses. I wasn't sure which, so I brought one of each."

She looked at his hands quizzically for a second, then laughed that musical laugh which curled his toes. "I'll take the punch, if you please," she removed her gloves and reached out with both hands. He carefully delivered the cup into them. She took a sip, then patted the bench beside her and eyed the champagne glass. "Would you care to join me with the other glass? It seems a shame to carry that all this way for nothing."

Thomas didn't need a second invitation. "Why, thank you."

They sipped in silence for a moment. Then she turned those sharp black eyes on him in that way that made him feel positively naked. "Now, it's one thing for an obscure guest to slip out for some fresh air, but for the guest of honor to be escaping into the garden—talk about being a recluse."

Her eyes were giving him the invitation to talk, if he wanted to, and to merely smile at her teasing, if he didn't want to. Her ability to read him thrilled and unsettled him. So many times in his life, people shook their heads at him. "I don't understand you, Thomas." He never realized that he got a perverse pleasure out of that element of mystery. Now he was sitting beside a woman who understood him, perfectly. And he barely knew her.

"Escaping is a very apt word," he observed laconically.

"I thought it might be."

Thomas sighed. "I've wanted to escape from more than just a party for some time, but I didn't know how," he admitted honestly.

"I seem to recall telling you recently that the mating rituals of money were dangerous," she observed. "Of course I've heard any number of stories about your—engagement. I'm sure the choices you faced were not pretty."

Not pretty! She didn't only have a gift for reading him. She had quite a gift for understatement. He was abashed, yet extremely grateful, for the glimmer of pity he saw in her eyes. "How did you know?" he asked, hoping she knew what he meant.

"Because you've got the most honest face I've ever seen," she answered.

"If you ever want to hear what really happened, I'd be pleased to tell you an honest tale to go with my honest face," he said earnestly.

Her hand fell lightly on his arm. "I would be honored to share your confidence," she answered sincerely.

"In the meantime, pray for me," Thomas asked, certain that the force of Regina's spirit must carry extra power.

Her lashes dipped to her cup as she finished her punch, then flicked back up to meet his eyes. "I don't pray," she answered him with her own honesty. "God can't help you, since there is no God. But I will help you, any way I can."

He stared at her, uncertain what to say. He knew there were quite a few freethinkers among the elite of Pittsburgh, but he'd never known who any of them were. Before his mind could form any coherent questions, Henry Waring appeared on the path.

"I am exceedingly grateful for your good wishes," he said gallantly, standing up and bowing over her hand. "May I return your glass?"

Regina stood up as well. "Yes, thank you." She handed over the cup and gathered her skirts about her. "I'm sorry, Henry, I didn't mean for you to have to come search for me."

"Headache?" Henry Waring asked his wife as he approached with a tender frown.

"I think I was getting one, but Mr. Baldwin seems to have helped. Either his punch or his company seems to have had a curative effect upon me."

The three of them drifted along the path back toward the house. "Thank you for both, Baldwin, nice to know there are true gentlemen in the world who will attend to my wife, when I'm not paying attention," Mr. Waring said, somewhat ruefully.

"It was my great pleasure," Thomas answered with complete honesty.

****

There was no sign of the bride and her bridesmaids yet, which suited Thomas perfectly well. He was in no particular hurry to depart. Lacking most bridegrooms' haste to be alone with his bride at last, he elected to join his father and a few of his colleagues at the bar, accepting their well-meant jibes about the rigors of married life, and listening with quiet interest as they fell back into talking business.

Industry was the first love of each of these men. Work was not a duty. It was a love surpassing all other loves. Anyplace else in the house, one would hear conversations about family, fashion, hobbies. But in the company of these men, there was but one topic of interest. Business.

Pittsburgh was the center of the industrial world. The resources of Pennsylvania—the coal, the oil, the iron, and the people gathered at the three rivers. Iron and steel mills lined the banks. The trains were firstly consumers, and secondly transporters of the plentiful and useful commodities.

People, raw materials and money poured into the city. Builders, bankers, even grocers forged empires as the booming population created a booming need for their services.

The adventurous, the ambitious, and the visionaries were chasing their fortunes through the hills of Western Pennsylvania. And the most successful ones were trading jibes with Thomas over scotches and bourbons.

"He's already acting like a husband," Mayor Blackmore laughed, as he handed Thomas a new glass of scotch, and held up the empty glass for all to see. "He's keeping up with the rest of us!"

Thomas raised his new glass in salute to the assembled gentlemen and downed the contents. His father slapped him on the back.

"What do you think of him, Tom?" he asked the Scotsman beside him. "He takes his scotch not only like a man—but like a Scot!"

Tom Carnegie eyed the bridegroom. "Aye," he answered with jovial skepticism, and a fair imitation of his older brother's thicker accent. "But can he *hold* his Scotch like a Scot? That's something else, entirely."

Thomas took the bottle of Scotch from the bar and presented it to the other Thomas with a flourish, as if offering him a trophy. "Since I was not raised on it as if from mother's milk," he said grandly, "I would not presume to be in the same league as the admirable Mr. Carnegie."

"Well said!" someone at the bar shouted as the others applauded. "These Carnegies always like to be recognized as the best at what they do."

The brother of Andrew Carnegie turned an arch look over his audience. "And with such meager competition as the likes of you, 'tis a wonder we're still at the top of our form."

"None of you will be in any form, whatsoever, if you don't relinquish the groom into the care of his bride," said a voice at the door.

The entire room stood at attention as Lucy Carnegie entered. Her petite figure, looking much less imposing than the blast furnace which had been named in her honor, stood in a posture of reprimand. But she couldn't quite keep the amused smile off her lips.

"But we're not done with him, Lucy," her husband Tom protested with a fond look. "We haven't finished warning him about the wicked ways of womanhood."

"Well, he'll just have to find out for himself," she answered lightly. She approached the bridegroom and laid a gentle but firm hand upon his arm. "Your bride is waiting for you," she told him. "As much as you're enjoying the company of these fine hooligans, 'tis time you took her away."

Deadpan, Thomas reached out with his free hand, took the scotch bottle back from the other Thomas, and took one last swallow, straight from the bottle. The men roared with laughter.

"Don't be so nervous, lad," he heard them call to his retreating back. "I'm sure your father here has told you everything you need to do."

Nervous? Thomas thought as he walked into the ballroom and spotted Meredith. No. Miserable, yes. He stumbled slightly as his hand missed the stair rail. He felt Mrs. Carnegie's hand turn from a decoration upon his arm to a supporting stone. Realizing he hadn't said a word to her, he stopped and turned to her.

"I make a very rude escort," he started.

She corrected him graciously. "You've been preoccupied with more important people than *me*. My husband—and your father—can be corrupting influences. Which goes hard on anyone not used to liquor. But I suspect she'll go easy on you."

Oh, fine. So now Mrs. Carnegie thinks he's worried about how his new wife will react to his getting inebriated on their wedding day. He wanted to correct her illusions, but somehow the liquor wasn't strong enough to make him wipe the understanding smile from the pretty face beside him.

As they crossed the floor together, and Meredith loomed larger and larger in his vision, he realized that no amount no liquor could really help. He was married to the sweet-faced little blonde monster before him. Barrels and barrels of alcohol would not change that.

Meredith stood at the top of the stair, having changed from her bridal dress into the dove-gray "Away Suit." He guessed from her expression that she must have emerged some time ago. She smiled, a trifle stiffly, as they approached. "Thomas? We've been looking for you."

"She sounds like a wife already, doesn't she?" Thomas asked his escort. "Never fear, Meredith, your devoted husband stands before you. I was tucked away with this excellent lady's husband and a few other mutual friends, getting lessons on matters of astounding complexity." The Scotch was bringing a wealth of suppressed sarcasm bubbling to the surface. "The ravishing raven-haired Mrs. Carnegie tells me you'd like to leave? In that case, *dear*," he continued without waiting for her response, "Shall we away? Say your goodbyes, then."

There was a flurry of merriment as guests crowded around to say goodbye. There was a collective squeal as Meredith untied the ribbon of her bouquet, and distributed the now-smaller bouquets among her bridesmaids. Janey Mason screamed happily upon discovering that hers held the hidden gold ring predicting the next bride.

Then Thomas and Meredith were deposited into the gaily-decorated carriage amidst a flurry of rice, slippers, and well wishes.

Then—they were alone.

The silence in the carriage was deafening after the hours of noise. Thomas closed his eyes and leaned his head back, listening to his ears ring. His head didn't quite feel attached to his body—and his body felt amazingly relaxed. Tom Carnegie was right—he certainly didn't have enough experience with hard liquor to drink like he had.

A sigh in his ear warned him the woman beside him wasn't going to vanish simply because he was ignoring her. When a small warm body started to press up against him, he reluctantly opened his eyes.

Meredith was snuggling up to him, eyes full of sweet romantic innocence, while she pushed her body up against his, and inserted her hand inside his.

With an impatient gesture, he removed his hand, and slid away from her on the carriage seat.

"Thomas?" she said inquiringly, smiling in expectation.

"What do you *want*, Meredith?" he asked, wishing he could simply jump out of the carriage and start walking to—anywhere. Wyoming Territory was sounding pretty good. Or maybe Alaska Territory. "What exactly do you want?"

Meredith dropped her eyes prettily with a coquettish flutter. "We're married now, Thomas. I thought most brides and bridegrooms took advantage of their first opportunity to be alone together."

Thomas sat and looked at her for a very long time. He knew she was shallow. He'd learned that she was calculating. But he still had to ascertain the depths of her stupidity. Entrapping him into matrimony was a canny, calculated move. But did she honestly think that forcing him to the altar meant compliance with her fantasy world for the rest of their lives?

Eventually, she got tired of posing with her eyes downcast, and she peeped back up at him.

"Most brides," he pointed out in a voice laced thickly with equal parts Scotch and venom, "do not entrap their bridegrooms with a cheap trick. You know, I'm amazed you managed to get all the pomp and circumstance into the bargain. If there had been any truth to the picture you succeeded in painting for our parents, we would have been married quietly, in disgrace, the day after my birthday party.

"Instead, you managed to manipulate your way into the wedding your little heart was set on. After all your despicable machinations, did you honestly expect us to have normal marital relations?"

Meredith sat looking dumbfoundedly at him, her mouth dangling open, her eyes full of surprise. "But Thomas, we're married now!"

Thomas sighed bitterly. "Failing to inspire a proposal from me out of love, you thought that I'd love you if you found another way to marry me?" Her vacant face flushed a little. "Yes. I see you did. I do wish you'd consulted with me on the matter first. I would have been happy to convince you otherwise."

He turned away to look out the carriage window, but the swift current of his anger turned him back. "Why me? You could have trapped any male with your little display. Of all the bachelors in Allegheny County, why did you have to pick me for your wretched little scheme?"

Unable to look him in the face, Meredith's eyes were glued to the edge of her fan. "I don't know," she shrugged. "Because every girl in town wanted to marry you. You're very handsome, you know."

Thomas watched the glowing street lamps passing outside the carriage window. "So you inflicted yourself upon me 'til death do us part' because everyone else in town thinks I'm good-looking?"

"A girl wants a handsome husband to be proud of," Meredith sounded scandalized that she actually had to explain this to him. "The other girls are going to be so jealous when they see us. You've got the nicest carriage. And your father's so very rich."

"So you married me for my family's money," Thomas stated flatly.

"Well, so many men lost their businesses a couple years ago, there just aren't as many worth marrying as there used to be. Some of the other bachelors in town are still rich, but they're always working. Even when they do come to parties, all they do is talk business. It's so hard to get them to come and dance! At least *you* like to dance."

Feeling the world close in around him, Thomas sighed. The anger drained away, leaving only a terrible dark feeling closing around his soul. He sank back inside himself, where he had spent the last three months, and made no more notice of Meredith for the rest of the drive.

Chapter 3

One wedding custom was solely the groom's responsibility—making the arrangements for the honeymoon. Seeing how this was the only part of the wedding tidal wave which did fall under his control, Thomas chose to exert his power. He refused to go on one.

The wedding trip was always the best-kept secret of the wedding plans. Only the groom, the best man, and sometimes the parents had any idea where the bridal couple were traveling. Thomas merely had to shrug and say "I thought that was supposed to be a secret" when the mothers hinted at him to disclose a destination, and they couldn't say much more on that score. As for the best man, Thomas simply told Edgar that he'd already given George, his coachman, all the instructions they would need and dropped the subject.

"Sorry, old man, I guess I should've asked you earlier," Edgar had answered, obviously disconcerted by Thomas' reticence. Discreet and loyal George, of course, had nothing to say on the subject to anybody. So it would no doubt be more than a little surprising to a bride when, instead of the carriage rolling up to the train station, George pulled up in front of their new house.

Thomas' parents had been more than enthusiastic in helping him select a house suitable for a young couple just setting up housekeeping. His mother dearly wanted to find a place close to theirs on Penn Avenue in Pittsburgh. Out of perversity, Thomas chose a house across the Allegheny River in Pittsburgh's twin city of Allegheny, on one of the less fashionable Mexican War streets, a small section of town north of the park where each street was named after a battle in the Mexican War.

It was a modest three-story house, nestled among the other tidy three-story houses running the length of Buena Vista Street. Furnished with carpets from Bovard, Rose & Co., furniture from Wm. Semple's, new gas fixtures from Tate, Munden and Tate's, and even some new wallpaper from Walter Marshall's, it was still a generous wedding present from both of their families.

Meredith smiled quizzically at Thomas when they'd stopped, and George came around to open the door and help her out. "Where are we, Thomas? Is this where we're staying?"

"You could say that," Thomas answered. "For quite some time, I suppose. I knew you'd be impatient to set up housekeeping, so I didn't plan any trip. This is your new home."

He suffered for her to throw her arms around his neck. "Oh, Thomas! How romantic!" she exclaimed. Releasing him with a piercing, high squeal that made him flinch, she turned around and clasped her hands to her breast to admire their new abode.

Her face fell in disappointment as she took a good look at the building. "This is it?" she exclaimed. A petulant pout pushed out her lower lip. At least this time, it wasn't just an attempt to arrange her face into a cute pose. "Surely our parents could afford better than this!"

"That might be," Thomas answered, his head filling with visions of long years of ingratitude. "Times aren't what they used to be, you know. Our parents were hit hard in '73. This is quite large enough for the two of us. There is still one more level than there are of us. I don't think we're in danger of crowding the servants too much."

As he expected, she missed his meaning—that they'd never have to be on the same level of the building at one time. "Servants? How many have you hired, Thomas? You didn't hire any Irish, did you? They're so dirty. You should have told me. I'm sure Mother could get us some nice, clean Swiss people."

With a sigh, Thomas looked up at his selected abode. He'd liked it for its clean lines, for its charm and simplicity in an age that seemed to get more elaborate with each passing year. He hoped he would continue to appreciate this building. He hated the idea of his cohabitant dulling his appreciation for a good piece of architecture. "Now, did I say I'd engaged any servants? The servants' quarters are mostly empty at the moment. Fill them with Swiss, Bavarians, Prussians, Welsh, or emancipated slaves. Whatever your grasping little heart desires. I only insist that you keep the people I've already employed. Joseph is not only a fabulous butler, he makes a darned good valet. You won't find a better cook than Mrs. Bishop, and George, of course, is indispensable."

Meredith was obviously mollified at the idea of hiring the rest of her servants, and curious to see her new house, even if it wasn't the grand mansion she was hoping for. She took his proffered arm, and he escorted her up the short walk, up the three steps, and across the front porch. Thomas turned the key in the lock, pushed open the beautifully-carved front door, and gave an exaggerated bow. "Your new home, Madame."

Meredith stood and looked at him, waiting. Thomas straightened, and stared back at her. "Yes," he prodded with a poor attempt at patience. "What is it?"

"You're supposed to carry me over the threshold," she reminded him gently.

He laughed abruptly. "Under the circumstances, I should think our roles would be reversed, considering you carried *me* off by force, so to speak. But, if I must." Stepping forward, he bent over and unceremoniously threw her over his shoulder and hauled her inside the door, backside first.

Meredith squealed in protest. "Thomas! How entirely unromantic!"

He closed the door behind them and turned up the gas lamps before depositing her on her feet.

"T'was your idea, not mine," he shrugged.

"There are right ways and wrong ways of picking up a lady," Meredith chastised him with a sniff.

Thomas regarded her coolly. "Since your method of getting yourself married proved you are no lady, Mrs. Baldwin, I didn't see the need to concern myself with that," he said bluntly.

Offended, Meredith drew herself up as tall as she could. "You're only saying such awful things to me because you're drunk. I've been ignoring all your nasty comments because I know it's only the liquor talking. But some things are just too much. I do wish you would have refrained from getting so drunk—on our wedding night."

"You needn't worry, Madame," Thomas vowed. "No amount of liquor is going to solve my problems. After today I'll never touch it again." He handed her the long-handled key for the gas lamps. "I'm sure you'd like to see the rest of your new house. You'll need this to turn on the lights. I shall now remove my drunken self from your presence."

Ignoring Meredith's protests, Thomas replaced his hat on his head and reopened the front door. He needed to go for a walk. A very, very long walk.

****

Thomas mostly found the national craze for copying Queen Victoria's activities tiresome, but there were some fashion trends he relished. Separate bedrooms, for example. Meredith had visited him once to display her "charms." He never wanted to see them again.

He'd spent his wedding night walking the Mexican War Streets, Prospect Park, around the Market Building, up and down Federal Street, down to the river. It seemed odd, looking at the Point where the Ohio River began from a northern vantage point. He came home after he'd assumed his new wife would have retired to her room on the far side of the hall from his own, and left again the next morning before she had emerged.

He'd spent a restless night—perhaps due to the alcohol consumption, or to the unhappy knowledge that he was no longer a free man. He awoke early, his eyes bleary and dry, his mouth feeling as if a small animal had crawled inside during the night and died on his tongue. Some inexplicable impulse drove him out of bed, into his clothes, and tiptoeing down the hallway, out into the quiet morning.

His coachman, George, was already up and busily removing the wedding garlands from the carriage. He made no comment at Thomas' request to take him to Olympus Ironworks. He hitched the horses to the carriage, and soon they were rolling over the Federal Street bridge, across the point, and up along the Monongahela River.

Pittsburgh was called "The Smoky City" for a good reason. Industries lined both banks of all three rivers, spreading out from the central Point where the Monongahela and the Allegheny united to form the Ohio River. Glass, coal, iron, oil, and steel industries lined the banks for easy access to the barges flowing as steadily as the water. Railroads cut their own paths through the hills and across the rivers, carrying in raw materials and people, carrying out everything those people could create from the raw materials.

The sounds of industry hung in the air: train whistles, the hiss of steam from the river traffic, the screech of metals from the rolling mills.

From his carriage window, Thomas could see the smoke coming from Waring Glassworks. It sat across the Monongahela on the Southside, that part of Pittsburgh which only three years ago had been the city of Birmingham. Waring Glassworks was the largest glass factory in the city, buying up the smaller companies as they went out of business during the hardships of the last few years. The central tower rose above its collection of simple, square buildings, a long, elegant spire with a clock large enough to read the time across the river, and made entirely of glass.

It was her doing, Thomas was sure of it. Grace, beauty, and power emanated from it, much as it emanated from the Waring who must have put it there.

He was startled out of his reverie as the coach stopped. They had reached the outer gates of Olympus Ironworks.

There was a great deal of surprise on the faces in the Supervisor's Office when Thomas presented himself. He tried not to smile at the panic he was causing, as secretaries tried surreptitiously to straighten their desks, the message boy stood gravely at attention, and his supervisor, Ian MacDermott, apologized in a great flutter.

"We weren't expecting you, sir, or we would have redd up the place a bit," Ian said, looking around at the piles of papers scattered across every horizontal surface.

Thomas laid a friendly arm across the short Scotsman's shoulders. "It's all right, Ian. I didn't know myself until this morning." He waved a dismissive hand at the clutter of paperwork. "After all, it's your office."

The atmosphere in the room relaxed—a little. "Well, thank you, sir," Ian sighed. "You're an understandin' man, you are. Now, what did you come to see me about this mornin'?"

It was Thomas' turn to sigh. "I don't really know," he admitted candidly.

"So you've just come to look around?"

Thomas smiled. "Something like that."

Ian looked up at him quizzically. "Well then, do you want me to come with you, or shall I leave you to your own devices?"

Thomas hesitated. On the one hand, he really did want thc man's company. The world looked so simple when seen through Ian's eyes. Every day, he came to Olympus. He wrestled the tigers of the business—suppliers, workers, customers. He went home at the end of the day, no doubt to a pretty Scottish lass who had recently moved to America. Ian knew who his friends were, what dangers his demons represented; and most importantly, who *he* was. Thomas wished his own life had as much certainty.

But while he wanted to talk with the man, Thomas also realized that the workday was no time for socializing—and this was not a man appropriate for him to socialize with. Thomas had no business to discuss. This man had business to do. Specifically, keeping his father's foundry running.

"I won't interrupt your work schedule," Thomas demurred. "I know my way around." Feeling a little awkward, he backed toward the door. "I'm here if—you need me."

Thomas left the office employees looking at each other in puzzlement. "I could have sworn," Ian's secretary Jamie spoke up, "he wanted you to go talk to him out there. But then he said he didn't. What's he doing here *today*, anyway? Him just married yesterday an' all."

Ian stared after his employer thoughtfully. "Marriage'll change a man," he observed slowly. "Makes a fellow feel he needs to be more responsible. But that one's always been a serious lad." He shook his head. "Only a crazy workaholic comes to work the day after he's married—and first thing in the morning, to boot. I'll expect Andy Carnegie to be spending his honeymoon inside that monstrosity he's built upriver. But Tom Baldwin?" Ian stared out the dingy little window, where he could see Thomas crossing the yard toward the smelting furnaces. "I don't know what to make of him."

****

Thomas crossed the yard and wandered aimlessly toward the large building across from the supervisor's office.

He was sure his staff would be scratching their heads over him—showing up inexplicably, the day after his wedding, with no real business to conduct. Well, and what of it? The whole city had been talking about him since the day after he and Meredith had been "discovered" in the music room. He was used to notoriety by now.

Fighting the urge to turn around and see if there were curious faces pressed against the office window, he smiled to himself and entered the puddling facility.

The making of iron was an art. Ironworkers were skilled craftsmen with a special knowledge of their trade. They also exhibited a special pride in their work.

"I can't look at a kettle of molten iron and know when it's ready," his father would point out with a hint of awe in his voice. "A good puddler can. That's something." His profound respect for his employees had worked to his advantage only months earlier, when most of the puddlers in the city had gone on strike. Richard Baldwin ran up a beer tab "for his talented artisans" at the tavern across the street one Saturday night, (leaving Sunday for his men to recover from the hangovers) and business went on as usual Monday morning. On his occasional trips into the foundry, Thomas faithfully emulated his father's respectful manner.

As he stepped inside the blistering heat of the foundry, he recognized one of the burly puddlers, standing just inside the doorway. Jan Belusik had been a puddler at Olympus Ironworks for twenty years. Even involved with the innocuous task of lifting a ladle of water to drink, the man's muscular arms rippled with power. It took a lot of strength to stir the molten iron. Many a puddler did not last for twenty years in such a strenuous profession.

"Mister Belusik," Thomas shouted a greeting to the iron-worker over the noise. "How goes it with you? Weren't you training a new helper last time I saw you?"

"Could be, could be," the giant Slovak answered. "I has to train 'em less well, I think. Them last two has their own puddles, now." He pointed down the row of massive boilers. "Jake's down there on Number 40. Me last one, Mick, is on Number 14 now. I've had *this* man a couple of months. Thought he was hopeless at first. Had to throw out a couple of batches the first week, I'd get to explaining so much, the lot would be ruined."

Iron was a finicky metal. It had to "cook" just the right amount before it was poured off into ingots. Too much or too little, the entire batch had to be discarded.

Thomas could see that throwing out two batches in a week's time rankled the craftsman's pride. "We'll get you someone else if you think this man can't do the job. I know you'd prefer to live up to your reputation."

The man nodded once, and moved back toward his boiler and assistant. "Thank you, Mister Baldwin. That's not necessary—yet. But I'll say something when it is."

Thomas watched the man climb back up his ladder, then turned to look down the row of boilers.

Olympus Ironworks had started as a modest little forge on a bend in the river, run by a pair of immigrant brothers from Switzerland. The shrewd pair had seen their golden opportunity when rebels had fired on a fort in South Carolina some fourteen years earlier.

War would be coming. And wars required—iron!

The brothers had approached Thomas' father, who was already a merchant of significant means. Richard had come to Pennsylvania in *his* youth as a butcher. Armed with his father's love of hard work—and a good recipe for sausage—Richard built a little sausage factory. And then a bigger one. And then a full-fledged grocery. It was a more-than-comfortable living, but there was always room for growth, and even greater prosperity.

He, too, saw that war meant opportunity, and scraped together every cent he could find to invest in the little iron company.

The money repaid itself in three months.

Buying out the brothers who had approached him in the first place, Richard poured every profit back into his new-found venture. The success was heady. Through four years of war, the government bought everything that the growing forge could produce. The precious ingots went downriver, where they were cast into the canons which were sent out to the battlefields as fast as they left the Fort Pitt Foundry.

In the ten years since the war ended, the demand for iron only continued to grow. The damages of war needed repairing. Meanwhile, people were using the trains to go westward. Travelers still needed the durable smoked sausages on the journey, while the railroads needed the iron for the rails, nails, and bridges that would get said travelers to their destinations.

The Panic of 1873 had had the potential to put an end to Richard Baldwin's empire. The railroads were hit the hardest, and many a company capsized as the sea of debt came washing back over the financially overextended entrepreneurs of Pittsburgh.

It took some fast thinking and even faster talking to keep business afloat. Friends and family counted for a lot in Pittsburgh.

Richard relied heavily on both. A distant cousin got a contract for supplying iron for bank vaults. The cousin of a cousin still living in upstate New York brought in an order for iron to be turned into pot-bellied stoves. Production at the family sausage plant was increased, the money from which helped keep the bankers at bay. Richard's good relationship with his workers paid off: everyone agreed to accept a cut in salary until hard times were over.

For Baldwin interests, hopefully, those hard times were coming to an end.

Instead of sinking the interests of the ironworks entirely in the railroad industry, as the Carnegies' new facility had done, Thomas had just found a new source for Olympus Iron. Streetcars. People had been pouring into the city for fifty years, and the population spread along the riverbanks, then over the hills. Those hills were full of workers who were employed along the riverbanks; every morning there was a mass migration of people moving riverwards. Every evening the same masses returned to the hillsides.

Sean McAlister had noticed that, and had started a lucrative business running streetcars. His first one ran from the Point in downtown Pittsburgh out to the eastern neighborhoods. Now, he planned to send trolleys to other populous areas beyond the Pittsburgh city limits.

And all this required iron for the streetcars and their rails. Enough iron to keep Olympus Ironworks busy.

Thomas shook his head, realizing he'd been daydreaming. He also realized that his shirt and jacket were now clinging damply to his skin, and his face was coated in sweat from the intense heat. He removed a slightly damp handkerchief from his pocket to wipe his face, and stepped back out the door.

The outside air felt cool against his face. He took a deep breath, glad to get the acrid smell of molten metal out of his nostrils. Iron was certainly a smelly business. Thinking as he was about his upcoming streetcar contract, Thomas turned back toward the supervisor's office.

He stopped in surprise as another carriage rolled to a halt beside his, and Henry Waring alighted.

Thomas stood a moment, blinking stupidly. Recovering himself, he shouted a greeting over the noise. Henry Waring turned around and strode to meet him in the middle of the gravel courtyard.

Thomas had forgotten the bone-crushing strength in the man's handshake. How could he forget so quickly? It was only yesterday when the man nearly broke his hand in the receiving line. But he found himself warming to the man's irrepressible high spirits.

"Just swung by to leave a message with your supervisor," he said in his friendly manner. "Didn't want to disturb you after your wedding, but I have another business venture to discuss with you. Not that the streetcars won't be keeping both of us busy, but Sam Diescher was talking with Regina and I at your reception yesterday. He's got some rather elaborate ideas for putting up more inclines. I pointed out that he should be placing his iron order with the bridegroom who was *throwing* such a grand party. But I thought you'd better make a sales call; when you're up to working again, that is."

Streetcars . . . "another" business venture? Thomas gave the older man a searching look. "Are *you* responsible for getting my name to Sean McAlister on his streetcar venture?"

Henry looked mildly surprised. "Didn't you know? Oh, me and my big mouth. Maybe you weren't supposed to know." He glanced around, as if anyone on the noisy grounds could overhear them. Thomas shrugged, then made a motion with his head, and the two men strolled in the direction of the Monongahela River.

Henry Waring resumed, "Right when you got engaged, my wife told me she'd met you, and that you told her how all the girls were chasing after you, and you wanted nothing to do with the lot of them. She also knows your new in-laws. So she figured out what's what.

"We'd both been feeling mighty bad for you, especially when the look on your face tells the whole story. Anyway, did you know that McAlister is a relation of Gina's mother's cousin? Well, Sean told us he was putting together a contract to make streetcars, and of course he wanted us to do the glass. He hadn't talked to anyone about the iron yet, and since we'd both been thinking about you, we gave him your name."

The two men stopped at the edge of the river. Barges loaded with coke were resting in the Olympus dock, waiting for a crew to unload the precious cargo. The river was high at the moment, and the barge traffic was heavy. Two more tugs pushed loads downriver, no doubt headed for other Pittsburgh plants, while steamboats, rafts, and every other floating vessel one could imagine contributed to the familiar sounds of the river.

"Listen," Henry cleared his throat. "Would you mind not mentioning my little slip to Gina, should you happen to see her? She always laughs at me when I make a gaffe like this." He grinned crookedly. "Tells me she's going to put me back on the next turnip truck."

Thomas laughed, but he was puzzled. "Turnip truck?"

Henry looked at Thomas in mild surprise. "Don't you know the expression? I didn't just fall off a turnip truck." He smiled, and thumped Thomas merrily on the back. "Or, I guess *you* just have."

Thomas laughed, politely, wishing the man knew his own strength; he returned to the subject at hand. "I promise. I'll never say a word about you dropping turnips. And thanks for the business. These last two years have been tough."

"Well, the worst is probably behind us by now," the older man lightly dismissed the crippling depression. "Just you watch; in another year or two, we'll all be riding at the top of the world."

"That's all fine and dandy in a year or two," Thomas thought as he waved at Henry Waring's retreating carriage. "But I don't know how I'm getting through the rest of today."

****

Thomas' carriage wandered the streets along the riverbanks, pacing restlessly from the Monongahela to the Allegheny, to the Ohio, crossing bridges because they were there. He couldn't yet face his new house and its occupant. He couldn't go to his parents' house. He wished he could bring himself to pay a call upon the Warings—but his heart had taken enough for one day.

Getting out of the carriage at a distance from the city, he stood and watched the smoke drifting upwards from the various plants.

Times had been hard for businesses in Pittsburgh. But as long as there continued to be smoke rising over the Smoky City—it wasn't all that bad.

Like most Pittsburghers, Thomas loved his city dearly. Sure, he was an Allegheny City resident now—but eventually, he was certain, it would be annexed to Pittsburgh itself, just like Birmingham.

He admired the new Union Bridge, an elegant covered wooden bridge spanning the Allegheny River between the Point of Pittsburgh and the shore of Allegheny City. It had been built the previous year. The Federal Street Bridge rose behind the Union Bridge, the Sixth Street Bridge behind that just visible through the smoke.

Outsiders had a less romantic attitude about Pittsburgh. Some ten years ago, a writer for the *Atlantic Monthly* referred to the city as "Hell with the lid off." Pittsburghers at the time either laughed, or snorted derisively, and went back to work. Glass, iron and steel were fire-breathing industries, after all.

He was startled out of his reverie by a splatter of rain. A few drops on his head quickly turned into a downpour. He dashed back to the carriage, where George was patiently standing at the carriage door to let him back in. "Where to now, sir?" he asked without a hint of impatience for Thomas' meandering. Thomas' stomach grumbled at him. "I suppose there's no help for it. Let's head home."

George maintained his professional detachment, betraying no relief at the request to turn homewards. "Yes, sir," he answered, and closed the door behind him. As the coach moved forward, Thomas wondered what George must be privately thinking of their long ramble.

The carriage had not rolled more than a few paces when it came to a halt at a curve in the road. Thomas looked out. Ahead of them, a carriage had driven off the narrow road, and the side wheels were rapidly sinking in the mud. It began to tip at an increasingly steep angle. A woman's scream rose above the sound of the rain.

George jumped down and dashed over to help the other driver. Thomas turned up his collar and made another dash through the rain, pulling open the door of the distressed carriage with care, lest he make matters worse.

"Would you care to share *my* carriage?" He shouted over the rumbling of the rain pounding on the carriage roof.

A well-dressed young couple, about his age, looked at him. "I thought I'd give them a hand, but I would be grateful if you could shelter my wife," the young man answered.

"My shoes will be *ruined*, out there" the woman protested, in tones that made Thomas think of his wife. He smiled, involuntarily, as she turned on her husband with a whining pout he recognized. "Charles, I can't go out there. Why don't they just pull us out while we stay here?"

As if in answer, the coach lurched sideways, tipping to an even sharper angle. The woman screamed and clutched at her husband.

"You can go shopping for new shoes while we're here in Pittsburgh," he said to her patiently. "Why don't you go with our benefactor, who's getting soaked while he waits for you."

Thomas was indeed getting soaked to the skin. But he barely noticed it, caught as he was in watching this mirror image of his own marriage.

"I don't *want* to get wet," the woman complained. She peeked outside. Behind Thomas, the road had rapidly turned into a creek. "Look at that. How am I supposed to get over there? Will you carry me across?" She asked plaintively.

"I could," her husband sighed. "And it will take me twice as long and you will get twice as wet. And when I slip in the mud and drop you, you'll be a great deal muddier than if you just run over there on your own, Elizabeth."

The woman sighed. "Fine," she frowned, but she got out of the carriage. Thomas ran alongside her, and opened the door to help her into his carriage. She scrambled in, and he quickly shut the door behind her.

Soaked as he was, he might as well see what he could do to help dislodge the mired carriage. He could see George down with the horses. The young man and the other coachman were behind the carriage, trying to push.

Feeling like a small boy unconcerned with the destructive powers of mud and water, Thomas stepped right into the mud entrapping the rear wheel. "Try lifting, not pushing," he shouted to them over a clap of thunder. "Let the horses do that part of the work." The other two men nodded. All three of them shifted their grip. "Ready? One, two, three!" With a lurch, the carriage rolled back onto the road.

Thomas stepped up out of the ditch. Almost simultaneously, the pouring rain reduced to a drizzle. Wordlessly, the men watched the skies. Within a minute, the rain had stopped completely.

An ironic chuckle arose from the drenched owner of the mired coach. "Well, my friend," he said, offering Thomas his hand, "if our timing could have been slightly different, we'd all be a lot less wet right now.

"I brought my wife with me from Johnstown thinking she'd relax and do some shopping." He jerked his head in the direction of Thomas' carriage. "Did she seem relaxed to you?"

"Well, no," Thomas admitted.

The other man's friendly face turned chilly for a moment. "I'm sure I will be hearing about this for a long time."

Thomas felt a surge of recognition. "It's not your fault it decided to rain just now."

His sympathy was met with a bleak look. "Oh, it is," he answered. "Somehow, it always is."

Thomas was moved to ask on a sudden impulse, "Would you care to stop at our house to clean up a bit? I have a feeling our wives would get along very well."

****

Okay, Thomas admitted to himself several hours later, so he was no judge of character.

Rather than rising graciously to the occasion of unexpected visitors, Meredith regarded the McKays with open hostility when Thomas brought them in the front door, and their coachman deposited their trunk in the foyer.

"*Where* have you been?" she asked Thomas archly. "And *who* are they?"

This was not the way to get the acquaintance off to a good start. Thomas ignored Meredith's confrontational greeting. "Meredith, this is Mr. and Mrs. McKay. I've just dug them out of Carson Street. Would you take Mrs. McKay up to your room and help her clean up a bit? I'm going to take Mr. McKay straight back to the laundry. We're just coated in mud."

"I can see that, Thomas," Meredith replied icily. "Well, come on, then," she said to Elizabeth McKay and started up the stairs.

Meredith's manners obviously did not improve while the men were peeling off muddy layers downstairs. After piling wet and muddy socks, trousers, and other garments in thc laundry tub, the two men dressed in fresh clothes and moved into the parlor. Thomas was pouring hot tea for himself and a brandy for his guest when he heard their wives at the top of the stairs.

Thomas handed Charles his snifter. "Brace yourself," he cautioned his guest.

On cue, Meredith's mouth started before her body entered the room. "Thomas, we're not very well equipped for entertaining," she started, her mouth smiling prettily while her eyes glared at him accusingly. He looked back at her impassively. Realizing her guests would make a much better audience than her husband, Meredith dropped her eyes, then peeped coquettishly up at the McKays. "After all, we were just married yesterday."

"Really?" Both faces lit up with curiosity. Charles gave Thomas a penetrating look. "And today you're helping out strangers on the street." He was obviously well-bred enough not to say anything more about the oddity. "Well, you must let us take you out to celebrate!"

"Honestly, Charles!" Elizabeth chastised her husband. "Why in the world would newlyweds want to go out to celebrate? I would think they'd rather be left alone," she smiled understandingly.

"Why, not at all!" Thomas hastily interceded. "It's not too late for luncheon. Where shall we go?"

****

It was a half-merry, half-sullen party that spent the afternoon in the dining room of the Duquesne Club.

The two men slowly worked their way over a variety of topics. They had a lot in common: Charles McKay was the only son of Robert McKay, whose steel mills formed the backbone of the city of Johnstown, 80 miles away in the Allegheny Mountains.

It took them hours to cover a single topic of conversation, because Elizabeth could hardly let a sentence or two go by without interrupting. Piqued as she was at her husband, she began addressing herself almost entirely to Thomas.

"It was *so nice* of you to offer your carriage to us," she gushed, flashing an indignant look at her husband. "Charles would never have thought to be so chivalrous. I can't believe he hired that coachman in the first place. The man's *Irish*, after all."

Thomas used to think that only New York City snubbed the Irish. He decided he really hated the derogatory emphasis. Weren't the old immigrants and the new immigrants all Americans, now? Between Meredith's and Elizabeth's prejudices, he made up his mind to talk to his father about hiring as many new Irish employees as they could.

Charles' eyes met Thomas' over Elizabeth's speech. "The man had been a coachman in Ireland for years. I didn't think coaches, horses, or roads would be all that different here." He shrugged.

"Shows what *you* know," Elizabeth snapped. She turned a brilliant smile on Thomas. "You wouldn't happen to know any good coachmen willing to live in Johnstown?"

Thomas gave Charles an uncomfortable glance. "I . . . really don't know anyone. Maybe you could ask my driver . . ."

"Oh! What a clever idea!" Elizabeth gushed at him some more. "Who would know more about coachmen than other coachmen? Charles would never think of anything so clever . . ."

And so it went. In contrast to Elizabeth's incessant verbal abuse, Meredith sat quietly, sneaking an angry glance at her husband now and then. She bristled visibly, however, every time Elizabeth praised Thomas.

It was late when Meredith and Thomas deposited the McKays at the Hotel Washington, then took their carriage back across the Union Bridge into Allegheny City. Meredith was silent all the way home, Thomas noticed with detached amusement. Well, hopefully he could convince her to stay that way.

His wish lasted only a minute after they'd closed the front door. Wordlessly, he helped her out of her wrap, took off his own coat, then headed for the stairs.

"Thomas!" Meredith nearly shouted from the bottom of the stairs. He paused on his way up, threw an inquiring glance over his shoulder, and waited.

"You're deliberately ignoring me," she accused him.

Thomas turned to look patiently at his wife. "Did you think I was ignoring you accidentally, Mrs. Baldwin?" In the confused silence that followed his question, he resumed his steps up the stairs. "If you wanted an attentive husband, maybe you should have looked for a willing one."

There was a library at the top of the stairs. Thomas entered, then locked the door behind him. As he did so, he sensed that the heavy wooden door would often be employed by him as a barrier between the Thomas Baldwins.

****

Meredith respected the closing of the heavy library door. However, Thomas was not safe upon leaving his sanctuary. Meredith was almost always posed outside the door whenever he emerged. The window seat at the landing between the first and second floors became her favorite perch, where she could spread her skirts around herself artfully, before becoming absorbed in some activity.

At first she tackled any number of embroidery projects. Antimacassars, handkerchiefs, lounging boots, and smoking caps were all started on his behalf with wifely enthusiasm, then discarded, half-made, in favor of the next project. When she started a spectacle case for him, he felt obliged to point out to her that he didn't wear spectacles. Soon after that, she seemed to abandon the needlework for reading. He noticed she never picked any book so big that she couldn't hold it aloft in one hand, while the other toyed with a curl or tucked daintily under her chin. When poetry failed to impress him she went for prayerbooks, and he'd find her posing in some pretty attitude of devotion. He thought about pointing out that if she read the books she posed with, it might make her a better person. But he wasn't sure he believed it, so he held his tongue.

He would hear her pacing outside his door occasionally. One Sunday afternoon, while he was feeling trapped in his own house and in a particularly irritable mood, he strode to the door and opened it abruptly. "What are you *doing* out here?" he asked.

Her eyes fluttered up to his, and fluttered back down. "I've been such a nitwit today," she laughed gaily, peeping back up at him through her lashes. "I thought I'd go for a walk, but first I forgot my shade, then I nearly went out without my gloves."

Trying to draw attention to her delicate white hands (which had no gloves on them), she laid a hand on his arm. "You've been cooped up in there too long, Thomas," she cooed. "Why don't you come for a walk with me? It would do you so much good."

Thomas removed his arm from under her hand. "No, thank you Madame." Before closing the door, he could not help interjecting as he glanced her over from head to foot, "Before you go out, you might also consider changing into some walking shoes. Those slippers won't hold up very well outside."

"Yes, of course, how sensible of you, Thomas," she started to answer him. With an impatient sigh, Thomas locked his barrier and returned to his desk.

Thomas particularly disliked being seen in public with his wife. It seemed all of Pittsburgh and Allegheny spent the next nine months following their marriage, watching Meredith's waistline for any change.

One would expect their questionable marriage would be followed by a hasty retreat on the part of the bride, when pregnancy's advanced stages forbade public appearances. Six, eight, nine months after the wedding, Meredith was still at Thomas' side, with her waist cinched in tightly by her whalebone stays. As much as he disliked it, Thomas did feel vindicated parading Meredith and her trim waistline in public.

Performances at the Opera House, events at the Exposition Society, the opening of the new Point Bridge over the Monongahela, Art Society lectures, fundraisers for the old West Penn Hospital; Thomas grimly squired his wife to these events, deposited her into his mother's care, and escaped to the company of his father and his cronies.

The Warings were never part of this society. Thomas watched eagerly for them, but after meeting Henry outside of Olympus Iron, the Warings vanished from view.

Eventually, Thomas ventured to inquire after the Warings' absence. He tried to ask casually, self-conscious about the conflicting feelings raging inside—attracted to Regina, liking Henry, and indebted to the both of them for their compassion.

His father looked at him in surprise when he asked. "The Warings? Why, I suppose they're off to New York. Henry's mother might be sick again. Seems to me his father died a couple years ago, and he's an only child." He shrugged. "They disappear once in awhile. But at least *they* always come back," he added with a sniff.

The sniff was for Andrew Carnegie, who ran a stiff competition for the rest of the iron and steel businesses in Pittsburgh—but did it from a hotel suite in New York City.

There was a growing animosity among the Pittsburgh iron and steel families toward the steel magnate. While other industrial owners lived, worked, ate and slept close to the same sooty skies as their employees, Andrew entrusted his brother Tom to oversee his empire. While Andrew put in frequent appearances, he did not live in the town that had elevated him from a lowly bobbin boy in a textile mill to one of the richest men in America.

The Scots-Irish community, of which the Carnegies had been part, had a particularly hard time with Andrew's defection. On the one hand, they were proud that one of their own had achieved such stellar success. "But," they observed, "he got his start because we gave him a chance. Now where is he, to return the favor?"

The next time Thomas saw the infamous Andrew Carnegie in Pittsburgh, he was in the company of Regina Waring.

Thomas was waiting for his father in the bank lobby of Mellon and Sons, so they could meet with A.W. Mellon about some of Olympus Iron's debts. Pacing back and forth, his mind worrying in circles over the rising cost of shipping, it took him awhile to realize that a low, musical feminine voice was calling his name.

He looked around, and there, on the far side of the lobby, was Regina Waring.

"Thomas!" She waved, hurrying across the lobby toward him. As she approached she favored him with an open smile as if he were a dear old childhood friend, instead of the acquaintance of a few hours.

"Regina Waring! Welcome back to Pittsburgh!" Thomas wasn't sure how to address her—even though she'd used the familiar first name, it really wasn't appropriate for him to call her "Regina." But to call her "Mrs. Waring" seemed so very formal. So he fudged and simply used her full name. Then he contented himself with looking her over hungrily from head to foot.

Of course, she'd picked up all the newest fashions while in New York. He stared in fascination as she approached. She wasn't wearing a bustle! Besides allowing a longer train of fabric to tumble out behind her, it provided him with a less obstructed vision of her shapely figure. Each curve from bust to waist to hips was accentuated by the stripe of her dress fabric, and embellished lavishly with buttons, bows, and the inevitable miles of pleated ruffle.

While these feminine decorations always seemed silly affectations on his wife, they were magically transformed into graceful and dignified *objects d'art* upon the person of Regina Waring, who was now smiling up into his face. He felt positively emboldened by her reception, and caught up both her hands in his.

"It's very nice to see you again," he tried to sound at least a little casual, like he was greeting a friend, not a woman he was terribly in love with.

"It really is good to be home," she admitted radiantly. "New York is such a dreadful place. Rudest people in the world, and they're proud of it."

"I've never been to New York," Thomas confided. "I know it's big, and has a large park, and theatres. Lots of people."

"Lots of rude people," she reminded him.

"So what took you to New York in the first place?" he asked curiously. "You disappeared so suddenly."

"Henry's mother had another bad spell," she answered with a sigh. "Ever since his father died, his mother seems to be sick more often than she is well. She'd never been sick in her life, before this. I swear she just wants the attention. But she refuses to come to Pittsburgh. She swears the smoke would kill her. I point out to her that it doesn't seem to have that effect on the rest of us—well, I'm not going to repeat the whole argument. It gets pretty colorful at times."

Thomas smiled sympathetically. "Isn't family wonderful?"

Something in Regina's expression sharpened. Her eyes looking keenly into his, she asked, "And how is your family?"

"My father is here. I'm sure he'll want to say hello."

"Of course. And your mother?"

"Starting to ask when the grandchildren are going to come," he replied bluntly, then blushed at his own artless reply. His eyes flashed guiltily at the bodies brushing past, but no one seemed interested in their conversation.

Regina smiled up at him with understanding. "Well, under the circumstances, it's to be expected. So how is your wife?"

Thomas opened his mouth, but this time he restrained himself from an honest answer. He closed it again, and looked at her helplessly, at a complete loss. He didn't know what to say. "She's in perfect health, thank you," he ventured lamely.

"And married life is treating you tolerably well?"

"Tolerably? Perhaps." Thomas wondered if she remembered their conversation in the garden after his wedding. He hoped she was still interested in being his confidante. He had the perfect opening. He cast his mind about, looking for the courage to bring up the subject.

As if reading his thoughts, she broached the subject, herself. "It seems to me you once promised to tell me the story about your . . . proposal."

She remembered! The thrill that went through his body tingled all the way to the heels of his feet and raised goose bumps down the backs of his arms.

"Yes, I did," he admitted in a happy daze. "And I'm prepared to fulfill that promise whenever you command."

"A man who takes orders. I like that," she observed. There was something provocative in her smile that Thomas didn't dare define. Uncomfortably aware of the flush creeping back into his face, he couldn't quite meet her eyes. "Name the day, dear lady, when I can take you for luncheon and bare my soul." He tried to keep up a gallant front, but his voice sounded awkward to his own ears.

"I'd forgotten that you embarrass easily." Her voice had dropped to a gentle murmur. "Forgive me. You're not at all like your father."

"I know," he admitted, downcast. "I've always wished I could be charming, like he is."

"You're perfectly charming as you are," she contradicted him staunchly. "You don't have to be loud and gabby to be charming."

This surprised him into meeting her gaze. She smiled into his eyes. "And we'll have a perfectly charming lunch tomorrow?"

"Yes," he answered breathlessly. "Yes, we will!"

"Good," she smiled at him, then turned her smile over her shoulder. Thomas looked over, expecting to see Henry's tall form, and was surprised speechless when Andrew Carnegie appeared from out of the sea of bodies and put a hand on Regina's elbow. "Hello, m'dear. Ready to go? I'm sorry I've gone and kept you waiting again."

"I'm quite used to it." Regina dismissed the apology with a fond smile. "Have you met Mr. Thomas Baldwin, from Olympus Iron? Mr. Baldwin, this is Andrew Carnegie from Carnegie Brothers."

"I think we've met. Mr. Baldwin, how are you?" He held out a hand to Thomas.

With a start, Thomas realized that he was still grasping both of Regina's hands. They'd been standing there, surrounded by the moving throng, holding their entire conversation with her hands caught in his. He dropped them hastily, and reached out to meet the older man's extended hand.

"I'm great. Business has been wonderful, thanks to this fine lady throwing a few contracts our way."

"Oh?" Both Mr. Carnegie and Regina voiced the same question at the same time. Thomas realized belatedly that he'd promised Henry not to reveal the source of his new business. He quickly looked at Regina, glad that Henry wasn't here to catch him in the act of betraying his secret.

"You should know you can't keep a secret in Pittsburgh," he mock-scolded her. "Your act of kindness was bound to slip out, eventually. I'm wise to you now."

Regina looked at him suspiciously. "How did you find out?"

"I have my sources." Thomas was pleased with the sense of mystery he managed to put in his voice. "Your mistake was in making a secret of it. Then everybody wanted to get in on it. If you would have insisted people should tell me, everyone would have forgotten. Or resented the favor, and purposely neglected to say anything. People are perverse creatures."

Regina smiled. "You're right. I should have known better. The secret was more fun than the information." The suspicion in her eyes melted away. "I'm glad you know. Now I can tell you that my cousin has been sending me glowing reports about you."

Thomas grinned, pleased. However, before she could repeat the praises poised on her lips, Richard Baldwin burst upon them. "Regina! You beautiful thing! So you're the one who's been hiding this luscious creature from us, eh Andy?"

"Absolutely," Mr. Carnegie responded as they shook hands. "Henry put her in MY custody. Don't you forget it, Richard."

Once again, Thomas felt himself fading into the background in the presence of his outgoing parent. He changed from participant to observer as his father and Andrew Carnegie exchanged witticisms and laughed heartily.

He wanted to partake in these glib exchanges. Rather badly. It was this ability to talk easily, to walk into a room full of strangers and walk out of a room full of friends, which was the secret to the success of many of Pittsburgh's elite. But somehow, Thomas had inherited the blarney gene from neither of his loquacious parents.

He sensed Regina's sharp eyes upon him. Realizing how glum his expression must be, he forced a smile and tried to pay more attention to the clever exchanges.

"We really must be going," Regina was saying. "But, Thomas, I'll expect you at Waring Glassworks tomorrow, about 11:30?"

"Yes, of course," Thomas answered.

Richard looked at his son in surprise. "What are you and this lovely lady doing at Waring Glassworks?"

Regina answered for Thomas. "Well, honestly, Richard, do you think you're the only Baldwin in the family who conducts business?"

"No, of course not," Richard responded, looking a little flustered. "Do you need me along?"

There was an unmistakable plea in his father's voice. It was *his* empire. He loved the wheeling and dealing, and was as painfully aware as his son that Thomas was not the dealmaker in the family. Everyone could hear his thoughts; "What if his son botched it up?"

"Nonsense," Regina answered again for Thomas briskly, smoothing her gloves with a dismissive air. "I want to know his thoughts on a couple little matters. I can't get a fresh opinion from you. Everyone in Pittsburgh has already heard your opinion on every subject known to man."

She grinned wickedly and flirtatiously up at the elder Baldwin as she finished. Thomas watched in fascination at the effortless way she pulled his father's strings.

"I'm being pushy, aren't I?" He asked, and laughed when she nodded. "Well, of course you can borrow my boy if you need him. Just go easy on him. He's never dealt with the likes of you, before!"

"I'll be gentle," she promised with a wink, then she tipped her head in farewell and turned away. On Andy's arm she moved gracefully out the massive doors and into the gray July streets.

Chapter 4

Thomas realized that, as much as he admired his father, he resented him, too.

Rather than ride the streetcar back home, his father asked Thomas to drive him in the carriage. Ostensibly it was so Thomas could have afternoon tea with his mother, but the real motive was immediately apparent; his father wanted to lecture him about Regina. During the entire drive back to his parents' home, it never once occurred to his father to ask why he and Regina were meeting.

"Now, I don't know what she wants, but don't let yourself go too far gone over that beautiful face of hers," his father warned. "Believe me, when it comes to negotiating, she's a demon. Okay, a demoness. Don't sign anything until you've had a chance to let me read it. Then I'll have my cousin Henry read it. To think my uncle didn't want Henry going into the legal profession. I don't see how anyone can own a business without a lawyer in the family."

Thomas' attention wandered. Regina surely did look good in that outfit she'd been wearing. The black trim suited Regina's expressive black eyes.

He forced himself to listen to his father again, still busily absorbed in the sound of his own voice. ". . . so if my cousin Michael won't hire a chemist, why should we? It's an unnecessary extravagance, when we're struggling these days, as it is."

Once again, Thomas' ears had trouble keeping track of his father's rambling voice. He had seen the man almost every day of his life. He realized his father had no other confidante; he couldn't very well talk to his wife, and his peers were more often rivals than intimates. But Thomas wished his father had a better memory for what monologues he had already delivered to his son's overworked ears. Michael Baldwin had been considering hiring a chemist for his foundry in Connellsville for years, and Richard had been coming to the same conclusion about not doing the same for even longer. He'd been hearing the "thank-goodness-we-have-a-lawyer-in-the-family" speech for as long as he could remember.

Occasionally there was a new idea to be discovered among the bombardment of old ones. But Thomas had long since learned that if he missed it on the first telling, there would be plenty of repeats. He'd hear it eventually.

If it wasn't so sad, it would be rather amusing, he pondered. This was a man he should be close to. For nearly ten years, he stood next to his father at every important event for Olympus Ironworks. He signed his name on every agreement (somewhere below his father's impressive but illegible scrawl). He accompanied his father, as he did today, to any number of meetings. Yet, the hours together did not create a bond between father and son. Although he knew every aspect of his father's business intimately, Thomas felt only isolation in his father's company. All the more so because his father never seemed to notice.

At least his mother expected an answer out of him once in a while. If he gave the occasional "Mm hms" for too long, she gave him an irritated look, and asked sharply, "Will you pay attention, Thomas? Honestly! I don't know where you come from." Most of the time, Thomas resisted the urge to explain it to her. Occasionally, like at his disastrous birthday party, he gave in to the temptation—even though he knew he'd only confuse and anger her.

He sighed. So, they were a disappointment to each other. Thomas knew his wish for more sensitive parents was as futile as his parents' wish for more outgoing offspring.

He came back to his father's conversation with a start. He hadn't realized his father had perceived his sigh; but the elder Baldwin was patting his arm in an awkward but affectionate manner. "Yeah, I know," his father was saying. "It seems like we barely get the chance to say what's on our minds anymore, now that you're married and out on your own." Thomas looked out the carriage window. Indeed, the horses were clattering up the cobblestones toward the imposing structure on Penn Avenue. "Your mother was just saying how big and empty the house is now. She misses you."

Thomas noticed the jump in his father's logic. He didn't say *he* missed having his son at home: Thomas was just to infer that part. It was interesting, how his father could talk so easily about any other subject. He could flirt like a wild young man in the presence of Regina Waring, but Thomas could not call to memory a single time his father actually said he loved either him *or* his mother. Amazing how a man who displayed so little reserve in his public life used so much reserve in his private life.

Suddenly, Thomas didn't feel like having tea with his parents. If it weren't for the prospect of Meredith waiting for him at home, he would have loved to drive away saying, "No thanks, Father, maybe another time." But the impulse for mischief was stopped by the ever-present instinct to avoid the Tartarus on Buena Vista Street. So, he stepped dutifully onto the carriage block and looked up at his childhood home.

The house was a monument to the money that a man could make in the duration of one war. It had been a defining point in his father's life; he wasn't merely a well-to-do butcher anymore. He was a millionaire.

So, he'd built a castle. The Baldwin residence was a towering structure, turrets at all four corners, two stone lions protecting its ornate oak doors. The long, narrow windows looked for all the world like gun ports for cannon. The edifice commanded respect as it looked haughtily down at the passers-by on Penn Avenue.

"Thomas! Stop *standing* there and come in!" His mother's voice commanded from the open front door. He smiled to himself at the motherly admonition, and mounted the smooth stone steps. His father had already dispensed with his hat and cane and was heading down the wide marble hallway.

"Hello, Mother." He dropped a kiss on her frowning forehead. "Nice to see you, too."

"Well, of course it's nice to see you," his mother sighed with familiar exasperation. "You're the one standing outside rather than coming in to visit. What were you doing?"

Thomas looked fondly at his frustrated parent. Not only did she have a complete lack of sentiment (for anything besides her eldest dead son), she also had no appreciation for good architecture. Handing his coat to Newland, the old family butler, he folded his mother into a hug and put his chin on top of her head. "I was just looking, Mother. A lot of people have built some grand houses in the last twenty years, but you still preside over the grandest house in Pittsburgh. Have you looked lately at what a beautiful house you have?"

Eugenia chuckled a little, her good humor restored by the appeal to her vanity. "I must confess, I hadn't thought about it for a long time. Now *I'm* going to be the one standing outside, gawking. When I catch my death of heat stroke, it will be your fault."

"I'll be wracked with guilt the rest of my life," he assured her gallantly.

"Well, I'm sure you'll be the death of me, one way or another," she answered. But the look she gave him was not without affection.

Releasing her from his embrace, he tucked her hand into the crook of his elbow and escorted her in the direction his father had taken. "You've been saying that for twenty five years now, and you're still looking perfectly healthy for a dying woman." He changed the subject for an easier topic that his mother could keep up with. "I hope we're just in time for tea?"

"Of course," his mother replied. "You think your father could wait for me before he walks in. But that's the story of my life, isn't it? I always get to walk in late, by myself."

Despite his mother's lamentations, tea was a fairly pleasant affair. Now that her son was properly married, Eugenia had more patience for his wayward sense of humor. Of course, there was still the question of grandchildren, but, as Thomas had pointed out the last time she had brought up the subject, these things do take time.

As he sat with his parents in the afternoon sitting room, Thomas let his mother's voice wash over him. The sight of two lively black eyes, the pressure of two hands tucked in his; the thought made him want to chortle with glee. Today, he listened to his mother gossip about family, servants, and next-door neighbors. Tomorrow—tomorrow!

He doubted that Regina had ever had a trivial conversation in her life. The wise eyes, her knowing smile; this was a woman who did not need to gossip and speculate about people. Here was a woman who *read* people. She saw through the layers at a glance, looked straight at a person's character. Thomas wished he possessed that skill.

Realizing he had stopped listening to his mother's monologue altogether, he arranged his features in an exaggerated expression of horror to match her own. "Oh, dear," he added, reaching for another macaroon.

"Isn't it awful?" she sighed and rolled her eyes heavenward. "And she won't listen to me. I'm sure St. Louis is a perfectly nice place. But honestly, Missouri? It's too drastic. I know his business failed, but that's no reason to leave everything behind!"

"If you ask me, Jem's doing the right thing. If you can't make a go of it in one place, you pick up and take a stab at it someplace else," his father observed.

Ah ha. The "she" his mother was referring to must be Phoebe Parker. The Parkers were their neighbors to the west, owning the stately brick home down the hill. The Parkers had been one of the wealthiest coke producers in southwestern Pennsylvania; and one of the hardest hit in the Panic. Jem had sold all his operations to a crazy young speculator named Clay Frick for an appalling fraction of their former worth. And just in time, too! Everyone knew that the coke industry was dying. Jem Parker was lucky to sell his assets when he did.

"So, let me get this straight," Thomas said slowly. "Jem Parker wants to move to St. Louis, Missouri."

"That's what I told you," his mother said impatiently.

"Bear with me, Mother. And Mrs. Parker is willing to go."

"It's sheer craziness."

"Well, if both of the Parkers are willing to make this drastic change in their lives, why are *you* objecting?" The noise his father made could only be described as a guffaw.

Eugenia looked from husband to son indignantly. "Well! Leave it to the men not to see the practical side! While Mr. Parker is out gallivanting around doing who knows what, Phoebe's the one who has to leave her house—if they can sell that house, these days!—and pack up three small children and try to settle in a little frontier town without a single relative! She'll probably have savages for servants!"

The Baldwin men exchanged amused looks. "Well, I've never been to St. Louis," the elder Mr. Baldwin observed, "but I'm sure it's much more civilized than you think."

"Besides," the younger Mr. Baldwin pointed out, "your savages may be harder workers than the current house staff you and Meredith have both been dismissing lately."

"Oh!" Eugenia exclaimed, nearly spilling her tea as she jumped inexplicably. "Servants! I almost forgot. I've got a girl I'm sending over to Meredith. She's been so unhappy with your latest housekeeper. Since you're here, I'll send Mary back with you. She's young, but she's the tidiest creature I've ever seen. She's so careful. I hate to part with her myself, but Meredith's been *so* unhappy, poor dear."

Thomas refused to react to his mother's last comment. He didn't know what Meredith complained about to his mother, but she complained about enough that he just didn't care. "That's very kind of you, Mother," he said blandly, keeping his face as neutral as possible.

His mother wasn't listening. She was already ringing the little silver bell on the tea tray. When Newland appeared, she instructed him, "Newland, tell Mary that Mr. Baldwin will take her back with him to interview with Mrs. Baldwin this afternoon."

"Yes Ma'am," Newland said, and left again.

None of the Baldwin servants talked much, Thomas noticed. Not that it was their place to lounge around gossiping with the lady of the house; but in most homes the servants didn't speak in monosyllables. Here, of course, a servant was always in danger of having his or her ears talked off. No doubt they all were trying to beat a hasty retreat.

When Mary met him at the carriage block, however, she looked as though she might have a great deal to say, under the right circumstances. Thomas was shocked by her youthful age, as well as by her beauty.

High cheekbones, full lips, glossy light brown hair and seductive blue-gray eyes behind long sweeping lashes faced him across the carriage seat. He amused himself by imagining she was one of those maids who was passed swiftly from household to household, as she shook up old families by seducing their sons. In horror, one family after another would supply her with excellent references and send her to a new position as far away as possible. The romantic notion appealed to him. But he still couldn't think of a thing to say to her.

"So . . . how long were you in my mother's household?"

"Six months," she answered primly.

Ah, yes. The reserve of a Baldwin servant. A poker face seemed to be the most important requirement. Thomas had a sudden sense of challenge, a need to break through that superhuman reserve.

"And in that six months, you've heard more talk than you had in the previous six years of your life?" He asked, a little wickedly.

Her eyes sought his. Her lips twitched a little. "They do talk a lot," she admitted.

"That, Miss Mary, is a very charitable understatement."

It was working! He could definitely see the glimmer of humor across her face. "Come on, be honest," he prodded her, "at times it's all you can do to keep yourself from covering your ears and running screaming out into the street."

It was definitely working. He could see her face thawing, a smile warming her features. "They get in shouting matches," she observed. "Not that getting louder means they hear each other. They both keep going without listening to what the other one is saying." Thomas smiled at the description. He used to hide from that same rise in volume.

"So I take it the Richard Baldwin residence is not quite your typical residence?"

"There's no such thing as a typical residence, sir."

"You're probably right. Every family has skeletons in one closet or another." He sighed. "At least I believe you'll find my household is much quieter than my parents'. My—wife and I don't spend much effort in trying to outshout each other." Thomas found it very awkward, bringing up the subject of his home life to this pretty stranger. For that matter, he found the word "wife" still felt like sand in his mouth.

"Well, to be perfectly honest, sir, you aren't what I was expecting."

Somehow, this confession pleased him greatly. "Really? So, do tell me, what were you expecting?"

Mary's face looked uncertain. Being too familiar with one's employer was a boundary one did not cross.

Thomas saw her hesitation. "Come now," he prompted gently. "I've been enjoying your honesty. Don't clam up on me now."

Mary looked down, and blushed crimson.

"Is it that bad?" he asked, surprised.

Mary ducked her head, and Thomas could see that the neat part in her hair had even turned red.

The embarrassment emanating from this previously reserved creature astonished him. He realized that for all the women making eyes at him, he'd never made a girl blush before. It was rather a pleasant sensation.

Knowing full well, however, how little fun it was to be on the other side, Thomas looked out the window and tried his best to be nonchalant. "I suppose it must be fairly dreadful being marched off from one household to another."

"I don't mind, sir. So long as I'm working. You—your mother did say the pay would be the same," she ventured, shyly.

"She did, eh? Cheeky of her, to go making promises for us," Thomas said, amused. "And what has my mother been paying you?"

"Four dollars a week."

"Well, my wife spends more than that a day, on gloves and other fripperies. You needn't worry about your salary. If my wife asks, tell her my mother pays you five. I'm sure my wife will be harder to work for than my mother was. You might as well derive some economic benefit out of this."

A surprised, delighted smile spread across Mary's face. He'd entirely melted through her reserve. Embarrassment forgotten, she seized his hand in both of her warm little ones. "Thank you, sir, oh, thank you!" She said breathlessly. "You won't be sorry, I'll keep the most particular house in Allegheny!"

Why was it so much easier talking with employees than with his peers? Thomas smiled and patted her hands with his free one. "I'm counting on it, Mary," he said.

The coach rolled to a stop. They were on Buena Vista.

Thomas watched with interest as Mary stepped from the carriage. She had drawn her customary mantle of reserve around her like a cloak, and waited deferentially to follow him up the steps to the house.

She did throw in one last pleasantry, however. Looking up, she said softly, "It's a lovely house, sir." Then she fell silent as their butler, Joseph, opened the door.

Joseph was a rare and valuable find: a genuine person. He pulled no punches. He told you what he thought, when he thought it. There was little boundary between servant and master. He was the antithesis of Newland, who had a poker face and little to say for himself. Joseph was lacking in that tact, but he made up for it in possessing the wisdom of the ages. Thomas thoroughly enjoyed his servant's sharp observations about the world outside—and he'd occasionally acted upon them.

Meredith was intimidated by Joseph. In private, she complained to Thomas that he "didn't know his place." Thomas pointed out that Joseph knew everything else about the world, and flatly refused to dismiss him. Especially since he also did his job very, very well.

So Thomas was more interested in Joseph's opinion than Meredith's when he presented Mary to their combined scrutiny.

Meredith looked down her nose at the shorter young maid. She disliked her instantly. She instinctively disliked all pretty women. She never knew when her distant husband might take an interest in some other woman.

"You're awfully young to be a housekeeper, Mary," Meredith informed her loftily. "How old are you?"

"I'll be twenty-one this fall, ma'am." Mary answered. Thomas marveled at the young woman's self-possession. There was an unmistakable hostility coming from Meredith. But Mary wore an air of unshakable calm, which only succeeded in rattling Meredith more.

"Twenty-one! You can't be a housekeeper at twenty one. I need a person who can run this household. A responsible person, not a flighty young thing."

Thomas smiled to himself. Meredith was twenty two; and best described as a "flighty young thing."

Mary calmly spoke in her own defense. "I've been working in households since I was ten, ma'am. My mistresses have always been pleased with me. I keep a very tidy house."

Joseph had been watching the exchange from the doorway with great amusement. Now he spoke up, to Meredith's annoyance. "I've been keeping up the house since Mrs. Wilkins . . . left. Can you keep things as neat as this?"

Mary looked around the hallway where they were standing. With a glance, she took in carpet, mirror, chair, and hat-stand, then she walked over to the door separating the hallway from the front foyer. She ran the tips of her sturdy brown gloves along the grooved edge of one of the door panels and displayed her now dusty fingertips for all to see.

"I keep a *tidy* house," she repeated, a trifle loftily.

Joseph laughed heartily. "You're good people, Mary," he nodded in approval. "You're good people." Having made his judgment, Joseph vanished down the hall.

Mary's expression remained neutral. Meredith looked sourly at her husband.

"Joseph approves," she observed testily. "I suppose that means we're keeping her?"

"Looks that way," Thomas replied, attempting that complacent tone Mary achieved so easily. It occurred to him it would be a useful skill to practice. "Do you have any objections?"

His question took Meredith by surprise. "I . . . guess not," she floundered. "I suppose you get four dollars a week?" She asked Mary loftily.

Mary's eyes barely shifted in Thomas' direction. "The other Mrs. Baldwin gave me five."

This put the wind back in Meredith's sails. "Five! What is the world coming to?"

Thomas turned toward the stairs with a weary air. Meredith was performing for his benefit. Time to put an end to the show. "We can afford the spare change, Mrs. Baldwin," he said in a bored voice. "After all, I'm sure you don't want it whispered all over town that we can't afford the same luxuries that my parents can. Welcome to the household, Mary." He disappeared up the landing, ending the interview.

****

That night, as he sat barricaded safely in his library, Thomas heard a soft knock at the door connecting the library to his bedroom. Before he could get up from his chair, the door opened, and Mary came in, balancing a tray in her hands.

Thomas gaped in astonishment. All these months, he'd been locking the hallway door to keep his wife out. In a matter of hours, his new housekeeper had found a hole in his defenses!

Mary was completely oblivious to his reaction. "You didn't come down for supper," she observed. "Rather than let your cook's efforts be completely wasted on your house staff, I thought I'd bring supper up to you."

Mary's voice was calm and composed, but in the lamplight Thomas could see a scarlet flush creeping over her face. Astonished for a second time in the space of five minutes, he made a gentlemanly display of not noticing her blushes. "That is terribly thoughtful of you, Mary. Just put it over by my desk."

She flashed a knowing look in his direction. "If I do, you won't touch a bite, will you? This soup's better when it's hot."

Thomas' nose became aware of the aroma of ham-and-cabbage soup coming from the tray in Mary's hands. She was right—Mrs. Bishop was an excellent cook. His stomach, awakened by the smell, grumbled a protest.

"You're right, Mary. Why don't you bring that tray over here?"

She put the tray down on the table at his elbow. Next to the steaming soup, she'd arranged bread, cheese, and slices of sausage in decorative little patterns on the china.

"Why, Mary, this is a work of art!" Thomas exclaimed.

His praise brought a smile of pure pleasure to her face, before the mask of reserve — albeit a rosy pink reserve — settled back into place.

"Your cook told me you were fond of sausage," a mischievous twinkle rose in eyes that looked very gray in the lamplight, "despite your family's connection to it."

Thomas chuckled. "You've been here less than twenty-four hours, Mary, and you already understand me better than my own flesh and blood."

"Oh, I don't know, sir," Mary demurred. "I was only trying to be amusing."

"Well, thank you. The effort is most appreciated."

"So is yours, sir," Mary replied, the cool impersonal tones slipping from her voice. "The raise, your support when your wife didn't seem inclined to like me . . ."

"My wife will not be easy to work for, as I told you. Do you think you'll be able to work here?"

"I will, sir," she answered loyally, "for you. You're nice enough to make up for the missus. Everyone thinks so: Joseph, the cook, your coachman . . . ." She stopped, and an expression of horror swept across her face. "Oh, now you're going to think I'm a terrible gossip. But I'm not, really, I'm not, sir!"

Thomas was now vastly amused. "I believe you, Mary. Everyone needs someone with whom he can let down his defenses. And I am happy to know my house staff is all willing to put up with my wife for my sake."

"Oh, we are." Very aware she'd stayed too long and said too much, Mary was backing toward the door. "Good night, sir."

"Good night—and thank you, Mary." Thomas did not realize at the time that a new nightly tradition had just started in the Baldwin household; a dinner tray, the household gossip, and rosy cheeks in the lamplight.

Chapter 5

Thomas spent more time awake than asleep that night. Lunch with Regina Waring! His head swam with visions—rather than the usual haunts, the Duquesne Club or the Hotel Washington, he'd take her on a picnic on a grassy slope. Up to the Duquesne Heights, maybe. Or Fineview.

His fingers shook as he wound his cravat and pinned a ruby stud into place. He tried to imagine what he'd say. What she'd say. He tried to think up flowery compliments as he stared at his own reflection. They all sounded silly to his ears.

His voice shook as he asked Joseph to tell Mrs. Bishop to load a picnic basket. All morning, he sat at his desk, looking at the clock instead of the paperwork. In the carriage, his heart pounded in time to the horses' hooves. Clip-clop-clip-clop. He took a deep breath and held it. He had to calm down.

Finally they crossed over the brand-new Point Bridge into the recently annexed South Side of Pittsburgh.

The South Side, still called Birmingham, had most of the glass industry of southwestern Pennsylvania. The encroachment of the iron industry, then steel, then the Panic of '73 had been hard on the glass factories. Many of them had been doing business with the railroads, which had been hard hit by the Panic. With their clientele nearly bankrupt, and their shipping rates rising rapidly, glass factories closed their doors and sold the valuable land to the highest bidders.

A great many of their assets were bought by the Warings for a song. Waring Glassworks' headquarters mushroomed above the flat buildings surrounding it; topped, of course, by the glass clock tower Thomas could see across the river on his way to Olympus Ironworks.

Thomas was not even sure of what Waring Glassworks did and did not make. He knew they kept a crew of artisans who made the stained glass for the windows one saw in almost every home in Pittsburgh. He knew, also, that most of the factory was dedicated to making clear plate glass; cheaper to make, therefore cheaper to sell and more in demand during these hard times.

Regina's shapely figure was standing in front of the second building. When the carriage came to a stop in front of her, he scrambled out hastily, before George could get down from his box, and held the door open for her himself.

"Your flying carpet has just flown in, my lady," he announced a little breathlessly. "You haven't been waiting long, have you?" His eyes sought the clock tower. It read 11:28.

"Oh, no," she reassured him, stepping nimbly into the waiting carriage. "It was so hot inside I stepped out early to get a breath of air. Every furnace we've got is going full blast."

She turned merry black eyes on him. It took him a moment before he realized her pun. Then he slapped his head and groaned.

"Blast. Furnace. Okay. I get it. Very punny." He thought a moment. "I suppose I should *steel* myself for more such humor."

"Only if we can *iron* out the kinks," she returned.

"But I know you'll get the *Bessemer* of me," he grinned back. "Was that too much of a stretch?"

"Not at all," she said, settling herself more comfortably on the carriage seat beside him. "I think that takes the prize."

"So what did I win?" Only after he'd said it did Thomas realize how forward that sounded.

Regina seemed as surprised by his question as he was. "I don't know," she answered, a little puzzled. "Lunch with me?" She shook her head and frowned. "No. That was a foregone conclusion. Well — I don't know." She shook a finger at him. "But I'll think of something."

Thomas was a little embarrassed by the attention she was giving his last comment. “Oh, never mind. I was just trying to be clever.”

“You were clever. And it’s bothering me that I can’t think of anything for a good comeback. You’ve out-clevered me.”

The two sat for a moment in a comfortable silence. Thomas looked over curiously as his companion chuckled softly to herself.

“Are we going to the Duquesne Club or Hotel Washington?” she asked him.

Feeling very pleased with himself, he answered, “Neither.” He was even more pleased with himself at her mystified expression.

“There really are no other options. Far be it from me to ever say anything nice about New York,” she continued, “but at least when you need to go out for lunch, there are some options available.”

“Wait and see,” Thomas answered, and glanced out the window. “Well, at least you don’t have to wait long.”

The carriage stopped. They had reached their destination: the carriage block of the Duquesne Heights Incline. Thomas affected a more graceful exit from the coach this time, and handed his companion down as elegantly as he could have hoped.

She emerged, like Cinderella from her magic pumpkin coach, and turned to him with a smile. “The Duquesne Heights?” she exclaimed, a little puzzled.

Thomas couldn’t suppress a pleased grin as George handed him the laden picnic basket and Regina’s face lit up with delight.

“A picnic?”

He offered her his free arm and nodded to George, who clicked to the horses and drove away. “I take it you approve?”

Regina’s smile had already answered the question. She gave his arm a small squeeze as she took it. “It’s a delightful idea. I haven’t been on a picnic in, oh, I don’t remember how long.”

Thomas was thrilled by her enthusiasm. She took the basket from him while he paid their fare for the incline, and playfully lifted the edge of the hamper to peer in.

"No peeking!" he chastised her in as stern a tone as he could muster.

"No fair!" she stuck out her tongue at him, but obediently let the lid drop back into place.

Reclaiming the basket from her in mock haste, he escorted her up the ramp to a seat inside the car of the incline. She sat with her usual grace, her skirts seeming to fall in artistic waves around her.

He looked his companion over with pleasure as she smiled up at him. "You look like a poppy!" he exclaimed delightedly.

She was a picture in scarlet red, every flounce and furbelow trimmed in black. She smiled with feminine delight. "You approve? My dressmaker feared I was being too garish."

"Do I approve? Absolutely!" He grinned at her, entirely lacking his usual self-consciousness. "I've never had lunch with a flower before."

"Some people," she pointed out with a subtle, seductive twist to her pretty mouth, "find it easier to share their secrets with the flowers than with another human being. Maybe I can split the difference."

"Well, the Heights could certainly use another flower," he concluded gallantly.

The two spent the remainder of the trip up the hill admiring the view as the car rose over the city. Alighting at the top, Thomas led Regina to a grassy slope, and spread out the quilt packed along with the lunch hamper.

"What a lovely idea," Regina sank onto the quilt and smiled at Thomas as he handed her a glass and poured her lemonade. "It's hot and noisy inside—but you can actually talk out here."

And Thomas talked. Over delicate little sandwiches the story of his "proposal" poured out of him. Over a selection of summer berries the awful details of the engagement and wedding unfolded. Then, over tiny little pastries Thomas found himself describing the terrible, aloof prison he called his home.

It was cathartic. Thomas' story rolled out of him in cleansing torrents, the words sometimes tripping over each other on the way out.

Regina sat, almost completely silent, through it all. Her face mirrored his every emotion—horror, anger, frustration, sorrow. Her eyes never left his, full of sympathy, full of encouragement.

When, finally, Thomas was talked out, he flopped on his back and looked up at the new electric lights illuminating the park.

"You're an awfully good listener," he observed, feeling awkward for the first time all afternoon.

Her hand reached out and ruffled his hair. "Not usually," she answered honestly. "But you've got a particularly fascinating story to tell. The story of your marriage is like a stage melodrama turned on its ear. Instead of an innocent damsel, compromised by a handsome scalawag, we have an unsuspecting hero tricked by a ruthless young lady. I'm sure you're not deriving much comfort, knowing yours is a unique tragedy."

Thomas shrugged his shoulders despondently. "Pittsburgh is its own little oligarchy of intermarrying elite familics. Do any of them marry for love?"

He was instantly sorry he asked the rhetorical question. Her eyes focused beyond him, her face softened, a fond smile crept over her lips. She was thinking of her husband. She answered with one word. "Sometimes."

The warm magic of their lunch might have died away at that moment. A chill of jealousy shot through Thomas. He fought it back. He had no right, he told himself firmly. Oh, but if only he'd met her before Henry Waring had!

Hah! And then what? Regina and Henry were made for each other. Period. Had Regina been his wife, he would still have been on the outside looking in.

Her eyes had come out of her reverie and she shook her head sadly. "You seem so completely alone," she observed. "Don't you have anyone to talk to — besides me?" she added with a smile.

Thomas sighed. "Poor, friendless me. I haven't always been this pathetic," he assured her. "But I'll admit, since my best friend Michael moved to Cleveland after we graduated from Western University, I've been pretty much on my own."

"Except for your parents, harping on you to go out and make friends." Regina guessed.

Thomas rolled his eyes upward. "Only occasionally. My father usually doesn't remember that I might want a private life, and my mother was always too busy campaigning for a daughter-in-law."

Regina laughed as he pulled a tragicomic face. "So what does your mother do now that you've supplied her with one?"

"Complains about everything else, mostly. She'd been neglecting other topics in order to focus her energies on complaining about me. Now, well, there are neighbors, servants, my father, the stores; there's always something to complain about. I told you yesterday she started in on grandchildren recently. I seem to have stalled her, for now. I pointed out that fertilization and gestation both take some time. She was so horrified that I might go into more graphic detail, she rather quickly found another subject."

Regina chuckled wickedly. "Sometimes one has to make use of those delicate sensibilities of the weaker sex."

"You don't seem to be suffering from them, yourself," Thomas observed.

She shrugged carelessly. "So, my peasant stock is showing. The elite of Pittsburgh is comprised of former peasants who ended up here on the frontier looking for a living. But money breeds pretension. Your mother—and most of the women of her class—can afford their little delicacies. So, they hire a less delicate maid to do the work, and become a decorative part of a society which wholeheartedly approves."

Thomas smiled as Regina tossed her head disdainfully. "So how did you escape the delicacy that afflicts the rest of the leisurely rich?" he asked.

"Freak of nature, I think." Regina pursed her lips for a moment, and stared intently at nothing, seeing all the women of her childhood. "I really married above my station in life. My father's a clerk, and my mother's a housekeeper. To them, it's less about popular delusions than station. Wealthy women don't have to work. I do—and so they shake their heads because I prefer the inside of a bank to the inside of a parlor."

Thomas surveyed the feminine face before him. No doubt every parlor in Pittsburgh whispered about this woman who did not take her place among their ranks. "So are your parents terribly disappointed in you?"

"Horribly. They never look at me without wondering where they went wrong." Another wicked chuckle rose from the ivory throat. "Then of course my mother looks at the sky and entreats heaven to send me children, so I can become a proper woman."

"Is it horribly improper for me to ask why you don't have any children?" Thomas asked only out of interest, but realized after the words were out how forward his question was.

"I'm sure it's completely improper, but I don't mind telling you. Maybe it's because you didn't even think to hint that there must be something medically wrong with me. Well, it just so happens I don't want children, which is why I don't have any."

Thomas was intrigued. "But surely you and Henry must — indulge. How do you avoid . . ." Thomas felt the need for all those delicate parlor euphemisms they'd both scoffed at. ". . . . the usual consequences?"

The look Regina shot at him made his temperature rise several degrees. There was such a combination of mischief, seduction, knowledge and mysterious, womanly wisdom! She smiled, slowly, and shook her head. "I see the Comstock Laws are doing their job."

"The what?"

"A couple of years ago they passed a federal law which makes it illegal to send obscene, lewd, or lascivious materials through the mail. It defines medical information on preventing disease and pregnancy as obscene. Not to mention the actual contraceptive devices themselves. Just imagine," she chuckled, looking in his eyes in a most disconcerting fashion, "if you and I had a mad, torrid affair, we could be jailed not for the sin we're committing in the eyes of most churches, but for receiving condoms to prevent taking syphilis back to our respective spouses."

Thomas tried furiously to ignore the jumping warmth which was growing between his legs after her suggestion that they had a torrid affair. He was watching Regina with a new sense of wonder. Was there no end to the different aspects of this woman?

Her eyes fixed on him candidly. "I'm sorry. I suppose I've embarrassed you again. Did I tell you my mother thinks I'm not a lady?"

"No," he answered, amazed. "I'm actually not embarrassed. Intrigued, yes. But not embarrassed." He smiled at her. "Although I don't think a lady is supposed to know so much. Do you realize how rare it is for two people to discuss such delicate subjects in public?"

Regina pointedly surveyed the landscape. "I wouldn't exactly call this public."

Thomas looked around the empty park, realizing with a start that the sun was trying to peer at them from the skies west of the city—meaning it was well into the afternoon!

"It would seem we've both lost track of the time," Regina observed a little sheepishly, as Thomas pulled out his pocket watch: it was nearly quarter after 4:00.

"Henry is meeting with Judge Mellon this afternoon," Regina continued, tilting her head to read the time over his shoulder. "I said I'd join them. If I don't get moving, they'll probably mortgage something, just to be funny."

They hastily packed the picnic remnants back into the basket. Thomas stood up to help Regina extricate herself and her poppy red dress from her spot on the quilt. Her sleek form-fitting style involved unprecedented volumes of ruffled train dragging behind her; he could imagine Meredith wrapping such excesses around chair legs and other obstacles. Regina seemed to possess a mastery of silly feminine garments that other women lacked—she took the hand he offered, stood up, and stepped off the quilt without a moments' fuss.

She turned with a flip of the hand that pulled the excess yardage off the quilt, then bent gracefully to pick up the nearest corner.

In companionable silence, they folded the quilt, then walked the short distance to the incline station. Thomas followed her in, and together they watched the city emerge through the haze during the trip back down the hill.

George was waiting nearby, as implacable and patient as ever. Spotting them from where he had tethered the horses, he freed them from the hitching posts and drove the carriage to the block. Thomas handed Regina into the carriage.

Regina turned to him when the carriage rolled to a stop in front of the Mellon family's imposing building on Wood Street. She tucked both her hands in his, in much the same fashion as she'd done the day before in the lobby. "I've enjoyed our outing. Thanks for sharing the truth with me. I hope I'm not being hopelessly nebby, dragging the story out of you like this."

"Oh, no!" Thomas clung to her hands. "You're the only person in the world who even guessed there was another side to the story. It was pointless for me to try to defend myself. Who would have believed me? I'd have made an ass of myself, and hurt Olympus Iron in the process. I'm so grateful that there is one person out there who knows the truth."

The smile faded from her lips and eyes. "So you ruined your life for your father's enterprise. I don't suppose he appreciates what a truly selfless son he has."

Thomas didn't know what to say. He looked at her, while her words echoed in his head. "You ruined your life." "You ruined your life."

Without warning, she leaned forward and kissed him. "Keep your chin up," she whispered. "And if you ever need me—I'm here."

Then she was gone.

Thomas sat, stunned, his lips tingling with the feel of her lips pressed against his.

All the way home, he kept raising shaking fingers to his mouth. He was grateful for the long line of carriages waiting to pay their tolls to cross the Union Bridge. It gave him just a few more magic minutes to relive her—the feel of her fingers pressing his, the sadness in her eyes, that kiss—oh, that amazing kiss. He ran his hands over the cushions where she had been sitting. He could feel the sympathy emanating from them. Her sympathy. He kneeled on the floor of the coach, and lay his face against the hard cushions.

He closed his eyes and let remembered sounds wash over him. Her laugh. The rattle of the dishes as they'd pulled them out of the basket. The silence of the empty park when they'd realized what time it was. "So you ruined your life for your father's enterprise."

Her eyes were so sad when she'd looked at him.

How many times had he touched her? His mind flew back over the hours of their interview. Handing her into the carriage. And out. Her hand on his arm on the walk to and from their picnic spot.

He realized the carriage had stopped outside his front door. And there he was, sitting on the carriage floor, a lovesick smile on his face. George opened the door for him before Thomas could regain his seat.

"Sir! Are you ill, sir?"

"Yes, George, I believe I am," Thomas answered. "Help me out, please."

After being discovered in such a position, Thomas realized he'd better play his part to the hilt. Unfortunately, letting George help him up to the house meant Meredith got a cue to put on her theatrics.

"Oh!" she shrieked, opening the front door. "Thomas! Are you all right? Oh, my darling!" She clutched at his free arm.

"I don't believe his lunch agreed with him, ma'am," George reported calmly.

Thomas smothered a smile. Lunch had agreed with him. In fact, it gave him the fortitude to live through the household fuss that swept him up the stairs and into his room.

He thought Meredith was going to plant herself permanently at his bedside, taking full advantage of her first opportunity to get inside his bedroom. He was therefore filled with gratitude when Mary gently but firmly removed his attentive wife. "He's only taken a stomach chill ma'am. All he needs is a nap, which he won't get with you worrying next to him. Come along."

"If I paid that woman what she was worth," Thomas thought as the door closed behind the departing women, "I'd go bankrupt." Then he closed his eyes. He couldn't go anywhere for a while. A nap didn't seem like such a bad idea.

****

After that glorious afternoon, a steady flow of invitations moved from the Waring to the Baldwin household.

"We just thought you needed to get out more," Henry told him heartily when Thomas tried to thank him for the copious attention.

It was more than a chance to get out. Thomas could actually enjoy himself. Unfailingly, Regina found a diversion to occupy Meredith, and prevent that devoted wife from clinging to Thomas' side the entire outing.

It was skillfully done—and never seemed to come from Regina herself. The daughter of one of Henry's associates became Meredith's devotee, clinging to the older woman, demanding help with her hairstyle. An elderly friend of the family took a fancy to her, and sat talking with her for hours, horrifying the young wife with his frank speech. Another young lady of indeterminate relation to the Warings insisted on pouring out all her romantic woes to Meredith.

Meredith basked in the attention, blissfully unaware of the inventive bribes the Warings thought up to keep Meredith supplied with companions.

Freed from both his family and his wife's hovering presence, Thomas blossomed. The Warings kept their own company, separate from the social circles of the iron and steel families. This crowd hadn't known Thomas from babyhood, and he discovered his own wit and confidence in the friendly atmosphere of his new acquaintances.

His father even noticed, in his usual, unobservant way. "I don't know how you've managed it, boy, but it's a damn good business move. You keep cultivating those tanners, glassmakers, and whoever else it is you're keeping company with. Those businesses can grow, and where there's growth, there's pig iron."

And always—always there was Regina.

There was something fierce in her friendship, at times. He'd catch a glimmer of it now and then. She was his Protector Goddess, overlooking his social life and his career with watchful eyes.

Oftentimes he barely said more than "hello" to her, before he was whisked off for a game of croquet with the head of a tannery in Allegheny (who, incidentally, was achieving record profits and was thinking of investing in iron while prices were down). Or he'd be seated at dinner next to the charming but formidable Mrs. Helen P. Jenkins, whose bluestocking essays were such a controversial but indelible part of Pittsburgh's social elite.

When he had the chance to talk to his patroness, he knew better than to express his gratitude. She would brush it aside as lightly as her husband did. "You're a friend. We enjoy your company."

So Thomas threw his efforts into being the most engaging friend he could be. He couldn't have Regina's love. But she was offering her friendship. He could return that, vigorously. It became his all-consuming passion in life, thinking of ways to please Regina. No invitation was ever accepted without some token accompanying the response, and the day after every event flowers appeared at the Waring doorstep. Thomas even contrived to find out Regina's favorite flowers, and a florist on Penn Avenue who carried them.

"You send her more flowers than you send me," Meredith pouted.

Her injured looks fell on an indifferent head. "When you help me close as many business deals in a month as Regina Waring does, wife of my bosom, I will send you baskets of flowers every day," Thomas answered.

"Oh," was Meredith's only answer.

Closing business deals in the summer of 1876 was no small accomplishment. Many companies had closed their doors in the past year. Those still in business seemed to be able to struggle through the hard times, but only through heavy negotiating and a large network of family and friends. It was Darwinism at work; only the strongest could survive. So the strongest tightened their belts, and continued to plunge forward.

Chapter 6

Belts were tighter still, a year later. And tempers all over the twin cities were shorter.

Thomas tried to remember, as he stepped out of Merchants and Manufacturers National Bank that hot, grimy July Saturday, when the last time was he'd authorized payroll without worrying about how he'd meet the next one.

The lengthy Panic put a worried frown on everyone's face these days. He passed two men laughing heartily as he spotted his carriage. Okay, so maybe it was just him. Maybe it was simply the hot weather getting to him. The charms of living in "hell with the lid off" seemed less amusing in the sweltering noontime heat.

Grumpy and out-of-sorts, Thomas plopped himself despondently on the hard carriage seat. He stared sullenly at the finely polished wood of the carriage floor for a moment, before he realized the ever-patient George was still waiting for direction. "Is it me, George, or is the world in a bad mood today?"

"I can't speak for the rest of the world, sir. But this heat isn't likely to make anyone feel terribly friendly."

"No, I suppose not," Thomas sighed. "Drive out to my parents' please, George. We're expected to join in an excursion to the country for a picnic, or some such frolic."

"Yes, sir," George replied. "Getting out of the smoke for a while might even improve your mood, sir."

Thomas grunted noncommittally and stared at nothing in particular as the carriage rolled over the cobblestones. He'd endured these torturous family outings before. He couldn't recall them ever improving his mood. A few blocks later, however, he had forgotten his sorrows, as he watched a steady flow of people moving toward the rail yards. "George, is something going on with the railroad?"

"I couldn't say, sir. I'd heard there was a bit of a commotion yesterday. Freight men refusing to take a cut in pay with double workloads," he answered with characteristic complacency.

Thomas' bad mood evaporated in a puff of curiosity. "Follow these folks, will you, George? I want to see what's happening."

His curiosity grew when he saw a parade of workmen marching down the street, heading for the rail yards. He could smell agitation in the air. What was going on?

The carriage turned onto 28th Street—and stopped. Thomas stared. There were thousands of people crowding the rail yards!

"It's a strike," a deep feminine voice said in his ear. "Want to join me? I'm going to go take a closer look."

Thomas was hard pressed to know which startled him more—the voice in his ear, or the excitement he saw when he turned and looked into the eyes of Regina Waring. She was leaning mischievously against the side of his open carriage, which had apparently rolled up next to a carriage block.

"Take a closer look? Are you out of your mind?" Thomas gasped. "If that's a strike, we're the enemy," he pointed out.

"Nonsense. Neither one of us is railroad. As long as we keep our mouths shut and our ears open, we'll be fine. I intend to go listen and learn—those could be my employees someday. Or yours."

Thomas looked from the crowd to Regina's determined face and back again. "Tell the picnic to start without me, George."

"Yes, sir. Be careful, sir."

Careful? A careful person would have turned around and left with his carriage. They followed the crowd heading toward the 28th Street crossing. Thomas looked Regina over critically. She was a bright, fashionable bumblebee in yellow and black; a sharp contrast to the drab gray and brown laborers collecting at the rail yard.

She seemed completely oblivious to the danger she posed to herself, standing out as she did. She had the train of her buttoned, beribboned ensemble thrown carelessly over her arm, her attention entirely focused on the noise of the throng.

Well, he was here to protect her. A little thrill went through him at the thought. He would protect her. Not Henry, not one of her throng of admiring entrepreneurs. Him.

They were inside the press of people, now. A train had recently entered the rail yard, and most of the crew had willingly joined the strikers. It would seem a few members were not so willing. A man in a conductor's uniform was being dragged out of one of the cars. Thomas couldn't hear what he was saying, but the body language was clear enough. The mob pressed up against the train, and a sea of arms reached up. The protesting conductor was swept away by the human current, which cheered as he was swallowed up.

The mob was so thick, the train was moving only by inches. A few strikers were hanging onto the engine, waving their hats and yelling—apparently this engineer agreed to honor the strike and refuse to continue with his train. Triumphant voices rose on all sides. "No freight's going out today!" "If everyone sticks together, those rich bastards can't do a thing!"

Thomas was intensely aware that, in this crowd, he no doubt qualified as a "rich bastard." Feeling uncomfortable and out of place, he glanced down at his companion.

He was astonished by the expression on her face—she was as intensely involved as the rest of the crowd. As he looked at her, she raised her voice. "It's time those railroad thieves came down a peg or two!" She felt him looking at her, and met his gaze.

She seemed abashed but amused by his shocked expression. "Well, what are you paying for freight? It feels good to fight back for a change."

Thomas looked around as the people closest to them voiced their agreement. "Yeah—we're fighting back, all right." "It's about time, too." "Them railroad men ride around in their fancy private cars while the rest of us pay for 'em." United by a common enemy, no one seemed to care what economic class a protester came from. This was not simply a case of workingman against rich man. People of all walks of life were crowding the rail yard; shop owners, factory workers, bookkeepers, male and female, young and old. They weren't here only to support the strikers. Regina was right. They were here because they all felt victimized by the railroad.

Thomas seemed to be the only person not gripped by a festive mood. While he was frowning at nothing in particular, the crowd around him began flowing in a particular direction: another train was entering the yard.

"Well, speakin' of them fancy cars," he heard someone sneer. "That looks like Superintendent Pitcairn's own private car."

"Something tells me he's not here to give his freight workers a raise," another voice chimed in.

"If he sold the car, he could hire back the ones he laid off," a third voice volunteered.

As they watched, the train crept through the crowds, and stopped. Eventually, Thomas, Regina, and the crowd in their proximity realized that people were moving toward the rear of the train. The motion swept them up as well, and soon they were able to see the town's Sheriff Fife, standing head and shoulders above the crowd on a gondola at the rear of the train, attempting to address the crowd.

He was flanked by a couple of understandably nervous-looking men: Robert Pitcairn, superintendent of the Pennsylvania Railroad and General Pearson, from the Pittsburgh National Guard. Below on the tracks, a handful of railroad employees stood guard.

Sheriff Fife was reading aloud from a piece of paper. He could only get in a few words at a time, between the jeers of the listening crowd.

"Governor Hartranft has instructed me . . . . that in order to preserve the peace . . . . I am authorized to use military force . . . . if necessary . . . ."

Finished reading the page, the Sheriff leaned forward, crushing the paper as he gripped the rail. "Peace-loving and law-abiding citizens of Pittsburgh," he lectured sternly but earnestly, "I beseech you to return to your homes. No one wants to use force, but it is our job to protect the peace, and we will do what we must."

He was drowned out by a wave of hoots and yells. "We're doing what we must!" "Protecting the peace, hell! You're just protecting the railroad!" "The Mayor understands the difference between the city and the railroad—you should take a lesson from him and go mind your own business!" "We're not leaving—it's blood or bread with us!"

The sheriff's response was lost against the myriad voices assaulting him. Eventually he gave up, shook his head at the other two men, and retreated inside the private car. A contemptuous cheer rose among the crowd, followed by the chants, "No freight trains leave this yard!" and "Blood or bread!"

"Round one goes to the rabble," Regina observed.

"That may be," Thomas answered skeptically, "but the final knockout will go to the railroad. You know that."

"Yes, of course," she sighed, her face falling. "But I always hope. Money and power can't always win, can they?"

Thomas looked at Regina in disbelief. "You are money and power. Why are you rooting for the other side?"

Her eyes wandered affectionately over the grim and grimy crowd. "Because somebody has to. My God, Thomas," she continued, indignation rising in her voice, "you know the railroads as well as I do. Greedy, corrupt bastards. They've been bleeding Pittsburgh dry for years. Every manufacturer in this city has been paying twice the rate it costs New York or Chicago. Meanwhile, every railroad president in the country has fired hundreds of men, while they give themselves raises and bonuses. Then they work the surviving employees to death, all the while preventing them from unionizing so they can protect themselves.

"Now, I don't want my employees unionizing, either. But I also don't give them a reason to. I don't abuse them."

Thomas thought about the puddlers' strike two years ago, and his father's particular attention to his artisans. "The railroad owners probably don't think they're abusing their employees."

He didn't expect the surprised smile Regina turned on him. "You're right. They're thoughtless, corrupt and greedy, but they don't spend much time among their manual laborers. They may be unaware of the abuses they're committing. Or they simply don't care. Today, however, every man involved in running this railroad should be afraid of what might happen. The people of Pittsburgh are calling the Pennsylvania Railroad on the carpet!"

****

There was a certain pleasant excitement in the air that afternoon. People laughed, talked, shared stories of their runin with the Pennsylvania Railroad. Factory workers who finished at midday came in from the South Side. The local militia floated about, having been called in the day before. Being sympathetic to the strikers, the local regiments held no formation once General Pearson left with the sheriff. They stacked their arms and mingled with the crowd, chatting as happily as the rest.

The pleasantry was broken by a line of uniforms marching eastward through the crowds. "Those aren't our boys," a hostile murmur rumbled through the crowd. "Those are Philadelphia brigades." The festive mood of the day turned icy in that moment of recognition. "They've got no business being here. This is between us and the railroad." The same sentiment was repeated over and over by voices which grew louder and more indignant as two Philadelphia brigades pushed their way to the center of the tracks at the crossing. "Leave it to the railroad to bully honest men out of an honest protest." "The governor's a filthy coward to send troops out to help the railroads." "The governor? Hell, it's them railroads that are the filthy cowards." "These Philly boys need to go home and mind their own business."

Thomas and Regina could almost hear the orders being barked to the soldiers. Regina made a move to get closer to the soldiers, as Thomas spotted the ladder up one side of a nearby water tank. He took hold of Regina's arm and pointed. "I've got a better idea."

"We won't be able to hear much, but we'll certainly be able to see better," she agreed, and they pushed their way through the dense crush of bodies.

It was only when they'd reached the tank that Thomas remembered that ladies don't generally climb ladders. He hesitated, looking dubiously at her fashionable attire. "Maybe this isn't such a good idea."

"Nonsense." She gathered her train more tightly together and threw it over her shoulder, displaying two stylishly-appointed black boots. Thomas tried hard not to stare, since she was also displaying a fair amount of black stocking as well as a shapely leather-covered ankle. With an effort, he kept his eyes glued to her face as she continued, "But if you're worried, I'll go first. You can catch me if I fall." She turned to put her hand on the nearest rung, but paused to throw over her shoulder, "Besides, you're enough of a gentleman not to tell me if you look up."

She was several steps up the ladder before Thomas closed his mouth and followed.

The tower's walkway put them well above the heads of the crowd. The Philadelphians stood in formation awaiting their next orders. As they watched, the command was obviously given. The soldiers lowered their rifles to point into the crowd. Step by step, they began to move forward, driving the people away from the railroad tracks.

The Pittsburghers were not so easily deterred. An eerie, sullen moment of silence was followed by a roar. A shower of rocks came raining down upon the Philadelphians.

A moment later, a single shot was heard—and then the collective fire of the two regiments.

Thomas pulled Regina out of sight of the militia and threw himself over her. He pressed them both against the shelter of the tank, listening to the shots and the screams of the crowd fleeing in every direction.

"And you were worried we wouldn't be able to hear much from here?" Thomas couldn't refrain from asking.

Just as abruptly as it started, the shooting stopped. Thomas and Regina raised their heads and listened. Thomas could feel Regina's hair tickling his cheek. He was instantly aware of her—the heat of her body pressed against his, her face only inches from his, the smell of her in his nostrils. His breath caught in his throat. "Regina . . ."

"I'm sorry I dragged you into this, Thomas," she interrupted. "You'd be on your way home, if it weren't for me. Instead you're pulling me out of the line of fire. What awful things you must think of me right now!"

Awful things? Like the way the smudges on her cheeks highlighted the beautiful shape of her nose? How all this excitement had put the most spectacular glow in her eyes? He wanted so badly to kiss her—if he looked at her any longer, he'd have to.

He pulled his body off of her, and leaned his back against the wall of the tank. "I don't mind," he dissembled. "You forget—facing gunfire is much more pleasant than facing my family." He smiled self-consciously. "The company's much better here."

She laughed and nudged him with her shoulder. "How chivalrous of you to say so." The smile faded from her face, and she looked away shyly. "My curiosity would have taken me right in front of those rifles, if you hadn't been here with me. You've saved my life, you know. Thank you."

"You're welcome," Thomas answered with equal sobriety. He pictured her lying dead under the soldier's guns, guilty only of sympathy and intellectual curiosity. The vision filled him with rage. There were people out there lying dead; maybe even people he'd talked with that very afternoon. Some of his or Regina's employees could be among the dead or wounded. Or even his house staff. George, or Mary, or Joseph could be among those he could hear moaning. He was filled with the need to see. "Why don't you stay here—I'm going to take a look."

He moved slowly sideways toward a point where he could see the troops. He was not surprised when Regina followed him. "What did I just say about my curiosity? Do you think I'd pass up another chance to die?" Thomas knew better than to protest, and together they crept around the tank, and cautiously peeked down at the tracks.

The troops had achieved their objective. The tracks at the crossing were clear. They stood in formation, at attention, their arms at their sides, guarding the tracks. Their faces were impassive, and not one of them looked down.

The dead and dying lay scattered about the rail yard. There were men, women, even children lying face down in the dirt. A young man in the uniform of the 14th National Guards, one of the Pittsburgh regiments, was crawling away from the scene, his right arm and leg both covered in blood.

From his elevated viewpoint, Thomas could see movements beyond the rail yard, as people half-dragged, half-carried dead and wounded away from the crossing. He could see the shock on people's faces—he could also feel the anger. It was a burning, deadly anger. These Philadelphians shot down protesters in cold blood. By God, this wasn't over yet.

Thomas and Regina both sat down on the hard metal deck of the water tower. They sat in silence, too appalled by the scene below to say anything.

"They could have shot over people's heads, and probably had the same effect without killing anybody," Regina said eventually.

"Could be," Thomas answered, only half paying attention. He'd seen movement on the streets below. Yes, indeed: the protesters were returning. He nudged Regina—easy to do, since she'd been leaning against him—and pointed. She looked, and a grim, glad smile reached her lips, if not her eyes.

As afternoon stretched into evening, Regina and Thomas remained at their perch, watching. They did not move; the soldiers did not move. But the people of Pittsburgh were on the move. The protesters of the afternoon began to return. As the news of the massacre spread, even more citizens of the city turned out from their houses and crammed the streets. The rail yard once again filled with bodies—and now, instead of the happy faces of the afternoon, there was a sea of angry, determined ones.

The Philadelphians were perfectly aware that the mood had turned ugly. They stood rigidly at attention, still keeping the tracks clear at the crossing. As the numbers of angry people blocked the rest of the tracks, it became obvious that the soldiers' objective was moot: no trains were going to be running any time soon.

Regina and Thomas regained their feet in order to stretch their legs when the troops began marching along the tracks below them.

"Do you suppose they're leaving?" Regina asked, puzzled. "After all, they can't possibly get a train through this rail yard."

Thomas scanned the panoramic view afforded by the water tower. There were now thousands of people crowding the rail yard, outnumbering the hundreds of soldiers leaving the crossing. He realized the regiment's objective and pointed as the first men entered the roundhouse nearby. "They're not leaving," he observed. "They're going to ground."

"But they'll be surrounded in there."

Thomas looked over the still-growing mob. "They're surrounded anyway. This way, at least there will be a wall between the troops and the crowd."

"Somehow, I doubt that will improve matters," Regina muttered, mostly to herself.

"Well, it has improved matters in one way," Thomas pointed out. "We can get off this water tower now."

As they climbed back down the ladder, Thomas and Regina could see that people were following the troops toward the roundhouse.

Thomas felt a surge of relief as his feet touched the ground. As he turned to lift Regina down from the ladder, he also felt a twinge of regret. Discounting the draining emotions of the afternoon—the fear of being shot, the anger at the deaths, and the long uncomfortable wait on the rough, narrow platform—he'd had Regina entirely to himself.

****

At some point, as the soot-blackened skies were growing noticeably darker, Thomas realized that the crowds had thinned—rather considerably.

"Where did everybody go?" Regina turned and asked him.

Thomas shrugged and shook his head. His eyes scanned the thinning crowd. He thought he detected a "flow" of people moving eastward. "It looks like people are heading toward downtown."

Regina looked at him seriously. "The armory's downtown."

They didn't wait long before the mob spilled back into the rail yard. As far as Thomas could tell, people were converging from everywhere—and, as Regina had pointed out, the rioters now had weapons.

Then he saw the cannon.

Several men were pointing it at the roundhouse, while others were straggling behind, toting cannonballs. The war was about to escalate—and they were right in the middle of the battlefield!

Thomas scanned over the heads of the mob. It was definitely time to get Regina out of there. But where to go?

He spotted the steeple of St. Philomena's Church, across from the railroad. There were already people leaning out of the bell tower, and others sitting on the sloped church roof. "Come on," he took Regina's hand, and pulled her through the thickening crowd.

They were struggling against a strong current of bodies going the other direction. The church across Liberty Avenue seemed very far away. Thomas put his head down and pushed forward, using his shoulders to create a path between the rioters.

The people thinned only when they crossed Liberty Avenue. Onlookers lined the street; Thomas decided not to try the front doors of the church, for fear of creating another human stampede.

He led Regina down the side of the building. Sure enough, there was a side door. He pushed against it, and then he and Regina stumbled into the relative quiet of the sanctuary.

They stood panting for a moment. "Feel like a buffalo yet?" he asked her between breaths. Regina nodded her agreement.

Thomas looked around. There had to be stairs to the bell tower here somewhere . . . . aha. A narrow circular staircase behind a well-carved wooden door curled upwards like a wisp of wrought iron smoke. Anxious to see what was going on, they were up the steps in a flash.

As he stepped onto the steeple platform, the first thing Thomas noticed was that the roof of every building along Liberty Avenue had people on it. They weren't the only onlookers putting a little distance between themselves and the spectacle below! He turned to point out the rooftop crowds to Regina, but she was gripping his arm and pointing back toward the rail yard.

Thomas wasn't sure what she was looking at, then a resounding boom filled his ears and he knew. The rioters had fired the cannon at the roundhouse!

Another boom crackled through the air. And another. The rioters had succeeded in ripping a hole into the side of the building.

The hair rose all over Thomas' body at the next sound which filled the night air. It was the roar of voices charging into battle; in this case, making a charge at the hole they'd opened in the roundhouse wall.

Between the darkness and the smoke, it was hard to see. Thomas strained to make out shapes when a now-familiar sound followed. For the second time that day, the Philadelphia troops opened fire.

Once again, shouts of anger turned into screams of pain. But this mob was not the festive crowd of strikers from that afternoon: a handful of dead and wounded would not scatter them. The crowd was too large, and far too angry.

That anger was shared by the spectators across Liberty Avenue. The onlookers were screaming for military and railroad blood, along with the protestors. He looked at Regina. The same hot bloodlust was in her face, too. "That's twice in one day, Thomas. Twice that Pittsburghers are lying dead."

A brilliant light flared up from the rail yard. "Well, I don't think Pittsburgh is going to simply accept this," Thomas predicted.

"That crowd wants its pound of flesh, and they'll stand out there until they get it."

They turned to look at the new light source. Flames were illuminating the rail yard; an oilcar was on fire! As they watched in horrible fascination, the rioters were running behind the flaming car, pushing it toward the roundhouse.

Regina covered her nose and mouth as the acrid smell of burning oil reached them. Blinking back stinging tears, they watched as the burning car rolled forward, tilted on the track, and crashed into the sandhouse.

There was a collective groan from the rooftops. The sandhouse was too far from the roundhouse to pose any danger. Then a cheer rose as another car was set on fire.

All through the night, Thomas and Regina watched from the church steeple as the mob lay siege to the roundhouse. The rioters sent burning cars crashing toward the building, while the troops scattered obstacles on the tracks and turned the roundhouse hydrants on the closest blazes. Occasionally a small crew would attempt to load and fire the cannon, only to be stopped by sharp-shooters firing through the previously-made hole. Even across Liberty Avenue, Thomas and Regina could feel the intense heat from the fire on their faces.

It was morning when Regina spotted the first ranks of the regiment through the smoke, marching in formation in an orderly withdrawal. She touched Thomas' shoulder. "Look—they're leaving."

Alternately illuminated by flames and obscured by thick clouds of smoke, Thomas could see the troops marching away from the roundhouse. They kept the building between them and the mob's instruments of destruction; neither burning cars nor cannon were in a direct line of fire.

They watched as the troops disappeared out of sight. The people of Pittsburgh had succeeded in driving the troops away. But to Thomas, it felt like a hollow victory. Maybe because the rules of sportsmanship required the winner to show charity toward the loser. Maybe because the troops had put up a valiant fight, successfully defending the roundhouse against the onslaught of cannonballs and burning cars. Or maybe because the anger and need for revenge had cooled during the long night.

Thomas was alone in his sentiment. There was a murmur of approval rumbling across the rooftops. "Good riddance," seemed to be the general reaction.

Down below, the rioters realized their target had vacated. Part of the crowd cheered and hugged each other for their victory, others gave pursuit to the retreating troops, waving their guns and still shouting for blood. Still others had apparently decided to finish what they'd started, and turned their attentions to the demolition of the roundhouse. They manned the cannon and cleared the tracks of obstacles, so that more burning cars could be sent crashing into the roundhouse.

A mad frenzy of celebration ensued. With the roundhouse now engulfed in flames, people set fire to anything on railroad property that would burn. Then a new activity began to occupy the rioters—looting.

No doubt the logic, if one could call it that, was, "since it'll be lost anyway, why burn the stuff that we can use?" The rioters had assumed possession of the rail yard and everything on it; literally as well as figuratively.

Thomas stood rooted to the spot. This was no longer railroad property! People were walking away with bundles of all sorts: hams, sides of bacon, eggs, umbrellas, calicos and laces, blankets, and countless shapeless sacks which could contain just about anything.

Yet, even as he knew it was wrong to be carrying off the non-railroad goods, it was hard not to be amused by the proceedings. A small boy was slowly dragging along a bag at least twice his size, tugging it forward inch by inch, occasionally stopping to rest before resuming his Herculean task. A woman went by, completely covered in flour, carefully keeping a large mound of it in her apron. A crowd of people ran past, all rolling barrels in front of them. One barrel smashed open, and a lake of molasses poured out. Now unfortunate people stepped into the molasses and got stuck in the sticky mess.

It was theft, it was lawlessness. As he watched the chaotic crowds which packed Liberty Avenue, Thomas saw a hundred little human tragedies.

His eyes were constantly searching, in fear that he would recognize a face. Were his employees part of this carnival? Did he pay his men so poorly that their wives were jumping between burning cars in hopes of stealing an apronful of flour? He wondered if Regina was thinking the same thing.

"I suppose we shouldn't be watching this," he said in her ear.

"Why do you say that?" she asked, never taking her eyes off the scene below.

Thomas wasn't sure what to say. "I don't know—it makes us accomplices or something."

She turned her head to look at him. Thomas suppressed a smile—her face was covered with oily soot. "We are accomplices. If every one of us spectators stopped watching and did something, we could try to stop the looting. It would be a damned foolish thing to do, but we should try. But the truth of the matter is, we're not inclined to. The railroad brought this on themselves, and yes, we know this is wrong, but we're still angry. If our employees want a free barrel of molasses out of this, they're welcome to it. I'm just hoping those goods down there are from New York or Chicago—that would be even sweeter revenge."

Thomas was a little surprised at her vehemence. "Remind me never to get on your bad side. Although I can't take you too seriously when you've got big black smudges on your face!"

"Your entire face is one big black smudge!" Regina countered. "So I'm not taking you seriously, either."

They grinned at each other a moment. Then a collective cheer rose among the crowd. Turning their attention back to the spectacle before them, their eyes searched for the cause. It didn't take long to spot: at the end of the rail yard, the Union Depot was on fire!

The news spread on the street faster than the fire was spreading through the building. People were running down the street to get a better view of the blaze. Looters abandoned their activity to go watch.

From their elevated view, Thomas and Regina could see the flames leaping out of the windows of the three-story building.

Given the activities of the afternoon, there was no question in anyone's mind that the depot was deliberately set on fire. Burning cars could easily have been pushed right up to the depot, under the awnings where passengers disembarked.

Regina laughed, pulled on Thomas' sleeve, and pointed. Thomas looked where she was pointing, and his jaw dropped in astonishment. The crowd of onlookers watching from the rooftops had doubled—maybe even tripled. Those who would not watch the siege of the roundhouse or the pillaging of the rail yard were now gleefully standing to watch the burning of the Union Depot.

Pittsburgh had collected its pound of flesh.

The onlookers cheered when the flames claimed a new portion of the building. They cheered as a nearby grain elevator caught fire. They cheered as the grain elevator collapsed, and again when the roof of the Union Depot collapsed.

Suddenly, the riot was over. The property of the Pennsylvania Railroad was a smoldering ruin. Thc collcctive anger had been satisfied in a cleansing outpouring of destruction, and people just—went home. It was Sunday evening, and people had to go to work in the morning. The crowd simply dissipated.

It was time for Thomas and Regina to go home, as well. They took a last look at the fire still smoldering in the shell that had been the Union Depot, and surveyed the wreckage that had been the rail yard. Even the intense heat of the fires had not bent the steel rails, which were strewn with piles of axles. They looked for all the world like the discarded chicken bones after a giant's picnic.

There was nothing left of the roundhouse but a pile of rubble. There was also nothing left of the water tower which had given them shelter during the first massacre at the crossing.

The hours they sat leaning against the tower seemed like a very, very long time ago. Thomas realized with some surprise that he was tired.

"We've been up for two days," he realized out loud.

"Tired?" Regina asked him. He looked at her smudged face—she was looking tired, too.

"Yes, I am," he admitted.

"Mother Nature is going to succeed where every other authority figure has failed," Regina observed. "She's convinced us all to go home."

With a backward glance at the panorama of destruction, they turned toward the stairs.

At street level, the scope of the damage seemed much more real. They had to watch their step to avoid the remains of the molasses quagmire. The acrid smell of still-smoldering remains seemed stronger in their nostrils, the axles across the tracks larger. The length and breadth of the charred rail yard seemed to stretch into forever.

Night began to fall as they walked down Liberty Avenue. They passed the last of the burned buildings, and the city became familiar again. The smell of burning oil and wood was replaced by the faint smell of hops as they passed the brewery, and later, the smells of grease and fennel as they reached the Italian grocers.

They said very little. Thomas hadn't even asked permission to walk her home—it just seemed natural that he would. His head was full of visions from the last two days. The bodies lying dead on 28th Street. The crush of people in the streets as they carried back weapons looted from the armory. The flaming cars as they careened toward the embattled roundhouse. Regina's hair tickling his cheek. Stop—plenty of time to savor the memories of her later. Right now, she was still only inches away from him.

He looked down at her. He could see that the same exhilarating and disturbing images were playing in her mind. "The newspaper ought to be interesting tomorrow morning," he joked, softly disturbing her reverie.

"I don't know if I'll want to read it, the account will be so badly skewed," she answered with a scornful toss of her head.

"The out-of-town papers will be better," Thomas agreed. "Just remember to keep your sense of humor while you read."

"I'll bet you I lose my sense of humor while I read," she answered dryly.

They fell silent again for a long while. Finally, they reached Fifth Avenue. The gas lights in the houses shimmered at them through the hot night air. They passed house after house, large stately homes which proclaimed wealth and power. A few were probably even owned by railroad men.

Tired as he was, Thomas was sorry when they turned their feet up the drive to Regina's house. She'd been his for two days of glorious chaos while the world had gone mad. Now they—and the world—were returning to normal.

The front door was wide open to catch any hint of breeze which might pass. Regina stepped through the doorway, and almost immediately the quiet house erupted into sound. The fuss of the house staff was drowned out as Henry's voice came thundering down the stairs. "Regina?!" Thomas could hear equal parts anger and relief in the single word.

The large man was down the stairs so swiftly, it was hard to believe his feet ever touched the stairs. Henry swept his wife up in a bear hug, lifting her so her feet didn't quite touch the ground. "You're safe," he sighed.

"Of course I'm safe," Regina answered with a kiss. Henry put her back on her feet as he realized Thomas was standing with the servants in the foyer. "Nothing could possibly have happened to me. Thomas was watching over me like a hawk the entire time."

Of course she noticed. She always read him like a street sign. Thomas didn't know what to say. Regina had her hand stretched out toward him. He stepped forward and took the hand, looking from Regina to Henry.

"What else could I do?" he shrugged at Henry, then looked back at Regina. "If you were going to be in the thick of things, at least I could provide escort." He spoke as casually as if they were discussing a tea party, not a riot.

"Well, I'm glad you were there," Henry told him. "I've heard people were actually killed!"

Regina looked innocently at Thomas. "Yeah. We heard that, too."

Thomas was astonished. So Regina wasn't going to tell the whole story to her husband!

On second thought, he didn't want Henry knowing how close they'd come to death, either. "Everybody heard that—it was all over. That's what got people worked up, in the first place."

"I can give you all the details in the morning," Regina promised Henry with a yawn. "But right now, I'm so tired. We need to get Thomas home."

The carriage driver was called, and Thomas was bundled inside with great ceremony. The familiar feel of horsehair cushions felt reassuring after the hours of standing in the rough wooden steeple. Thomas fell asleep almost immediately as the carriage rocked over the cobblestones.

Chapter 7

He woke as the Warings' coachman opened the carriage door to let him off at his own carriage block. He blinked a moment; he'd been dreaming of brushing Regina's long, black hair. He'd taken out the pins, watched the silky waves tumble down over her shoulders. He brushed the black mass until it shone, then reached under it to undo the top button at the nape of her neck . . .

And then reality forced his eyes open with the click of the door latch.

He'd barely stood up when a shriek came from the house. "Thomas!" That was why he had sworn off alcohol. His wife had a voice that would not mix well with hangovers. It was probably peeling the paint; he'd better ask Joseph to check for damage.

Meredith flew down the stairs. Thomas could see she was ready to put on quite a performance, and mentally braced himself. She bodily threw herself at him, flinging her arms around his neck. "Oh, my darling," she sobbed.

Before he could remove her clinging hands, two more voices shouted from the front door. "Thomas!" "Son?" Now his parents rushed forward to greet him. His mother reached out to grip his arm in both her hands, reassuring herself that he was real. His father held back, already regretting such a show of feeling, and stood clearing his throat in a manly fashion.

All three of them were talking at once. The sound assaulted his tired ears, and Thomas tried to separate the cacophony into voices. "You're alive!" "I was afraid you'd been killed by that mob!"

"We heard there was shooting." "That was a dangerous thing to do, son, wading into a strike."

Thomas raised his arms over his head and waved. "Whoa!" he shouted. The voices died. "I'm fine." He turned to thank the Warings' coachman, but the driver had already returned to his seat and was clicking to the horses. They trotted away up Buena Vista. Oh well—it gave him an excuse to send a thank you note to the Waring household tomorrow. He turned back to his hovering family.

"Have you been with that Waring woman all this time?" Meredith asked accusingly.

Of course they knew. George would have told them that he'd waded into the morass in Regina's company.

"When Mrs. Waring told me she intended to take a closer look, it was my duty as a gentleman to look after her. But if that holds no value for you, remember this," Thomas gave his wife a cool, steady look. "Our association with the Warings has been extremely profitable. If you want new dresses this fall, my dear, Mrs. Waring needed to stay alive. So protecting her was also my duty as your husband."

He did like taking the wind out of Meredith's sails. She stood with her mouth still open for a moment. "Oh," was all she finally said.

"Regina's a wild woman," Richard Baldwin observed. "Her instincts are always sound—but this was pure lunacy." He shook his head, but his eyes looked at Thomas with shrewd appraisal. "Henry Waring owes you a great big favor for this."

Thomas felt filthy, letting his family think that he'd protected Regina for economic strategy. But—better that than the truth. He tried to smirk at his father. "Yes, that has occurred to me," he answered, trying to put a touch of smugness in his voice.

His father nodded once in approval, and turned back toward the house. Thomas and the women followed behind. Thomas noticed that the entire house staff had assembled to peep out the windows. They discreetly vanished as the small party climbed the steps, except for Joseph, who opened the front door.

"Would you tell the staff I'm quite all right, Joseph? And thank them for their concern."

Joseph shared his warm, gruff smile. "We've been worried about you. Mary's been white as a sheet since George told us where you'd gone. We all knew you were good people, and that's why you went there in the first place, but we're all real glad you're home."

Thomas felt genuinely warmed by his house staff's concern—more so, indeed than by his family's cloying hysteria. He touched Joseph briefly on the arm, then followed his family into the parlor.

"Honestly, Thomas," his mother scolded him as he entered behind them, "you talk to your servants as if they were equals."

"They're people, Mother," Thomas answered her wearily.

"Well, of course they're people, whoever said they weren't?" Thomas knew better than to argue with his mother. He just forgot sometimes. Eugenia continued, "But you shouldn't go making friends with them. You've got to consider your position."

"That's wonderful advice, Mother," Thomas tried to answer, when an immense yawn nearly split his head in two. "Can I sleep on it?"

Just then the chime on the mantel began to sing. It was midnight.

"We've all been up late, Thomas," Meredith interjected. "And we can't send your parents home at this hour." She smiled dotingly at him. "We'd better give them your room for the night."

Thomas desperately tried to clear the cobwebs from his brain. The little bitch had got him good. He'd turned the third bedroom into his library—to serve as a barrier between his room and hers. But it meant they didn't have a guest room to offer. If they had planned guests, at a reasonable hour, he could have fled to the Duquesne Club for the night. But at this hour, there was no escape. He couldn't think of any way around it.

"Of course, my dear," he answered silkily, remembering the settee in his library—unfortunately his mother thought of the same thing.

"If it wouldn't be too much of a bother, Meredith, dear, Richard has such a snore, can we find him a bed in Thomas' little library? Otherwise I'll never get a wink of sleep all night."

Meredith smiled happily. "Of course."

Now Thomas was really trapped. With a tired sigh, he turned toward the stairs as Meredith rung for Mary. "Mary, please bring a set of spare bedding to the library. We're having company tonight."

"Yes, Ma'am."

He and Mary met on the landing after he'd gathered his nightclothes from his bedroom. "Mister Baldwin," she whispered his name. It was half a whisper, half a sigh.

"Hello, Mary," Thomas felt a certain gratification from the intense relief in her face. She turned pink, then white, then pink again.

"It's good to have you home, sir," she finally smiled back.

"Thank you, Mary. Although I fear this long night keeps getting longer," Thomas sighed candidly, looking at the nightclothes in his hand and the bedclothes in hers.

"Yes sir." The beautiful eyes twinkled mischievously, and she impulsively blurted out, "If you have trouble sleeping here, you can always come up to the servants' quarters. We'll hide you." She turned a bit rosier at her audacity, and her eyes dropped to study the floor.

Thomas was surprised and amused by her offer. "'We'll hide you?' Mary, what kind of gossip goes on up there?"

Mary shrugged her shoulders, hugging the bedding to herself and putting her chin on top of the pillows she was carrying. "You know I don't pay any attention to idle gossip, Mr. Baldwin."

"Mary," he said, mock-sternly.

"There are never two people in the same room in this house. Mrs. Baldwin takes to the parlor, you take to your library. If she has her tea in the morning room, you'll have yours in the dining room. We never need to place more than one chair before a fire, or bring more than one place setting," she paused delicately before continuing, "or fluff more than one pillow."

Thomas was interested by her observations. “I had no idea I was so obvious.”

“It’s not a matter of being obvious, sir,” she explained simply. “Any good worker knows the preferences of his employer. You prefer to be apart from Mrs. Baldwin.” She shrugged again. “As your staff, we all know that as a fact, so we can plan accordingly.”

The sound of voices rose from the hall—his wife and parents were following him up the stairs. Mary vanished into the library in a puff of pillows and he resolutely opened the door to Meredith’s room.

He had not set foot inside since she had taken up residence on their wedding night. He remembered approving the pink roses-and-lilies wallpaper (“it’s so sickly sweet, I’m sure she’ll approve”). The room was filled with lamps, cushions, curtains; everything frilly and feminine. As he looked around with distaste, he tried to imagine what Regina’s room would look like. Elegant, no doubt. An occasional, restrained use of a floral pattern. Or maybe exotic, with Moroccan or Arabian accents.

Another yawn interrupted his survey of the room. Well, at least with his eyes closed, he wouldn’t be able to see it.

Fearing the scene Meredith no doubt had in store for him, he hastily undressed and donned his summer nightshirt. He was dragging a coverlet and pillow off the bed by the time Meredith finished depositing his parents and entered the room.

“Why, Thomas, what are you doing?” Meredith demanded in amazement.

“Close the door, Meredith,” Thomas instructed. “My parents don’t need to listen to your performance.”

Meredith gave him one of those uncomprehending stares which he found so nerve-wracking, but she obeyed and closed the door behind her.

“To answer your question,” Thomas continued wearily, “I’m making myself a place to sleep. It’s hot enough that you won’t be needing the comforter. But I can use it. The floor is rather hard.”

Meredith saw her opportunity. “You don’t have to sleep on the floor, Thomas.”

As she stepped toward him, Thomas recalled her predatory movements in the music room over two years ago. "Yes, yes I know—we're married. That doesn't mean I have any intention of ever getting into the same bed with you."

He hadn't even slowed Meredith's momentum. "Why not, Thomas? Since we are married, why not make the best of it? You've never given me a chance, Thomas. I can make you happy, if only you'll let me."

Thomas sighed. He was so tired. The only happiness he wanted right now was the blissful oblivion of sleep.

He hadn't realized he'd been backing up until he stepped on the comforter arranged under the window. Meredith was still moving forward, in an uncanny repeat of the morning in the music room. In a moment she'd start undressing.

This is ridiculous. It was time to take control of the situation. "Do you really want to make me happy, Meredith?" he asked softly.

"Oh, yes, Thomas!" she was breathing seductively against him, having succeeded in cornering him between the window and the armoire.

"Then let me get some sleep. I haven't slept in two days, and I'm very tired."

That was not the answer Meredith wanted. She frowned, and sparks snapped in her eyes. "Thomas!"

He hated when people used his name frequently. Usually salesmen, or shifty foremen, or bankers—it was a signal for untrustworthiness. Not that he didn't trust Meredith—he knew exactly what to expect from her.

But as he gave her one of his loathing looks which usually quelled her protests, she actually surprised him by meeting his gaze, squaring her shoulders, and gathering some semblance of dignity about her.

"We've been married for two years, Thomas, and you've never treated me like a wife," she began archly.

"I think I just did," he retorted dryly.

She was not to be deterred. “You’ve ignored me, locked me out, and embarrassed me whenever you could. You hardly ever dance with me. Sometimes I think you’ve even hid, so I wouldn’t have a partner for the Grand March.”

“Oh, what powers of perception,” Thomas thought coolly to himself. But he didn’t interrupt her string of grievances.

“How do you suppose it looks, that you will hardly dance with me? You ask other women to dance, but not me. You make me wait, and wonder. I practically have to ask you. And I haven’t done the last waltz since we were engaged. Either you disappear as soon as it’s announced,” her lips curled down in an angry pout, “or you’re dancing with your mother.”

Thomas was rather proud of that particular dodge. He looked at her in mild surprise. “Can’t a man dance with his own mother sometimes?”

She was not about to be mollified by his offhand excuses. “People still talk,” she answered steadily.

Thomas was unamused. “And what precisely do they say, Meredith?” His voice cracked like a whip. “That, gee, they don’t seem to be a very happy couple? That he can’t even stand to be in the same room with her, much less put his arms around her long enough to dance with her? It does, of course, make it less surprising that they haven’t produced any offspring, even though they were immediately engaged after that shocking indiscretion . . .”

“That’s another way you’ve embarrassed me,” Meredith interrupted him. “Janey and Elsie both got married after me. Janey has a baby now, and Elsie . . . .” Meredith stopped and dropped her eyes. Babies were fine—but having them was not a subject discussed between men and women. Even in private, in the middle of a fight. “Elsie will have one soon.” The fight came back into her eyes, and she lifted her face again. “I was married first—I should have been the one to tell them things.” A blush crept over her face. “Instead, they tell me about,” her face now crimson, she had to stop and take a deep breath, “what people do when they’re married. Do you know what it’s like, hearing them describe these—these things” (Thomas noted with offhand amusement that sexual acts were "things" to Meredith), "and then they ask me questions, and I can't even answer them!"

Thomas smiled—almost sympathetically. "I don't generally get approached for sexual advice, no. But you see, my dear, I'm a gentleman. A gentleman doesn't discuss his wife's bedroom talents with other gentlemen. But do tell me, dear wife, do ladies discuss their husbands'—or do they ask you since your method for getting married proved you were no lady?" Meredith gasped at the insult as he continued, "And now I am curious—in what terms have you bragged about my sexual prowess, considering you've no firsthand knowledge of it? Or have you actually told your bosom friends the truth about our unique marital relationship?"

"I told them you were a gentleman," she answered loftily, "and that I couldn't discuss such matters."

"Well, well," he murmured. "My wife is capable of telling the truth, if you put her under enough duress."

Meredith could see that she was losing ground. She stamped her foot like a child. "You're hateful!"

"Well, at least we're alike in one regard," Thomas agreed smoothly. "I'm providing you with a rather nice roof over your head, a generous clothing allowance, use of the carriage you'd admired so much, and a staff of highly competent if under-appreciated servants. Since you're waving the Baldwin name all over the city, you're at least entitled to that. But that's all you're entitled to. I'm not part of the deal. I won't dance with you. I'm past caring about anything the town gossips say about us. And I'm not performing my marital duties. You'll be the envy of town, my dear. Other married women are forced to submit to their husbands' demands and engage in this rather undignified act. It's part of their duty as wives. I'm releasing you from that duty."

"It's her isn't it?" Meredith asked suddenly.

The abrupt change of topic threw Thomas. He blinked at Meredith for a moment. "Who?"

"That Waring woman." The dislike rose bitterly in her voice. "You're in love with her. You have been since before we got married."

Thomas was surprised. Insight, from Meredith? Well, even a blind squirrel will find a few nuts. And Meredith did seem to have a fascination for mating rituals.

For one free mad moment, he imagined spilling out the truth to her. "Love her? I adore her. Worship her. I've memorized every word she's ever said to me. I ache with the beauty of her every movement. I'd wait all night in the rain just to see her tilt her head to the side, the way she does when she's listening. I'd walk to the ends of the earth just to see her smile. I lay awake at night thinking of things to make her laugh. I will never love a woman the way I love her."

But that was his secret. It was locked in his heart, a familiar pain he would live with every day until he died. It was a part of him too sacred to share with anyone.

"My dear," he answered aloud, "you needn't go looking among my business partners for the source of my inattentiveness. All you need to do is look in a mirror."

"I don't understand," Meredith said.

"Of course you don't." His distaste at being shackled to this woman bubbled up to the surface. "Ignorami such as yourself aren't generally equipped with the mental capacity for much comprehension, are they? Every glimpse I get of your vapid countenance is a mnemonic that I've been saddled with an imbecile. Some men may not be so punctilious—but I'm not about to engage in coitus with such a repugnant vessel as you provide. And so, madame, you might as well resign yourself to the fact that your inquisiturient tendencies on this subject are going to remain unsatisfied.

"Now, if you'll excuse me, I'm taking my rest in the only room still unoccupied." Feeling drained by his soliloquy, he turned and scooped up the bedding off the floor. Time to start using his mother's technique—deliver a threat then leave the room.

"Wait!" Meredith was crying now. "Thomas, you know I didn't understand half of the words you just used."

"If you did understand them, wife of mine, you wouldn't have to worry about dying a virgin." He walked to the bathroom door. "I will be sleeping in the bathtub tonight," he informed her. "If you disturb me, I will kill you."

As he threw the pillow and coverlet inside the big porcelain fixture, he thought he was going to have to inform her that her sobs qualified as "disturbing." But he was asleep as soon as his head reached the pillow.

Chapter 8

1878 seemed to start out as badly as 1877. When things began to improve, it happened so gradually, it took a while to realize that the Panic was over.

Thomas sat at his desk in the Olympus tower, staring at the open account books without actually seeing them. It was nearly eight o'clock at night; the building was empty. It was so silent his ears rang, and his thoughts seemed too loud.

His mind wandered aimlessly, thinking over things that needed to be done, wondering what Mary would bring him on his nightly supper tray. Memories of college shenanigans with his friend Michael rose unbidden to the surface. He wanted a bigger house. Meredith would no doubt like a few more servants to harass.

He jumped a foot high when a cough sounded from the doorway. He whirled around in his chair, knocking books, papers, and inkwell to the floor.

Henry Waring hurried forward to help him clean up the mess. "I'd definitely say you've put in too long of a day when your friends can't even come to visit," he said with his usual hearty chuckle. He picked up the accounts ledger and laid it back on the desk. "Money worries?" he asked gently.

"No—that's just it," Thomas answered. "I can meet my payroll and I don't know why. The money's there. It's been years since I've just paid my people. Usually I have to beg, or borrow, or at least pray really hard. My bookkeeper, Fred, hasn't asked for money for weeks. I had to see for myself what's going on."

"Things are definitely improving," Henry observed. "Orders are up—I'm even hiring people. It's not over yet, but the end is coming. Which is why I came to see you. The Panic will be over soon, and when people have money again, they'll want something to spend it on." Henry pulled up a chair and sat facing Thomas. "I'm here to invite you to join me on a venture into architecture."

"Architecture? You've lost me, Henry. I make iron, remember? Not too much of that in most buildings. I'm not set up to do wrought iron railings."

Henry leaned back in his chair and grinned at Thomas. "You're not thinking about the right kinds of buildings. I make glass, you make iron. Put them together, you get the kind of luxury buildings people haven't been building much lately."

Thomas slapped his forehead. "Wintergardens! You want to build wintergardens?"

"That's right." Henry sat upright, and Thomas could feel the explosion of pent-up enthusiasm. "Here's what I'd been thinking. They've been putting up custom greenhouses for seventy-five years or so—why hasn't someone standardized the parts? If we did, and offered a variety of sections that could fit together in any number of ways . . ."

"Why, hell, we could sell them through the Montgomery Ward catalogue!" Thomas' eyes filled with visions of greenhouses. Little, private hothouses. Huge exhibition-sized palaces. He knew just the drafter he'd need to talk to about this . . . .

Henry interrupted his rapidly spiraling daydreams. "I guess you can see where I was going with this. I take it you're interested?"

"Am I! When do we start?" Thomas asked with a grin as wide as Henry's.

"Right now, if I can convince you to leave your desk and go eat. I swear I could smell roast pheasant when I passed the Duquesne Club, and it's been at the back of my mind ever since."

****

Waring-Baldwin Wintergardens began that very night, with the rough draft of a contract scrawled on a napkin in Henry's nearly illegible handwriting. It added a new interest—and a new complication—to Thomas' life. Here was a business that was his own, not a set of tasks passed down to him from his father. His own venture, where he could take his own risks and revel in his own successes.

It also put him into a much closer relationship with both Warings. He honestly enjoyed Henry's company—very much. He was Thomas' senior by several years, but always treated him as a partner and an equal, not as a son to whom he dictated. But the frequent glimpses he got into Regina's perfect relationship with her husband gave Thomas an almost unbearable pain.

Still, being able to work together, to dream together, was worth the moments of agony. Regina laughed at them one night, when she discovered the two men in the kitchen at two o'clock in the morning, surrounded by blueprints and half-eaten muffins. Thomas didn't mind being laughed at. The vision of her, her hair tumbling free to her waist, the red and gold wrapper making her skin glow, kept him awake for many a night. The three of them had a champagne toast when the company became official—and again when the first order came.

It was a large one, for a conservancy in St. Paul, Minnesota. Henry brought the news himself, in a typically Henry sort of fashion. He blew into Thomas' office one afternoon, and thoroughly confused his secretary, David, by chatting away about the closed deal without stopping to give the least bit of context.

It was hard not to overhear Henry's happy loud voice in the next room: "You ready to put in the long hours, son? This is going to be a whole new adventure, but it's going to be work, make no mistake."

"I'm sure it is, sir," David Smith was a tactful fellow, which made him a very useful secretary. Thomas pushed his chair back away from his desk and stood up to go rescue him. Mr. Smith made an excellent gatekeeper; it seemed a shame to waste his talents on someone he was as glad to see as Henry Waring.

"Henry, are you telling my secretary that we actually got an order for a wintergarden before you tell me?"

"Would I do that?" Henry looked from David, to Thomas, and back again. "Oh. I guess maybe I just did. Well, I had to tell somebody. We're in business, Thomas! We're going to Minnesota!" He handed Thomas a bottle of champagne and looked around. "You mean Gina isn't here yet? She went to send the telegram while I went to get the champagne. I thought she'd beat me here."

"I'm not hiding her anywhere. Smith? Are you hiding Mrs. Waring in a desk drawer somewhere?"

"Not last I looked, sir." Thomas had never been able to decide if the man had no sense of humor, or an exceedingly deadpan one.

"There you have it—you beat her here, so you get to tell me the news. Do you want to start over? I'll just go sit in my office and pretend I haven't heard anything." Thomas didn't know what possessed him, but he playfully turned around and went to sit back down, aware of the somewhat incredulous stare of his secretary.

Henry had no such sense of reserve. He followed Thomas into his office and tapped him on the shoulder. "Give me that," he reclaimed the wine bottle from Thomas' hand, walked back out of the room, and closed the office door.

He knocked on the door, and threw it open, waving the bottle in one hand. "Guess what, Thomas? We got it! We're going to be building a wintergarden in Minnesota!"

Enjoying the silliness, Thomas reacted in kind. "Really? Wow, that's great news!" The two men looked at each other, and burst out laughing. They laughed even harder when they realized both Smith and Regina were watching from the desk outside Thomas' door.

"Is someone going to fill me on the joke?" Regina smiled at them both quizzically.

Thomas and Henry looked at each other, and laughed all the more. "No," Henry finally answered his wife. "I don't think we can."

"In that case," she shook her head at the both of them, "why don't I go find some glasses for that champagne. We've got some celebrating to do."

****

Several months later, Thomas was sitting on the veranda on a surprisingly warm April evening, when the Warings' carriage rolled up to his carriage block.

"Now, why on earth," knowing Henry was supposed to be out of town, Thomas felt a guilty pang of disappointment when Henry stepped from the carriage, not Regina. Thomas was further mystified by the box Henry extracted from the seat beside him. Curious, he leaned over the balcony rail. "Why, Henry! It's not even my birthday!"

"So, I'm early!" Henry laughed in response. When he set the box on the porch, Thomas saw there were two black puppies sleeping inside. "Actually, it's Gina's birthday next week," Henry continued. "And I've come to ask you a favor. I've just got back from Ligonier with her birthday present, here." He scratched one of the dogs on the back of its head when it looked up and yawned. "Full-blooded Labrador Retrievers. Gina was promised the pick of this litter.

"Her birthday's not for a week yet, and between now and then I have to go to St. Paul to check on our project. Since I'm going out there, I might as well visit St. Anthony's Falls and check out the new Hungarian rollers a pal of mine installed at his flour mill. Don't know how long it'll take me. In case I'm not back in time for her birthday, I was hoping you'd have it in your heart to take charge of these two?"

Fully awake now, one puppy had its paws on the edge of the box, and was busily cleaning Thomas' hand with its little pink tongue. Thomas rubbed the silky ears. "I don't see why not."

****

Three days later, Thomas was standing in the telegraph office trying to decide whether to use the word "purchase" or "acquisition" on the telegram he was sending when he heard the word "Waring" spoken in the back of the room. Instantly, he was all ears.

"I have no idea where you'll find Mrs. Waring," a freckled teenaged clerk was telling a young messenger boy who gripped a telegram in his hands. "This is going to be difficult, since she could be at any one of her businesses. But you can't leave this at her home for her to find tonight. This is bad news, and she needs it now."

Thomas realized he'd better speak up quickly, or the boy would be halfway to the Glassworks. "Excuse me for eavesdropping, but is that bad news going to Mrs. Henry Waring? I'm Mr. Waring's business partner, if I might be of help," he volunteered.

The freckled clerk looked from Thomas to the messenger boy for a moment. "Well, actually sir, this is pretty hard news, so if you're willing to take this to her, I'd be obliged."

Thomas accepted the telegram from the youngster. He looked down at the card in his hand, then the world stopped as he stared at the message:

MRS WARING EXPLOSION AT MILL STOP HENRY WARING BADLY HURT STOP MAY BE DYING STOP COME IMMEDIATELY STOP

G. CHRISTIAN
WASHBURN CO

"Dear God!" Thomas maintained the presence of mind to tip both the clerk and the messenger. "You've done well to give this to me, gentlemen." His own telegram forgotten, he rushed out the door. Thank goodness for the ever-present George, waiting patiently outside the office door.

"George—to Waring Glassworks as fast as you can. Mr. Waring has been hurt!"

It was an endless, anxious ride to the Glassworks, only to be told Regina was not in. She might be at the bank—or at the newspaper—or the dressmaker's.

There were too many places to look. Thomas told George to drive out to Fifth Avenue, on the off chance she was home. No such luck. But her maid volunteered that Regina had taken both her duster and her heavy boots, which most likely meant she was planning on visiting the flour mills.

Thomas groaned. The flour mills were all the way out in Sewickley, on the Ohio River. He thanked the puzzled house staff, shouting on his way back to the carriage, "If Mrs. Waring returns, please ask her to stay home! It is most urgent that I find her!"

It was a long, feverish ride to Sewickley. The unflappable George had been infected by Thomas' frenzy and whipped the horses into a gallop down the winding river road.

They pulled with a clatter into the small yard of the mill. Thomas was out the carriage door before George could get down from the driver's seat. "Mrs. Waring's carriage is here," George called after him as he sprinted toward the office.

Thomas burst in the office door, making everyone in the room jump. "Where's Mrs. Waring?" he cried.

There was a moment of puzzled silcncc as half a dozen faces stared at him. Then Regina's voice floated through the quiet.

"Thomas? Mr. Baldwin, is that you? I'm right here." Regina's poised figure appeared in a doorway off the main office. She was smiling—then her face froze and she, too, simply stared at him.

Thomas realized the state he was in. He was hatless, breathless, coatless, his cravat was under one ear, and he had no idea where the telegram was. And, now that he'd succeeded in actually finding Regina, he had to find a gentle way to tell her the bad news.

He felt the stares of everyone in the room. Well, no use worrying about it now. Emulating Mary's trick, he pulled a mantle of composure around himself. "I beg your pardon. Sorry to disturb everyone. Mrs. Waring, may I have a moment of your time?"

He saw the amused gleam in her eye. "Of course—please join me in my office?" She turned. Thomas followed, and gently closed the door behind them. Regina was gracefully reseating herself behind a large mahogany desk. "So what brings you to my mills—and in such a state? Have you killed somebody? Your lovely bride, perhaps? I'll be glad to lend you the money to get to Mexico . . ."

Thomas threw himself on his knees at her feet and took both her hands in his. "I only wish that were the case. But I'm afraid it's worse. I happened to be in the telegraph office and intercepted a telegram for you." He took a deep breath. "Henry's been hurt," he told her. "There was an explosion. The telegram said he may be dying—and you should come immediately."

Regina stood up so quickly, Thomas was knocked off balance. "I'm sorry," she apologized, and offered her hand to help him up. But Thomas was already using the solid mahogany desk behind him to get back on his feet.

"Let me drive you to the train. George is waiting," Thomas offered. They half-walked, half-ran through the office under the puzzled stares of the mill employees.

Regina broke into a full run as Thomas opened the door for her. George opened the carriage door as soon as they appeared. Regina was down the stairs and across the gravel in a split second. Thomas was right behind her. "To the train station, George," he directed.

George was up in his seat with a bound, and with an ungraceful lurch which sent both passengers sprawling, they were galloping back down the river road toward Pittsburgh.

There was nothing to do but wait. They sat together in a terrible silence, listening to the clatter of hooves over stones, and the creaks and moans of the carriage. Thomas realized that Regina's hands had curled into fists as they rested in her lap. He reached over and pried one loose from where it was clutching a fold of skirt. He tucked it into the crook of his arm and sat patting it as reassuringly as he could. She reached across with her other hand and clutched his arm with both hands.

"It will be all right," Thomas finally said. "It has to be."

"I just thought of something awkward," she confessed to him in a small voice. "I don't believe I'm carrying enough cash to pay for a railroad ticket all the way to St. Paul. Would you be willing to—um—"

"It would be my privilege to get your ticket." Thomas answered, the gallantry rising to the surface as it always did in Regina's presence.

"I'll pay you back when we return."

Thomas declined her offer. "Thanks to you and Henry, I can afford a train ticket," he pointed out fondly.

"Oh, it wasn't our doing," Regina protested.

"Maybe. But I acknowledge my debts," Thomas countered. "Times have been hard for so long. Other companies have not fared so well. One of the many closures could have been us, if not for your amazing connections. And you singled me out. I'll always be grateful for that."

Regina smiled up at him. "You needed a break. You're good people, you know—you're loyal, decent, and do everything you can to hide that wicked sense of humor of yours. Although I don't suppose you get much opportunity to use it."

"You are my best audience," Thomas told her candidly.

"So, I'm easily amused," she shrugged self-deprecatingly.

"Easy? You think it's easy, keeping you amused? It's a lot of work, trying to be clever," Thomas protested.

"Aha," she pounced. "So you do have to work at it. I wondered."

The moment's levity over, the occupants of the carriage returned to tense silence. It was a long time until they actually pulled up at the train station. Thomas threw himself out of the coach, and held up a hand for Regina.

As she alighted, George volunteered from the driver's box, "Why don't I drive to Mrs. Waring's house while you stay here with her, sir? I can deliver a message to your maid, ma'am," he finished with a respectful nod to Regina.

Regina looked blankly up at George. "Tell my household what's happened. Ask Margaret just to put a few things in a valise—whatever she thinks I'll need."

"Yes, ma'am," George answered solemnly, then looked back at Thomas. "Anything else, sir?"

"Just go. I don't need to ask you to hurry. Thank you, George."

The carriage rolled away with another lurch. Gently, Thomas turned Regina toward the entrance. "Let's get you on a train."

It was two hours before the next passenger train was due. Thomas bought Regina's tickets: Pittsburgh to Chicago, Chicago to St. Paul and all the way back again, with a companion one-way ticket for Henry. Regina was surprised when he explained all the tickets in the little bundle he handed her.

"You needn't have done all this," she exclaimed. "I can wire my bank for money once I get there."

"Well, it's one less thing to worry about," Thomas answered.

Her expression became grim. "You're right. There's no telling what I'm going to find when I get there."

The pain crackling through Regina's voice felt like a jolt of electricity. Thomas' mind created a barrage of horrible images; Henry's large, powerful body lying broken and bleeding. The hands with their bone-crunching grip lying weak and helpless on a thin hospital blanket. The kind eyes staring at nothing, and the hearty voice reduced to a delirious whisper.

Fear swelled in his heart. Fear and guilt. He'd spent many an hour dreaming that Regina was free. But not this way. Dear God, not this way!

He took a shaky breath. "You're going to torture yourself all the way to Minnesota if you think like that." He stood up, and offered her a hand with what he hoped was his most charming smile. "Let's see what the newsstand has to offer."

When they walked back into the waiting room with copies of *Frank Leslie's Illustrated Newspaper* and the *New York Times*, they found George looking for them. He was carrying a small satchel and a white box.

"What on earth—" Regina wondered, peeking inside the box. Then she chuckled. "A box lunch! That woman thinks of everything."

"Yes ma'am, she does," George answered. "You have an entire trunk traveling with you. I've already checked it in for you ma'am. You'll need to claim it when you get to Minnesota." He handed her the baggage ticket.

"You're the soul of efficiency, George. Thank you," she smiled at him.

Thomas dug in his pockets, and discovered a scrap of paper and a pencil. "I'm going to see Mrs. Waring onto her train," he said while he scribbled. "In the meantime, would you send this telegraph to Mr. George Christian at the Washburn Company in St. Anthony's Falls and let him know when Mrs. Waring's train is due in?"

"Of course, sir." He was moving the moment the paper touched his hand.

Once again, all they could do was wait. They tried to talk, but most of their attention was absorbed with listening. They listened to the rumble and screech of train wheels, to the myriad echoed voices in the busy waiting room, to every announcement of the conductor.

At last, Regina's train was announced. Thomas carried the satchel and bundle of papers and followed Regina to her compartment. He put away the satchel, tucked the box lunch away on the shelf overhead, placed her hat beside it. He found a cushion to place on the opposite seat so that Regina could put her feet up. At her bidding, he opened the windows.

Then he couldn't think of anything else. He looked at her, feeling at a loss. He couldn't help her any more.

"You've been my gallant knight all day," she observed, offering both her hands in the familiar gesture. "I can never thank you enough, Sir Thomas."

"No thanks are necessary, dear lady. I am ever at your service." Thomas took both her hands in his, and bowed over them, gallantly.

"Then thank your George again for me. I am in his debt, as well."

"I will, My Lady. Any other commands?" Thomas was enjoying the role she had assigned him. It suited them both—he, the adoring knight, she, his royal queen.

"None." The train whistle blew a warning. "You'd better depart. Thank you, Thomas."

"You're welcome, Regina."

He turned and left her compartment. Leaping down to the station platform, he ran along the train until he came to her window.

"A favor, My Lady?" he shouted up at her.

Regina's face appeared in the window. She smiled down at him, and held out a hand. "I was hoping you hadn't left me yet."

He could just reach her fingertips with his. "Of course not. I'm your knight, and I take my duties seriously." The humor dropped away from his voice. "Would you telegraph me when you have news?"

Regina's jaw trembled suspiciously, and her eyes blinked back an excess of moistness. Not trusting her voice, she nodded.

"I'll take that as a promise," Thomas spoke lightly again, his own voice sounding terribly wobbly.

The whistle shrieked again, and the train started to move forward. Thomas walked along, still touching Regina's hand, until the train picked up speed, and her fingertips slipped away from his. "Goodbye!"

Thomas stood on the platform and waved until the long fingers in the ruffled sleeve were no longer visible in the sooty air. "Please God," he prayed as he watched, "let Henry come back with her. Don't make her suffer because I am committing the sin of loving her."

Chapter 9

The next evening, Thomas was surprised by a knock on the door. He checked the time: it was 6:50. A little early for Mary's visit with his dinner tray. But then, perhaps Mary had the evening off.

But it was Meredith, not Mary, standing in the hallway, with a very determined look on her face. "Thomas, I must speak to you."

She put her head down and seemed about to charge into the room. Thomas, who had been holding onto the doorframe with one hand and the door with the other, didn't move. Meredith only took a step before she realized he was intentionally blocking the door.

The big blue eyes stared at him accusingly, but she said nothing, simply waited, assuming the force of her stare would be enough to push him back and allow her to enter.

Thomas impassively returned her gaze. "About what, wife of mine, must you speak to me?"

"Well, I'm not going to stand here in the hall and tell you," she answered loftily.

"Why not?" Thomas asked.

"This is . . . private," she insisted.

"Why? Are you pregnant?" Thomas asked. "Who's the father?"

Right on cue, Meredith gasped with indignation. Thomas had to admit, there was an element of fun in goading Meredith. Not that it was hard—she was much easier to upset than his mother—but it was rather satisfying.

Meredith glared at him, looked up and down the hall, then whispered to him angrily, "It's about Mary."

Mary? Aggravating Meredith was forgotten in a swell of concern. What happened to her? Oh, no—maybe she'd quit. Meredith had been particularly odious to the girl recently—he'd heard Meredith's shrill complaints echoing down the halls. Of course he couldn't hear Mary's calm, quiet answers. But when he'd asked Mary about the altercations during her evening visit, she had nothing to say on the subject. What if Mary left, angry at Meredith's abuse?

Without a word, he stepped back and let Meredith step into his sanctuary. Thomas caught the look of mingled curiosity and excitement as she glanced swiftly around the room: she'd succeeded in reaching his inner chambers!

"Not too much to see in here, my dear," Thomas resumed his place at his desk, preferring to have the massive wooden barrier between himself and his spouse. "Just me and a lot of paper." He spread his hands to indicate the rolls of blueprints strewn all over the desktop. Mary chided him in amusement that he was not a very tidy person. "Now," he tried not to sound worried, "what's this about Mary? Has she left us?"

"No," Meredith took one of the seats facing the desk. "But I certainly wish she would. Thomas, we've got to dismiss her."

Hmm. Meredith had never liked Mary—Thomas' instincts told him that Meredith's only real objection was that he did like her, and Meredith saw her as competition for his affections.

"Really? Has her standard of cleanliness dropped?"

"Well, no," Meredith admitted.

"Stolen anything?"

"No."

"Has she been slow in responding to calls? Or arriving intoxicated?"

"No."

"It can't be that she's asked for too much time off. I've never seen someone so devoted."

Meredith's eyes snapped in anger over the word 'devoted.' "Oh, no, she's very devoted—to you, at least. It's most improper."

Thomas thought to himself that if Meredith tried to lift her nose any higher, she'd get it stuck in one of the gas lamps.

"Improper? To have happy, competent people working for us? Who go beyond the call of duty to make us comfortable?"

"I'm not comfortable," Meredith interrupted. "She makes me uncomfortable. She's—she's—insolent."

Thomas gave his wife a piercing look of appraisal. "My dear, I've never seen her so much as look at you disrespectfully. She's never talked back to you, even when you're yipping at her like a bad-tempered Bedlington Terrier. How can you possibly call her insolent?"

Meredith sat silently for a moment. "She just is," she insisted uncertainly. "She looks at me as if she's better than I am."

"She is better than you," Thomas replied bluntly. "She's honest, a hard worker, doesn't generally go sticking knives in other people's backs—and she's a lady. I simply can't imagine her going around exposing her breasts to men in an attempt to elicit proposals of marriage."

Meredith sat for a moment, silent. Thomas watched remorselessly, as the resentment burned in her face.

"We were discussing Mary, not me," she said finally. "Why do you always have to bring that up?"

"I'm pointing out, my dear, that you are not without sin, so you shouldn't go casting stones," Thomas got up and paced the floor. "Our parents and friends and relatives snickered behind our backs when we got married. What makes it any different if the servants speculate about us now? Maybe you should try treating them with a little more respect. I'll bet then you could stop worrying so much about how they're looking at you."

He had had all he could stand of this conversation, and strolled over to pull back her chair. She stood up reflexively, and he put a firm hand under her elbow and guided her to the door.

"If you have a legitimate reason to dismiss someone—theft, say—you can come talk to me. But don't come complaining to me about their attitudes. They put up with you more hours a day than I do, and I admire them for it."

"That's why they're insolent toward me," Meredith answered bitterly. Thomas noted with amusement her grievance was no longer just with Mary. "They all know you prefer your servants to your wife!"

"I got to choose the servants." Thomas looked down into the petulant face he'd been shackled to for three years. He wanted to say something much cruder in answer to her implied accusation that he was having an affair with Mary. But that would only encourage Meredith to treat the servants even worse than she already did.

He gave a mental sigh. They would all be happier without Meredith in their lives.

That was it! Inspiration flowed through his body. He smiled almost seductively at Meredith, and pinned her against the broad oak door. "I know you're not happy here with me, Meredith. But you have it within your power to change things for the better."

"Oh, yes!" the breathy voice sighed, her hands fluttering up to clutch his lapels, the blue eyes wide and eager, the red lips tilted up toward his. "Anything, Thomas! Name it!"

"Leave me," he answered, amused by her grasping romantic overtures. He kept his voice soft and seductive, continued to pin her between the door and his chest. "You could go anywhere—Italy, France, England, or only as far as New York City. Someplace where the social life is gayer. I'll buy you a house on whichever fashionable street you want. You can hire and fire servants to your heart's content. You can take however many lovers you want—although you should change your name, for the sake of the Baldwin fortunes. You can pass yourself off as a widow. If you think you'd want to get married again, you should divorce me; but one thing at a time. For now, you could do whatever would make you happy."

It took a while for his meaning to sink in. Then the blue eyes got bigger. "Thomas!" Meredith chided him. "What would people say?"

Thomas pressed his sale. "That such a lovely American widow can't possibly stay a widow for long."

Concepts were not Meredith's strong suit. Thomas realized he should have known better. "Oh, Thomas, do you think I'm lovely?" she leaned against him eagerly.

He broke the contact by stepping away. "Somebody might think so," he answered coolly. "I was speaking figuratively."

"Oh." She obviously did not know what 'figuratively' meant. His eyes dared her to ask. But as usual, she simply ignored what she didn't understand and moved on.

"I couldn't go places by myself, calling myself a widow," she announced, the indignation in her voice rising as the impact of his suggestion began to sink in. "It would be dishonest."

"Why, my dear, you've proven that you have a remarkable talent for deception," Thomas countered smoothly.

She favored him with one of those uncomprehending stares which he found so particularly unappealing, then continued, "You wouldn't even come visit me, would you? You'd make me leave Pittsburgh, and my friends, and I'd never see you."

"To be a widow, my dear, by definition means your husband is dead," he answered patiently. "No, I wouldn't come see you."

Tears began to fill the big blue eyes. "I won't leave Pittsburgh. I won't leave you. I'm your wife and you can't just get rid of me."

"As you wish." Thomas shrugged to hide his disappointment. "But don't expect my manners to improve." To put an end to the interview, he opened the door.

There stood Mary, a loaded dinner tray in her hands. "Good evening, Mr. Baldwin, Mrs. Baldwin," she greeted them quietly.

"Good evening, Mary, won't you please bring that in and put it on my desk? Anywhere you can find room." Thomas chatted while Meredith glared. Her pout goaded Thomas to a realization, and he smiled as the maid turned to leave again. "Thank you, Mary. It's considerate of you, as always."

"T'weren't anything, sir," Mary answered deferentially.

"Oh, but it is," Thomas insisted. "Mrs. Baldwin and I were just discussing your services. Considering how you've been with us for almost two years, it's about time we gave you a raise. Could you use another, say, fifty cents a week?"

"Sir!" Mary's eyes were shining.

"Thomas!" Meredith gasped.

Thomas relished the outraged look on Meredith's face. "Oh, you're right, dear. A dollar, then, Mary. You're worth every penny."

Both women looked at him, stunned. Mary let out a happy breath. "I don't know what to say, sir."

"Try 'thank you.' It usually works for me."

"Thank you, sir. Thank you, ma'am. My mother will be so pleased."

She was gone in a flurry of excitement which made Thomas smile. He turned his smile down to Meredith's frowning face. "I don't know. She didn't seem very insolent to me."

Meredith left without another word. Thomas closed the door behind her and turned to savor his dinner along with his domestic triumph when there was a knock on the door. "Now what?" Thomas retraced his steps and opened the door.

This time it was Joseph, holding a telegram and wearing a somber expression. "This just arrived for you, sir." He handed it to Thomas, and swiftly left.

Leaning against the doorframe, Thomas looked at the ominous white card:

MADE IT TO ST PAUL 4:10 PM STOP
HENRY DIED 2:45 PM STOP
BRINGING HIM TO PGH TOMORROW STOP
AT LEAST WE TRIED STOP
REGINA

Chapter 10

Thomas was meeting with his father and the foundry managers when Regina returned to Pittsburgh with Henry's body. Then Regina was at the stonecutters when Thomas called at the Waring house. Soon after that, her family started arriving, and Henry's mother from New York; so Thomas didn't see Regina again until, following his parents, Meredith on his arm, he entered her parlor for the wake.

The house was filled with so many people come to pay their respects, it was a while before he actually caught sight of her. She stood in the traditional place for the bereaved, next to the casket. A fragile-looking lady sat next to her, and frequently Regina would rest a reassuring hand on the older woman's shoulder. People swirled around them with hugs, and kisses, and murmured words of consolation.

Thomas could hear any number of things in the whispered buzz. "What was he doing there? I thought he was building a factory, or something." "That man never did stop working, did he?" "He wasn't even in the mill when it exploded." "Well, of course not—they never even found the bodies of the workers inside." Thomas forced himself to stop listening. He didn't want to know any more.

People shifted forward, and they were standing in front of the casket.

"I hate to see you go like this, Henry," Thomas's father said. "You're a lot younger than I am. It doesn't seem right."

"Dear, you're talking to a dead person," his mother admonished. "He can't hear you."

"We're here to say goodbye, I'm saying goodbye," his father protested, as they moved along. Beside him, Meredith shuddered as she gave the barest of glances down at the coffin, and removed her hand from Thomas' arm. "I can't abide funerals," she whispered. "Dead bodies make me want to scream."

She retreated hastily after his parents, and Thomas was alone with Henry. A dead body, was that all Meredith saw? He was awash with feelings as he looked down at the kind face. He heard the surprisingly high-pitched voice of the big man, remembered the strength of his grip. He also remembered the way he always treated Thomas, as an adult, as an equal. It had been a new experience for Thomas, who had always traveled in his father's wake, always feeling like "The Son." Henry had unknowingly shown him a new standard to expect from people.

The awful weight of responsibility crushed down upon his heart. He'd killed this man. He'd loved Regina, and wished that she hadn't been married to Henry. Well, now she wasn't anymore. He'd died in the process of visiting the construction of the first Waring Baldwin Wintergarden. It was his fault. If there hadn't been a Wintergarden, Henry would still be alive today.

It was the most awful kind of betrayal imaginable. "I'm sorry, Henry," he whispered aloud to the serene face on the satin pillow. "I'm so sorry."

He backed away, his vision blurring, and he bumped right into Regina.

"I'm sorry!" he repeated again. "How clumsy and stupid of me."

"It's all right, Thomas. I'm pretty clumsy and stupid myself, right now."

A look of perfect understanding passed between them, then both pairs of eyes were too wet to see through. Regina dropped her head forward until it touched Thomas' chest.

Thomas' throat was constricted. He swallowed hard against the rising tears, and laid a comforting hand on top of the dark head. For one suspended moment, the room, the people, the coffin vanished, and they were alone together.

Regina's shoulders rose and fell with each ragged breath. She rubbed her forehead against him, then, with an effort, she pushed away. "Thank you, Sir Thomas," she murmured.

"I'm yours to command, My Lady, whenever you need a knight," he responded gently.

"I do have a favor to ask of you, Thomas. I want you to be one of his pallbearers."

Thomas was surprised and gratified. "Me? I'd be honored to. But—surely he has closer friends and relatives . . ."

"You were his business partner—and he thought a lot of you," Regina answered sadly. "So do I."

"Well, thank you," Thomas answered simply, guilt and delight fighting wildly under his waistcoat. "I'm pleased to be of service."

"I knew I could count on you."

There wasn't anything left to say, and the line of mourners behind Thomas was getting longer. He patted her shoulder, a little awkwardly, and moved on to where Henry's mother was sitting.

"Mrs. Waring? I'm Thomas Baldwin. I was one of Henry's business partners," he introduced himself.

The face was wrinkled and the body frail, but the eyes of the elder Mrs. Waring were still keen. She looked him over critically. "Baldwin? Oh, yes. You must be the iron fellow, with a fast piece of baggage for a wife."

Thomas tried to keep a straight face. "I see you've heard of me."

"You and Henry started this business building these wintergardens."

Thomas could feel his face flushing, the guilt making his heart pound loudly in his ears. "Yes, ma'am, we did. I feel his loss terribly, Mrs. Waring."

"Bah! You businessmen never feel the loss of anything but money," Mrs. Waring looked sternly up at Thomas. "Just you make sure that wintergarden up there gets finished. You understand me? And a dozen more like it. He was all excited about the plans you two were making. Now you've got to finish what you started."

Thomas was speechless with amazement. If he'd tried to tell his mother about his business alliances, she would have interrupted him with speculations about the neighbors and offered him another macaroon. This woman, by contrast, had obviously listened to what her son was doing, enough to remember the people in her son's life and what dreams were closest to her son's heart.

He took the old matriarch's hand in both of his. "I promise you at least a dozen completed wintergardens. It's the least I could do to pay tribute to a remarkable man—with a remarkable mother."

He kissed the withered hand. She smiled a little, then waved him brusquely away. "Forget the flattery. Don't forget the promise."

As he joined his wife and parents, Thomas tried to imagine any of them extracting such a promise at his funeral. The very idea was ludicrous.

Having paid their respects, the Baldwin clan seated themselves in a row at the back of the parlor. It was a strategic location on his father's part; everyone waiting to pay their respects would notice him sitting nearby.

And, of course, every man of influence in Pittsburgh lined up to pay his respects. The city turned out in force, expressing shock and grief at the sudden death of one of its own.

Thomas was struck by the similarity between weddings and funerals. There was a receiving line with a woman at the head of it, an assembly of people in a church for a few words marking the significance of the occasion, and for those not directly involved with the event, it was a party, a reason to drink, eat, and talk.

The volume of the murmuring voices was increasing, as was the number of guests in the stuffy room. The Mrs. Baldwins left for the relative coolness of other parts of the house, but Thomas elected to remain with his father. It meant he got an occasional glimpse of Regina.

"Well, once again, there she is, the center of attention," he could hear the woman in front of him saying to her neighbor. "Trust Regina to milk every last drop of attention that she can possibly get."

"She's always been good at that," her companion agreed.

"I could have been the one up there now," the first lady sniffed. "I was visiting Regina in Newport when she met him. He danced with me first."

"You never told me that!" The second one exclaimed.

"Mmmm hmmm. He even flirted with me. But who knows what Regina said to him when he danced with her later. She's got no sense of decorum. I'm surprised Henry was taken in by—whatever it was she said. But that could have been me up there, not her," she concluded importantly.

"She does look better in black than you do," the second one observed pragmatically, as if, Thomas thought, this was at all relevant to the subject at hand.

"Oh, I know—and so does she! Although someone ought to give her a fresh handkerchief. Her nose is turning red. Doesn't she look perfectly awful?"

"Did you ask about her clothes?"

"I did—and you're not going to believe this! She won't give them to me. She told me that Henry didn't like women wearing mourning, and she was going to keep wearing her wardrobe after he's buried! His mother, too. Regina said something about them respecting his wishes."

"Don't you think that will make her look bad?"

"I don't know. I think it's shocking. But then, she always was stingy. When she bought us our house in Johnstown, I wanted this big beautiful place, right on Main Street. But she insisted on buying us the brick one on Jackson, because it's farther from the Stony Creek. She said she didn't think it made sense, living in a house where it floods every year. But every house gets flooded every year. Everyone pulls up the carpets and lives on the second floor for a while. I think the truth is, our house was cheaper. She actually said it was safer—and Mother and Da believed her! But I'm not so easily fooled.

"Look at that!" The speaker Thomas guessed must be Regina's sister changed the subject without stopping to take a breath. "Did you notice? I never would have worn that broach with that dress. What on earth could she possibly have been thinking?"

"With all her money, you'd think she'd have better jewelry," her companion added. "If she's not going to give you her clothes, I suppose that also means she won't give you her jewelry?"

"She won't. I've been after her for years to give me that black and red piece. I've got much better skin color for it than she does—at least, when I remember to lotion every night. Have you tried that new pearl cream?"

Thomas was increasingly amazed by how quickly they could talk about absolutely nothing. He realized Regina never talked about her family. He could see why. He also understood the source of her sympathy toward him. Meredith and Regina's awful sister were cut from the same cloth. He wondered what the rest of her family was like.

He got to find out a little bit later, as people began to move from the parlor to the dining room, where pots of coffee and tea were surrounded by the assortment of baked goods that had been arriving with the guests.

"Did you see that? She and Henry must've paid good money for them." A voice behind him commented.

"Good money?" Thomas wondered to himself. "As opposed to what, counterfeit money?"

"Those two have always been kind of strange about money," a second voice responded. "She's really been strange about Henry's funeral. That monument she's ordered is such a simple thing, and half the words don't make sense."

"I think it's supposed to be Latin," said the first voice.

"Have you ever heard of anyone having Latin on his gravestone? And it's so small. I told her she needed to get a bigger one, but you know her. She never listens. She just said substance was more important than size."

"What's that supposed to mean?"

"I don't know. But then I've never known what that child was talking about. I don't know who she takes after."

Thomas strolled casually over to the large mirror to tidy his cravat and get a look at the two speakers. They stood in the corner, a man and a woman looking a little out of place among the finery. He searched for a resemblance between Regina and either person while trying not to stare—the running dialogue made him sure at least one of them was related to Regina.

Oblivious to Thomas' scrutiny, the couple continued gossiping. "Did you know she and her mother-in-law fought about the arrangements? That mother-in-law always struck me as a little strange. I've never liked her all that much. It seems she wanted to take her son's body back to New York. I guess Regina wasn't going to let her tell her what to do. Besides, I don't think Henry and his mother were that close, so why should he be buried back there?"

Thomas sipped his tea to suppress a smile. And he thought his mother was a terrible gossip? Yes, indeed, obviously in the same family.

It offered an intriguing question, he pondered, watching from the doorway as Regina received the condolences of well-wishers. How did a woman of subtlety, insight, and elegance come from this family of shallow backbiters?

He started when he was tapped on the shoulder. He turned around to gaze into his father's face. "We're getting ready to go now, son," Richard told him softly.

As he followed his father through the crowded room, Thomas realized he was looking at the answer to his question. Lineage was irrelevant in the creation of the sophisticated Regina Waring. Same as it had been when two outgoing but unobservant Baldwins had managed to create his quiet, world-watching self.

Chapter 11

Thomas thought it was supposed to rain at funerals. But the day they buried Henry was dry, dry as a bone. It was unseasonably hot, and the sky overhead was thick and black. Allegheny Cemetery was simply too close to the industrial districts.

Being one of Henry's pallbearers put him standing side-by-side with William Henry Vanderbilt, John Rockefeller, George Westinghouse and the Carnegie brothers. Having borne out their sad duty to escort Henry's body from house to hearse, hearse to church, and church to cemetery, they stood together, silent black sentinels, hands folded but ready.

Uncomfortably warm, his legs starting to tire a little, Thomas barely heard the priest's voice. From his advantaged position, he could observe the unfolding events from a close proximity, an unobtrusive part of the scenery. He watched as Mrs. Waring, Junior, supported Mrs. Waring, Senior, before turning her over to someone from the large crowd of mourners who'd come from New York. Half the city of New York seemed to have come, joining the crowd of familiar faces from Pittsburgh and Allegheny.

Regina's family stood in a cluster behind her, and Thomas noted with amusement that they couldn't even stop talking during the funeral services. He strained his ears, but couldn't quite make out the words. Still clucking over Regina's clothes, or jewelry, or some other minor detail, he imagined.

His eyes were constantly drawn back to Regina. Surrounded by people, she seemed to be standing alone. Her hat and heavy veil hid her face completely, but her posture had not lost its natural poise.

Even in this, the most awful moment of loss, her elegant figure filled him with admiration. The tiny waist and straight back projected strength—like an ancient oak tree defying a blizzard.

As he watched her, however, he caught a subtle reminder that she was not feeling as strong as she looked. It was a tiny gesture of the hand—a lost, almost fluttering motion; the impulse to reach for Henry's hand, stopped by the realization that it wasn't there for her any more. That source of comfort lay cold and motionless inside the casket, now.

His eyes began to sting. Swallowing against the tightness in his throat, he tore his gaze away.

His family was well back in the crowd. His father looked properly solemn. His mother and Meredith simply looked bored. At least his wife had shown enough breeding to do all her complaining while they still had been at home.

"Why do I have to be there, Thomas? I wasn't in business with Mr. Waring. I hate funerals," she had moaned before they left. "My feet hurt for days afterwards."

He'd watched unsympathetically as she pouted at him. She was so convinced she was cute when she pouted. So far, he'd been unsuccessful in disabusing her of the notion. Of course, he could be more direct in his approach and simply tell her it made her look like an overdressed monkey.

"Maybe you should consider wearing more sensible shoes," he had offered helpfully. "Beats me why women's feet hurt, when they put things on which are shaped nothing like their feet."

"I can't help the fashions, Thomas." Meredith sniffed loftily.

"You don't have to wear them, either," he had answered, pulling on his gloves and taking up his hat to leave. "Why don't you try setting them? Find a cobbler who will make you a shoe that's fit for wearing, and I'll pay any price he asks. Of course, that would leave you with one less thing to complain about."

People were stirring, and Thomas looked at the priest in surprise. The service was already over. Regina and Henry's mother stepped forward to take the shovel and drop the first clods of dirt on the coffin.

****

It was over. The six pallbearers shook hands, and turned toward their families. Regina's black hat could barely be seen, she was surrounded by so many well-wishers. Thomas lingered at the edge of the crowd, uncertain whether to try to speak to her now, or wait until later.

"You really ought not to be standing out in this heat, Mrs. Waring. Can't I escort you to your carriage?" Thomas heard a strange voice behind him with the strong accent peculiar to New York.

"If I did, who would see to Regina?" Thomas had not realized Henry's mother was lingering beside him on the periphery.

"Mrs. Waring, your daughter-in-law may be occupied for some time," Thomas pointed out. "If you'd prefer to get out of this heat now, I'd be happy to take on the responsibility of driving her home when she's ready to go."

The old woman looked over the gathered crowd of well-wishers with critical eyes. "She should be taking me home, and all these people should go home, too."

Thomas and the New Yorker looked at each other with some amusement. "I'm sure she's feeling that way, too, Mrs. Waring," Thomas soothed, while the New Yorker nodded his agreement. "But she really has no choice in the matter."

Now Mrs. Waring was looking at him with critical eyes. "No choice? Of course she has a choice."

Pulling out the conciliatory smile he often used on his mother, Thomas shook his head. "Those are Henry's business clients. Men that your daughter-in-law will have to rely on if she's going to keep your son's interests alive. If they want to talk to her now, she's going to let them talk. Henry would have done the same thing if he were alive, and she was the one we'd just buried."

The sharp eyes were now looking at him with interest, not criticism. "I always told my boy he loved those mills more than he loved me. So—things haven't changed quite so much, after all."

The New Yorker offered his arm with new authority. "It sounds like the other Mrs. Waring can take care of herself. Let her handle your son's friends, then she'll come to take care of you. Sir—" the New Yorker tipped his hat to Thomas, then led the older Mrs. Waring down the hill toward the line of carriages waiting on the cobblestone road. Thomas watched them go, amazed at his own glibness and insight.

Maybe, when he found the right people, they brought out the best in him.

The Baldwin women were still standing on the grassy hillside. Thomas strolled over to them, scanning the crowd around Regina. No doubt his father was in there somewhere. Thomas murmured to his mother, "Would you mind terribly taking care of Meredith? The older Mrs. Waring wasn't feeling well, but she wouldn't go home until I promised to see the younger Mrs. Waring home. But I don't know how long this will go on—and," he continued without bothering to hide the malicious twinkle in his eyes as he looked at Meredith, "I'm sure Meredith's feet are already hurting terribly."

"Why, of course we'll take care of her," his mother answered. "But honestly, Thomas, how did you end up with such a bother? Surely her family can take her."

"Mrs. Waring asked me. I was loathe to say no. After all, mother, if I'd died, I'd like to think that if you asked a favor of one of my colleagues at my gravesite, they'd show you the same respect."

The appeal to her motherhood worked. Her eyes filled with tears, and she patted his arm. "Of course, Thomas. It was kind of you to offer. Meredith can come have dinner with us. You can join us when you're done."

The crowd around Regina was thinning perceptibly, now. He was able to push his way in beside her. "Your mother-in-law took your carriage," he murmured near the hat, presumably close to her ear. "I shall escort you home when you're ready to leave."

She gave his arm a light touch in acknowledgment, and continued talking to the circle of well-wishers.

Thomas removed himself to a nearby tree and watched. "She must be getting tired," he speculated, but her posture never wavered. It seemed she had all the time in the world for each mourner who offered her the same inadequate words of solace. He wandered back over to stand close to her as the numbers dwindled away to nothing—and only after the last well-wisher released her hands and walked down the hill, she turned to him with a tired sigh.

"Take me home, Thomas."

He offered her his elbow, then looked back over his shoulder at the newly-formed mound of dirt. "Do you—need to be alone first?" he asked.

"I've been alone all day," she answered, her voice sounding tired and very far away. "I don't want to be here anymore."

George was waiting with the door open by the time they descended the hill. "Thank you, George," Regina acknowledged. "To Mrs. Waring's please, George," Thomas directed.

George nodded once, and closed the carriage door with a respectfully muffled thud.

In the silence, Thomas studied the heavy veil and listened to the irregular sound of her breathing. He searched his mind frantically for anything he could do or say.

"Why don't you take that thing off your head," he suggested solicitously. "You must be stifling in there."

"If I do, I'll frighten you to death," she said hoarsely, but with the barest shadow of her sense of humor. "I've been crying for four days, straight."

Thomas took her hand and squeezed it, gently. "I'm sure you're a perfect fright," he agreed amicably. "But it doesn't matter. It's only me. You're not in front of an audience anymore. And it's a long trip back to Fifth Avenue."

Regina sighed again. "You're right. Vanity seems awfully silly right now. I am terribly hot." With a despondent gesture, she pulled out the long hatpin and threw the offending hat on the seat opposite her.

Thomas was shocked at the sight of her face. Swollen eyes, red nose, puffy cheeks, skin almost yellow—he could have passed her on the street and not recognized her. Hoping she hadn't seen the look on his face, he smiled at her. "See? That must feel better. Shall I fan you?"

Regina shook her head. "No." She put a hand on his arm. "Please—stop trying to be kind to me. People have been trying to be kind to me for days now, and the pity doesn't make it any easier. Makes it harder, even. It's this incessant reminder of what I've just lost."

He could see she was trying to fight back the terrible pain, the tears; but she was losing. She sniffed long and hard, while two tears slipped out from under her control and slid down the well-stained cheeks.

Trying to keep the "kindness" out of his face and voice, he found his handkerchief and offered it to her. "I'm sure mine's drier than yours," he observed, practically.

Was that a chuckle? Yes, indeed. There was a trace of a smile on her face as she looked down at the square of linen in her hand. "Quite a bit drier," she admitted, and laid her face against it.

A moment later, a soul-wrenching, screaming sob erupted from the grieving woman. Thomas felt a few tears running down his own cheeks as he watched, helpless, as Regina slid to the floor of the carriage, curled up in a ball, and sobbed.

Thomas did not try to intervene. He'd never seen two people who were as close as the Warings: it only stood to reason that no one would grieve so deeply as Regina Waring.

Eventually the storm quieted. She curled up at his feet, her head on his knee. He stroked her hair soothingly, silently, for what could have been hours.

"They're much kinder to widows in India," she finally broke the silence. "They burn their dead there—unlike our wholly disgusting custom of sticking our deceased in boxes and burying them in the ground, to rot slowly at their leisure.

"When a man's remains are being burned, his wife climbs up and throws herself on the funeral pyre. A much more compassionate society than ours. She's allowed to die with him, unlike our system of expecting women to go on with a dead heart."

She spoke flatly. This was a statement of fact, not an expression of self-pity. But Thomas was horrified.

"You wouldn't really kill yourself? You're not planning—something, are you?"

Regina was silent a moment, then answered slowly, "No. I don't suppose I will. I'll do what my society expects of me, living out my days as a poor little widow."

Thomas leaned sideways in his seat, so he could actually see her face. He scrutinized the puffy red features, and frowned. "That does not sound like you, at all."

She smiled a bitter little smile. "In case you haven't noticed, I'm not myself, lately."

"No, you're not. Which is why I feel compelled to discount anything you might say right now."

She glared at him for a moment, then her expression softened. "You're not going to let me feel sorry for myself forever, are you?"

"No, as a matter of fact, I'm not."

"That's what grief really is, a most profound kind of feeling sorry for ourselves."

Thomas thought about that for a moment. "I suppose that's true. Since, after all, the deceased has presumably gone on to a better world."

Regina's body twitched impatiently. "Which is the most horrid of all the lies we tell ourselves."

"What do you mean?"

Regina stared up at him almost condescendingly. "You don't really believe any of that, do you? This whole notion of an afterlife is nothing more than a fairytale we tell widows and children because it's more comfortable than telling the truth—that you'll never see your loved one, ever again. The loss is really as horrible as it seems, so cherish that last look he gave you, that kiss before he walked out the door. You didn't know it at the time—but you'll never have another one again."

The awful self-pity was creeping back into her eyes. Thomas was horrified at the bleak vision she'd painted for him. There couldn't possibly be any truth to that—it would make every death unbearable by its sheer magnitude of loss. No wonder she was going crazy with grief. He searched his mind frantically for something comforting to say.

"No God could be quite that cruel."

The look she gave him shot that down in a hurry. The corners of her mouth turned down in amusement.

"You don't think so? Read the Bible sometime. God is a nasty, malevolent being. He's all-knowing, all-seeing, but He creates Man and gives him free will, all the while already knowing that Man will fall from grace and get tormented for it. Thus—God specifically created Man in order to torment him. That's sadistic at the very least, if not downright evil. I refuse to worship such an evil being."

Thomas' head was spinning. He'd never really thought about God before. He went to church every Sunday, with every other Scots-Irish Presbyterian in the city, and not quite half-listened as the minister's words washed over the congregation. He tried reading the Bible once, as a child—but got bored somewhere through Deuteronomy. "But, God is a comfort to people during times of grief."

"If that were true, I would be the only one crying, wouldn't I?"

"What do you mean?"

"When a Christian dies, if other Christians really believed in Heaven, they wouldn't be crying. They'd be celebrating. Instead of expressing condolences, they'd be offering congratulations. Like graduation. The custom would be to shake hands and say 'congratulations, you must be thrilled for Grandpa.' But we don't.

Because, deep down, we know the truth. Life is finite. This is all we have. There is no God, all we have is each other."

The carriage had come to a halt at the grand Waring front door. The two of them sat, looking at each other for a long moment.

"I dread the thought of going in there," Regina confessed. "The entire house is going to ring with silence. I can take the memories that are staring at me from every wall. But I can't stand the silence. In other countries, the women are expected to wail—and the wife doesn't do it alone. At least if I'd been Jewish, the entire community would come sit shivah with me. We'd sit up all night and talk about him. Real talk—stories about his life, not that cold, meaningless "insert-name-of-dead-guy-here" speech we just suffered through. We'd celebrate the man who had touched our lives. But we—we don't talk. We don't make any noise. We whisper."

Thomas heard the dangerous quiver returning to Regina's voice, and realized he had in his possession the cure for the silence. It was time to change the subject; Henry's birthday present might not be the tragic reminder Thomas had feared.

"Would you like to avoid your house a little longer?" he asked, mischievous and mysterious.

It worked. He saw the glimmer of curiosity in her eye. "What do you have in mind?" she asked.

"Well, first I think it's about time you get off the floor." As she obediently took his hand and rose to sit on the slippery cushions, Thomas leaned out the carriage window. "Home, please, George. We're keeping Mrs. Waring with us for a while."

"Yes, sir."

Addressing her questioning gaze, Thomas answered, "I have something of yours. This seems like a good enough excuse to get it to you."

"Something of mine? What could I possibly have lent you . . ."

"Oh, it is nothing that you have lent me." Thomas answered before refusing to offer any more explanation on the ride back out to Allegheny. When they reached the Baldwin gates, Thomas told George to drive around back.

"No reason for you to put that contraption back on your head," he answered her surprised look. "If we go around to the rear, you won't need to."

Man, he was getting to be a better liar.

Thomas dismissed George as they rolled to a stop. "This won't take too long, George, but we won't need you for a little while."

"Very good, sir."

Thomas jumped lightly out of the coach and handed Regina out himself. He delighted in her puzzlement as he led her to the back door. Wordlessly, he pointed out the two Labradors, who were lounging on the cool stone steps. Seeing potential playmates, the pups scrambled to their feet and started toward them at a loping gallop.

"Oh, the sweet things!" Regina exclaimed, sinking to the ground and reaching out with both hands. As if recognizing their new mistress, both dogs ran straight up to her, wriggling with excitement as they vied for attention. "I love Labs," she confessed to Thomas, as one climbed into her lap in order to chew on her chin, while the other was lying belly-up on Regina's skirts, getting her stomach rubbed. "Where did you get them, Thomas? Are there any more in the litter? I'd been wanting to get a pair, myself."

Thomas knelt beside her, and rubbed the furry head which appeared under his hand. Jet-black, just like the feminine head beside him. "I know," he said gently, realizing that he'd just come to the hard part. "That's what Henry told me when he asked me to hide these two for a few days. They're your birthday present from him."

As he expected, her eyes filled with tears. She ducked her head and wrapped her arms around a small black body. The dog wriggled in her arms until it could reach, then busily started licking her face.

"Was there ever such a man?" she asked softly. "Even after he's dead, he's still busy showing me how perfectly he understands me."

Thomas noticed that she phrased "understands" in the present, not the past tense. But he said nothing. Intellectual constructs were all fine and dandy, but cold comfort compared to warm, wriggling symbols of a husband's love for his wife.

****

There was a slightly less unhappy shape to Regina's mouth when Thomas returned her to the Waring manse on Fifth Avenue.

He followed her into the kitchen carrying one of the dogs. Regina preceded him with the other. "Kate," Regina called into the hallway. "Can you find an old blanket? I've got visitors here who could use one."

A voice, presumably Kate's echoed back from the stairs. "I was starting to wonder about you, Mrs. Waring. The funeral must have been over hours ago. What kind of visitor could possibly want an old blanket? Why . . ." Kate appeared in the doorway, a pretty, plump woman with her arms filled with a faded patchwork quilt. Her mouth dropped open at the sight of Thomas and Regina and their black bundles. "For law's sake, Mrs. Waring! What have you brung us?"

"One last gift from Mr. Waring, Kate. Mr. Baldwin had been keeping these for him—they were to have been my birthday present."

At the mention of Henry, Thomas saw the sudden transformation in Kate. She lowered her voice, dropped her eyes, and moved stealthily, like a nurse in a sickroom. "I'll see to them, ma'am. No need to fret yourself." It gave Thomas an insightful peek into the quietude Regina had been enduring.

A commotion was heard from the front of the house. "Your folks keep asking if you're back yet," Kate groaned, rising from the floor.

"Of course," Regina's smile faded, and her hands automatically brushed over her collar, her skirts, her hair. "Wish me luck, Thomas. I've got an audience again." She listened to the chorus of voices for a moment. "Or maybe I have that backwards. Maybe I am the audience." She sighed, and led him toward the kitchen door where they'd entered. "You'd better slip out the back, while you can," she advised sardonically.

"Do you need me to stay with you?" Thomas asked. He'd heard enough at the funeral to realize Regina could use some moral support to survive her relatives.

In a spontaneous gesture of affection, she had kissed him before Thomas realized what was happening. "You're a dear, sweet friend, Sir Thomas, but I wouldn't ask anyone to put up with my family. Go. And thank you."

Feeling swept up by romance, like a knight, or a bandit, Thomas kissed her hands, and left out the kitchen door.

"Almost like an illicit lover," he thought to himself as his carriage rolled away. Considering the heat in his body, and the tender look she gave him as he left, that might not be so far off the mark. Naturally, she was in the depths of mourning now. But someday . . . he daydreamed all the way home.

Chapter 12

As much as Thomas appreciated the clean lines of the house on Buena Vista Street, it was time for a new home. There simply wasn't enough space. Sure, the Commons was down the street, but he wanted more yard. More rooms—more space between his room and Meredith's.

He realized it was the result of his interaction with Regina. She seemed so close to him throughout the ordeal of Henry's death; since then, he only saw her occasionally, usually to get her signature on Waring-Baldwin Wintergardens documents. His heart ached at the shadows under her eyes and the pain in her face. He loved her more insanely than ever, which made his imprisonment with Meredith all the more unbearable.

When he ended up on the same streetcar as John Herron, a realtor who knew of "just the house" out on Hiland Avenue, he didn't stop to think. He went out to see it that very day. He bought it the next.

It was a sprawling place—an untidy, asymmetric and whimsical collection of porches, bay windows and field stone chimneys under a no-nonsense slate roof. The floor plan rambled from one parlor into the next. The library was so full of nooks and crannies it would take Meredith an hour of determined searching to find him.

The grounds were large enough for a wintergarden, which Thomas was building in his mind's eye, running alongside the carriage house in peaks to match the roofline of the house.

The construction was only a couple of years old. The owner, Lawrence Phillips, was a railroad man who was moving his large brood to Kansas City. "The railroad tells me to go, I go," the congenial older man said to Thomas as they signed papers at the bank. "I do hate to leave the place behind", he confessed. "Those floors are a work of art. There will never be a finer set of floors in town."

Thomas had to agree. The delicate wood mosaics had captivated him the moment he walked through the door, as had the painstakingly-carved staircase grandly marching up the center of the house. The workmanship was impeccable and Thomas felt very pleased with himself.

He was in a thoroughly jovial mood when he walked up the narrow steps on Buena Vista. "Well, wife of mine," he announced from the doorway of the dining room, where Meredith was halfway through her soup, "I've just bought you the single most expensive birthday present any woman in Pittsburgh is likely to receive this year."

He astonished the entire household by ordering his dinner brought to him in the dining room, where he could continue to tease Meredith with hints about her "birthday present."

"How expensive is it?"

"Very."

"Is it big?"

"Huge. You won't believe how big it is."

"Is it nice?"

"A whole lot nicer than you deserve."

"Don't be mean, Thomas. But really, is it pretty?"

"If you don't think it's the epitome of beauty, there's something very seriously wrong with you."

She gazed at him with that blue incomprehension he always found so annoying. Well, 'epitome' had four syllables in it, of course he confused her. "Your dinner's getting cold," he chided her, then refused to answer any more of her questions while he tackled the roast pork, new potatoes and carrots on his plate.

He didn't know where the idea of calling the house her birthday present came from. It had simply popped out of his mouth when he'd seen her sitting in the dining room. He'd imagined her complaints about moving; maybe by calling it her present she would be less likely to whine.

It was only after he'd finished relishing a generous slice of Mrs. Bishop's raspberry-chocolate torte and set aside his fork that he took up the subject again.

"So tell me, my dear, just how many weeks is it until your birthday? It is close to your birthday, isn't it?"

"Over three weeks away," she said in a rather small voice.

"Uh huh. Seems a shame to have to wait that long. But, I suppose I'll just have to. I'd hate to spoil your birthday by giving you your present early. You won't get anything on your birthday, then, if I give this to you early."

As if he'd ever paid much attention to her birthday! He neglected to produce the appropriate baubles after they were married; his mother had taken to giving him unsubtle reminders before birthdays and anniversaries.

Meredith gazed at him mournfully. "Oh, Thomas! You're not going to make me wait three whole weeks!"

"Well," he answered slowly—very slowly, "I won't if you can get your bonnet on and your bustle into the carriage while I send for George to hitch up."

"Honestly, Thomas," Meredith protested. "Bustles are so out of fashion. Don't you know anything about women's styles?"

Thomas smothered a smile. He still remembered quite vividly his first sight of Regina Waring in the lobby of Mellon and Sons, in a striped dress that molded to the curve of her hips . . . .

"So," he said aloud, "you'd rather enlighten me on women's fashion than see your present?"

Meredith quit the table before Thomas had finished removing the napkin from his lap.

He refused to answer any of her questions on the ride to Hiland Park. When George stopped at their new carriage block, Thomas handed Meredith out with a great deal of ceremony.

"There you are, my dear," he said with a grand wave of his hand. "When your little girlfriends are waving their new birthday jewelry under your nose, you can now point out that your birthday present is too big to wave."

The blue eyes gazed at him in puzzled incomprehension, so Thomas reached into his pocket and found the front door key. He held it up, then placed it in her hand. "Happy Birthday, Meredith."

Understanding dawned in the little face. For a second, she was almost pretty. "You bought me a house?" she squealed.

Thomas winced at the high-pitched sound, but he forced himself to remain pleasant. "Well, I suppose if that doesn't fit in the lock, all I've bought for you is a key." When she gave him the predictable look, he told her patiently, "Go open the door and see your new house."

She understood that. She dashed up the stairs as fast as her skirts would allow, and fumbled eagerly with the key in the lock. When the massive door swung open, she stood stock-still, dumbfounded. "Ohhh."

Only a soul with a complete insensitivity to beauty would be able to walk in the front door without coming to a standstill. The gleaming walnut staircase served as a frame for the imposing stained glass windows on the landing. The twelve-foot ceilings (which seemed immense after their modest ten-foot ones) demanded that you look up, admiring the tall doorways as the eye was drawn upwards to the figured tin overhead. It made Thomas feel like he'd entered a palace, not a house.

He took his time admiring each room. Meredith dashed ahead, her high-pitched squeals echoing fainter and fainter. The house was big enough and solid enough that he soon couldn't hear her at all. He was definitely going to like living here.

The house gave him an odd serenity. Thinking about the pocket doors and the towering fireplace in the new library gave him the patience to listen to Meredith's happy inane chatter on the carriage ride back to Allegheny.

"... it's the most perfect shade of blue, don't you think? Blue is such a hard color. My mother always likes blue, but there are some shades of blue that I like, and others that don't seem to work, if you know what I mean. Of course, lots of blues are just fine for clothes, but that doesn't mean I'd want them on my walls. It's important to have the right shade of blue in one's dress, since it brings out the color of the eyes. Have you noticed how different shades of blue will make my eyes look a different shade of blue? Oh, why Thomas, do you suppose the color of the room affects what color my eyes are? Maybe I should repaper the drawing room in blue! Then I'll receive guests in a room where people will stop dead by how blue my eyes look. Mrs. Phillips has loads of taste. I suppose if she didn't, she wouldn't have found that perfect shade of blue ..."

Thomas tried to remember which room was blue. He honestly had no idea.

He was brought back from his thoughts by a squeeze on his arm. Meredith usually managed to obey the unspoken rule prohibiting more than minimal physical contact, but in her excitement, she'd forgotten.

"Oh, Thomas," she said, her face aglow, "thank you. It's a wonderful birthday present. Can we be moved in before my birthday? I want a party in my new house!"

Thomas actually smiled down at his wife's eager face. "Yes, Mrs. Baldwin, you may have your birthday party in your new house, if it pleases you."

Meredith let out a high-pitched squeal and threw an arm around his neck. Thomas suffered the gesture. There were so few moments of marital harmony in his household. Letting one slip through once in a while wouldn't kill him.

****

Meredith's birthday party was an exceedingly grand affair. The new house was in perfect order. The old furniture was settled into new locations, new settees ordered and delivered to embellish the more copious parlor space, new carpets, lamps, and curtains applied as needed. The new house was more than twice as large as the previous one, so it was going to take a little while to fill it; but it was a start. The entire building had been thoroughly scrubbed while it was empty. It would probably never be so clean again, and the freshly-polished woodwork gleamed in the glow from the gas lamps.

After the fuss of cleaning the place from attic to cellar, followed by the chaos of moving their possessions from Buena Vista to Hiland Avenue, the great flurry of decorating began. Thomas eventually took refuge at the Duquesne Club for a couple of nights rather than climb over mystery boxes and trellises and floral garlands.

But even he had to admit that the end result was beautiful. He assumed Mary and the house staff were responsible for the air of charm about the whole thing; he couldn't imagine Meredith having this much artistic vision. The dining room was a fairie's paradise, the parlors looked like garden hideaways, the drawing room had been transformed into some Tennysonian idyll.

Best of all was the main hallway. It was an Indian paradise of palm trees. The palm fronds brought back fond memories of his parents' greenhouse—and his first meeting with Regina. He could still remember his chagrin at her startled cry. The wry amusement in her voice as they'd talked. She'd been wearing dark red. He'd been mesmerized instantly by her laugh. How desperate he'd felt to find something clever to say. How devastated he was when he'd found out she was already married.

Thoughts of marital status wiped the foolish happy grin off his face. Well, now she was available, but he wasn't. Would she even be interested in him? The shadows of grief fell so dark and deep across her eyes. Would she ever consider marrying again? He certainly was no Henry Waring. He wasn't clever or gregarious. He didn't have Henry's way of making everyone smile with the simple act of stepping into a room.

No, he was just dull, ordinary Thomas. No doubt Regina would find far more remarkable suitors than him should she ever decide she was willing to marry again.

Since Regina was still in mourning, she was not expected to partake in festivities, public or private. He'd sent her an invitation, anyway, offering lamely, "In case you'd like a chance to get out of the house a little." He wasn't surprised when she'd sent her regrets.

"As your friend and business associate, can I request a private viewing of your new domestic arrangements? You're right in that the house does feel like it's closing in on me, but I'm not ready for society yet. Thank you a thousand times over for thinking of me. I do realize that you're watching over me, and I appreciate it. Never in my life have I ever had such a good friend as you, my dear Sir Thomas. I am most grateful for you. Your most humble friend,

R"

Ah, well. Her friendship was certainly nothing to sneeze at. He was looking forward to giving her a private tour. Any moment alone with her was bliss. Even if he was only showing her the contents of his library, instead of the contents of his heart.

The hall clock struck eight. Guests should be arriving at any moment. Joseph appeared in the hallway, straightening his already impeccable livery. "You're perfectly beautiful, Joseph," Thomas smiled at his fastidious butler.

"If that were the case, I wouldn't need all these pretty clothes to hide behind," Joseph joked back as he passed him.

Both men looked up as the rustle of silks announced Meredith's descent down the staircase. Good God, what was the woman wearing? He'd been hiding with proper masculine horror from all her prattle about the newest fashions and how they applied to her dress for her birthday party, but even with his admittedly automatic dislike of any garment on his wife's figure he had to appreciate that her much-lauded reception dress was—absurd. The heavily-decorated cylinder that passed for a skirt seemed to give her some trouble in providing adequate room to take a step; the missing fabric leaked out into a ridiculously long train behind her. Or gotten puffed up into the funny little flaps hanging on the side of each hip. Thomas stared at his wife, trying to imagine the dress without the stigma of its wearer. No, it was still the ugliest thing he had ever seen.

Meredith obviously mistook his bemusement for admiration. She tossed her head expectantly. "Well? You may tell me I'm even prettier than Joseph."

Thomas caught the sour undertone in her voice, and answered bluntly, "I'm a lousy liar, Meredith."

He could always count on her to not understand when she was being insulted. She paused a moment. He wasn't sure whether she was waiting for him to continue, or trying to figure out what he'd just said. Then she caressed the flaps of fabric over her hips coyly and peeped up at him through her lashes.

"I didn't think my birthday dress was going to be finished in time, but Mrs. Conway worked wonders, didn't she?"

"Yes, I'm definitely wondering," Thomas admitted with perfect candor.

"Of course, it had to be blue, to bring out the color of my eyes . . ."

Thomas recited a quick prayer of thanks as the doorbell rang, heralding the first of their guests. He didn't really want to hear another soliloquy to blue—and her eyes.

"No need to fish for compliments from me, wife of mine," he stopped her cheerful chatter. "Your arriving guests will be full of birthday compliments for you. Shall we receive them?"

****

The house may have been different, but it was still a typical Baldwin family party. Meredith took gleeful, clinging advantage of his proximity in the receiving line, managing to keep at least one hand wrapped around his arm at all times. It made it a little difficult to greet people, but Thomas eventually gave up trying to extract his arm from her grasping fingers and just shook hands with her hand on his elbow.

Eventually he was able to escape her clutches with the excuse that he had other hosting duties to attend to. He wandered through the house, listening to the sound of voices resounding through the halls, off the grand high ceilings, floating over the stair rail. He supposed he was going to have to hold parties more often. He could feel how pleased the building itself was to be festively decorated and filled with people.

His mother, Aunt Eleanor, and Aunt Louisa were in the front parlor, heads together, frowning and whispering about something dire. Meredith and her mother were on the landing, seated in front of the stained glass window, their heads also together. Thomas had a feeling whatever the two groups were talking about, it had something to do with the other group. Come to think of it, it had been some time since he'd seen the two mothers fawning over each other. Or even his mother fawning over Meredith. Odd.

Predictably, his father and uncles were on the opposite end of the house from the women, deep into the brandy and grumbling about the favorite topic of the day, the scarcity of Bessemer steel ingots. Now that the Carnegies were using everything that they produced, it seemed the entire city of Pittsburgh was suffering from the shortage.

One old friend of his father's, Andrew Kloman, who had a personal grudge against Andrew Carnegie, was complaining more bitterly than anyone else.

"He's starving us to death, that's what he's doing," he said, pounding his hand against the table for emphasis. "When my lease ran out on the old Superior Mill, I bought a nice chunk of property out in Homestead. But now I'm afraid I'll get the mills built, and they'll just sit there. I'll have hundreds of workers from the Amalgamated looking at me . . . I promised them something to do, instead I'll be sending them home with an apology because Andy Carnegie doesn't want us building bridges anymore."

"That's okay, we'll take them," Curtis Hussey teased. "We could use a few more good Union men." Almost every man in the room employed members of the Amalgamated Association of Iron and Steel Workers: Amalgamated men were steadier and more responsible than non-union employees.

"So why are you doing bridge struts?" Bill Singer was also a steel manufacturer feeling the pinch from the ingot draught. "Build yourself a blast furnace, then we can all go back into production again. You'd make a fortune."

"A fortune? Yeah—Holley's patents alone cost the fortune. Not to mention the rest of the startup costs. I don't have that kind of money."

"Maybe you don't," old Dr. Curtis Hussey, who had never borrowed a dime of money in his life, and owned copper mines, copper rolling mills, AND one of the biggest crucible steel operations in the city, pointed out. But perhaps we do."

The younger Hussey was obviously well-used to his father's business adventures. "Now we're going to build a blast furnace? Kloman's right. Bessemer Steel Association royalties are going to be pretty darned steep."

"I'm not talking about us," Hussey senior gestured between himself and his son. "I mean," he spread his arms to indicate everyone in the room. "Us."

Thomas' father's face lit up. "A bunch of you need Bessemer ingots. We all appreciate a good business opportunity."

Kloman's habitually sour expression had lightened considerably. "We can give Andy Carnegie a run for his money!"

"It certainly would be nice not to need him anymore."

The excitement in the room was palpable. Everyone started talking at once; the ideas were flowing thick and fast, and varied from speculations on how to avoid the royalty fees to opinions on where to position the blast furnace on Andrew Kloman's strip of riverfront land in Homestead. Without a word, Thomas slipped out to fetch paper from his office. Someone ought to start taking notes and getting something down in writing.

Chapter 13

Even though they had talked for hours, the forging of the new company was cut short when the entrepreneurs were dragged away by weary wives insisting on going home. Despite this, the plans for the venture, now being called the Pittsburgh Bessemer Steel Company, grew by leaps and bounds. What started as a solution to the shortage of Bessemer steel ingots grew into a grand scheme to go into direct competition with Andy Carnegie making steel rails for the railroad. The flurry of excitement was heady; here was the chance to punish those upstart Carnegies who had the gall to make good in Pittsburgh and then leave the city for the society of New York.

As the agenda changed, Thomas began to have his own private doubts on the matter. It seemed to him that emotion and business were not a good mix. There was a demand for Bessemer steel. That was a sound business idea. On the other hand, Carnegie was already taking care of the market for steel rails.

His father didn't see it. He was as excited as the rest of them at the prospect of going into competition in the railroad market. "Everyone's making fortunes in the railroad. My cousin Matthias sure did all right for himself back in Philadelphia," he commented over Sunday dinner. "Why not us, too?"

"You've already made a fortune, father," Thomas observed. "You built yourself a mansion here without having to touch railroads. It seems so, I don't know, unimaginative, to jump on someone else's bandwagon."

"Well, who the hell cares about imagination? This is about making money," his father snapped.

Thomas wasn't cowed. "If it was about making money, we'd be making Bessemer steel—not competing with Carnegie over steel rails," he argued back.

Richard stared indignantly at his son. "You don't know what you're talking about, son," he dismissed him. "It's always about competition. The better man edges out the other guy, the market goes on—the money goes to the better competitor."

"I beg to differ," Thomas thought to himself. He chose not to pursue the argument, but he still found the rationale unconvincing. It's about revenge, not money. At least if they called it by its true name, he'd have fewer reservations on the topic.

****

It was only a week after the debate with his father when he found himself revisiting the topic with an unexpected ally.

He'd arrived home to find a most surprising spectacle in his front parlor: Meredith sitting rigidly in her chair, attempting to entertain Regina Waring!

He was astounded to see her. She'd been thoroughly reclusive since Henry's funeral, leaving the running of Waring-Baldwin Wintergardens entirely in his hands. After her mournful reply to his attempt to entice her out for Meredith's birthday, he thought it would be a while before he saw her.

Now, here she was in his front parlor, looking for all the world like any other woman in Pittsburgh making a social call.

At least, it had the outer appearance of a social call. He doubted Meredith wore such a sour expression when she was receiving other visitors. She was smiling, but it was the artificial nasty-nice smile Thomas knew all too well.

Regina, of course, graced the opposite chair with her characteristic elegance. Grief enhanced her ability to live up to her name. She looked like a queen in her royal palace as she sat balancing a teacup and saucer delicately between her fingers. Only royalty could make a saucer look like the natural extension of one's left index finger.

She must have felt him staring at her, the mesmerizing black eyes turned and smiled solemnly at him from across the room. "Hello, Thomas," she greeted him, and he thought he detected the smallest hint of amusement in her voice. "Your wife and I have been discussing the latest fashions."

Meredith stiffened and sniffed; Thomas wasn't sure if it was due to Regina's use of his given name, or because of something about the fashions being discussed.

Regina's next sentence solved the mystery. "Apparently your wife is embracing the very excesses that I am absolutely refusing to wear."

Thomas was so delighted to see Regina's face looking at him from one of his parlor chairs it took him a long moment to remember the ugly new dress his wife had worn at her birthday party. God, he loved a woman with sense. Of course, even that ridiculous frock would probably look magnificent on Regina's lovely form.

He gave his best ignorant masculine shrug. "There isn't a man in the state of Pennsylvania who would argue with your sense of fashion, Regina." He studied her red and blue suit with its long enticing row of buttons extending all the way from the lace under her chin down to her feet, the saucy bonnet perched on her head, and the black armband around her right arm. Of course. Henry's funeral instructions against discarding her wardrobe for a black one. But wearing a black armband, as was the masculine custom, still gave Regina the means to express her mourning. "I'm sure more husbands will be requesting their wives to take up armbands instead of black crepe."

Regina shook her head. "Henry didn't impose this on me, you know. He and I both agreed that it's silly, the way people do things because Queen Victoria does it. We're Americans for goodness' sake. We cut the umbilical cord to England a hundred years ago. We're supposed to think for ourselves."

Thomas hadn't actually known the reason behind the no-black edict. Of course the answer would be both sensible and profound. "You do excel at that," he answered admiringly. "I'm looking forward to having you back at the Wintergardens. This was supposed to be a joint business venture. I'm missing the Waring half of the input."

"Actually, I did come here to discuss business with you, not fashion," Regina stood up. "As well as to collect the private house tour you promised me." Regina turned back to Meredith as Thomas offered his elbow. "Thank you for the tea and company."

"You're welcome," Meredith answered, staring balefully at Thomas. He knew he'd hear from her later about offering his arm to Regina. Well, then, he might as well enjoy himself. When Regina rested her fingers on the proffered arm, he put his hand over them as he guided her out into the foyer to begin the house tour.

He only got as far as the foyer when Regina abruptly came to the real reason of her visit. "Thomas, we need to talk about your family's involvement with Kloman's new steel venture."

Thomas was thoroughly surprised by the abrupt change of topic. "How," he sputtered with astonishment, "do you know about that?"

Regina rolled her eyes. "Everyone always talks to me. Sometimes I think it's a curse. I frequently know a lot more than I want to." She turned to admire the front staircase that was his pride and joy. "Breathtaking piece of craftsmanship," she sighed appreciatively.

Thomas felt like he was being drawn and quartered. He couldn't concentrate on the length of her eyelashes, the pride in his house, and the new steel venture all at once. "No. I mean, yes. I mean, can we sit down and talk about this?"

"About the staircase?"

He took her by the elbow and escorted her to the window seat on the landing. "You know perfectly well I'm not talking about the staircase. Even if it is breathtaking. What do you know about Pittsburgh Bessemer Steel?"

"Well, I hadn't known the name until now," she answered, looking amused for a moment. "See what I mean? Everybody talks to me." She frowned earnestly. "I also don't know how far you're in, but Thomas, I'm urging you to get out. This venture is doomed from the outset."

Thomas laughed at her melodramatic choice of words. "Doomed? I have some reservations of my own, but—doomed?"

Regina's serious face didn't twitch. "Thomas, going into direct competition with Andy Carnegie is suicide. It's stupid. Yes—it's doomed."

Thomas felt a strong twinge of dislike. "So what makes Andy so impervious to competition? He's just doing business like the rest of us."

"Yes and no," Regina answered. "Yes, he's just a man making and selling a product, like the rest of you. But no—he doesn't DO business like the rest of you. You forget where he came from. He doesn't simply sell rails to the railroad. He got his start at the Pennsylvania Railroad. He doesn't need to put out any effort whatsoever—he just sells to his buddies. You're going to tell me Kloman's going to convince Andy's friends to buy from him, instead? Are you going to sell to other railroads? How are you going to get steel rails out of Pittsburgh—if not on Pennsylvania Railroad lines? What is freight going to cost you?" She let out a long breath. "Andy's going to eat you for dinner."

Thomas laughed at her odd expression. "He's going to what?"

Regina was almost glaring at him. "I'm serious, Thomas. Andy Carnegie's going to bide his time, let you build him a pretty new facility, wait for you to fail, then he'll buy out your entire works for pennies on the dollar. Mark my words. You're going to lose every dollar you sink into this."

Thomas searched Regina's face. "Does Andy Carnegie know all about our business plans?"

Regina's eyes became oddly shielded. "He knows enough. Don't do it, Thomas. It's pure folly. Not to mention just plain bad business."

"All right, all right, I'll see what I can do," Thomas had no idea how he could possibly convince his father to get out, when he had already voiced his own reservations to the plan.

"Well, I hope you can do something. At least you've been warned. Now," she stood up from the window seat and looked at him expectantly. "How about that house tour you've been promising me?"

Thomas offered his elbow for the second time that afternoon, and this time actually got to show off the new house.

****

How to approach his father? On a subject that had already been, well, sort of discussed? Under the curious gaze of his father's secretary, Thomas paced outside his father's office door the next morning, having no particularly brilliant ideas. Deciding that stalling was not an effective technique, he finally knocked on his father's door.

The first problem, he realized upon entering, was not merely broaching the subject. It was getting a word in edgewise. As soon as he showed his face, his father began a typical monologue.

"Ah, Thomas. I've been thinking we need to expand our office space. At the rate we've been adding bookkeepers, and secretaries, and salesmen, we're going to be too crowded for this building before too much longer. Not that this is a bad thing—I'm glad we need all the personnel. It means business is doing well . . . ."

Thomas patiently sat down and looked at his father. He'd been repeating the idea of expanding the office space for some time—Thomas wished he'd just do it, instead of talking about it. He made a mental note to send an architect over to talk with his father as soon as possible.

He listened as the monologue drifted over the familiar topics—when he finished with the office, he went over the usual complaints about the high shipping costs, the price of coke, and the list of people they were going to be having lunch with that day. "After lunch, I'm going to drop by Andy Kloman's office to see if . . ."

Aha—an opening. Thomas decided to take a direct approach. "I had an interesting visitor the other day," he interrupted, forcefully enough to be heard over his father's voice.

Richard stopped and looked at his son with some surprise at the interruption. "What?"

Thomas dropped his voice, forcing his father to actually look at him and listen. "I had a—very—interesting visitor waiting at home for me yesterday," he repeated. "Regina Waring came to talk with me about Kloman's grand plans."

His father groaned. "That woman's got a nose like a bloodhound," he groaned. "I suppose she wants in on the deal?"

"No," Thomas was glad his father trusted her business instincts. More than his, obviously. "She came to warn us both away from having anything to do with this deal."

"Why would she do that?"

Thomas had to smile. "Because she likes us, father. She's got some inside information she wasn't willing to share with me, but it was enough to warn me not to sink Olympus Ironworks money into Pittsburgh Bessemer Steel."

He did it. He'd floored his father. He was sitting at his desk, looking back at him, his face full of surprise.

"It's up to you, of course," Thomas continued mildly. "But like you said, she's got a nose like a bloodhound. She came out of mourning to warn us to get out before the financial losses start pouring in." He paused, wondering what tack to take next. "Henry Waring always trusted her instincts. Bragged about them. The two of them didn't do too badly together."

"Yes, yes, I heard Henry brag about her enough times," his father had his voice back. "I don't need you to tell me about her ability to sniff out a good business proposition." Thomas found himself facing a very searching look from his father. "So she wouldn't tell you exactly what she knows?"

Thomas shrugged. "Not all of it. She knows more than she's letting on. But I don't think she's trying to swindle us in some fashion, if that's what you're wondering."

"I wouldn't put it past her," his father answered sternly. "I think you can be too easily charmed by that pretty face, son." Thomas thought about the foolish grin that always lit his father's face when confronted with Regina's pretty face, but he held his tongue and let his father continue, "She's ruthless."

Thomas wasn't sure whether that was an insult or a compliment. Either way, he fought the need to defend his idol's actions. "I think she ruthlessly broke confidence with someone else in order to warn us, because I'm more than a friend—I'm a business partner," he reasoned. "It might be enlightened self interest on her part. If we lose money, I lose money, that could affect Waring-Baldwin Wintergardens. It's not merely a sentimental legacy to Henry, you know. It's also a moneymaker."

His father looked at him. "By God, son, I think you're right. That explains it. I wouldn't trust anyone to show up on my doorstep and hand over business advice for my own good. But if it's for their own good, too, well, that's not as suspicious. Maybe we'd better weigh anchor. We'd be asses to lose our shirts after being warned ahead of time."

Thomas was afraid to say another word. He'd done it. He'd managed to convince his father to pull out of Pittsburgh Bessemer Steel. Of course, there was going to be hell to pay if he and Regina were wrong.

Chapter 14

After the chaos surrounding the move to Hiland Avenue and the withdrawal from Pittsburgh Bessemer Steel, Thomas settled down to the daily obligations of being a Baldwin. He went to the Olympus Building, met the payroll, attended the meetings of the Freemasons, and contributed generously to the Pittsburgh Association for the Improvement of the Poor. He traveled to Chicago to negotiate the construction of wintergardens as part of George Pullman's grand plans to create an entire company town on the outskirts of that city. And, occasionally, he got to meet with his business partner—the Waring half of the Waring-Baldwin Wintergardens!

As much as he looked forward to them, the meetings always wrenched at his heart. True to her word, Regina continued to dress like a fashion plate in browns, blues, cardinals, and violets; but there was no mistaking her grief. She wore the pain on her face like a veil. She smiled, and talked, and frowned with a numbness Thomas hated to see. She never cried, and she never laughed.

One chilly April afternoon as he helped her off with her mantle, she seemed even glummer than usual. Even asking after the dogs, which she'd named Anthracite and Bituminous after the two types of coal, only brought a shadow of a smile to her lips. She listened listlessly to his description of his successful transactions with Mr. Pullman, and supplied none of the usual witticisms, acute observations or enthusiastic congratulations he had come to expect.

Certain at one point that she was looking straight into his face without seeing or hearing him, he started to stray from the subject matter to see when she'd notice.

". . . so I thought I'd take up your suggestion from a few months ago and do away with my wife. I'd have to move to Mexico at that point, of course, so I thought I'd see if you'd like to come with me. We could relocate the whole Wintergardens headquarters to Mexico City. What do you think?"

"If you think it's a good idea," she answered automatically.

He watched her a little more sharply, and continued, "Well, in that case, once we get down there, we might as well get married. It would save on expenses and . . ."

Regina's eyes snapped into focus. "Wait. What did you say?"

Thomas leaned back in his chair and smiled. "Nothing of consequence. I wanted to gauge how much you weren't listening. You're obviously not up for this. Shall we table this discussion for another time?"

She almost—but not quite—smiled. "What other time? I always seem to be walking around in a haze."

"Yes, I'd say you do," Thomas agreed. At least she'd reacted to his proposal of marriage. His mind prodded him on an idea he'd had for some time but was reluctant to bring up. He still didn't want to bring it up, but his conscience wasn't just pricking at him—it had moved on to beating him with blunt objects. "Regina, can I make a suggestion?"

Regina's black eyes were now very much in focus on his face. "If you ever withhold your suggestions from me, Sir Thomas, I shall be most displeased with you," she answered loftily. Then her face softened with affection. "In case you haven't realized it, I rely upon your wisdom a great deal."

Thomas shrugged in pleased embarrassment. "I don't know that I possess any great wisdom."

"Well, I do. I know you're wise beyond your years, and you're full of talents you don't even know you possess yet."

Thomas was taken aback by the praise. "You're giving me an awful lot of credit."

"Yes, I am. So say 'Thank you' graciously, and promise to live up to my high expectations."

"Thank you," Thomas answered obediently. "But I'm afraid of promising more than I can deliver."

Regina folded her hands complacently. "I have faith in you."

It felt so good to hear the words! Was it any wonder that he worshipped this woman, whose most casual utterance made him feel—well, all manner of things.

"So what's your suggestion?" she asked with the warmest smile he'd seen from her in a very long time.

Oh, he couldn't. He just couldn't.

He had to. For her sake.

"I wish you'd consider going away for awhile," he forced his lips to say the words. "Find a change of scenery. Spend a few months in Europe somewhere; Italy, or Spain, or England, whatever strikes your fancy. But get far away from Pittsburgh."

Regina looked doubtful. "I haven't been to our mills in Johnstown for a while . . ."

Thomas shook his head emphatically. "No, no, no. I mean, go someplace you've never been before. Someplace that has absolutely no memories of Henry attached to it."

He managed not to hesitate before saying Henry's name. Most people paused delicately before they'd drop their voice and say his name in Regina's presence. Thomas knew how much she hated that. But he realized why people did it. It was hard to watch the horrible pain that came into her eyes at the sound.

She frowned a little at him. "If I run away from everything that reminds me of Henry, there's not much left."

"I know that," he answered gently. "But at least if you're in a foreign country, battling with foreign languages and currencies and exchange rates, it will offer some distraction."

"I don't know." Thomas could see she was giving the idea some serious thought. "I get lonely now; what would I do among strangers?"

"You could take Anthra and Bit with you, of course, so you wouldn't be completely alone."

"Although they do remind me of Henry," she pointed out practically.

"Hm. True. There's certainly a lot of ways you could benefit our wintergardens, if you can bring back some business. The United States doesn't exactly have a monopoly on expositions."

A spark of interest illuminated her face. "I've always wanted to go to Venice, to see the glass factories at Burano."

"Well, there's a start," Thomas encouraged her. "I'll bet that's not the only place where you've got some professional interest."

"I don't know," Regina frowned reluctantly. "To leave the mills, the glassworks, my house, you . . ."

Thomas was pleased to be included in the list. He swallowed his pleasure and shook his head dismissively. "Oh, you've left all of us a long time ago. Your body may be here, but your mind has been elsewhere. Why don't you go someplace and find the rest of yourself? Then you can all come back together."

Regina was looking at him with eyes that had the old sense of humor peeking through. Her head tilted, eyes narrowed, then she pursed her lips suspiciously. "Awfully eager to be rid of me, aren't you?" she observed, a smile playing at the corners of her mouth. "If you try to buy me out while I'm away, you've got another thing coming."

Thomas laughed with relief at the glimpse of the old Regina. "I wouldn't dream of trying to buy you out!" he answered easily. "You're my partner, and you're stuck with me. Just like I'm stuck with you. Which is why I'm trying to take care of you."

"I can take care of myself, thank you very much."

"Which is why you're going to Venice?"

"Which is why I'll think about it. I might even talk to Andy when he gets back to town. He's been overseas recently, he may have some recommendations."

****

Regina had her "talk" with Andy Carnegie, and it turned out that another Pittsburgher, Clay Frick, a raw young entrepreneur whose gamble selling coke, instead of coal, had recently made him a millionaire, had just invited Judge Mellon's son, A.W., to go explore Europe with a couple of other Pittsburghers; Frank Cowen and A.A. Hutchinson.

"The boys," as Regina took to calling them, were delighted to include the pretty widow in their party. They understood the need to shake Regina out of her ennui, and lightheartedly bombarded her with details on London, Paris, Ireland, and, to Thomas' delight, Venice.

"Why not?" Clay Frick had answered when Thomas slipped in the suggestion. "It's a little farther than we were planning on going, but it'll make for a bigger adventure."

It was two months from the day that Thomas first broached the subject until he sat on Regina's veranda, watching as George and Regina's servants loaded the trunks onto his carriage. Going away was the best thing she could do, but he was going to miss her terribly. He may have won, but it was an extremely hollow victory.

His resolve was strengthened when she stepped out onto the veranda with a mournful little sigh. When she realized he was watching her, she stopped fiddling with the buttons on her gloves and gave a small shrug. "I shouldn't be doing this."

"Yes, you should," he answered firmly—and almost meant it. "You're going to mourn Henry the rest of your life. But I'm not going to let you mope the rest of your life. Henry would never forgive me."

There, nicely said. Casual, lighthearted, he didn't sound like a man whose heart was breaking because he was sending the love of his life away. He leaned forward and attracted Anthra and Bit's attention. The two dogs trotted eagerly over to him.

Regina watched him as he scratched the silky black ears. "You play me like a newly-tuned violin, my friend," she said fondly. "I think I shall be worried for my assets while I'm away, and I shall have to send spies to check your every report to me."

"I shall bribe your spies into giving horrible reports, so you won't stay away too long," he answered. "But you're not allowed home until there's some color in your face again, and you can hear me when I'm trying to give you a report."

Her eyes narrowed. "I don't know about this 'not allowed' business," she started, then continued contritely, "but I'll play by your rules, since I haven't been a very good business partner to you. You deserve a lot more support than I've been giving you."

She held her hand out to him, which he took in both of his. He kissed the back of it, feeling the smooth leather under his lips and wishing he could peel back her glove and kiss the warm flesh underneath. "My lady, you've recently lost a very cherished husband. As your partner, it's my job to provide you with support. Which at the moment includes sending you off to foreign countries for some much-needed recuperation. When you come back, no doubt I'll be in a state of crisis, and you can order me to take time away from Pittsburgh to go climb mountains in South America, or something."

"South America? Why South America?"

"Why not? I've never been there."

She gave an approximation of the rich deep laugh he missed hearing from her.

"See?" He pointed out. "You haven't even left, and you're starting to sound better already."

"So I don't actually have to go now?" she asked pertly.

"Foolish question! Of course you do. If you don't complete the cure, the malady will return with alarming acuity."

"I don't know what sounds worse, the cure or the disease."

"Oh, the disease is worse, I assure you."

"In that case," she turned and closed her front door, then looked at him expectantly. "Would you be so good as to escort me to the train station?

Chapter 15

With Regina gone, decisions about the Wintergardens fell on him, alone. For all practical purposes, it had been up to him since Henry died, and Regina's grief had meant limited attention to business matters. But she had at least been nominally involved. Now she was completely absent. It was an odd feeling; their enterprise had evolved from a trio to a solo. He seemed to be getting along well enough. The orders kept coming in, the finished products kept shipping out. But it was lonely without the Warings to consult on the financial, artistic, or administrative decisions.

He was capping his inkwell after sending off a long missive to his architect when his office door opened, and David admitted a tall lanky stranger with an oddly familiar look about him.

"Mr. Baldwin? I've got a Mr. McKay come to see you, sir."

Thomas stared, puzzled, as the stranger stepped forward and bowed. Thomas stood to return the courtesy and frowned. "I'm sure I know you, but I hope you'll forgive me . . . ."

"I figured you probably wouldn't remember me," the man smiled apologetically. "Charles McKay. Some four, five years ago you fished my wife and I out of a ditch on Carson Street."

A jolt of recognition spurred Thomas to offer his hand for a vigorous handshake. "McKay! Yes, yes, I certainly remember you, and a very excellent lunch at the Duquesne Club. Haven't seen you since. What brings you to Pittsburgh?"

"My father's sent me to open a Pittsburgh office. Just to have better railroad contacts. We're not trying to give you any competition," he added quickly. "I've never forgotten your hospitality when we were here, and so I thought I'd do things properly this time and bring you my letters of introduction."

Thomas took the prim envelope with a laugh. He appreciated the niceties, but it seemed so unnecessary under the circumstances. Charles McKay's likeable manner made him feel instantly like an old friend.

"Well, now that we've dispensed with the proprieties, welcome to Pittsburgh! Even if I don't believe your disclaimer about not being competition," Thomas couldn't help but joke.

Charles was obviously too earnest for that sort of humor. He frowned and repeated, "No, honestly, it's really to help with shipping and supplies . . . ."

"I'm kidding, I'm kidding," Thomas quickly reassured his newly-renewed acquaintance. "I'm sorry, I must be a little giddy today. I've just waded through quite a few big revisions. It's been a long morning. It's obviously going to my head. Care to adjourn with me to the Duquesne Club? If you're going to be here a while, you might want to join. I use my membership all the time."

"Lead the way!" McKay exclaimed heartily.

****

It was the best invitation Thomas had ever made. Charles was a born storyteller, and kept Thomas so thoroughly entertained, he had to send his beef brisket back to the kitchen, as it had gotten cold while he sat listening. He seemed to recall that upon their last visit to the Duquesne Club, Charles' wife had spent most of the meal interrupting him. Without the interruptions, Charles' stories seemed to flow from an endless fountain. By the end of the meal, Thomas felt he'd found a new best friend.

The friendship solidified quickly in the weeks that followed. Charles became a frequent visitor at both the Olympus office and the Baldwin's dining room table. Charles' good nature even had Meredith charmed into laughing at his anecdotes. Supper at the table was a new experience for Thomas, who still habitually escaped to the shelter of his library.

Now Charles' voice flowed through the meal, and Thomas noticed even the servants were lingering over the dinner service in order to listen to larger parts of Charles' conversation. He imagined that there was a heap of household staff on the other side of the kitchen door, their ears pressed against it.

By the time Charles' wife Elizabeth joined her husband in Pittsburgh, Thomas had even helped the McKays locate a suitable house, not too far from his old place in Allegheny, among the grand homes on Ridge Avenue. It was a formidable brick structure with tall windows and a fashionable mansard roofline decorated with the nicest wrought iron railings Thomas had ever seen.

Elizabeth McKay was as awful as Thomas had remembered. She seemed to have a special knack for malapropisms, and a complete disregard for her patient husband. She was obviously unhappy at the prospect of leaving her house and friends in Johnstown, and seemed quite determined to dislike everything about Pittsburgh.

"The soprano at the musicale last night was SO off-key," she began her litany of complaints, when the McKays and Baldwins had assembled on the McKays' front porch one particularly pleasant summer evening. "The seats in Library Hall are SO uncomfortable. I miss our little opera house," she sighed plaintively. "And I know that there are more merchants here in Pittsburgh, but why on earth can't they ever carry anything nice? I must have tried on a dozen pair of gloves before I found some that didn't have something wrong with them. I declare, the poor quality that these shops are willing to sell to customers is perfectly disgraceful."

She could be very imaginative in her grumbling. There were the obvious things to complain about: the weather, the cost of shoes or groceries, or the difficulty in finding good domestic help. Thomas had a hard time keeping a straight face when she complained about the sidewalks on Wood Street, and the other people at social events.

"I'm sorry Mrs. Waring's overseas," Thomas offered helpfully when she paused for air. "Once she gets back, you'll have a fellow Johnstonian to commiserate with."

Charles' face lit up with interest. "You know the Warings?"

"Yes," Thomas answered, "I'm in business with them. Well, her, now. You didn't know that Henry Waring died in an accident a couple years ago?"

"You know, I had heard. I'd forgotten. I shall have to pay a call. You say she's overseas?"

"I sent her there, myself, with orders not to come back until she's herself again. Pittsburgh society isn't the same without her, but . . . ."

The mention of Regina's name had put an exceptionally sour look on Elizabeth's face. "Pittsburgh people might think of Mrs. Waring as fit company in polite society," she interrupted in a huff, actually turning rather red in the face, "but that woman wouldn't be received in decent homes in Johnstown. No woman THERE is fooled by her, even if she does have awfully nice dresses." There was no mistaking the envy in her voice. "I don't havc anything as nice as she does. Not that I know anyone here, so what's the point of having a new visiting suit, anyway," she sniffed disagreeably.

Charles had retreated back into his usual reticence in his wife's presence. Thomas squirmed internally for his friend, then looked from Elizabeth to Meredith, who was posing primly in her newest dinner gown with a somewhat smug smile on her face. "I know," he exclaimed, "why doesn't Meredith take you with her when she goes calling? There must be several people here in the city to whom you haven't been properly introduced. And of course Meredith must know everyone worth knowing in Allegheny County, both seamstresses and society. She ought to be able to help you out."

Both women looked at him indignantly. He wasn't quite sure which code of feminine conduct he'd violated with his suggestion, but he was sure there was some sort of vanity associated with keeping one's favorite seamstress a secret, or perhaps visiting needed to be done individually, to allow for grand entrances when wearing new visiting suits. He had no idea. But the looks on their faces goaded him to even greater friendliness and generosity. "Oh, I insist," he smiled as sweetly as he could. "I certainly can spare George for longer periods of time so that Meredith can help you get better situated here in town." Thomas enjoyed being one of the few families who still kept stables and his own carriage and driver. The extra expense was well worth the convenience it afforded him. Not to mention he enjoyed the ability to be generous with the luxury when he chose. "Pittsburgh's a wonderful city, you just need to get to know it better."

Elizabeth's face sported an eerie copy of Meredith's own nasty-nice smile. "I'm sure," she answered, looking very sure that she had no interest in getting to know it any better than she had to.

****

It had been so many years since Thomas had had a good friend. He'd been a loner as a child, preferring to go off on his own and climb trees, rather than get into horse races and ice skating and the rest of the more sociable pastimes that his brother Benjamin had delighted in.

At Western University, he'd somehow gotten himself attached to Michael Watson. They seemed an unlikely pair: Thomas was quiet, tall, reserved, and admittedly the better-looking of the two. Michael was a talkative round fellow with few, if any, inhibitions. If it weren't for Michael, Thomas doubted if he ever would have sown a single wild oat in his youth. He probably would never have tried alcohol, or seen the inside of a brothel, or learned the words to several songs that were not sung in polite society, if it weren't for his best friend.

Soon after graduation, however, Michael had left Pittsburgh to explore the oil industry in Cleveland. Neither man being much for correspondence, they had pretty much lost touch. Last he'd heard, Michael was worth about four times as much as Thomas, expanding his oil refineries along the shore of Lake Erie, and had married the daughter of the man who owned the railroad that he was supplying with oil.

When Michael left, Thomas had been too busy getting indoctrinated into the Ironworks to think much about his missing friend. They were adults now, time to grow up and get down to business. Until the Warings had come along, he hadn't thought much about the fact that he no longer had a confidante.

Now he had someone to talk to. Granted, he spent a lot more time listening than he did talking, but it was still nice to have a companion close to his own age and situation with whom he could talk about the gas-versus-electric debate, or the changing cut of men's vests, or whatever neat innovation George Westinghouse was working on NOW. As much as he valued the Warings' friendship, it wasn't the same sort of friendship. Regina loved the haggling and dealing involved in doing business, but was far less interested in technological advances. Henry had been several years older than Thomas, and somehow, while Thomas appreciated that Henry treated him like an equal, he never felt like an equal.

Charles was very much an equal. Similar family histories, similar occupations, similar tastes. Even, to a certain extent, similar marriages. When the McKays met with the Baldwins, Charles' chatty voice died away to nothing in his wife's presence, his shoulders hunched forward, no doubt against the barrage of her voice, and his cheerful face picked up a resigned expression that pained Thomas to see. He found himself checking his face in mirrors when he was in public with Meredith—did his face take on that same expression? He didn't think so. He seemed to have more of a will to fight back than Charles did. After five years of marriage, he was fairly inured to Meredith's sweetly-smiling glare, and her private fury at his inattentiveness only inspired him to make even greater attempts to be charming and amusing in company. The irony did not escape him—he wanted so badly to be more outgoing, and he had two women, polar opposites, bringing him out of his shell. Regina through inspiration and encouragement, Meredith through sheer perversity.

Perhaps because of a mutual recognition of unhappy situations, neither man ever discussed his home life.

There were plenty of other things to talk about. Besides technology and fashion, Thomas greatly enjoyed playing native guide in his home city, and answering Charles' questions on everything from history and geography to the best place to find lighting fixtures.

He also found himself enjoying Charles' love of activity. Spurred by a mutual desire to avoid their homes, both men frequented the excellent archery clubs that dotted the city, purchased beautiful, tall bicycles which required a great deal of practice to gain proficiency riding, and started serious collections of poles and tackle to partake in the very fashionable pastime of fishing.

Thomas had no idea such a simple concept as dropping a string in the water with bait on the end of it required so much equipment. Not to mention a special wardrobe. Cycling and archery, sure, but fishing? Absolutely. This simple and solitary hobby also required a special place to wear said clothing and use said equipment. He found himself buying two shares in a private sportsman's club, the South Fork Fishing and Hunting Club, which was in the Allegheny Mountains beyond Johnstown. It was a newly-formed organization, with grand plans to create a sparkling mountain lake, utilizing an old dam that had been part of the canal system.

The plans were to stock the lake with fish, maintain the lands around it as a game preserve, and create a sportsman's paradise. Having to travel a goodly distance away from his wife's voice for all of Saturday and Sunday sounded even better than paradise to Thomas. He looked forward to the following summer's fishing with great anticipation. Why, it would be a fine thing even if the fish never bit at all.

Chapter 16

The new friendship and hobbies served as a distraction from the gaping hole in his life where Regina had been. She had sent him a cable from London, letting him know they had made it at least that far in safety, and a brief card from Paris, saying that the city was beautiful, but it wasn't Pittsburgh. Just for spite, Thomas sent a card with artwork of Pittsburgh to her hotel, to help her compare. Her last message, sent before the group was supposed to move on to Ireland, said simply, "You brat." Thomas was immensely pleased by the playful message.

She started sending small packages, and even a glass chandelier from someplace near Venice. Thomas guessed it was from one of the factories she'd been wanting to see. He was pleased to see she was having fun.

Clay Frick returned with most of the rest of his party, but apparently A.A. Hutchinson and Regina had elected to extend the trip. Thomas tried to sound casual when he asked Clay if there was a romantic attachment between the two of them.

"With A.A.? That would be awfully amusing! I loosened him up enough to get him to sell me his coalfields in Connellsville so he could keep on traveling—he's going to continue all the way around the world. I expect it'll take him longer than 80 days. I knew if I showed him a good time I'd be able to get somewhere. A.A.'s always been a dull fellow, but seeing some of the world has made quite the improvement."

"And does he have designs on my business partner?" Thomas really didn't like the idea of Regina off on a romantic jaunt around the world with this 'dull fellow,' especially if traveling had 'improved' him.

"He'd be showing awfully good sense if he does. The fellow doesn't have much of a head for business, she could probably do a lot better with his assets than he can. Just as well for me there was no attachment while we were all traveling together, I can't see her ever selling me his coalfields, if she had them. Or else she would have charged me at least three times as much to get them. A.W. Mellon thought I was daft bringing A.A. along in the first place, but I knew if I showed him a good time . . ."

Thomas could see he wasn't going to get anywhere trying to glean useful information about Regina from Clay. His mind was perpetually occupied with his business ambitions. Not much room to think of anything else.

A.W. was no better. Thomas tried a more direct approach the next time he was in the Mellons' bank. "So how's my business partner?" He asked by way of greeting.

Mellon's eyebrows went up for a moment. "Who? Oh. Mrs. Waring. She's fine, I imagine." No one would ever accuse A.W. Mellon of being a talker.

Finally, a letter came from Regina herself.

My dear Thomas,

Well, you were certainly right. Sending me away and making me wrestle with foreign currencies has been the sort of mental challenge that has pulled me back to the land of the living! The boys made for excellent travel companions, and I'm finally beginning to look at things without wishing Henry was here to see them, too.

To that end, I'm hoping you're willing to do without me for a while, yet. I admit, I'm daunted by the prospect of coming home and facing my life again. When A.A. announced his intentions to stay on, I thought I'd follow his example. He's a decent traveling companion, a keen observer, but very quiet and deliberate. There's more to him than meets the eye. Not unlike you, that way.

I suspect he's also taken a fancy to one of the young ladies here at the hotel, and I shall soon be called upon to play chaperone. We'll see how it goes. The young lady is also terribly quiet, I can see the two of them simply perishing in agony, each sitting there trying to work up the nerve to say something to the other.

I certainly trust you to continue doing the same excellent job running everything for the Wintergardens without me. I'm agog at the success you've had running solo. In the meantime, of course, please cable me if you want my vote. I guess I'll be home when I'm ready.

Thank you for sending me on this quest, my dear friend. So far it's been successful. I remain gratefully yours,

R

At first, Thomas felt red-hot pokers of jealousy at her warm appraisal of A.A. He wished he could have been her 'decent traveling companion.' But when she talked about playing chaperone for A.A. and a young lady, he felt mollified. And, of course, he appreciated the affection she was showing him. Her gratitude was certainly pleasant to have, and Thomas realized that, almost spouse-like, she considered herself accountable to him.

All he could do was send an encouraging reply and go on. He split his days between the Olympus Ironworks office and the Wintergardens. He spent as much time as possible at the Duquesne Club. He and Charles McKay reluctantly put their bicycles and fishing gear away when the weather turned cold. And he came home to his house on Highland Avenue, greeted at the front door by Meredith's voice and Regina's chandelier.

The winter months seemed to drag by. He finally talked his father into renting a telephone for Olympus Ironworks. He turned down an invitation to leave the Duquesne Club and join some of the harder-drinking members, who were starting their own club, which they were calling the Pittsburgh Club. Since he didn't drink, liked to brag about the chef, and was definitely starting to improve at billiards, he didn't see the point of changing loyalties.

Charles seemed to be getting more and more restless. He'd pick at his food at lunch, or send things back to the kitchen over slight offenses. He couldn't seem to sit through a performance at the theatre, without getting up to stand at the back of the box at the Opera House, and he was no better at Library Hall. Even while sitting in a chair, he'd bounce his leg or tap a finger. After a while, Thomas started to get irritated. He tried to remember when his friend had picked up these nervous tics, but he had no idea. He was certain, though, that these were new habits.

He finally decided to beard the lion in his den, and point-blank ask him.

They were settled into their favorite comfortable chairs in the big lounge at the Club, and Thomas had been deep into one of Herbert Spencer's books on Social Darwinism. He couldn't seem to read more than three sentences in a row, when Charles would shift positions. He found himself watching Charles more than reading, and wishing for a clock within eyeshot, so that he could see whether Charles actually sat still for an entire minute before shifting again.

Finally, he gave up, closed the book, and looked at Charles. "Well," he set the book on the reading table and folded his hands. "Why don't you tell me what's going on? I'm not going to get any reading done until you do."

Charles looked back at him. "What do you mean?"

"I mean, you've been fidgeting like a schoolboy. And not just tonight. For several weeks, I think. If you're having some sort of medical issue, I can recommend a good physician . . ."

Charles, predictably, stood up and began pacing. "No, no, it's nothing like that," he demurred.

"Well, then, what's wrong?" With almost anyone else, Thomas never would have asked. If Charles wanted to talk to him, he'd talk to him. Goodness knows, his friend liked to talk, after all. But somehow Thomas felt obliged to open the topic.

Charles stopped pacing and just stared unhappily at him. "I wish I knew. I guess I'm—restless."

Thomas smiled in an imitation of Regina's 'go-on-I'm-listening' smile. "Miss the bicycles?"

Charles shook his head and paced over to lean against the fireplace mantel. "No, it's not that kind of restless. At least, I don't think so. Maybe I thought if we bought the bicycles, I could go fast enough to leave the restlessness behind me."

He began charging up and down the room again. Thomas was getting tired watching him. He imagined that being married to Elizabeth would definitely make any man restless. He could certainly understand that. Being married to Meredith used to make him restless. Now he was merely resigned. Besides, he seemed to have found a way to live with her. It wasn't ideal, but it was all he had.

Even if the unhappy marriage was the reason, this was something Thomas couldn't bring up. So he watched, and waited.

Charles did another lap of the floor, then flopped into the chair opposite Thomas and looked at him helplessly. "Does life ever seem pointless to you?"

The question surprised Thomas. "No." He wasn't sure how to answer. "I mean, we're here; we didn't have a choice in the matter; I guess I do what's in front of me that needs to be done," he finished rather lamely. Charles was right—what was the point? This was obviously going to be a depressing conversation.

Charles nodded. "See what I mean? Pointless. At the end of the day, I've done some work for my father, made some money, talked to some people, ate a few times, and if it's a good day, you and I had a chance to do something for fun for a while. Is this it? There's no meaning, no drive, no—no point."

Thomas didn't know what to say. Charles had just summed up his life pretty accurately, as well as his own. It never occurred to him to ask the same questions. He sat and stared at his friend. "What about church?" he asked.

"What about it?" Charles asked. "I sit there and wonder what to pray for." He clasped his hands together and lifted his eyes. "God, I'm unhappy, but I don't know what to ask for. I don't know what I want. All I know is, I don't want this." He looked back at Thomas. "I do that, God'll laugh at me and call me a jackass and send me a plague for being ungrateful. I have a pretty wife, who wears pretty clothes while sitting in my pretty house while I ride the pretty streetcar to my pretty office. Isn't that the American Dream? I'm a living example of the success that all my employees dream of achieving."

Thomas nodded. "You're right. You are an ungrateful jackass."

Charles joined in Thomas' laugh. "Yes I am. Makes me feel good about myself."

"'The mass of men lead lives of quiet desperation,'" Thomas quoted. "'What is called resignation is confirmed desperation . . .'" He stopped quoting. Wasn't that the word he used to describe his life? Resigned?

Charles looked at him inquisitively. "What's that from?"

"Thoreau. Didn't you read Walden in college?"

"Sure, but do I remember any of it? I wasn't paying attention. Latin declensions, literature—if it wasn't about making iron, it wasn't going to be relevant, was it?"

"Pointless. I'm beginning to detect a theme in your life." It occurred to him that perhaps his advice to Regina might be the answer to Charles' restlessness. "Have you thought about taking a trip somewhere? Business has been pretty steady, and everyone seems to be heading off to Europe these days. Clay Frick seemed to enjoy his belated Grand Tour. My business partner, Mrs. Waring, is still overseas."

"Oh, yes. I forget you had a connection with her. You know we went to school together?"

"You did?" Thomas hadn't known.

"We started in the same primer class. We must've been, what, eight? Seven? Something like that. So where is she, exactly?"

"In the south of France, I believe. Although she wrote to say she's contemplating moving on to Madrid, or back to Italy."

"France, Spain, Italy, it all sounds pleasant. Maybe we should follow her example."

For all his advice to other people, somehow it had never occurred to Thomas that he could travel, too. Well, and why not? After all, Andy Carnegie, Clay Frick, and Regina Waring found ways to leave their businesses long enough to travel. His mind began to make a quick mental checklist of what tasks he could leave to whom.

"We could do that," he said aloud.

"Let's!" exclaimed Charles. "A little travel would be good."

Thomas could hear the blood pounding in his ears so loudly, he could hardly hear Charles listing off ideas of places to go. If Regina wouldn't come to him, he'd just have to go to her.

****

The following month was a tizzy of excitement. Of course, neither wife was terribly crazy about the idea of traveling, until both men dangled the prospect of a trip to go dress shopping in Paris before their feminine eyes. Then they heard nothing else but raving about someplace called Worth. Both men hid with masculine horror from such raptures, and spent more pleasant time contemplating the museums, theatres, architecture and landscape that were all possible destinations. Differing visions aside, an impatience to leave gripped the foursome.

Thomas' eagerness to be on the train bound for New York, and boarding a steamer that would bring him closer to the sight of Regina's black eyes, made the time until departure almost unbearable. But they couldn't simply jump on the next train leaving Pittsburgh; they needed time to plan their destinations and time to get business to such a state that they could leave for a while. Neither of their fathers had ever really traveled, and neither understood why anyone would want to leave Pennsylvania to see something of the world.

"Land, water, buildings. We've got all that right here," Richard Baldwin protested when Thomas told him he wanted to go travel. Richard had always been Thomas' staunchest defender when people wondered at the lack of a wedding trip. "There's work to be done," Richard had said to anyone who commented on the odd omission. "Why go someplace else? Pittsburgh's as good a place to be as any."

Thomas had appreciated his father's lack of curiosity at the time. But it did mean now he had to find a reason to explain the sudden desire to travel. "Consider it a belated wedding trip," he heard himself saying. "Now that times are better, it won't matter as much if I'm away."

"It wouldn't matter if you were away or not, anyway, I guess," his father answered. "Go ahead, you might as well take your trip."

Thomas ignored the rather hurtful nature of the comment, and took him at his word. A glamorous-sounding itinerary slowly emerged: New York to Liverpool, Liverpool to London, then across the channel to France. After several days in Paris, where the husbands expected a great deal of freedom while their wives were completely absorbed by the local dressmakers and whatnot, they would travel south to Spain, then along the Mediterranean back through France, to Italy.

Thomas wrote to Regina, informing her of the plans to come to Europe, and casually suggesting she could join them, or they could find her. He waited in vain for a response, which he took to mean he'd missed her at her hotel and she'd moved on. But then, it could also mean the mail in southern France was unreliable and she hadn't even received his letter yet.

It didn't really matter. Thomas knew he could track her down once they were on the same continent.

Less than a week before departure, however, all dreams of catching up with Regina in some romantic Italian villa came crashing to a halt. Meredith's father, Warren Burke, was found dead on the floor in his office. The doctors said his heart had given out. He'd walked into his office that morning, with no idea that he was sick, then several hours later his staff heard a loud thud. They came in to see what the noise was, and there was their employer, lying peacefully on the floor, dead.

Now in mourning for a man who'd never liked him, married to the daughter he hadn't actually despoiled, Thomas was forced to stay in Pittsburgh and bid his friends a good journey.

He tried to bear his disappointment with good grace, but as he sat through the funeral services, knowing the McKays were probably boarding the steamer for Liverpool, he felt like throwing himself on the floor, kicking his heels and screaming like a two-year-old.

His mind flew back to Charles' self-mocking prayer; "God, I don't know what I want, but I don't want this."

In his case, he knew what he wanted. He wanted to look into the depths of those black eyes. Using the reliable old excuse that she was his business partner and therefore he had to look out for her, he'd extracted a promise from Charles to find her, wherever she was, and check on her. It wasn't the same as being able to see her for himself, but under the circumstances, it was all he could do.

****

Now without Regina or Charles to provide a glimmer of cheer, life went on. Thomas put his head down and threw himself into his work. New orders for the foundry, new orders for the Glassworks. More employees to do the work, more money for the payroll. Look for a way to make everything cheaper, or faster, or prettier. Meanwhile, Meredith's brothers surprised him with a large number of shares in her father's brewery. Both boys were even quieter than Thomas, and they candidly told him they needed both his business experience and his way with people.

"My what?" Thomas had exclaimed.

"Everyone likes you," James Burke answered matter-of-factly. "Besides, you're in the family, it's only fair you should help us keep the family business going."

So he spent some time going over the breweries' books, got better acquainted with the premises, talked with the employees. He was part-owner of a brewery, which was mildly amusing for a man who didn't drink the stuff.

He was lonely, which seemed odd. Most of his life, he preferred to be alone. He never really needed company. Now he found himself wishing for companionship, but while he was surrounded by people, he had no companions.

It made him short-tempered and easily irritated, so he said less and less to anyone, and tried very consciously to be patient and kind to his employees and domestic staff. The family didn't matter; he never got a word in edgewise with them, anyway. They talked at him. He looked back, nodded, and thought about other things.

Business poured in. He turned the money into stock, back into expanding the foundry, into a wintergarden behind his own house. He experimented with stained glass designs instead of clear glass on his wintergarden. Even his father noticed that the long hours he'd habitually put in had become even longer. "See? You don't need any vacation time. There's work to do."

When the warm weather came, he was able to take out his bicycle and fishing tackle again, but both activities were less fun without Charles' company. He tried to show interest in developments up at the Fishing and Hunting Club, but those, too, reminded him that his best friend was away on the trip he expected to be taking, too. He kept half an ear on the improvements to the dam and the progress on the new clubhouse because he felt he should, but he didn't actively venture any opinions.

At last, May came and, at least according to their original plans, the McKays should be returning on the steamer from Liverpool. He watched for any correspondence from his friend, although he didn't really expect any. Charles was even less of a writer than him. He watched the calendar, counted off the ten days' crossing, and wondered if they would stay in New York for a while, or stop off to see family in Johnstown before returning to Pittsburgh. He'd heard precious little from Regina lately, getting only a note that she had embarked on some shopping spree that he would be sure to laugh at.

He hoped Charles had kept his promise and checked on Regina—he desperately wanted news of her.

At long last, a cheerful whistle sounded outside his office, and Charles stepped through the door, unannounced.

"McKay!" Thomas was so glad to see his friend, he could have hugged him. He jumped up from his chair, nearly spilling his ink bottle, and all but ran around his desk to shake hands. "It's about time you got back. The fishing's been fabulous all spring, and you've missed out on some good hauls!"

Charles returned the handshake heartily. "Well, as long as you haven't caught them all, I'll catch up to you," he answered. "Have you been to lunch yet? Not that I'm sure I know how I'm going to choke down plain old American cooking after the amazing repasts I've had in Europe. Look at me, I've gained at least ten pounds."

Thomas looked. Charles was still as thin and lanky as ever. "Yes. I can see you're getting downright portly. Well, we can ask for some bread and water for you." He capped his ink, grabbed his hat, and led the way out the door.

He listened patiently as Charles gushed about the trip: what they'd seen, what they'd done, where they'd been. He didn't really want to hear any of it. After all, if it weren't for his usual lousy luck, he would have been able to experience all of it for himself. But Charles was his friend, and of course, he wanted to find out if he'd seen Regina.

He had his chance an hour later, when Charles needed to pause in his talking to take a long drink of water. "So," he asked as casually as he could, "did you manage to find Mrs. Waring anywhere during your wanderings?"

Charles nearly choked as he swallowed. "I'm so sorry, old man," he sputtered as he dove to pick his napkin off the floor. "I forgot to tell you. Yes, yes we did find her. Perfectly by accident, as it happens. I didn't find her so much as she found us. She showed up at our hotel in Nice. We saw quite a bit of her. She's pretty good company. Very handy to have around when you're looking at a lot of old buildings or art. That reminds me—did I tell you about Venice?

Now I understand what this craze of building things that look sort of Italian is all about . . . ."

That was it; Charles had seen "quite a bit of her," and that was all he had to say about her. No doubt she was less interesting to him than the Venetian structures they'd admired together, but that wasn't what Thomas wanted to hear. Her eyes were probably sparkling as she leaned back in a gondola in some canal, smiling in appreciation as one beautiful building after another floated by. In a red dress, maybe, like the one she wore on their picnic at the Duquesne Heights.

He realized he wasn't listening to Charles anymore—he couldn't stand hearing anymore. He put up his hands. Charles stopped talking and looked at him curiously.

"I know you've got days and days of stories I want to hear. But right now I've got to get back to the office. Want to tell me more over a fishing pole?"

"Oh, of course. I'll walk back over with you. I'm easing my way back into work. My fellows are so used to my absence, they're getting along perfectly fine without me."

So it was several more minutes before Thomas' ears were able to ring in the quiet of his office, and he was able to indulge in a nice, quiet sulk.

Living vicariously through others was not something he could do. He was happy for Charles that he'd had a good time. He seemed so relaxed and happy, devoid of the restlessness that had possessed him before the trip. Now Thomas was the restless one. He wanted to see something of the world. He wanted to have stories worth telling people. He wanted to see Regina.

"Mr. Baldwin?" his secretary David Smith interrupted his dour thoughts. "Mr. McAlister from the streetcar company is calling on you, sir. And there's a messenger from the Misters Burke; looks like they've got another question for you. And this package came for you from Mrs. Waring."

Package? Thomas nearly knocked his chair over, standing up to take a long cylinder from him. In his eagerness, he nearly forgot to thank his surprised employee.

"Thank you, Smith. Tell Mr. McAlister I'll be with him in a couple of minutes."

He'd been waiting to hear from Regina for months. Sean McAlister would have to wait.

The cylinder contained a thick roll of blueprints, with one of her typical scrawled notes on top.

> *Mon cher Sir Thomas,*
>
> *Just when I think I shall stop gallivanting around Europe and come home, someone else comes along to tempt me into staying a little longer! The McKays have left, and now the entire Carnegie clan of Gay Charioteers is coming overseas and have invited me to join them in Scotland. Well, and why not? I've made it to the rest of the British Isles.*
>
> *In the meantime, I've sweet-talked my way into an order for the Wintergardens—hold onto your hat, my friend, and take a look at the size of this place! We wanted to get into the industrial and World's Fair markets, I think we're there. This place is a theatre, but big, and visible, and I'll be pretty surprised if it doesn't lead to plenty of other large projects. Unless they want to see me again in Leipzig, I'll be coming home with Andy et al to get to work. I've been away quite long enough.*
>
> *We've got a glass palace to build!*

Thomas set aside Regina's note and unrolled the enclosed sketches. She wasn't kidding! This wasn't a modest little greenhouse. This was a behemoth.

The woman was amazing. For all the bragging Henry used to do, he was still selling her short. She had vision, ambition, and a knack for making things happen. He certainly never would have envisioned the places his life would go because of his association with her.

With a sigh, he allowed the paper to roll up, and called for Smith to let Sean McAlister in. His association with her meant associating with a lot of other people, too. Time to get back to taking care of them.

Chapter 17

She was coming home. Not now, but soon.

That thought sustained Thomas through the remainder of the spring and into the summer. It was nice having Charles back. They both joined the Keystone Bicycle Club, taking out the fishing gear became fun again, and the updates on the construction of the clubhouse up at Conemaugh Lake became more interesting.

It was a typically stifling Pittsburgh July day—hot and dark without a hint of breeze coming though the windows to relieve the heat. Thomas was glad for his usual Saturday morning stop at the brewery. His brothers-in-law allowed him to install a new-fangled refrigeration system behind the old icehouse; he loved slipping into the building for a delicious moment of cool air.

Thomas found to his surprise that he enjoyed being a brewer. At first, he had felt a bit lost among the hops, and yeast, and barrels, and cooling pans. But he soon realized that business was business: instead of a recipe for pig iron there was a recipe for lager, and instead of searching for places to turn the ingots into streetcar parts, or cannon, or stoves, (or wintergardens), the output merely needed to be barreled or bottled and taken to the front tavern, and people came to you. How much easier, by comparison!

The Burke boys seemed to have little enthusiasm for their profession. For that matter, they never seemed to question anything about life. They went along with the flow, doing whatever was in front of them the same way they'd done it the day before. It never occurred to them to build, or change, or grow. At least their policy of non-resistance gave Thomas free reign with all the interesting possibilities he'd found in the business.

"We understand that if you want to keep up with business, you've got to stay modern," James Burke had said when Thomas had suggested adding the refrigeration system. "You go ahead—just don't explain to me how it works." Walt Burke had grunted his agreement. Thomas came to the conclusion that Walt never actually spoke—he simply grunted, and James translated for him when necessary.

So, every Saturday on his way downtown Thomas stopped at the brewery to check the week's progress—and to remind the crew that he was watching. Workmen were frequently sloppier on Saturdays; either you had the sort of men who started dawdling, because the week was almost over, or they started rushing, because the week was almost over.

Since he had instituted a policy of half-price beer for brewery workers at the end of the workday, and extended the privilege to include the construction crew, he knew they were well-disposed to do a good job. But showing up once a week to admire their handiwork didn't hurt.

The moment he stepped inside the brewery doors, he was inundated with demands from all sides—from the barkeeper waving tavern orders, the clerk waving receipts from the cooper, the floor manager giving him dirty looks while asking a long list of questions. James and Walt Burke stood in the midst of it all, looking at him with their usual, vaguely bemused expressions.

The stream of questions seemed endless. Thomas had made it to the far side of the lobby, although he was beginning to despair of ever making it out to the icehouse, when a voice at the door shouted, "The President's been killed!"

A shocked silence fell over the entire building. Everyone stared at one another for a moment, then turned to stare at a perspiring drayman standing in the doorway.

"What did you say?" Thomas prompted the man, quite sure he didn't hear what he thought he heard.

"I just passed Freddy, who has to drive past the newspaper office, and he says they've got a bulletin up. It says 'Garfield assassinated this morning at the B & O depot in Washington.'"

The silence lasted a moment longer, then everyone started talking at once. "It's a hoax—papers will say anything to make a sale." "Who would want to assassinate Garfield?" "It was one of those socialists, I warrant." "Not again. Oh, not again."

Not again, indeed. It had only been sixteen years since Abraham Lincoln was felled by an assassin's bullet. Every man in America who was over the age of two at the time could remember where he was and what he was doing when he'd learned the news that the man who'd successfully defeated the rebellion against the Union had been slain by a lone, crazed rebel.

Thomas looked at James and Walt. "There isn't going to be a soul in this city who will be able to work once the news gets out. Do we give up now and send the men home, or do we at least attempt to keep them here until noon and send them home at dinnertime?"

Both of them shook their heads mutcly. Thomas sighed. He wished Meredith was as quiet as her brothers. "All right, there's probably not really going to be any news of real substance for awhile, yet," he guessed. "No reason to spoil today's batch if we can help it. We still don't have a telephone up here, do we? See about getting a reliable message boy to go stand at the newspaper, or maybe at the telegraph office, and bring a report back every hour. If all we do is wait for news all day, sales may be better than usual. Make sure the message boy stops at the tavern every hour, too."

Fortunately, the floor manager and foreman were standing there with James and Walt. The lot of them nodded at his instructions. Thomas didn't know what else to say. "God help us all, gentleman. I've got to get over to Olympus. I'm sure there's an iron mill full of men wondering what's going on, too."

George had the carriage at the carriage block when he stepped outside. "The office, the mill, or the newspaper first, sir?"

"The newspaper, please, George. No sense sending everyone home if this is all some big mistake."

****

It was hard to get the carriage down Smithfield Street, there were so many people hurrying in the direction of the Commercial Gazette office. They came to a complete stop when they reached Fifth Street, which was packed with bodies.

Absolutely every head was turned in the direction of the newspaper office. Thomas stood up in the carriage and craned his neck, trying to see anything useful over the heads of the crowd. The closer people got to the newspaper office, the more densely they were packed in. There was no getting close, not right now.

"Excuse me, what's the news?" he started asking. The answers were, of course, varied. "The President's been shot." Well, at least that was already more information than he'd previously had. He wasn't the victim of a bomb or a maniac with a knife. All information was, of course, suspect. One person told him the President was dead. Someone else said he wasn't dead, but he was seriously wounded. There was some variation about where he was—whether he was still at the depot, or if he'd been moved back to the White House. One person was quite sure the President wasn't even in Washington at all.

Thomas decided to give up. There was no way of getting information unless he walked on the heads of everyone standing there. People were all trying to get the same information, which was coming from the same office. Eventually, everyone would know. For now, all anyone could do was wait. "We'd best get out of here while we still can, George."

George needed no urging. He clicked to the horses, and the carriage began to creep slowly through the thickening crowd.

Movement was even more difficult than before. Instead of flowing with the traffic, they were now attempting to go against it. It took the better part of an hour to make the short journey to the Olympus offices.

Every head looked up to stare at him when he walked through the door. Smith was on his feet and at his side in a moment.

"Have you heard, sir?"

"The President?" It seemed silly to ask, but knowing how his life seemed to work, he thought he'd better. Otherwise he'd be awfully surprised to find his house had burned down, or the mill workers were striking, or his wife was waiting in his office.

Smith nodded. Okay, so only one crisis at a time today.

"Yes. I've just come from Fifth Avenue. I was trying to find out what's happening."

"Any news?"

Thomas shook his head. "Nothing substantial. The President's been shot. He's either dead, or he's not. He's either in Washington somewhere, or he's not."

****

Thomas' description held true for a very, very long time. The nation went on vigil together: they watched and waited until after midnight, while the bulletins had little new information to report. To relieve the waiting, the owners of the Fifth Avenue Lyceum opened the lecture hall's doors to a public assembly. The mayor and a number of other dignitaries made speeches and resolutions deploring the villainous actions of the assassin, expressions of sympathy for the family, and of course prayers for the recovery of the President.

It wasn't terribly comforting, but it was all anyone could do while they were waiting. Thomas received a telegram from Regina in Scotland, begging for news. He had almost none to give her. He summarized the details of the shooting as reported in the papers, but he knew it would offer little comfort.

The night's vigil turned into days, the days turned into weeks. Day after day, the morning paper offered the thin reassurance that the President had survived the night. The heat wave briefly replaced the president in the headlines, followed by a relapse and recovery, followed by more daily reassurances. Worn out by the continuing melodrama, people uneasily turned back to their daily activities.

The opening of the new clubhouse at South Fork proved to be a very welcome distraction.

It started out with a party, of course. Benjamin Ruff, the new club's president and Colonel Unger, the caretaker, looked understandably pleased with themselves as they played hosts to some of the most powerful men in Pittsburgh. Clay Frick was there, enduring endless teasing from A.W. Mellon over a Miss Childs he was smitten with. Curtis Hussey was a member, and Thomas felt more than a little awkward when Curtis and his father, Dr. Hussey, pointedly looked in his direction while loudly talking about how well Pittsburgh Bessemer Steel was doing, and the wonderful new man they'd found to be general superintendent, now that Andrew Kloman had passed away.

Thomas decided that he didn't really want to have to sneak around them whenever he visited the Club. "I'm sorry to hear about Mr. Kloman," condolences for a death seemed like a safe approach. "He died before you actually got the mill running, didn't he? I'm sure he'd be gratified by your success." He carefully kept his voice neutral and respectful.

"Thank you," Dr. Hussey was looking him over with a certain amount of suspicion. Thomas could only assume the Husseys were expecting him to try to join in, now that the venture was actually up and running.

"So Mr. Clark isn't giving you any trouble? I heard he was pretty unhappy with Amalgamated." The Amalgamated Association of Iron and Steel Workers was as deeply embedded at Pittsburgh Bessemer Steel as it was at Olympus Ironworks. Thomas had heard, however, that when William Clark was compelled to give in to workers' demands, he had flat out vowed revenge. Thomas didn't see the point of antagonizing your work force. But then, he knew he was a product of the Old School, who were by and large gentlemen who respected the value of labor. It was a mutual relationship. Men wore their best suits and hats when they came to pick up their pay. It was the working-man's gesture of respect for the job, and his employer.

The Husseys shrugged noncommittally at Thomas' question. "Mr. Clark does differ from the rest of us on the subject of unions, but he is otherwise a very capable manager."

"Glad to hear it. Congratulations, then." Realizing he'd not performed brilliantly in his overtures, Thomas decided to cut his losses. He nodded pleasantly and excused himself with the pretext of refilling his empty glass.

The rest of the evening seemed to go more smoothly. He and John Hunt had a perfectly pleasant conversation anticipating a first crack at the black bass with which Conemaugh Lake had been stocked. He got to meet Robert Pitcairn, who had been one of the central figures in the railroad riot several years ago. There was no doubting that the Pennsylvania Railroad owned Mr. Pitcairn's soul: he did whatever needed to be done for the good of the railroad, he traveled in his private car wherever the railroad told him to go, he was now a member of this club in order to protect the railroad's interests. Apparently, the powerful and paranoid railroad had some questions about the safety of the dam, and since there were railroad tracks along the Little Conemaugh River, they wanted a man present at South Fork to keep an eye on things.

Clay Frick watched him curiously as he asked for a refill on his lemonade. "Are you a Temperance advocate?" he asked with a slightly guilty glance down at the glass in his hand, which no doubt contained something a little stronger than lemonade.

"Certainly not—that would be bad for business," Thomas answered, amused. "I personally don't drink. But it's a free country. What anyone else does is his business. This whole notion of one group of people forcing everyone else to live by their standards of morality is completely anti-American. People can do what they want to in their own homes—or with their own bodies. Don't tell me I have to drink, and I won't tell you not to." He raised his glass in a toast. Clay nodded appreciatively, and clinked his own glass against Thomas'.

"Andy Carnegie feels sort of the way you do," he told Thomas after they'd each taken a pull on their respective beverages. "Though I think he's a little more critical of the evils in our society that come from liquor. He figures if men drink less, and work harder, they can better their lives that much more."

Thomas shook his head. "Of course Andy Carnegie would say that—the man doesn't know how to stop working."

Clay grinned. "Part of his genius."

Thomas was detecting a serious case of hero worship. "Genius? He's certainly formidable, but I don't know that I'd call him a genius."

"Oh, you've got the same old sour grapes as everyone else in Pittsburgh," Frick answered a trifle dreamily. "The Carnegies have changed the way business is conducted in America, or maybe all over the world. I'd like to work for them someday."

Thomas couldn't believe what he was hearing. "You'd give up being president of the Frick Coke Company to work for the Carnegies? You haven't actually ever met Andy, have you? How do you know you'd want to work with him? He's not always that great to his own people, you know."

Clay's grin never wavered. "Sometimes his own people don't live up to his standards. I'd like the chance to try."

Clay Frick was undoubtedly off his rocker. Thomas decided it was time to firmly plant his tongue between his teeth and clamp down. "The world's a crazy place, who knows? Someday you may get your opportunity. Assuming they ever come home from this trip they're on."

Clay looked a little surprised. "The Gay Charioteers should be departing for the States in a couple of weeks. Didn't Mrs. Waring write you?"

Jealousy stabbed through Thomas. "Yes," he lied. "why?"

"I heard from Tom a little while ago," Clay continued. "He said the lot of them should be coming home the middle of August." Clay looked around the new clubhouse appreciatively. "Now that I've seen what a charming retreat this is going to be, I'll have to bring her up here sometime. See if she'd be interested in becoming a member. She's such a hiker, she'd probably like it here."

Thomas imagined Regina's figure gracing the parlor where they were standing. Or disappearing among the trees. Or out in a rowboat on the lake. It was certainly an appealing thought.

"It's a good idea," he said aloud. "I hope you can convince her. Once she's home, knowing her, she may be so eager to get back to work it won't occur to her to spend time taking in fresh air and exercise."

****

It took some doing, but Thomas was able to find out the details of the Gay Charioteers' travel plans. It helped that the Carnegies were such widely-known celebrities. Eventually, he learned they were boarding the steamer in Liverpool on the thirteenth of August. As luck would have it, he'd discovered a new architect based in Manhattan with whom he wanted to meet. He cabled Regina, and boarded a train for New York.

Two days later, he prowled the dock, trying to look everywhere at once. How on earth was he going spot anyone in all this chaos? The entire port was packed with moving bodies, heading in every direction at once. Finding one woman in the midst of it all was simply impossible.

"Thomas!"

He whirled around so quickly he nearly ran over an overworked porter dragging two trunks at once. He apologized, frantically searching for the source of that wonderfully familiar voice.

There she was. Coming down the gangplank, her figure a vision in gray and red, her hair gleaming under the pert red feather on her hat, her face—smiling!

"Regina!" Thomas dodged between passengers, porters, dock workers, and various other obstacles standing between him and his objective. He reached the bottom of the gangplank at the same time she did, in time to put his hands around the slim waist and lift her down to solid ground. In a fit of exuberance, however, he changed his mind while she was still midair, and he folded her into a big bear hug.

Her squeal of laughter let him know that she forgave him the familiarity. "Oh, Thomas, it's so good to see you again!" she laughed, her arms squeezing his neck. "I couldn't believe my eyes when you cabled that you were coming!"

"It was pure luck that I had to be here, anyway," Thomas set her down on the dock. "But I would have been happy to come meet you if I knew you wanted me to," he finished gallantly.

"Oh, Sir Thomas, I'm sure you would have, and you know I'd never ask for anything so silly. I'm a big girl, and this is America. I managed to get around Europe by myself when I needed to; I should be able to manage on home soil."

Thomas was a little disappointed that Regina deemed it "silly" for her to ask for his company. But he wasn't about to let anything spoil the joy of seeing her again.

"So where's the rest of your party?" he asked, scanning the ship for signs of other Pittsburghers.

"Still attempting to get packed up, I'm sure." Regina rolled her eyes good-naturedly. "Of all the people I've traveled with, this group takes the prize. Tom and Lucy are marvelous, but Margaret is a handful. I swear the more Andy tries to cater to her, the more difficult she becomes." She sighed. "He's completely devoted to her, but I don't think she's necessarily got his best interests at heart."

Thomas smiled. "Sounds like you're done with traveling for a while."

She smiled back ruefully. "Let's say that living alone doesn't sound very frightening right now."

"I'm glad to hear it." He picked up her hand, kissed the back of it, then tucked it into the crook of his arm companionably. "I've needed you back. I've been running things the best I can, but I didn't get into the wintergardens business as a solo venture. Half the business is yours, and I don't like trying to make decisions for you."

He'd forgotten how much he missed the tilt of her head when she'd look up at him! He wanted to wrap her up in his arms and hug her again, right there in front of God and the entire Port of New York.

"It's an unusual man who's willing to have a woman for a business partner—and really treat her like a partner." Her smile turned the smallest shade wistful. "Henry used to say you were probably the single most decent gentleman he'd ever known."

There was that hint of sadness around her mouth, but the shadows didn't reach her eyes. "Henry put more faith in me than anyone ever had before. Although you listened to me before he did. I owe a lot to the both of you."

"Well, then, one good turn deserved another, and we're even. I pulled you out of your shell and made you use your talents; you picked up all the broken pieces after Henry died and glued me back together, so I can continue to use mine."

"You're a pretty strong person. You didn't need me," Thomas demurred.

"Even strong people need friends sometimes. Yes, I daresay eventually I'd have pulled myself together. It's not in my nature to live a life of 'quiet desperation.' Life's too interesting for that. Nonetheless, you helped pull me together, and I'm grateful."

Thomas was surprised and gratified by her Thoreau reference. Before he could comment upon it, or tell her any of his conversations with Charles, there was a commotion behind them, and the Carnegie clan appeared on the deck of the ship. Several reporters materialized, including a gentleman from the rotogravure, who was lugging his camera equipment and trying to keep up with the rest of the group.

Regina groaned. "I've seen plenty of newspapermen, too, traveling with that lot. Shall we move along? My trunks must be in by now. You still haven't told me about this architect you've found. I think it's the same person Alva Vanderbilt uses. And I haven't confessed to you all about the crazy artifacts I started collecting. It's turned into one serious project . . . ."

They strolled more briskly away from the Carnegie party, which was swallowed up by people as soon as they stepped off the gangplank.

Chapter 18

Regina was home.

Thomas could swear the air felt different, having her back in the city. She wasn't merely a charming or beautiful woman; she was a force of nature. She affected the world around her with her presence. The Duquesne Club gave out free slices of coconut cake, since it was her favorite. Judge Mellon was actually heard whistling in the bank, and Andy Carnegie offered to build a library as a gift to the city of Pittsburgh.

"It's great to have our girl back, isn't it?" Durbin Horne, the son of the drygoods merchant, ran into Thomas at the florist shop. Thomas, who was signing a card to send to Regina's office at the glass factory, looked up in confusion.

"Our girl?"

"I'm sorry. Mrs. Waring. I guess she's more your girl than anyone's since she's your business partner. But she does have this knack for making an impact, doesn't she? I doubt there's a man in this city who would deny that she's our Pittsburgh girl."

"She's certainly made an impact on my life. I guess I couldn't speak for anyone else." Was every other man in the city as much in love with her as he was? He wasn't sure he liked that idea, but he certainly couldn't blame them if they were.

"She always tells me we're put on this earth to make the world a better place, and she certainly seems to live by that. Our family was having something of a crisis a few years back, and, well, she was a lot of help when we really needed some."

Thomas remembered Regina's quiet assistance on his behalf right after he'd gotten married, when Sean McAlister gave Olympus Iron their streetcar contract.

"Yes," he said simply. "She does have a knack for that."

Inevitably, the conversation drifted to the popular gossip of the day. "So what do you think of Mr. Bell's trumped-up claim about being able to find the bullet in the President? What a load of malarkey."

Thomas had followed the daily news on the President's condition as anxiously as everyone else. When Alexander Graham Bell traveled to Washington with an invention he claimed would be able to detect exactly where the bullet was lodged, he was as hopeful as everyone else. The invention didn't work. Bell claimed it had worked perfectly at home, but as he passed it over the President's body, lying in bed in the White House, the device simply hummed, no matter where on his body he tested. Bell packed up and returned home in defeat, still claiming the invention seemed to work perfectly everywhere else he tested it.

Thomas shrugged. "The man is a scientist and inventor, not a grandstander. If it were Thomas Edison, I'd believe he made the claim just for the attention. Not that Edison doesn't invent amazing things in that lab of his. But I think Bell honestly thought he invented a way to find the bullet. I feel sorry for him. I'm sure he feels like the world's biggest failure right now."

"I have to agree with you there." Horne obviously had no sympathy for the inventor. "After getting all our hopes up, he's probably getting hourly reminders that he failed. Well, next time he'll be more careful." He looked down at the large bouquet of lilies in his hand. "I'd best be getting home with these. Are you going to be at Mrs. Waring's house party?"

Regina must have sent out the invitations, but Thomas hadn't seen his yet. He would have to check when he got home. Meredith was not above throwing pieces of his correspondence straight into the trash from time to time.

"Wouldn't miss it. See you there."

Regina had approached him with the idea of her house party well before the invitations were written. "Thomas, can I ask you an etiquette question?" She'd popped her head in his office door one afternoon, nearly startling him out of his chair.

"Etiquette? Me? You can ask, of course, but I doubt I'll be able to answer."

"Oh, pish posh," she'd responded, bustling into the room and settling herself comfortably in the chair across from his desk. "You've got enough common sense for any two people, and if I'm contemplating something questionable, you'll tell me."

"What do you have in mind?" Thomas was intrigued by her hint.

"I want to know if it's unseemly for a widow to throw a party to show off her new treasures." As Clay Frick and A.W. Mellon had gleefully begun purchasing artwork during their European adventures, Regina had taken up the notion of overhauling her entire house with artisans' handiwork. Each room of her house represented a particular mythological creature. She'd planned a "Dragon Room," a "Griffon Room," a "Mermaid Room," and so on. Apparently, she'd been shipping home stained glass windows, lighting fixtures, mantelpieces, and other assorted bric-a-brac.

"You've been widowed for three years. I should think you're allowed out of mourning." He looked at her speculatively. "Considering you never officially went into mourning in the first place, I'm finding your concern rather odd. Why do you care what people think now?" he grinned. "You never have before."

"Quite a few people have been clamoring to see all my ill-gotten gains. But if I throw a big fete to let everyone see what I've brought home, I will doubtlessly be seen as coming 'out,' as it were, and I'm back in society. That could be good for business, or bad for business, depending on how people perceive any number of variables."

Thomas couldn't help but smile at Regina's statement. "You're developing a one-track mind, my dear lady."

Regina laughed in protest. "A girl can't be too careful, you know."

Thomas leaned forward and scrutinized her suspiciously. "Who are you? You're definitely not Regina Waring, darling of the industrial world, flouter of conventions, snubber of ladies' drawing rooms, lone world traveler, member of the men-only Duquesne Club . . ."

"Okay, okay, I take your point," Regina stopped him. "You're quite right. I never have worried much about what people think or say. I do what I do, and for some reason, people are willing to go along with me. Goodness knows why I get away with it, but I do."

"You lead a charmed life," Thomas observed, not without a hint of jealousy. He wished he had her luck!

"Funny thing to tell a widow," she observed caustically. "But you're right, I do. I guess that's why I was questioning this party—I used to have Henry to protect me. Whatever I did, he approved, so what was anyone else going to say? I didn't care what anyone thought after he died. I was too busy feeling sorry for myself. Then when I left to go travel, it didn't matter to me since I wasn't at home. Now I'm home again and trying to function normally for the first time, and I guess I'm feeling a bit alone."

"You're not alone, Regina. You should know that by now." Thomas had trouble keeping the fervor out of his voice.

"Thank you, Sir Thomas," she smiled and stood up to leave. "Perhaps I just needed you to remind me. You'll get the first invitation, of course. I'm sure you're as curious as everyone else to see what I brought home on this extended shopping spree of mine."

****

Shopping spree? Somehow that didn't seem like an adequate term for the volume of architectural and artistic treasures Regina proudly displayed to an astounded Pittsburgh that September evening. There had been whispers that her house was entirely unrecognizable, but rumors didn't prepare him for the shock when the ornate new front door—with seven different panels depicting scenes from Homer's *Odyssey* (an eighth depicted the blind scribe himself)—swung open.

Regina's front hall had been transformed from a typical Victorian reception area, buffering the public from the private worlds, into a gothic art gallery—not so much welcoming as very, very entertaining. It was an imposing shrine—to dragons.

The walls were covered with golden fabric. If you looked closely, Chinese dragons and lotus blossoms were woven into it. Dragons were cleverly intertwined around each other and chasing each other around the intricate brass chandelier, and dragons featured prominently in the tapestries on the walls (but nothing, Thomas noted with amusement, depicting Saint George slaying the dragon). Best of all was the new carved banister; it, too, was a clever and subtle homage to the grand imaginary creatures.

"Isn't it horrifyingly magnificent?" Regina welcomed the gapers who were milling about. "I defy anyone to try to describe my new staircase without making it sound gaudy."

"Oh, but it isn't—not in the least!" Philander Knox's new wife, Lillie, hastened to assure her. "It's SO tastefully done!"

A quiet, petulant sigh came from somewhere in the vicinity of Thomas' shoulder. He looked down at Meredith, who was the only one in the room not looking around with a face full of delight and wonder. He'd tried, half-heartedly, to convince her not to come, but of course she wouldn't have any of that.

"Everyone is going to be there!" she protested. "It will be the perfect chance to wear my new turquoise evening dress."

And here the hostess was talking about the staircase being gaudy . . . .

"I told you, you didn't have to come," Thomas murmured in his wife's ear.

Her response was to give him the overly-sweet smile that always meant she would complain to him all the way home.

"Why don't you go find your friends, so they can admire your new dress," he prompted her. "The rest of us are going to be taking our time here and admiring this house."

There was nothing artificially sweet about the look she gave him then, but she did leave in search of more attentive company.

Thomas didn't realize he'd let a sigh of relief escape from him until he felt Regina's hand on his arm. She didn't say a word to him; she'd just slipped in next to him, tucked her arm around his, and squeezed. "The dragons are what got me started on this whole project," she confessed to the assembled admirers. "Clay and A.W. had been gleefully collecting paintings, and I was having fun laughing at their new avocation, when we came across both the chandelier and the staircase at an estate sale. They were going to be destroying anything they didn't sell, and, well, I couldn't let such craftsmanship be lost forever. No one else wanted it. After that, we found the dining room table, then the first of my mermaids. I was lost."

Regina had released Thomas' arm as quietly as she had taken it. His eyes followed her as she flitted among her guests, her bright figure one more piece of artwork among the collected treasures.

Regina must have felt his eyes on her. She turned from pointing out the dragon design on the doorknobs to one of the Clark children, and smiled at him. "I ought to see how some of my other guests are faring. Please feel free to investigate the rest of my new rooms."

Thomas and Lillie Knox caught each other's eager expressions. Thomas offered his elbow. "Well, Mrs. Knox, what are we waiting for? We heard our hostess."

She took his arm and nodded eagerly. "Let's see what else there is!"

****

"What else" included griffons holding up the dining room table, fanciful fairies peeking out from among the draperies, and glass mermaids combing their glass tresses in an entirely glass chandelier Thomas recognized as the same make as the one hanging in his foyer at home.

After gawking their way through the house, the guests congregated on the porch, among the centaurs, and spilled out onto the lawn, where a new fountain of water nymphs bubbled in the midst of newly-blossoming mums. As dusk fell, lanterns being held by other creatures from Neptune's realm were lit—by electricity, no less. The powerful lights gleamed as brightly as daylight, and guests lingered on the porch enjoying the last of the summer weather.

No dancing had been planned, but the pocket doors between the music room and the ballroom were opened, and various ladies took their turns at the piano and an impromptu ball broke out. Saratoga Lancers, Glide Lancers, Centennial Lancers, College Lancers, New American Lancers, an occasional waltz or polka, then the Irish Quadrille, Prince Imperial Quadrille, and the new Polo Quadrille. No doubt the inevitable German dance games would eventually take over. Normally, Thomas wasn't too fond of Germans, but the company was so pleasant, he imagined he wouldn't mind the ritual humiliations so much.

Lillie Knox proved to be as delightful a quadrille partner as she was a tour companion. Lucy Carnegie was a lively polka partner. Judge Mellon's wife even favored him with a rare appearance on the dance floor, when her husband was called upon, as the oldest person present, to lead an old-fashioned barn dance.

He contemplated leaving the dance floor once Meredith appeared, as he usually did, but he was having enough fun, he decided he'd suffer the consequences of listening to her for the next several days. After all, he already knew he would be getting an earful, anyway, as soon as they were alone. Maybe she'd get tired early and he could send her home without him.

He looked around the crowded room, imagining being the host, having a right to stay after the rest of the guests had left. He hadn't realized he'd sighed aloud again, until once again there was a light squeeze on his arm.

He looked down into Regina's black eyes.

"So what's wrong?" she asked him. "You seem so wistful tonight."

What was he supposed to tell her? That he wanted her to run away with him, ruin both their lives, abandon her grand, newly-refinished house, and live in sin with him in Mexico? Ask for her help in poisoning his wife so that he could propose to her from a prison cell? That he loved her?

"I am," he answered with a glibness that surprised himself. "You haven't danced with me yet. I thought you liked dancing with me."

His reply seemed to take her by surprise. "I do," she laughed, protesting, "but you haven't asked me yet."

"Well, I am now," he bowed over her hand with a flourish, and led her grandly onto the middle of the floor.

She wasn't fooled by his gallantry. She danced with him, laughed at his antics, flirted with him, returned the pressure of his hand with her own firm grip, but her eyes were appraising him sharply through all five figures of the quadrille.

How well did they know each other? He knew the tilt of her head, the nuances of her voice. He'd memorized every curve of her figure from her neck to her ankle—of which he'd seen occasional glimpses. He knew a fair amount about the workings of her mind. But there was still more to learn. How well did she know him? She'd always seemed to look right through him, reading him like a trade journal. Did she know he loved her?

The music stopped, and he escorted her toward the refreshment table. She was still looking at him with more than casual interest. He wondered what she'd do if he bared his soul to her, threw himself on his knees and made love to her. She'd probably run away, laughing at him as she did.

If she were going to press him about what was on his mind, she never got the chance. One of her servants met her at the refreshment table with a small envelope. It was a telegram.

"This was delivered for you, ma'am," the servant told her quietly.

Regina took the envelope and glanced up at Thomas, obviously puzzled. "Who would . . ." she looked at the message, and her voice trailed away. "Oh."

She stood there looking at the telegram for a long while. Then she looked around the room uncertainly.

"What is it?" Thomas asked gently.

"I don't know what to do," she answered. "People will want to know, but I hate to spoil their good time."

"What do you mean?"

In response, Regina handed him the telegram. It said simply,

PRESIDENT GARFIELD DIED HALF PAST TEN TONIGHT STOP

CR

Thomas stared at the words. Garfield was dead. The long months of vigil were over, but not with a happy conclusion. He handed the slip of paper back to Regina. "How is it you're getting telegrams from the White House?"

"It's not from the White House; it's from the friend of a friend of . . . never mind. I know a lot of people. Henry's family was from New York, you know."

"Neighbors in New Jersey, huh?"

Regina smiled. "Essentially. I didn't ask for the personal news service, but I've been getting my own private updates since he got there." The smile faded, and she looked around at the assembled guests. "Almost everyone here's a Republican—not that it matters at a time like this . . . ."

Thomas plucked the telegram back out of her hands, folded it in half, and slipped it into his breast pocket. "The news can wait. The morning paper will be soon enough. No reason to spoil everyone's evening." Knowing her one-track mind, he added, "Besides, it would be bad for business for people to associate your house with the place where they learned that the President was dead."

"There you are!" George Westinghouse found them talking earnestly in the corner. He handed Regina a glass of champagne. "It's nearly midnight. You said you wanted to say a few words before supper?"

"Yes, I did. Thank you, George." She took the arm offered to her, and gave Thomas a glance over Westinghouse's broad shoulder. He knew she was going to heed his advice to keep her silence.

Westinghouse escorted Regina into the middle of the ballroom, and raised his voice to carry above the rest of the happy chatter. "While a very splendid-looking supper is being set up outside, our hostess has something to say to us."

Thomas saw the brief flicker of uncertainty cross her face. She certainly did have something to say to everyone. He waited, wondering if she were going to keep to her silent resolution of moments ago, or if her honesty would get the better of her.

"I wanted to thank all of you for your kind stroking of my vanity while I show off this creative endeavor of mine." She actually colored a little at the spontaneous round of applause that followed. "Mr. McKay has christened this new-old house of mine Elysium—literally christened, since he spilled wine on the new mosaic floor—and I think the name's going to stick. So, ladies and gentlemen, I give you—Elysium."

There was a hearty response from the assembled, and those equipped with glasses drank to the health of the newly-named house. Her eyes swept lovingly around the room. "It's not the building that makes the home, it's the people in it." Thomas could swear her eyes lingered briefly on him, but he wasn't sure. "Thank you, all of you, for being part of my paradise."

This time, a larger chorus of voices drank to her health. Regina looked pleased, but a little sheepish, and when the voices died down, she announced, "Now everyone go eat before we start getting sentimental."

The casual buffet meant there was no need to wait for one's assigned dinner companion. Thomas lingered a moment, but he knew it would be impossible to reach Regina's side through the pressing crowd squeezing through the French doors. Might as well get in line. He spotted Charles McKay also holding back a little, and walked over. The company of one's best friend was, after all, sometimes better than the company of even the most beautiful of women.

Chapter 19

President Garfield was dead. It was sad, and in a way, it was also a relief. Uncertainty was far worse than plain bad news. Bad news could be dealt with: you cried, or raged, or prayed, but you could act appropriately and move on. Uncertainty meant waiting, with no real course of action ahead.

Chester Arthur was sworn in, the country grieved, and people got back to their lives.

Thomas felt he was getting back to his life for the first time in over a year. His best friend was back, his idol was back, business was more fun when it was occasionally interrupted by Charles' cheerful voice, or when he discussed Wintergarden business while looking into a pair of endless black eyes.

Thomas was overjoyed when Regina suggested sending one of their best project managers, a capable, tall fellow named Matthew Jacobson, to oversee the Crystal Palace in Leipzig, rather than going back to Europe herself. The telegrams came back and forth across the Atlantic so frequently, the Wintergardens staff knew the names of every delivery boy at the telegraph office. But Regina stayed in Pittsburgh.

The excitement over the large overseas project, however, couldn't mask the growing anxiety at home. The entire iron and steel industry watched with a great deal of interest in March when the newly-opened Pittsburgh Bessemer Steel plant erupted into labor conflicts, and the labor conflicts erupted into violence. Thomas had thought Clark was a fool when he announced that the plant would be non-union and attempted to force his employees to sign contracts to keep the Amalgamated Association of Iron and Steel Workers out of the company.

He felt a little more in sympathy with Clark's position three months later, when the Amalgamated called a nationwide strike.

"Business is dropping everywhere," Thomas' father had protested as he and the union leaders discussed wages. "How am I supposed to keep my head above water and all you boys in jobs, if we can't fill what orders we do have coming in?"

"I'm sorry, sir; we know times are hard. They're hard for us, too. We've got families to feed, you know."

Thomas never said a word while sitting at the negotiation table next to his father. He hated being there. He wished everyone could get what they wanted. His father had always coached Thomas that "You have to treat your people well." Now it didn't seem to matter. The people they had done their best to keep happy apologized politely, but stayed loyal to their union and struck, anyway.

Fortunately, the opening of the Crystal Palace was not affected by the growing troubles at home. Neither glass, nor flour, nor any of Regina's other businesses seemed to be affected by the growing depression, and Thomas alternated between envy at her lack of worries and gratitude that between his involvement with glass houses and the brewery, he still had a steady income.

He was even more grateful to be able to escape on Saturdays to the cool, simple comforts of Conemaugh Lake.

Charles McKay was having a worse time of it than Thomas was, since his family's business was not as diverse as the Baldwin interests. The two men would often talk on the train out to South Fork, or in a rowboat in the middle of the lake as they dangled their fishing lines into the clear, sparkling water. They would complain in general terms about the frustrations of keeping business afloat, and how it seemed they'd just recovered from the last round of hard times. But Thomas got the feeling Charles wasn't saying how truly worried he really was.

To Thomas' great delight, Regina also bought shares in the club. She even came fishing with them, and good-naturedly took their coaching on techniques for dropping the line into the water, and pulling in the fish when she caught them.

On the other hand, to Thomas' chagrin, Meredith decided to come to South Fork. What had started as a sportsman's retreat quickly devolved into a family gathering spot. Several members were building cottages along the water, set back from the shore and up the hill to catch the mountain breezes. These men sent their wives and children out to the country—for the entire summer.

Getting rid of Meredith for the entire summer didn't sound like a bad idea. But Thomas still felt that his private escape had been invaded. It would be wonderful if he could have afforded to build one of the roomy wooden cottages with plenty of windows and porches—and numerous bedrooms. But with the iron business wallowing in the doldrums, he couldn't justify the expense.

So Meredith packed her valises, boarded the train with him, and moved into his room at the clubhouse.

A thirteen-by-fourteen foot room did not leave a lot of space for him to escape his persistent wife. After successfully dodging it for seven years of marriage, Thomas was faced with the prospect of being forced into Meredith's bed.

He avoided the clubhouse that weekend. He and Charles were out on the water by sunrise. Regina had declined to join them, electing to wander through the woods that afternoon with "the young people," as she called the tribe of unmarried young adults now inhabiting the cottages. While Thomas missed the quiet, he did appreciate the great sense of fun the crowd brought with them, as they swam, hiked, boated, staged elaborate plays and pageants, and generally made things much jollier.

Regina and the young people were planning to end their scramble with supper at the picturesque spillway on the far side of the dam from the clubhouse. It was Charles' idea to take their day's catch to the kitchen, have the cooks clean and fry it right then, and transport the still-hot bundle across the lake to join the picnickers.

The surprise and delight on her face when they showed up with their dinner offering was terribly gratifying. As was the lighthearted company. Thomas could see why Regina elected to spend time with them. They laughed a lot. Sitting back and watching, Thomas realized he didn't laugh much in his life. Not much to laugh about.

No time like the present to try to fix that, was there? He slid off the rock he was using for a seat, determined to try to play with these youngsters.

He started by sneaking up on two of the youngest lads of the party, who were pretending to throw each other into the water, and pushed the both of them in. He got a sound dunking in return when he tried to help them back out. He held his own pretty well at spitting watermelon seeds; almost as far as the Willock boys.

The girls contented themselves with being spectators; all except for Regina, of course. She had instigated a contest with Charles and a couple of the other young folks, throwing rocks in an attempt to drown a leaf that was floating in the still water to the side of the churning waterfall.

Such simple entertainments preoccupied the party until dusk, which fell rapidly in the old mountains. Thomas had been watching the light sinking but had been singularly unmotivated to be responsible and suggest it was time to start back toward the clubhouse. Meredith was lying in wait back there, somewhere. And even if Regina wasn't specifically playing with him, he could hear her laugh, and look around to see her. It was double incentive not to leave.

Eventually, however, it got dark enough to be dangerous. People and picnic supplies were handed into the boats, which became precarious in the dark, since the boats were moored against the relatively steep sides of the spillway. Several young ladies elected to walk over the dam, instead of risking the clamber down to the boats. Regina elected to take the walk with them, to provide adult supervision.

Charles sprang back out of their boat. "I'm going to go with the ladies. It's not right for them to be without an escort, even if we are out here in the middle of nowhere. You don't mind, old man?"

Thomas didn't have much choice—someone had to row their boat back across the lake. He wished he would have volunteered first.

He rowed slowly enough to be able to keep an eye on the party as they walked along the dam road. It was a pretty sight—the colors of the sunset provided a glowing blue and purple background behind the silhouettes of the party. The girls walked in small groups, arms linked, while Regina and Charles lingered behind, like two ducks herding a little flock. Laughing voices drifted down to him; he tried to make out Regina's low laugh, with no success.

The sky darkened considerably, and the silhouettes started to blend into the falling twilight. Thomas pulled harder on his oars. Since it was getting too dark to see Regina's trim figure strolling along the top of the dam, he might as well head for the boathouse.

Always in the back of his mind was the specter of Meredith, waiting for him back in their room at the clubhouse. As soon as he had the boat back to the boathouse, he found a couple of lanterns and set out to meet the walkers. He heard their laughter well before he saw them.

His lights inspired shouts of "Haloooo!" and "Hark! Who goes there!" His favorite was "But soft! What light through yonder trees breaks?"

"I am east of you, but I assure you, I'm no Juliet," he called back.

"Oh, no, you're much prettier," he could hear Charles' voice.

"Hey! And here I thought I might find an honest man," he answered.

"Watch out, or we'll steal your lamps," Regina's laughing voice joined in.

"Diogenes never tried looking for an honest woman," Thomas pointed out, not needing to shout anymore. He lifted one of the lamps to illuminate everyone's faces. "And since none of you are flying away, I'm obviously no Psyche."

"Nah, you're still much prettier," Regina said.

"Oh, well," Thomas sighed playfully. "I'd rather have brains than beauty, but I guess I'll have to work with what I've got."

"Oh, you poor thing," Regina answered dryly. "With lashes like those, you're never going to get an ounce of pity. At least," she chuckled, "not from any honest women."

Thomas shrugged at the compliment. He'd always hated when people commented on his looks. Even coming from Regina, it made him feel awkward. He was glad for Charles' interceding. "Come on, old man, hand me one of those lanterns. No reason you have to carry both of them to light our way."

The party formed into a marching order: Charles leading Regina at the front of their little parade, followed by the Misses Lawrence, Thomas following to light the way for Miss Sharpe and the Husseys.

After seeing the young ladies returned to their families, Thomas suggested a cool drink after all that walking. Regina gave him a knowing look after glancing at the grandfather clock in the hallway. "I guess eleven isn't all that late," she observed softly. "There must be some cold buttermilk or something in the cellar."

A raid on the kitchen produced a bottle of wine, a pitcher of water, crackers, cheese, and a selection of ripe summer berries. The trio settled themselves on the front porch with their light repast, and watched the moon rise.

It was a beautiful night. Following the stillness of dusk, a soft breeze sprang up, wafting across the lake with a slight scent of water, and fish, and mountain. Sometimes they talked; sometimes they lapsed into a companionable silence as they admired the moonlight shining on the lake. It was peaceful, and beautiful, and Thomas didn't want to leave.

Unfortunately, he could see that both Charles and Regina were having trouble keeping their eyes open. They were both making valiant efforts to stay awake with him, but it was a losing battle.

After nodding off so thoroughly he cracked his head on the back of the rocking chair, Charles was the first to concede defeat. "It's awfully late—we've been up since before dawn. I think it's time for some sleep."

Regina was using her hands to cover a yawn. "I concur. I wasn't up as early as you gentlemen, but I'm quite ready to retire."

Thomas felt bad about pushing his friends to the end of their endurance. His answer was interrupted by a large yawn of his own.

"All right, old man, bedtime," Charles stood up, and tilted Thomas' rocker forward, dumping him onto his feet. "You're as bushed as we are."

"I'm sure your wife has been asleep for hours, by now," Regina assured him softly.

Thomas was too tired to dissemble. He blurted out honestly, "I sure hope so."

He caught the look that passed between Charles and Regina as they climbed the stairs. Yes, indeed, both of them realized he'd been avoiding going up to his room.

"You two are the best friends a man can have, you know that?" Thomas said.

The three of them had paused outside his door. Regina stepped close and kissed his cheek. "Get some sleep. Good night."

Charles nodded to him. Thomas nodded back. There wasn't much left to do but go in.

There was no need to open the door as softly as he did; the lamp on the little table was lit, and Meredith was sitting in the chair beside it, waiting for him. "It's about time you got in," she said, her voice barely above a whisper. "Where were you?"

Thomas closed the door behind him and looked at his wife. She was obviously furious. No doubt she had been harboring romantic notions about their forced close quarters, and hadn't counted on his prolonged absence.

"Where was I?" he repeated coolly, wondering if he started walking now, if he'd make it to Pittsburgh by daybreak. "Just now I was watching the moon rise over the lake with good friends who appreciate beauty. I suppose you sat here with your back to the window the whole time, and missed it."

"I've been waiting for you," she answered loftily.

"So I see." Thomas was half-inclined to turn and walk back out the door again, and she could wait for him some more. Only the fear of her following him into the hallway and waking the entire clubhouse with their domestic unhappiness kept him inside the room. He could see she wanted a confrontation, and she wanted it now.

"Well?" he prompted her when she said nothing. "You've been waiting for me. I'm here. What do you want?"

"What do I want?" she repeated indignantly. "I want what everyone else here's got." The words started tumbling out, faster and faster, as she listed her grievances. "All the other women here had someone to sit with during dinner. The new Mrs. Frick got a necklace from your friend Mr. Frick, and it wasn't even their first anniversary. He just felt like giving it to her. Mrs. Suydam had an afternoon tea to show off her cottage, which is so much nicer than only having one tiny room here, and if the Suydams can afford a cottage, I don't see why we can't. Whenever the younger ladies go out walking, they come back with flowers from the young men. I never get any flowers," she finished with a pout.

Thomas folded his arms, leaned back against the doorframe, and looked at her in silence. In their long years of marriage, she still had failed to learn that posing with her face in a pout and her eyes downcast failed to inspire him to great demonstrations of love.

He didn't have long to wait. Her patience for posing wasn't what it used to be. The lashes fluttered up to look at him.

"Are you done posing?" He asked her unkindly. "You can continue all night, if you like. No need to stop on my account."

"I'm not posing!" she protested. "I'm angry. I had dinner with Mrs. Clarke today, and she knows everything that goes on with her husband. I never know anything." The tears were welling up in the big blue eyes. "When you leave, you don't tell me when you're coming back. You haven't surprised me with any presents since you gave me the house for my birthday. You never bring me things when you've been traveling. You—you don't even have any pet names for me."

"Oh, I do," Thomas reassured the little Blonde Monster. "But I don't think you'd like them very much."

Meredith characteristically focused all her attention on the little part she wanted to hear. "You have a pet name for me?"

"In a matter of speaking."

"What is it, Thomas? I didn't know. You've never told me."

"And I'm not going to. You wouldn't like it." When Meredith opened her mouth to wheedle, he continued, "It's not flattering."

She closed her mouth and gave him another resentful glare. "Why don't you ever flatter me, Thomas?"

Thomas nearly laughed. "Because we're married. You've been spending too much time with the unmarried people. Flattery is what the young men do to convince a young lady to marry him. I don't recall having to work hard on that score. You seemed rather convinced without requiring any encouragement from me." He said the words without any bitterness. After seven years, it was a statement of fact.

"Mr. Frick compliments Mrs. Frick," Meredith disagreed. "Mr. Suydam brings flowers for Mrs. Suydam. Dr. Hussey is still sweet to Mrs. Hussey, and they're as old as our parents."

"Well, look at my parents, Meredith. I am as thoughtful to you as my father is to my mother. I guess it runs in the family."

Meredith's eyes flashed. "Speaking of families!"

Uh oh. Here it comes, now.

"When are we going to start a family, Thomas? Elsie, Janey and Rose have all been married for less time than I have, and they all have at least one baby. They look at me with such pity. I go to call on them, and all they can do is talk about their children."

"If you like children so much, I'm sure your friends will let you play with theirs," Thomas suggested helpfully. "You can be a doting aunty."

"I don't like their babies. I want my own," Meredith snapped. "Everyone's talking about me and staring at me and thinks there's something wrong with me."

An amused snort emanated from Thomas, but Meredith ignored him.

"It's humiliating, everyone pitying me and whispering behind my back," she complained bitterly. "My girlfriends don't have time for me anymore, they're mothers now, and I'm not. Your cousins look at me and flaunt their children to your mother. They make me feel—like I'm not as good as they are."

Thomas' lips twitched. "Well, since you've proven to be defective, my dear, maybe you need to take up some other interests in your life," he suggested. "Philanthropy is a noble profession that many women of your class engage in. There's plenty of charity work to be done. Who knows? It might even improve your mind."

"I don't want to improve my mind!" she snapped. "I want a baby."

"Well, Mrs. Baldwin, how unfortunate for you. I've told you before. While there are many men out there who will to copulate with anyone who's willing—and yes, I'm thoroughly convinced you're quite willing—I'm not one of them. There are women in the world who are mate-able, and those who arc not. You are most emphatically NOT mate-able."

He was oh, so familiar with the uncomprehending blue-eyed stare his wife gave him. And with her response. "But we're married!"

Thomas looked at her. "And what does that mean, Meredith? We've been married for seven years. Don't you think by now, we've established what sort of relationship we've got?"

"What relationship?" Meredith shot back resentfully. "We don't have a relationship."

"Oh, but we do. You just said it, my dear. We're married."

She gave a sigh of frustration that would have been comical if the situation weren't so unhappy. "Married people aren't like us." Thomas was somewhat amused by the understated observation. "All the married women are—well, they—they act like—" she frowned with the effort of grasping toward definition. "They're important."

"All the more reason you should consider taking up some good works," Thomas pointed out. "There are plenty of hospitals, and schools, and benefit societies who would find a pair of willing hands very important."

"I don't want to be important to them," Meredith obviously didn't like his suggestion at all. "I want to be important to you!"

Thomas was filled with a mixture of revulsion and pity. "I wouldn't fret on that score, Meredith. You've made an important impact on my life."

"Have I?" she asked desperately. "I don't feel important. Not since you bought me the house for my birthday. You don't bring me flowers or presents, you don't say nice things, even when we're going someplace and I've got a pretty new dress and all my friends tell me I look perfectly smashing. You don't even notice."

Why, oh why, Thomas wondered, did society 'educate' women to be so stupid? Why were they taught piano and needlework, instead of Latin and logic? He thought of Regina's intelligent black eyes, her talent for understanding that went beyond her knowledge of Thoreau, her keen business acumen. The notion that women's constitutions and their mental sensibilities were too delicate, and must be protected, was absurd.

"That's because no matter how prettily you pose, you stir nothing in this male breast. You shouldn't expect flowers, or pet names, or love poems, or any other sentimental tokens from me. You don't inspire that sort of sentiment. I will burn in hell before I plant my seed in you. If that isn't plain enough for you, try this. You're not going to be having my babies." To illustrate his point, he took a light quilt from the foot of the bed.

"I'm sorry the other ladies make you feel inadequate, Mrs. Baldwin," he continued. "I suggest you look for some other way to raise yourself in their eyes. It won't be through me."

"Where are you going?" she asked, panic in her voice as he opened the door.

"The rocking chairs on the front porch are comfortable enough. Far more comfortable than staying in this room."

"But . . ." she began to protest, as Thomas closed the door. "But we're married," he finished for her.

Chapter 20

Summer slid into fall amidst a flutter of excitement when Andrew Carnegie brought the famous Social Darwinist writer, Herbert Spencer, to Pittsburgh. Excitement turned into embarrassment, however, when the illustrious man couldn't take Pittsburgh's soot-filled air. Most of the first families enjoyed a satisfying snicker behind closed doors; during his visit Mr. Spencer clearly preferred the more congenial company of Tom Carnegie, staying at the younger Carnegie's house in Homewood and shunning the luxurious hotel suite Andrew had engaged in the city.

Fall slid toward winter, starting with a controversy at the pig iron convention over a tariff hike, and ending with a lot of unhappy Republicans when the Democrats took control of the House of Representatives at election time.

Thomas endured another Christmas married to Meredith. She glared at him as he played with his nephews and nieces. That January, he learned another delightful escape South Fork had to offer: ice sailing. When Charles lured him up to the mountain to investigate the joys of ice fishing, the younger men had been scooting across the ice on funny little flat craft that were mostly skeleton and sail. He didn't need to be asked twice when one of them offered Thomas the opportunity to try it. It was distinctly less cold riding with the wind, instead of shivering in it while waiting for the fish to bite.

Regina kept disappearing to New York the following spring. First it was a visit to her fellow "Charioteers," then it was for some big costume party thrown by another friend, then she hopped the train again in May to attend the opening of a new bridge.

"Should we just set up a Wintergarden office for you out there?" Thomas asked when she returned. He felt a little nonplussed; she missed the party at the Clubhouse for the opening of the next Season. He and Charles had spent most of that Saturday and Sunday in the company of their wives, and it had been a thoroughly unpleasant experience. Thomas couldn't remember when he'd missed her deep chuckle so much.

"Don't be too annoyed with me," she begged with a hint of that chuckle now. "I did bring you back a nice, fat contract."

"You never go anywhere without bringing back a nice, fat contract," Thomas observed, unable to stop the smile tugging at the corners of his mouth. "As long as you keep coming back with your eyes sparkling and a nice, fat contract up your sleeve, I can't complain." There, spoken like a business partner, not like a lover who deeply deplored each and every departure. Playfully, he eyed her tight sleeves, trying not to be obvious as he also admired the intriguing, lace-frilled keyhole of her bodice. It afforded occasional tantalizing glimpses of ivory skin between neck and breast. "Uh-huh."

"What?" she laughed, holding up her arms in some confusion.

"You're going to need bigger sleeves. I hope trends in fashion can shift to accommodate you."

"Oh, you," she laughed. "Now that the bustle is back, I can hide all sorts of things, back there." She looked behind herself. "Contracts, contractors . . ." She grinned at him wickedly.

"I"—Thomas just looked at her. "I have no idea what to say to that. You've got me cornered."

There was something unbearably sensual in the look she gave him. "Then I'd better stop. Some men get very dangerous when they're backed into a corner."

Thomas definitely had no idea what to say to that.

He knew she was the best one to go on sales calls; what man wasn't charmed by her? Every exposition she went to, every dedication ceremony, every party seemed to yield a new contract. Apparently she even managed to coax a smile out of the dour Mr.

Rockefeller up in Cleveland. Thomas nearly fell over when Mary delivered a letter from his old college friend, Michael.

"You've got clever tastes in business partners," his old friend had written. "Here I am, signing a contract with you when you haven't even paid me a call. Well, what's a fellow to do? When that partner of yours can get money out of Rockefeller, mere mortal men haven't got a chance."

Thomas was glad for Regina's abilities to bring them a steady flow of business. But he wished it didn't take her away from Pittsburgh so much.

He tried not to let her absence affect him, but he watched himself get crankier and crankier while she was away. He found himself saying less and less, so as not to offend anyone he shouldn't. He realized he was too far gone when he sat down to lunch with Charles at the Duquesne Club, and the two of them sat there, saying nothing.

He must've been really surly to stop the loquacious Charles from talking. He'd better clear the air a little. "I've been pretty lousy company lately, haven't I?"

Charles looked surprised by the question. "You have? I wouldn't say so. I think I've been the one who's been off lately." They stopped talking again, as a lad carefully set down their plates of Beef Wellington. "Look," Charles said in his old earnest manner, as soon as the waiter had departed. "You might as well know. You will, sooner or later, I guess I'd have told you by now, but I'm still deciding how I feel about it . . ." Thomas simply waited while Charles went through his monologue. If there was indeed news he intended to impart, Charles would get around to it eventually.

Charles took a large gulp of water, then toyed with his fork. "My family is . . . that is, Elizabeth's . . . . I'm going to be a father."

He looked—Thomas wasn't sure how he looked. It seemed like such an odd blend of apprehension and excitement and unhappiness. Well, and was he surprised by any of it? Apprehension for the responsibility, for the unknown changes about to take place in his life. Excitement for the possibilities. And unhappiness—since

Elizabeth was probably even more unpleasant company now than she usually was.

"Congratulations," Thomas answered. "Your family must be quite pleased."

Charles smiled crookedly. "Yeah, the usual stuff about carrying on the family business," he answered. "I'm sure Elizabeth will have a girl, to spite my father. Either way, my mother will be happy."

"You'll be a good father. I'm sure you'll find as many ways to get a girl into trouble as a boy."

Charles gave him a funny sort of smile. "I hope so. Do you think—if it's a girl, I hope she turns out more like Mrs. Waring than like, well, than like our wives."

Thomas wondered if Charles was as smitten as himself, or if it was a general wish that his potential daughter could be as witty, insightful and intelligent as their friend. "You'll have to ask Mrs. Waring what her parents did to make her so different."

"I know it's nothing her parents did," he answered. "Her family's from Johnstown, remember? They're very . . ." he stopped, unable to come up with a useful description. "Ordinary."

Thomas remembered the catty sisters and bemused parents he'd overheard at Henry's funeral. "Maybe extraordinary things come from ordinary beginnings."

"Seems so in her case." Charles answered.

"It happens. Where do any of these new-money people come from?" Thomas reasoned. "The Carnegies, or Rockefeller—there's a good one! They both started out as clerks, and now they're both filthy rich, and getting richer every day."

"You go in for that Social Darwinist stuff, don't you?" Charles asked, looking amused.

"I don't know; maybe I do. I think it's great that here in America, anyone who works hard can achieve anything. Maybe what Mrs. Waring proves is that gender doesn't matter. Just smarts."

Charles snorted. "And luck. I think a lot of guys out there are plenty smart, but most of them aren't climbing from hovels to mansions."

"Hm. If I had to chose, I think I'd rather be lucky than good. Although maybe I'd like a little more skill AND a little better luck." A sobering thought hit him. "I suppose that's the difference between us and our fathers."

"How do you mean?"

"I was thinking about Social Darwinism. If the best, and the strongest, naturally rise to the top, what happens to us? Our fathers are the ones that started out without much. But what happens then? We're the offspring of the best and strongest, and we start at the top. We were, one could argue, born lucky. I must admit, I personally don't feel very lucky most of the time. And I don't think I'm more skillful at anything than any other man. I was simply born with more access to resources."

Charles looked at him and shook his head. "All I know is, I'm about to be a father, and if it's a boy, I know he'll get stuck in the family business, and if it's a girl, I hope I can make her as interested in business as Regina Waring is. It's nice having a woman who's as good to talk to as she is to look at."

"No argument here," Thomas agreed.

****

It was hard to talk to Regina, though, when she wasn't around much. As Elizabeth went into confinement, Charles was around less, and harder to talk to, as well, when he was around. Thomas felt a bit deserted. He'd just gotten used to having both his best friends back. Now both of them were once again absent from his daily life.

Ah, well. Must be time to focus on business . . . .

Business took a fascinating turn that October, anyway. People were still gossiping about the shock of seeing the exposition halls burnt down, when a new and even more personally interesting topic took over the conversations at the Duquesne Club. The Husseys and the rest of the partners who formed Pittsburgh Bessemer Steel had approached Andrew Carnegie, and offered to sell.

It was rather satisfying, when his father told him the news. He'd driven out to his parents' house to bring his mother her birthday present, prepared to hear the usual litany of family gossip. He was rather surprised when his father met him in the hallway—and much more surprised by the greeting he received.

"My boy! My brilliant boy!!" his father looked ready to hug him. "You were right. You were absolutely right. If you weren't so far ahead of the game, we'd be the ones going out there with our hats in our hands and our tails between our legs."

"Father?" Thomas had no idea what his father was talking about. He had never called him 'brilliant' before. He wasn't sure he had ever admitted he was right before.

"I got the most interesting apology from Dr. Hussey. Things have been a little strained between us, you know, since we didn't go in with them on their venture. I told him that business is just business, but, well, you know how it is."

Thomas had felt a little bad about that. He knew the two men's relationship had been much less cordial since they had dropped out of the venture.

"Well, I ran into him at Mellon's this morning," his father continued. "And wouldn't you know it? They're giving it up. They've put together an offer to sell the lot to Carnegie. Hussey told me he couldn't be mad at me for being right. He called me a smarter man than he is. Imagine that!" His father chuckled, looking quite pleased. "I told him no hard feelings; I'm easy to underestimate."

Thomas noticed his father hadn't given him credit to Dr. Hussey. Well, to be fair, he didn't deserve any credit, did he? All he'd done was pass along Regina's advice, and urge his father to listen to it.

He did want to know, himself, how it was she knew not to gamble on the venture. The moment he knew she was back in Pittsburgh, he paid her a call at the Glassworks.

She was sitting in her office, which was already decorated with flowers from the businessmen welcoming her home. She was absorbed in the papers on her desk, and didn't look up as he stood in the doorway, watching her.

"Red really does suit you," he finally said when he got tired of waiting for her to discover his presence.

Her reaction was certainly satisfying. She jumped with a shriek, sending the papers in her hands flying in all directions.

"How long have you been standing there?" She asked, as he fetched the papers that landed on the floor in front of her desk.

"Long enough to wonder what on earth you were reading that was so absorbing," he answered with a chuckle.

"A very exciting contract, I assure you," she gasped, her hands still pressed to her bosom in a very entertaining manner. He was sorry when she removed her hands to reach for the papers he had collected.

"So what brings you here?" she asked, sifting through the pages, trying to put them back in order.

He settled himself in the chair in front of her desk. "Have you heard Carnegie's buying Pittsburgh Bessemer?"

"Yes, I heard."

"I thought you might have." He leaned forward and propped his elbows on the desk to look into her face. "How did you know?"

"Andy told me himself."

"No, no. You knew before the company was more than scribble on a napkin that things would go badly—that it would end like this. You warned me, and now you've saved us a couple years of fiasco, ending in abject humiliation. How did you know?" He repeated.

"Look at the people involved. It was inevitable." She answered simply.

"How do you figure? All the players were successful in their other businesses."

"Not Andy Kloman. And this wasn't about success in other businesses. This was about trying to outdo Andy Carnegie. This was about revenge, not about steel ingots."

"That's what I'd been thinking beforehand."

Regina looked at him with that tilt of her head that gave him gooseflesh. "So why didn't you say something?"

"Who would've listened to me?" Thomas asked.

"Men of good sense," she answered. "Which might normally include these gentlemen, but not when they were acting without thinking things through." She sighed, and her face took on an odd expression. "Any number of unpleasant complications can arise when people fail to think things through."

Thomas scrutinized Regina's face. "Is something wrong?"

Regina's eyes stopped looking through him and looked at him. "Nothing serious."

"Why don't I believe you?" he asked, still studying her expression.

"Because I'm a lousy liar," she answered with a rueful smile.

"All right. What's going on?" Thomas asked with his best Father Confessor imitation.

"Even I can be insanely stupid about people from time to time." She reached across the desk and gave his hand a squeeze. "But don't worry—I'll never let an error in character judgment touch the Wintergardens."

"Hang the Wintergardens!" Thomas exclaimed. "It's you I'm worried about."

"It's just—call it 'family foibles.' I won't bore you with the details." She stood up and reached for her pelisse and bonnet. "I once horrified an introverted friend of mine by saying that the antidote to people is more people. Since I firmly believe it's true, why don't you take me to lunch and force me to be sociable? I need a reminder of how many terribly interesting people there are in the world."

What was a gentleman to do? Burning with curiosity to know more about the family Regina never liked to talk about, Thomas opened the door for Regina and followed her out to where George stood waiting.

Chapter 21

The South Fork Fishing and Hunting Club was proving to be popular enough; the members decided to add an addition to the clubhouse which would more than triple the size of the building. There would be three stories, with the front rooms offering even better views of the sparkling lake. The front porch would be extended all the way across the face of the building, allowing more space for rocking chairs.

In the meantime, families continued their high-spirited amusements with what space they had. To start off the season, a small brass band made up of local musicians provided the music for a dance on the front lawn. It was a pretty scene, the young people laughing in the lanternlight with the moonlight on the lake behind them. As always, Thomas' eyes searched for Regina's dark hair. She was hard to spot as the lawn swirled in large concentric circles. Forward and back, to the left, to the right. Then the circles split, the men moving clockwise, the women moving counter clockwise. Leaning against a pillar, Thomas spotted Regina as she offered her hand to each gentleman she passed: left, right, left, right. She smiled and flirted with each person she passed; even with the women who gallantly danced "the gentleman's part" rather than sit out a dance for lack of enough male partners.

So absorbed was he in observing her, Thomas had not even heard the approach of the two women who leaned over the balcony rail on the other side of the pillar.

"See?" The first voice startled him. "She can hardly take her eyes off him. She's been watching him all evening."

Thomas smiled to himself. That same description could certainly apply to him, keeping his mute vigil over Regina.

"Oh, my! Her whole face lights up. Does he know?" asked the second voice.

"I'm sure of it," replied the first. "He very carefully does not watch her; but every so often he can't help himself, and peeks in her direction. Probably to make sure she's still watching."

"He does? I don't see . . ."

"Keep watching," her friend admonished.

The two were silent a moment, then they laughed together. Apparently they caught him "peeking."

"You don't believe they're actually — involved, do you?" voice number two asked.

"Well, I wouldn't put it past her," her companion sniffed. "She's been a widow for years, and every man in town is falling over himself, helping her keep her fortune together. She owns an empire, you know."

"More than that glass factory?"

A bolt of lightning seemed to rip through Thomas' body. They were talking about Regina!

"My dear! You are new. She's got assets in flour, copper, tin . . . . I'm not sure what else. If she were a man, she'd be the most eligible man in town. As it is . . . ."

"Is she going to remarry?" the second woman asked.

"If only she would," the first answered. "Then she'd be less odious. But she keeps the single ones at arm's length, saying she doesn't want to remarry, and flirts with our husbands instead."

"You seem to think she has one particular husband in mind."

"And it's not mine, thank goodness. We should be glad she does have one man in her sights. She'll leave the rest of ours alone."

Their voices died away. Thomas remained at his observation post until the music ended, vainly trying to catch the telltale expression the women had observed on Regina's face. By the end of the dance, he decided they were making it up. He couldn't distinguish anything significant in the direction of her eyes or the brilliance of her smile.

He shook his head. He didn't like the idea that Regina could be in love with someone. A stab of jealousy shot through his heart. Especially since, considering he wasn't on the dance floor, that someone could not have been him.

He needed to talk to her. If it were true—well, he had to know.

He bolted down the stairs, two at a time. The strains of the next waltz were starting. Where was she? No doubt her dance card was already filled.

"Thomas?" Her voice was next to his ear. "For whom are you searching with such urgency?"

"Why, you," he answered. "Come on, I'm taking the next dance." Without waiting for her answer, he put an arm around her waist, and guided her into the swirl of dancers.

"Okay, what's wrong?" Perceptive as ever, Regina's sharp eyes studied his face. "Why are you frowning like that?"

"Oh, I've heard some unpleasant gossip."

"About what?"

"About you."

"Oh." She seemed to lose interest, but seeing Thomas' expression had not changed, she decided to pursue the subject. "Well, come on, then. What nasty rumor have the good ladies concocted about me, now?"

"How did you know?"

"What else would it be? The worst gossips I know are all men. But the most malicious gossips I know—when I am the subject matter—are all women. You can't spend your life worrying what other people think," Regina rolled her eyes. "Some people want to think the worst. It's more entertaining than thinking good thoughts about you."

Thomas realized that talking with Regina was not making him feel any better. "Has anyone pointed out to you that you take a very dim view of human nature?"

Regina laughed. "I know. How can I sleep at night? For your information, I sleep very soundly, since I have the universe figured out. It's a comforting feeling. It means fewer surprises in my life."

"I think the gossip I heard would surprise you," Thomas predicted.

"All right, get it off your chest," she offered merrily. "What awful thing are they saying about me now?"

"That you're in love."

That did surprise her. She said nothing for a moment, while her expressive face went blank.

"With whom?" she asked in a strange voice.

"I don't know," he answered. "The women I was inadvertently eavesdropping on didn't say, except that he's married."

"How interesting," she commented, mostly to herself. "Well," she smiled up at him, the mischief returning to her eyes, "at least no one's accusing me of getting married again."

"What's wrong with that?"

"Besides being inaccurate, it's also terribly dull gossip. At least this has a wonderfully naughty edge to it. No doubt it will snowball into something really racy. Do keep your ears open. This could get entertaining."

Thomas shook his head, feeling a little dazed. "You're unbelievable. You're being accused of committing adultery, and you're just amused and glad they're not speculating on something more harmless?" He took a breath, then decided to pursue the issue that interested him most. "So why don't you want to get married again?"

"Why on earth would I?" She asked in surprise. "Women marry out of economic necessity. I obviously don't need to worry about that. I'm not lonely, so I don't need companionship. I have no maternal inclinations, so I don't need someone to have children with . . ."

"And you're not in love?" Thomas added softly, desperate to hear the answer.

"Well, I sure hope not," she retorted. "I've been telling every man who proposes to me I'd feel like I was betraying Henry."

"Every—are you getting proposed to?" Thomas asked in alarm.

"Goodness, yes. Henry wasn't even dead a month when I received my first proposal. I've been turning them away ever since."

A desperate feeling of helplessness washed over Thomas. What would he do if she ever accepted one of those proposals?

"Close your mouth, Thomas. I see I've astonished you," Regina's amused voice called him back to her. "I thought you knew me better than to be surprised by anything I say. These gentleman see me as nothing more than a conveniently rich woman. Not as me. It used to appall me, too. Now I just piously mention Henry's name, then laugh in my sleeve as they turn tail and flee."

Thomas smiled down at her, relieved. "You're a cruel woman, Regina."

She grinned back up at him. "And you wouldn't like me any other way."

****

The moonlight streaming brightly through his open window certainly didn't help Thomas get to sleep later that night. But then, neither did the hard floor, the pillow, or Thomas' churning thoughts. Scores of faceless suitors, rich, handsome, and free, kept offering their hands to Regina every time he tried to close his eyes.

Giving up, he quietly rose, dressed, and snuck out, careful not to disturb Meredith's deep, regular breaths. He was terrified of rousing her—she'd insist on taking a walk with him, and the last thing he wanted right now was company.

Conemaugh Lake shimmered as a light breeze rippled across the surface of the water. It looked ethereal, unreal, this lake in the mountains. He sprang down the steps and headed for the boathouses. Maybe he would take one of the rowboats out into the middle of the lake.

He was stopped dead in his tracks by the sound of voices coming from the water.

". . . problem is, dear, I know what I want. But are you willing to spend an eternity in limbo so that I can have it?"

Thomas' heart stopped. That was Regina's voice! The low, soft chuckle that he'd fallen in love with the first time he'd heard it—but laced with an underlying current of feeling he'd never heard before.

"Limbo seems like Paradise after Hell. No, that's not it. I'm still in hell. This is hell. My god, I can't look at you from across a room without wanting you again." And that—that was Charles McKay's voice.

"Thank you for that," Regina was saying. "After all the time I've spent worshipping you from afar, it's nice to know why you still won't look at me."

"In public, silly bunny, in public. I'm looking at you now, aren't I? If I look at you any harder, my eyes will fall out. Have I told you how magnificent you look when you dance?"

"I thought you weren't looking."

"I can see. You're the brightest light in the room. It's hard to miss you. You shine so much, I could probably still see you with my eyes closed. Here—I'll try it now."

There was a pause, then a giggle. A giggle! From Regina?

"Hm—yes. Don't you look lovely? That's a rhetorical question, of course."

"Honestly, dear. Such silly little pretty compliments."

"Survival skill. I'm married, you know."

"You've never told me how you ended up married to her," she started with a strong hint of mischief in her voice.

"No, I haven't. It doesn't matter, anyway. Money marries money. The damage was done a long time ago. Until that miraculous moment when you slipped under my armor, I'd accepted the fact that I didn't need a heart, and I'd never feel anything again. Now I've got my heart back. With you, I can give up things I'd never thought I'd do without."

The tone of Charles' voice suggested he was leading up to something. "I can leave her if you want me to—we can disappear. To—to California, or Brazil, or someplace."

Thomas heard a bitter version of the low, soft laugh he loved so well. "And leave everything? Your family, all your businesses?"

"There's steel in California," he muttered rebelliously.

"Do you think you'd be able to sell your steel, with every businessman in the country aware of your perfidy?" she pointed out with ruthless pragmatism. "And me! We know what I'd be. It's one thing to flirt with the men I do business with. But those same men who flutter over a smile and a kiss on the cheek won't do business with a fallen woman."

"We'll go farther—to Europe. Africa. China. We'll do business with people we've never done business with before."

"Even if you could start a business without the all-powerful McKay family behind you, would you be happy? Would we be happy?" She answered her own question before he could protest. "I'm sorry, my own, my dearest, but I know myself. You were born into an empire. I had to marry and build mine. I can't give it up. Not even for you. I've been your slave since the moment I first laid eyes upon you—but I'm that weak. I can't give up either of my two greatest passions. I'm not strong enough."

"Not strong enough to live in sin with me?" he asked with tender irony.

"Bah! There's no such thing as sin. Every time I look at you, and I get a tingle that goes from the top of my head to the tips of my toes, I know that loving you like this can't possibly be a sin."

"My sweet angel! Every time you get that tingle, you're committing another sin."

"Well, then, I'll gladly burn in your Hell for the sin of looking at you."

"Come here, pretty one. I can't stand just looking at you anymore."

There was a rustle of skirt, then a prolonged silence. Thomas fled, having a clear picture in his mind's eye of what was happening beside the moonlit waters.

****

The next morning, Thomas went down to the Clubhouse early after a sleepless night. He was surprised to see Regina already in the dining room, attacking her French toast with relish.

"May I join you?" He felt awkward standing over her table, where she was absorbed in the latest Crockery and Glass Journal.

"Oh! Thomas. Of course. Do sit down."

"Thank you. Just coffee, please, John," Thomas told the waiter who had materialized out of nowhere. "Lovely weather we're having this morning," he commented neutrally to Regina.

"Isn't it perfect out there?" she asked, so cheerfully Thomas winced. Yes, she'd obviously been having a very good time last night . . .

"Some of the kids are taking me sailing this morning," she smiled. "It's sweet; they've claimed me as one of their own."

"What do you mean?" Thomas heard himself asking.

"I'm old enough to be the mother of some of these young folks, but they've officially declared they don't believe it, or don't care. So I get a lot of invitations."

Thomas felt the oddest feeling of power as he encouraged her small talk. She didn't know what he knew. For the first time since he'd known her, she couldn't look into his eyes and tell him what he was thinking. He was enjoying the sensation. But he couldn't keep this secret to himself. He needed her to know.

"Before your nautical expedition, how about taking a walk with me down to the shore?" he asked, abruptly changing the subject.

Something in his tone of voice gave him away. She looked at him in her usual piercing fashion, then answered agreeably, "What a nice idea. We might as well enjoy this gorgeous morning to its fullest."

It was an effort not to hurry. He toyed with his empty coffee cup with an outward show of idleness while she finished her tea. A friendly argument ensued over which of them would put the tab on their club bill, then they strolled leisurely out the door and down to the boardwalk.

"I overheard the most interesting conversation last night," he approached his subject casually. "I didn't see the couple in question, but voices can carry very well when the sound bounces off the boathouse. On a still night, you can hear people on the dock from a good distance away."

Regina's cheeks had acquired two bright red patches. "And what were these two youngsters talking about?" she asked, completely failing in her attempt to sound casual.

Thomas guided Regina away from the boathouses—and their dangerous acoustics. "Oh, the usual love triangle stuff. He's married, she's not, he's ready to throw away everything for her, she's not. I had the bad timing to be taking a walk last night. Apparently I wasn't the only one with the romantic notion to see the lake by that amazing moonlight."

Regina had been stunned into silence. Thomas glanced sideways at her, and continued his casual observations, "As far as I could tell, I was the only person around to hear their guilty secret. But anyone could have heard. It was late, but it was such a beautiful night, we may not have been the only people out for a stroll. Now, I'm not going to go around gossiping about that conversation to anyone. But other people? This place thrives on gossip, my dear lady."

Regina put a hand on his arm to halt the flow of his words. "You know." She managed to get a lot of different emotions into two words—embarrassment, guilt, and relief.

"Yes, I know." He stopped and faced her, taking her by the shoulders and shaking her gently. "And I shouldn't know. What if one of these catty gossip mongers had been out for a walk, instead of your sympathetic old friend?"

The hand still gripping his arm tightened convulsively. "We weren't thinking about the acoustics," she answered softly. With a burst of feeling, she looked up into his face. "If anyone had to know, I'm so grateful it had to be you!"

"You lied to me," Thomas didn't try to hide the hurt and disappointment.

"I had to. Thomas, you don't go around bragging about this sort of thing. It's too private. There are also businesses and a marriage at stake. People generally don't approve of this sort of behavior, even if it isn't any of their business."

"No," he agreed. "I know you're not worried about your immortal soul—or what people think. With this, you have to worry about what people think. If you two are found out, it could cost you both your businesses. The risk seems too great for the reward."

She smiled; a half-complacent, half-wicked smile. "The risk is part of the reward. Every day, I face the usual cast of characters, but all the while I'm thinking, 'I've got the most extraordinary secret.'"

"Is that worth risking Waring Glassworks?"

"No. And yes." Her eyes looked earnestly into his. "Have you ever been in love, Thomas? Mindlessly, passionately in love?"

Had he ever been in love? How could she look at him, her endless black eyes boring feverishly into his, and ask if he'd ever been in love? His heart thumped painfully. He stared at her a moment before he remembered to answer her question.

"Yes," he choked out.

"Then you know how exhilarating it is. I feel like a kid who's stolen a cookie from the cookie jar. I know I shouldn't have it, and I'll be in trouble if I'm caught, but it's an awfully good cookie."

It was on the tip of his tongue to point out sourly, "And when you've spoiled your appetite?" But an image rose before his eyes—the image of Regina's face on the train as she left for Europe. The contrast was stark. The pale face with the lackluster eyes had been replaced by rosy cheeks and sparkling eyes. She had transformed from a grieving, miserable haunt back into a happy, vibrant woman.

It wasn't the travel which had brought Regina back to life. It was Charles. Thomas wished fervently that it could have been him.

He would be willing to risk the Baldwin fortune if he could be the one to put that light in her eyes.

He sighed, took her hand, tucked it back into the crook of his arm, and resumed their stroll along the water's edge. "Keep in mind," he admonished gently as they walked, "all those adages about kids caught with their hand in the cookie jar."

She laughed—a heedless, heady version of her sensuous chuckle. "Well, so long as you're the one catching me, I know I'll be forgiven."

"Hm. I may not always be there to catch you, you know. But if I'm going to be privy to your guilty secret, I might as well know all of it. How exactly did you get into this whole sordid affair?"

"When we were in Europe," she admitted, looking almost eager for the chance to talk about it. Almost as eager as he must have looked, years ago, when he'd been able to pour out to her the truth about his ill-fated marriage.

"In Europe! That was—three years ago!" Thomas felt like a complete fool. "You've been carrying on under my nose for three years, and I haven't figured it out?"

"No. But you asked how it started. I would say it got started when we were both in Europe. You'd told him to check on me; he made a point of keeping his promise to you. He'd invite me to dinner, or the theatre, or something, whenever we were in the same place. We ran into each other all over the Continent."

"You know that we've known each other since we were children. He'd always been so inaccessible to me—I was the daughter of a bookkeeper, he was the son of the man who owns Johnstown. But now we were equals. It was like a challenge. Now that the playing field was more even, could I get this one aloof man to notice I had a charm bracelet, let alone any other charms?"

Thomas said nothing. Aloof? Impersonal? No doubt Charles' interest in Regina went back much farther than Regina realized.

"All I wanted was a smile, a compliment—the usual foolish nonsense," she confessed. "I thought I was getting nowhere. Then when we were both back in Pittsburgh, and we'd see each other in connection with you, and away from Elizabeth, he was a different person. He was relaxed. Cheerful. He actually plays when you're around. If you don't realize it, you mean the world to him."

"Nice to know." It was nice to hear, especially since he'd been feeling neglected since Elizabeth had presented Charles with his son Robbie, and Charles saw a lot less of Thomas. On the other hand, it was exceedingly painful hearing it from the woman he adored, while she was demonstrating her intimate connection to Charles. "Go on."

Regina took a deep breath, and continued, "The—complicated part started out here. Last year. One night a few of us had stayed up late, drinking a fair amount, and having a good time talking. I must confess I'd been flirting rather outrageously. Men with a few drinks in them are such devoted admirers. When I said goodnight, Charles was next to me and walking me to my door. I was still flirting terribly with him, and enjoying myself, because for a change he was flirting back.

"Then suddenly it wasn't flirting anymore. It happened so quickly—he'd taken me in his arms, and walked me back into the corner. I could feel my heart pounding. I could feel his legs pressed against mine. My arms were wrapped around his neck—I wasn't even sure how they got there."

"He didn't even try to kiss me. He just held me, looking at me. I panicked and ran. I don't even remember touching the doorknob—the next thing I do remember is being alone, and unable to catch my breath.

"I trembled all night. I trembled for an hour leaning up against that door. I trembled for a couple of hours laying in bed staring at the moon through my window. I trembled when I woke up the next morning.

"I realized that this wasn't some foolish flirtation. I had been trying to make him flirt with me—but Charles doesn't flirt. I had started much more than I realized. It scared me. But it thrilled me, too.

"When I saw Charles the next day, he was his reserved self again. But something wasn't the same. The three of us had dinner together. Purely by accident—I came in as they came in, and Elizabeth insisted we sit together. And then she went on in that . . . . uniquely Elizabethan way of hers."

"Ah, yes," Thomas remarked. "That painful propensity of hers for making you wish you could crawl under the table, rather than be mistaken to be in agreement with any of her uncharitable observations."

"The very same," she agreed. "Somehow, Charles and I bonded over that dinner table. While Elizabeth went on and on with that uncomfortable monologue of hers, Charles and I would glance at each other in understanding. Sometimes we'd look at each other, and nearly laugh. All the while, my heart was pounding so hard I thought I must be making the whole building shake."

"So when did you go from bonding to—bonding?" Thomas asked, endeavoring to sound as disinterested as a good Father Confessor should.

"In Pittsburgh," she answered honestly. "The three of us were going to go to a play. Elizabeth took to her bed with a headache, because of the heat. Charles showed up at my door alone." Regina was breaking out in smiles and blushes. "We never made it to the theatre that night."

"I see," Thomas sighed.

Misinterpreting his reaction, Regina stopped and gripped his arm urgently. "Oh, tell me you understand, Thomas! I—may not care what the world thinks. But I do care what you think."

Well, that was something, at least. Thomas looked down into her upturned face. "What I think," he said slowly, "is that when I put you on that train to Europe, I never expected to see you smiling again. I don't care why you're smiling. I'm grateful to see you happy again."

He smiled at the relief in her face. Yes, she really did care what he thought! "I also think," he continued, "that Anthra and Bit will be upset with us for taking this walk without them!"

The serious part of the conversation over, Thomas dismissed the subject of Regina's love life, and escorted her back into public hearing with an animated discussion of the joys of large dogs.

Chapter 22

Thomas' attention was so wrapped up in the business of trying to navigate between banks, suppliers, clients, his workers, and the various disastrous elements of his personal life, he only slowly began to notice that something was wrong with his father. Once he was aware that things were amiss, he still couldn't put his finger on what it was for a couple weeks. His father seemed to be getting a little thinner . . . he didn't seem to eat as much . . . and, worst sign of all, he wasn't talking as much.

When his father failed to offer any explanation, Thomas eventually decided he was going to have to use a direct approach. The perfect opportunity came one afternoon, as they left the Masonic Temple after the annual selection of officers.

"You're awfully quiet, these days," Thomas observed out loud.

When the only answer Thomas received was a grunt, he knew that something really was wrong.

"Are you sleeping all right?" Thomas asked, realizing that the only way he'd find out what was troubling his father was if he could stumble onto the truth with a lot of questions.

"Fine," his father answered, digging in his suit pockets to avoid his son's eyes.

"You're not worried about the Ironworks—or the sausage factory, are you? Times are pretty tough, but . . ."

"Of course not," his father interrupted. "We've survived Panics before. We'll weather this one, too."

Thomas listened to the silence after that brief statement. Compared with the usual monologue his father conducted when they were alone, it was positively alarming.

"You're not upset with me, are you?"

"Why should I be upset with you?"

Once again, the eerie silence descended between them. His father, for all he loved to talk, did have one subject he preferred to avoid: health. Thomas knew only one question was left to ask. "Have you been sick, lately?"

The lack of answer was answer enough. His father looked out the window as if Thomas never asked the question.

Once upon a time, Thomas would have dropped the subject when his father ignored him like that. But somehow, that wasn't the right answer today.

"Father, the only times I've ever seen you quiet is when you can't talk, like when you're in church or sick, or when you won't, like the time you didn't speak to Mother for a week when she threw out your favorite shoes. Why don't you confess what's wrong, rather than listen to more of my questions," he suggested.

"I haven't been eating much," his father volunteered.

"No, I guess you haven't," Thomas recalled the last few times they'd been at the same table. His father pushed his food around on his plate quite a bit, but Thomas couldn't say he'd actually seen his father eat. "Why haven't you been eating?"

"I can't keep it down," his father replied. "Some days, I eat some of this, some days I can eat some of that, but I never know what will agree with me. It's not the same from one day to the next."

"I don't suppose you've seen a doctor about this?" he asked, already knowing the answer.

"Doctors? Bah—they don't know anything," his dismissed the entire profession with one wave of his hand. "They give you some nasty powder you'll be tasting for a month after, and tell you to get some bedrest. Well, I can do without the powders, and I don't need to pay a doctor to tell me to go to bed."

Thomas frowned. "And what if something's really wrong, father?"

His father's shoulders twitched. "Then I don't want to know."

****

It was only a few weeks later when the entire Baldwin family got to find out. Weak from starvation, Richard Baldwin collapsed early one afternoon, crossing Wood Street. He was carried into the back office of Carr and McCandless' Dry Goods, and a doctor was summoned. Richard was, as Thomas described later, too unconscious at the time to protest.

An errand boy was sent to fetch Thomas from the Olympus building.

Thomas arrived hatless, coatless, and breathless from dodging carriages and pedestrians along his ten-block sprint. A clerk stood up as he threw himself, panting, into the office. "This way, Mr. Baldwin. Dr. Oldshue is with him right now."

The doctor was putting away his stethoscope when Thomas cautiously opened the door of the little back office. His father looked pale and weak as he lay on the floor. It frightened him. His father looked so—fragile.

"Hello, Father," he called softly.

"Sent for you too, did they?" his father grumbled. "What took you so long? You could have saved me from this fool."

Thomas smothered a smile at his father's lack of diplomacy and shrugged apologetically at the doctor. "I take it, Father, you don't like what he has to say?"

"He's trying to tell me I need an operation," his father waved his hand, weakly, to dismiss the idea. "Hogwash."

"Your father has a tumor in his chest," the doctor explained to Thomas. "I would say it's sitting on his esophagus and cutting off the route from his mouth to his stomach. His collapse today is due to starvation. If that tumor isn't removed soon, he'll die from it."

Thomas stared at the doctor. "Are you sure? It's not just a sour stomach, or something?"

The doctor shook his head as he plunged his arms into his overcoat and picked up his black bag. "I'm sorry I can't offer you better news. He's not going to get better on his own," he answered candidly. "And if he gets too much weaker, I can't promise that he'd even survive the surgery. If he decides to act, he'll have to do it soon." Dr. Oldshue handed Thomas a plain white calling card. "My office is on Grant Street—you know where to find me if my services are required. 'Til then, you might see what he can do with liquids—broth, milk, maybe some applesauce."

"Thank you, doctor," Thomas called as the doctor left the room.

"Damned doctors," his father fussed. "He was talking to you as though I wasn't even here."

"Well, you were calling him names," Thomas pointed out. "And I wanted to hear what he had to say. You didn't."

"No, I didn't." All this excitement was draining what little strength his father had. His voice was getting weaker. "I don't have a tumor. That butcher wants to cut me open because he can charge more for that than for those nasty powders."

"Which I notice he didn't even offer to you. You couldn't keep them down if you tried, could you?" Thomas asked.

He was answered only by silence.

"I thought so," Thomas continued, trying not to show the alarm he was feeling. "Well, I'll take you home so you can at least get some rest. Assuming Mother lets you get any rest."

His father's eyelids had been closing. He opened them in horror. "You're not going to tell her?"

Thomas' hand was already on the doorknob. "Well, how are you going to explain going home in the middle of the day? You'll have to tell her something." He opened the door. "You sleep. I'll be back with the carriage as soon as I can."

****

Thomas had no illusions that his mother was going to take the news of his father's illness with good grace. She did not disappoint him. No one got the chance to explain anything; the moment his father emerged from the carriage, leaning heavily against Thomas as he climbed the stairs, she was standing at the front door, arms folded, busily jumping to the wrong conclusions.

"Well! This is a new one, Richard! Coming home drunk after lunch at that men's club of yours? Honestly! You're not twenty-eight anymore, you know. When are you going to start acting your age? I suppose you're in a similar condition, Thomas?"

"He's not inebriated, Mother," Thomas answered with some asperity as she paused to take a breath. "He collapsed this afternoon in the middle of the street. Fortunately, there were plenty of Good Samaritans around . . ."

His mother wasn't listening anymore. "In public, yet! I suppose absolutely everyone saw him?"

In the back of his mind, Thomas could hear Meredith's scandalized voice. "What would people say?"

"Well, fortunately somebody did," Thomas answered sharply. "Misters Carr and McCandless took him into their store and called for a doctor."

"Witch doctor, more like," Richard spoke up for the first time. "Quack. Medicine man. I'll wait and hear what a homeopath has to say on the subject! At least they cure people, instead of killing us for our money!"

Thomas wasn't born until after the cholera epidemics of the 40s, but he had grown up with the aftermath. Cholera survivors were fiercely loyal to the doctors who saved them. Richard was one of the many patients cured by a homeopathic physician. When the army surgeons had failed to save his brother Benjamin, his father's belief that other doctors were worse than useless became gospel.

His mother, however, was less of a convert. "No one's going to kill you, Richard. I'm the only one who's going to die—of embarrassment. Come inside and stop making such a scene."

Thomas was hard pressed to say which was worse: his mother's lack of concern or his father's. When Newland stepped forward to offer his assistance, Thomas handed his father over to the steady butler, and turned to face his mother. "Well, if you don't want to know what happened, and he refuses to acknowledge what happened, I'll go back to work, now."

The threat worked. As he turned to walk back to the waiting carriage, his mother stopped him. "Wait, Thomas. I'm sorry. What did the doctor say?"

"He thinks Father needs an operation. There's something in his chest that's been blocking his stomach. Have you noticed if he's been eating lately?"

"Of course he's been eating!" she answered testily. "I still have to have Eliza keep a plate warm for him because of the hours he keeps. I suppose he's taught you the same bad habits, so Meredith never knows when to expect you, either . . ."

Patiently, he redirected the conversation back from whence it came. "But does he actually eat? Or does he push the food around on the plate without actually ingesting anything?"

He could see in her face that she didn't know. And that as his wife, she knew that she should know. And above all, she wished they could talk about something that didn't involve bodily functions!

He put an arm around her when she didn't answer, and guided her inside. "Never mind, Mother. It's apparently been happening for some time. He didn't want to talk to me about it, either. The doctor said Father needs an operation, or he'll starve to death. Father doesn't believe the doctor. That's the important information you need to know."

As soon as his father was settled in his room with a glass of milk and with his mother hovering over him like an anxious gnat, Thomas sat down and wrote a quick note to Dr. James McClelland, the Baldwin family doctor, requesting a house call. He planned on simply sending the note with George, and remaining at his parents' house. But as he stared down at the scribbled lines, he could vaguely hear his mother's voice drifting down the stairs. There wasn't much he could do here, anyway. George could drop him at the Olympus building on the way. He might as well go back to work for the rest of the afternoon.

****

One of the joys of a large family is the extended community in times of crisis. One of the curses of a large family is that same extended community in times of crisis. When Thomas returned that evening, most of the family was present. Uncle Alfred had heard when he'd stopped at Carr and McCandless', and came out on the next streetcar. Aunt Mary had heard while she was at the milliner's, and sent her daughter Anne to inform Uncle John and the boys, while Mary came straight out to the house. The brothers, sisters, spouses, and cousins all crowded into the parlor, or visited the invalid as he rested in his room.

Thomas couldn't say which was worse, establishing himself downstairs in the parlor while various family members announced what they thought his father should do, or sitting upstairs, while his father endured visits from family members trying to tell him what to do. Thomas had never in his life felt so much sympathy for Richard.

Not one person asked his father what he wanted. "Of course you won't go under the knife," Alfred obviously shared Richard's disdain of doctors. "Those surgeons killed your son at Stone River. No reason why they shouldn't try to kill another one of us." "I thought that McClelland fellow was supposed to be better than those other quacks; guess I was wrong," sniffed his father's cousin Lavinia. "We ought to schedule surgery as soon as possible," John announced with his usual brusque no-nonsense manner as soon as he walked into the sitting room. "The sooner the doctor does his business, the sooner you can get back to yours." Aunt Eleanor had apparently decided Richard was already on his deathbed. She sat beside him, sighing plaintively, stroking his hand and asking endless questions which Richard mostly ignored. Thomas, knowing how his father hated to talk about his health, broke his self-imposed silence and interceded.

"If you want me to go over what the doctor had to say, I can tell you later."

She looked at him with all the fondness she might have for a dog who had just tracked mud across her new Persian carpet. "When I want to know what the doctor has to say, I will send for him," she announced imperiously. "Why don't you leave, Thomas? I'm trying to talk to my brother!" she finished with a dramatic flourish.

Downstairs was no better. His mother vacillated between a hand-wringing urge to milk all the attention and sympathy she could from the moment, and an annoyance with her husband for causing so much commotion. The rest of the family hovered around, arguing, cajoling, and mostly airing their opinions. Since everyone was doing so at once, no one was left to actually listen to what anyone else had to say.

Was this the result of money and power? He heard in each voice the urgency to make itself heard above the other voices. But in none of the voices did he hear any genuine concern for the man upstairs.

Of course, that man upstairs was no different than the rest of his family. He liked solving problems out loud. He didn't like showing any emotional attachments to his family. Thomas realized he was watching his father reap what he'd sown. Nonetheless, his heart filled with pity.

****

It was late when the visitors decided it was time to leave. Thomas felt the need to remain behind as people trooped out the door, en masse. Leaving Meredith drowsily draped on the parlor couch and his mother still saying last goodbyes, he climbed the stairs one last time to check on his father.

He was astonished when his father asked him, "What do you think I ought to do?"

"What do I think?" he repeated stupidly. His mind did a quick inventory. No, he could not recall his father ever asking his opinion on anything. The very idea of his father wanting to know what he thought left him speechless.

The babble of family conversation returned with a rush. "I think," he answered slowly, "that what anybody thinks doesn't matter. What do you want?"

Unexpectedly, his father's face broke into a smile. "You know what I want? Sausage. Split open and fried with onions, the way my mother used to fix it."

"Really? Hmm," Thomas answered. "I think I know of a little factory around here that makes a pretty good sausage. Although I don't know about the fried with onions part. Eliza might be hurt if I try to tell her how to make it."

Father and son looked at each other, a moment. "I'm never eating sausage again, am I?"

Thomas swallowed hard, and answered practically, "That depends. If the doctor's wrong, maybe you will. If the doctor's right, it depends on what you do. If you don't get surgery, you won't. If you do get surgery, maybe you will. If, as you say, the doctors are fools, do you think any of them can operate on you successfully? It's like a life-sized card game, Father. You get to make the call, but there's no way of knowing what anyone else at the table's got."

"Damn your metaphors, son," his father pulled a hand out from under the covers to shoo Thomas out of the room. "I always was a lousy gambler."

"Aha," Thomas thought as he softly closed the door and tiptoed down the stairs to collect his sleepy wife. "So that's where I get it from."

****

The week that followed was frustrating and even humiliating for his father. Richard insisted on going back to work the next day, but he was so exhausted by the streetcar ride down Penn Avenue, he'd needed to rely on the kind arm of one of the Olympus Ironworks bookkeepers to get from the streetcar to his office. Thomas had a daybed brought into the office when he saw the distress Richard was in, which earned him a full afternoon's silent treatment from the elder Baldwin. But Thomas walked in that evening to find his father utilizing the offending furniture for a much-needed nap.

The following day, Richard accepted the use of Thomas' carriage and coachman to get downtown—then had to turn around immediately for home. He'd tried to eat breakfast that morning, and vomited all over himself and the carriage seat.

Without fanfare, Thomas checked with his father's secretary, and went to all his father's meetings. He knew better than to suggest that Richard stay home. His father would have to figure that out for himself.

The rest of the family wasn't nearly so reticent. "You're sick, for goodness' sake," Aunt Eleanor sniffed with dramatic flair. "You should be home in bed."

"And leave Thomas alone with my business?" Richard had reportedly answered with an indignant huff.

That stung, when it reached Thomas' ears. Richard had never expressed faith in the abilities of his only remaining son. Unlike his mother, his father rarely spoke Benjamin's name. But Thomas could hear the silent comparison. Their firstborn was handsome, clever, witty, brilliant, charming, and the perfect heir. Thomas was a dull second not worthy of notice. Benjamin died a hero's death with all the glories and honor of battle. Thomas had been merely dutiful and faithful, showing up every morning at the Olympus portals since he was sixteen years old.

But his father was sick, and frustrated, and frightened. So Thomas set aside his feelings and dutifully handled the company's business, writing copious notes against the day when Richard would demand a full report of the transactions he'd missed.

After a few days' struggle, his father gave up the quest to reach the Olympus building. He was exhausted by his efforts, and unwilling to endure more indignities. Thomas made the rounds of banks, boardrooms, and men's clubs, and failed to deliver all the sympathetic get well messages his father would have resented receiving.

He was the only member of the family who didn't express surprise and outrage when, after a week of battling sickness and fatigue, Richard Baldwin announced his willingness to undergo the operation—but only with Dr. McClelland.

As he listened to the fresh round of family tirades, it occurred to Thomas that the outrage was not at the idea of surgery, but rather at the thought that Richard had not consulted each family member before making his decision. He patiently endured the ritual airing of family opinion, and made the arrangements for his father's stay at the Homeopathic Hospital and Dispensary on Second Avenue.

Predictably, his father turned down Thomas' offer to stay with them after George drove them to the hospital. "I don't need you hanging around," Richard had responded testily. "Your mother's quite enough."

So Thomas spent the dreary December day of his father's operation in the Olympus Building, watching the clock and wondering.

At least he was not alone. Every employee in the building watched and wondered with him. The day dragged by with agonizing slowness, despite the fact that Thomas was trying to keep his father's schedule as well as his own.

At 8:15 pm he still had a tall stack on his desk. Normally he would have accomplished much more, but it was hard to be efficient while checking the clock every ten minutes all day long. With a sigh he capped his inkwell and turned down his desk lamp. He'd had all the suspense he could take. Time to go see his father.

Visitor's hours ended at nine, but Thomas managed to get there with a few minutes to spare. The doors were open, and the nurse at the desk was engrossed in the work on her desk, so Thomas simply slipped past her and up the stairs.

Three beds from the end of the ward on the third floor, Richard was laying, with his eyes closed, looking more dead than asleep. Thomas sat in the empty chair beside the bed. Whenever he looked at him, he realized, he'd seen the imposing presence who had forged his own personal tale of wealth and success. He didn't see the fragile old man. Now, Thomas scrutinized the familiar face with a fresh eye.

When had his hair gotten so thin? The short style Richard favored had gone from a dark brown to a steel gray long ago, but now he realized he could look right through the individual strands to his scalp. The wrinkles had been accumulating, too, and the skin on his neck sagged into folds. That could account for the beard. His mother had complained bitterly when his father had grown it. But Richard was not given to whims. He did not do things without a good reason.

The hands on the blanket weren't the powerful, capable ones Thomas remembered, either. He stared at the gnarled fingers. Some of the nails weren't quite right. They only grew halfway down the nail bed, and looked thick and rough. The skin sagged on his hands, too. The blue veins stood out stubbornly against the thin skin.

"You must be his son?" A nurse with a sweet, round face and compassionate eyes walked around Thomas' chair, and placed a light hand on his father's forehead. "Your mother kept wondering where you were all day, and whenever your father was awake he told her he didn't want you here."

"Was he awake much?"

The nurse shook her head. "Between the anesthesia during surgery, and the morphine the doctor gave him for the pain afterwards, he hasn't been with us much. It's perfectly normal for him to sleep most of the day."

"Normal, she says," Richard surprised them both by saying, without opening his eyes. "but how can I get any sleep with everyone yakking all the time?"

"Are you all right, Mr. Baldwin? Are you in any pain?" the nurse asked solicitously.

"I'm in plenty of pain," Richard answered. "But that doesn't bother me. You do. Now, both of you, get out of here."

"But Father, if you're in pain, she can probably help you," Thomas pointed out.

"These quacks have done quite enough," his father replied. "So have you. Now go. I don't want you here."

"Okay, Father," Thomas stood up. "I only stopped by to see how the surgery went."

"Don't worry about me," his father's voice was already drifting back into sleep. "You worry about not ruining my company while I'm stuck here."

Another big hearty vote of confidence from his caring parent. Thomas looked down at the bed, no longer seeing the fragile sick man. He saw his father again. "Good night, Father."

Thomas turned and looked for the nurse. She was going tranquilly about her business, giving another patient a glass of water. Thomas waited at the foot of the bed until she finished with that patient and joined him. "I wanted to thank you for caring for my father," he offered sincerely. "I imagine he's not an easy patient to care for, and I apologize for any grief he'll give you."

She smiled up at him cheerfully. "I was a nurse with the Union army, Mr. Baldwin. I've cared for much more difficult patients than your father. We'll get along just fine."

He wished her a good night and headed for the stairs, still smiling at her cheerful confidence. 'We'll get along just fine.' The smile faded a little. He wished he could have said the same.

****

Two weeks before Christmas, Richard Baldwin came home from the hospital.

Every family member looked anxiously for signs of improvement: a dab of color in his cheeks, a glimmer of energy in his voice. Everyone brought every sort of tempting morsel to the house: soups and broths, puddings, oranges, chocolates, caramels and candies of all sorts.

Too exhausted to put up much of an argument, Richard dutifully tried it all. Some days, he seemed resigned to his fate, and made attempts to eat only to quiet the incessant family voices. "You have to keep trying, otherwise you're going to starve to death." Other days, he rang for the servants, demanding his favorite onion broth. When that would not stay down, he would try something else—and something else, swallowing and throwing up in a determined biological battle against his own body.

Due to the indignity of his malady, Richard forbade visitors. But they came, anyway. The house always had at least one extra branch of the family tree hanging around. The cook quickly learned to plan dinner for twelve and keep a couple of Richard's favorite soups simmering on the stove.

"I don't know how long I can keep this up," Eugenia confessed irritably to Thomas. "Your father hasn't even been home a week, and we're being eaten out of house and home. Between your father's asking for something different all the time, and the constant visitors, I've had to hire another cook. Poor Eliza was going to quit on me, and I can't say I blame her." She sighed. "This is completely ruining Christmas this year, I can tell. Well, your father always was a good one for bad timing."

Thomas had listened to his parents complaining about each other as long as he could remember. He'd long since learned to listen without giving any response. As he looked at his mother, and thought of his father lying upstairs battling furiously for his life, he recalled his old conclusion that they deserved each other.

If that was true, his parents' marriage qualified as one of the great tragedies of the nineteenth century.

Chapter 23

His mother's words came back to haunt him. It was still dark as he buttoned his vest by gaslight, when he heard the bell ring on the front door. His eyes wandered over to the clock before he walked out into the hall. Seven o'clock in the morning?

Sudden realization hit him in a sickening wave. His father.

He was in the hallway by the time Joseph had closed the door behind the messenger.

"That was someone from my parents' house, wasn't it?" Thomas called as he pounded down the stairs.

Joseph cleared his throat as he handed Thomas the envelope. "Yeah. That was that new Hunkie servant of theirs." Joseph stood waiting while Thomas unfolded the note. Thomas held it so Joseph could read over his shoulder:

Christmas Eve, 1884
Thomas,
Come quickly. Your father has passed away.
Your mother,
Eugenia Baldwin

Thomas calmly handed the note to Joseph. "Would you please find out if George has left for his parents' house yet? If he hasn't, ask if he'd mind hitching the cutter before he leaves. I'll drive it myself. This is going to take a while. Almost everyone was going home today?"

"Yes," Joseph had to stop and clear his throat again. "You let Mary go home to her mother in Latrobe last night, the rest of us were leaving tonight."

"Tell everyone they're dismissed. The Christmas greens are on the back porch—someone should take them home. And whatever Christmas cooking that's already done. Ask Mrs. Bishop if she'd mind packing up anything I can reasonably bring to my mother's to help feed the horde, and divide up the rest for the staff. I imagine it will be a few days before we'll be eating a meal at home," Thomas felt oddly detached and pragmatic. A checklist of things to be done danced before his eyes. In the back of his mind, he was thinking that he was about to go through the public rituals of grief—for a man he'd come to realize he barely knew.

Joseph's voice called him back to the present. "I know you and your father weren't very close, but I imagine you'll still miss him, now that he's gone."

Thomas looked solemnly into the older man's face. "I hope so, Joseph." He turned and climbed the stairs to go wake Meredith with the news.

The knob on her bedroom door felt odd under his hand. He hadn't been near her room since the night he came home from the railroad riot. To avoid the squeamish feeling he got from being in her room, he marched briskly up to the bed and shook her shoulder. "Wake up, Meredith." His voice was barely more than a whisper. He felt like an idiot as he heard it. What was he whispering for? To avoid disturbing her sleep? He shook her again and repeated in a normal voice, "Wake up, Meredith. Bad news."

She stared at him sleepily for a moment before she recognized him. "Thomas?"

"The one and only. Sorry to wake you from your slumbers, but I bring bad tidings. My father has passed away."

Meredith sat bolt upright. "Oh, Thomas. No! Not on Christmas Eve! When will we open presents?"

Open presents? Well, there was a problem that hadn't occurred to him. "I don't know, Meredith. Eventually. There are a few things that are going to take precedence over your getting gifts for Christmas."

She threw back the covers and jumped out of bed, without bothering to make a big production for his benefit. "Everything always comes before me," she snapped. "When is it my turn?"

Thomas looked at her with some amusement. "Why, when you die, of course. Then you get to be the center of attention. Lots of flowers, everyone talking about you. It's kind of like being a bride, but I suppose there aren't any gifts to open." He retreated back toward the door. "If you can possibly manage it, hurry up and get dressed. It's going to be a long day and we'd best get started."

He wasn't swift enough. Meredith realized her opportunity, and glided forward in her nightgown, her hands reaching for his arm. "If you stay and help me dress, Thomas, I'll be that much faster."

Thomas hastily pulled the door open, wondering why he hadn't left it open in the first place. "Your maid, what's her name, Martha, must be awake by now, and since she's far more accustomed to solving the mysteries of female clothing than I am, she'll be far more useful to you. If she's not already on her way, I'll send her in."

He escaped into the hall as Martha came running down the stairs. She rounded the corner at full speed, and he put out his hands to keep her from running him over.

"Whoa there! You're just in time. I just woke her. And it's only fair to warn you, she's likely to be in a foul temper right now."

She nodded a little. He always got the feeling she didn't like him very much. "As you say, Mr. Baldwin." Thomas felt like she'd dismissed him as she opened the door to his wife's room. The subject occupied his thoughts for no more than a second, as he realized that since he was in mourning now, he'd have to change his vest and cravat.

Joseph was already in his room, laying out the very garments Thomas had been contemplating. "Mrs. Bishop has packed up most of the contents of the kitchen, and wants to know if you need her help at your mother's."

Thomas snagged the silk of his cravat as he removed the pin too hastily. “She’s a good, kind soul, but I wouldn’t dream of interfering with her family Christmas. Thank her for me. I appreciate how you all look out for me. If I could have grown up under so many watchful eyes, my life might have turned out better.” He smiled as the older man held up a black vest for Thomas to slip his arms through.

“I doubt we could have changed much,” Joseph observed practically. “Mrs. Baldwin is a pretty determined creature.”

“You’re right, Joseph,” he sighed as he did the buttons. “But you usually are.”

“Well, that may be so,” Joseph agreed candidly, “but it’s not all it’s cracked up to be. If you’re right too much, people call you a smart ass.” He headed for the door. “But then, I guess I’d rather be called a smart ass than a dumb ass.”

Thomas turned back to the mirror to fasten his black cravat, unable to stop the grin that had spread over his face.

****

The other Baldwin residence was filled with sad reminders that it was the day before Christmas. The kitchen was permeated with the smell of the almost-finished plum pudding, and a Christmas tree leaned against the back porch. Thomas smiled a little, remembering his father’s traditional grumble over the newfangled German fashion.

As the family legend went, his mother had begged for a tree for years after the papers published pictures of Queen Victoria’s family beside the tree Prince Albert had decorated for them. Eventually, she simply ignored her husband’s protests and hired a German gardener who not only brought her the coveted evergreen, but installed it in the front parlor for her and showed her how to decorate it. He’d even presented her with her most cherished ornament: a small glass pickle. The person who found the pickle on the tree, he explained, would get an extra present on Christmas morning.

He and Meredith found his mother, still in her dressing gown, crying inconsolably in her upstairs sitting room. As soon as she saw his mother, Meredith burst into tears and rushed into her arms. The two women rocked and wailed together in such an intense display of emotion, Thomas felt like he was standing at the open end of a blast furnace.

He stood rooted to the floor, uncertain what to do. He felt like he was intruding on someone else's private grief. Meredith hadn't known his father all her life, yet here she was, sobbing as if her heart would break. There was his mother, who had done nothing but complain about or to his father as long as Thomas could remember, wailing in her grief.

Maybe he just didn't understand women very well.

His mother drew a deep breath, then held out her hand to him. Obediently he stepped forward and took it. "Thomas," she gulped between sobs, "you have to make the funeral arrangements. I can't. Your father always took care of those sorts of things . . . ." Her wet face screwed up at the mention of his father, and she buried her face back in Meredith's shoulder in a fresh outburst of tears.

Still holding her outstretched hand, Thomas awkwardly patted his mother's shoulder. This wailing was making him really uncomfortable. He stood there, bewildered, trying to offer as much sympathy as he could through that one hand. But he had no tears of his own to shed. His father would have approved of that. "Crying's women's work, son," he vaguely recalled his father saying when he was a wee lad with a skinned knee. But it left him on the outside, looking in at an event he should have been part of.

Eventually, his mother let go of his hand in order to use her handkerchief. "If I'm going to make his arrangements, I'd better go do it," he said awkwardly. He realized he had no idea how funeral arrangements were made. Then practicality flooded his mind with details that needed to be seen to. "Has anyone else in the family been notified yet?"

"No," his mother sniffed, dabbing at her eyes with her soggy handkerchief. Thomas dug his out of his pocket and handed it to her. "That's what I wrote you for. I can't handle telling so many people, Thomas. You'll have to do the best you can."

The best he can? Wasn't that what he'd been doing, all his life? And he was even pretty darned competent when he did his best. Hell, even when he wasn't trying very hard he was pretty darned capable.

An angry knot grew in his chest and constricted his throat. Unable to utter a word, he turned and left the room.

He wasn't even sure with whom he was angry. His mother? Yes. Himself? Well, yes. His father . . .

His feet turned, and the impulse carried him back down the hall and into the sickroom.

Well, there he was, in bed, looking merely asleep. He'd died with a frown on his face. Although his father wouldn't admit it, Thomas suspected that he was in quite a bit of pain. Which, naturally, he wouldn't discuss with anybody.

Not, Thomas realized with a shock of self-recognition, that he himself would have behaved any differently, if he had been the one to lie, dying, in this room. After all, who was there to talk to in this house?

He sat in the chair next to the bed and looked at him. If his life were a novel, there would have been some sort of connection between him and his father. Some sort of sentimental goodbye. Something that made sense of their relationship, that made him feel less neglected, that gave him some insight, some sense of meaning.

This was life, not fiction. Life didn't work like that. The only meaning he had was the horrible realization of how much he was like his father. Married to a shrew, not prone to talking much; the company was the primary focus of his life. His father had excelled at making money. He certainly hadn't excelled at the art of living. Thomas was becoming better and better at making money. Was he doomed to be as big a failure as his father was?

No. Bigger. At least his father had been respected by everyone in the family. Thomas didn't even have that.

He shook his head and left the room, wondering why he'd even want the respect of his family. But the disturbing notion pursued him downstairs and into the study while he wrote the necessary letters and dispatched the necessary people.

He didn't want to be like his father.

And he didn't have the faintest idea of what he could do to prevent the similarities.

****

Thomas "did his best" for the next couple of days. He informed the family of his father's death, notified the Masons and Knights Templar, visited Mr. Rodney of Rodney and Smith in order to pick out a casket and order the hearse and carriages, went to the church for the minister, fielded questions and expressions of sympathy from well-wishers ranging from clients to business rivals.

The family held its own private wake on Christmas Day. There was a public wake the day after that, and the funeral was two days after Christmas. Two days after that, Meredith finally got her wish to open presents; the entire family congregated once more on the hapless Eugenia, ("Well, you DO have the largest parlors, you know," Aunt Eleanor pointed out with undisguised envy in her voice) and held one very large belated Christmas gift-giving.

His cousins Edgar, Lily, and John brought in a Christmas tree, decorated it, and even had the spare gift for the finder of the pickle. Meredith's elation from locating the little green ornament faded abruptly upon opening the gift. "What's wrong with a skipping-rope?" Edgar had to defend himself from her disappointment. "Everyone can use a little bit of exercise. It's good for the constitution! We almost bought a harmonica, but we realized not everyone in this family has a great deal of musical talent."

Eventually, everything was over. The last vestiges of holiday decorations were bundled off the same day that Henry Baldwin came over to read Richard Baldwin's last will and testament. Thomas wasn't terribly surprised by the contents. Even after death, Richard Baldwin had managed to find one more way to belittle his only surviving child.

He'd left Thomas most of the stock in Olympus Ironworks, oh, yes. But not quite a controlling share. He'd split up a significant portion among the other members of the family; his mother, his uncles and cousins, so that they would all maintain an interest in the company. Because he didn't think Thomas was capable of running the company.

One last, humiliating vote of no-confidence from his doting father.

He found himself pacing restlessly from room to room, anger eating holes through his insides. He drifted past the children playing lawn games in the ballroom (his mother would be horrified if she knew), the women discussing mourning fashions, the servants arguing as they cleared the last of the dishes in the dining room. His feet started to turn him toward the stairs up to his father's bedroom, but he stopped halfway to the landing. He didn't want to visit that room again. Maybe he never wanted to see that room again.

The house was simply closing in on him. He needed a breath of air. Where could he hide? Where he always hid—the hothouse! A fond smile reached his lips. It never occurred to him before, how terribly fitting it was that he'd first met Regina in a wintergarden. He wanted to go sit on the bench where they'd sat together. He hadn't even known her name then.

He passed the music room where Meredith had cornered him. Snippets of music floated out the door, interspersed with a murmur of feminine voices. He was idly following the zigzag pattern of the wood inlays on the hallway floor, as he used to as a boy, when voices from the parlor caught his ear, and the sound sharpened from distant babble into words.

"Well, someone has to help Thomas."

It was his mother's voice. His cousin Albert's voice groaned in response.

"Aw, Auntie. I know, but I've got my own business worries. I don't have the time to come and hold Thomas' hand."

The very idea! Albert's foundry wasn't exactly doing very well; he'd started using other foundries because Albert's was too slow; and with business so depressed everywhere, slow deliveries could be a death knell.

"Well, then, make the time," his mother answered sharply. "Your uncle left me with this huge steel company, and I don't know the first thing about running it."

"It's really not that hard, Euwie," Thomas recognized the voice of his mother's oldest brother Charles. "You and Thomas should be able to figure it out."

His mother's voice was rising in pitch. "We'll lose everything Richard made. I never had to worry about money—that was his affair. He just brought it home to me and told me I could spend it how I pleased. He was that generous." She stopped to blow her nose. "I don't know how things have managed to go on since he got sick . . ."

There was a murmur of agreement in the room, then his Uncle Alfred said gruffly, "It's a shame Benjamin isn't alive. He would have been able to run the business."

"It's a shame Thomas doesn't have a head for business," Aunt Eleanor sighed mournfully.

Thomas heard all that he could stand. He'd been living with his parents' disregard for long enough; he'd married to preserve the family name, honor, and business. Now to hear what sounded like his entire family discounting his abilities at the Ironworks—this was too much. He strode the rest of the way down the hall, and stood in the doorway.

The voices died away as they saw him standing there. He could almost hear them wondering how much he'd heard; well, he might as well confirm their suspicions right away.

"Actually, things have gone on quite well since Father's first collapse," he stated slowly. He couldn't believe how very calm his voice sounded to his own ears. "I've managed to meet the payroll without getting us any deeper into debt, got the Mellon boys to extend one of our big loans without increasing our interest rate, and I may have found a new buyer. Which, may I point out, is an awful lot like pulling off a miracle when other places are closing their doors and sending their workers home. I do rather well on my own, actually. I don't need any of you to come hold my hand.

"Olympus Ironworks is mine now. I'm the only one in this room who's invested an entire life in it. In iron. Not steel, mother. It's iron. Great flaming red-hot gobs of pig iron."

"It's not just about making iron, kiddo," his Uncle John pointed out quietly. "You've got to know how to sell it, too."

"And how else do you suppose I was finding new buyers—in a market like this?" Thomas asked, even more quietly. "I'm not making iron and heaving it into the Mon River. Give me the smallest modicum of credit, for once!"

He glared around the silent room, hating every single face he laid eyes upon. "Let's get something straight, right now. Every one of you who has stock in Olympus Ironworks can sell it to me. I've got the money to buy out the lot of you. And frankly, I don't need to be saddled with the interference of a bunch of inattentive ingrates who haven't the slightest idea what I'm doing."

He was out of air. He took a deep breath and continued, "I expect to see a stack of shares on my desk when I return to MY office at the Olympus Building tomorrow morning." His voice had dropped to little more than a whisper, but even he could feel the air crackling around him as he spoke. "Since that's your opinion of my head for business, I want you all out. You will have your checks by tomorrow afternoon. I suggest you be prompt. You don't want me to have to come find you in order to buy out your share in MY company." He looked around at the assembled faces one last time, turned on his heel, and walked out of the parlor.

There was laughter floating out of the music room, and he recognized one of the voices as Meredith's. He marched down the hallway, his heels echoing loudly in his ears. Meredith was sitting at the harp, while his cousin Lily and Albert's wife, Constance, were sitting together on the piano bench. It was actually sort of a pretty tableau, but his particular dislike of the music room and his current anger wouldn't let him acknowledge the fact.

"Meredith," he grunted from the doorway. "Say good night. We're leaving."

The blue eyes took one look at him, and for once there was no incomprehension in them. Without a word, she stood the harp upright and rose to her feet. Constance sprang up as well.

"I'll put the cover back on for you, Merry," she offered meekly, glancing nervously at Thomas.

Thomas turned on his heel and marched to the front door. He realized that he could hear no sound coming out of the parlor yet.

It was a silent ride home. The only sound came from the horses. The harness bells jangled loudly in the crisp air, their hooves crunched on the snow, and they snorted an occasional commentary to each other. Thomas folded his arms and stared stonily in front of him, aware of the nervous attention of the other two people in the sleigh, and ignoring it.

What exactly was he going to do now? He knew with great certainty that he wanted his family out of Olympus Ironworks. How the hell was he going to get them out? They weren't going to simply sign their shares over to him. How the hell was he going to pay for all those shares? Yeah, he could manage them if he'd had some time to plan for this. But paying for them all by tomorrow afternoon? How could he have said anything so stupid?

Well, no doubt the family was busily talking now about how he'd become unhinged by his father's death, and they'd be trying to drive HIM out of Olympus Ironworks. He'd put up a good fight, first. Of course, he'd have to find a new lawyer. Under the circumstances, he couldn't exactly use Henry Baldwin!

He was mentally trying to calculate how much money it would take to buy out everyone in the family when the sleigh came to a stop. He looked up in surprise. They were home.

Leaving George to wait for Meredith to finish fiddling with the lap robes so he could help her down, he stepped out onto the carriage block and strode across the walkway to the front door. Meredith was at his elbow by the time he got the door unlocked, so he opened it and held it for her to pass. Joseph hadn't heard them come in, so Thomas removed Meredith's cloak for her. She stood waiting while he threw down his gloves, muffler, and bowler, undid the overcoat buttons, and hung his overcoat next to her cloak. He wasn't sure what she was waiting for. When he finished, he turned and headed for the stairs.

His foot was on the first step when Meredith spoke. "Thomas, I'm sorry."

He stopped and looked quizzically at her. For what? He thought, but he only stared down at her solemn face looking up at him over the banister.

"I shouldn't have been laughing, so soon after your father's funeral," she apologized meekly, dropping her eyes guiltily and toying with the lace on her dress. "Lily and Constance and I just wanted to, um, well, we wanted to get away from the rest of the family for a while. We didn't think there would be any harm in playing some music. But Lily and Constance are both very out of practice, and so their piano duet was absolutely horrible, and it was quite funny," Meredith's voice was rising in pitch with a suppressed giggle. "But we shouldn't have been laughing. I mean, what would people think? I didn't mean to disgrace you in front of your family, Thomas. I understand why you're angry with me. I'm very, very sorry."

Thomas sighed. Of course she had no idea why he was angry. He looked down at her penitent face, and found that, at the moment, he couldn't quite dislike her. What do you know, she was capable of both sensitivity and decency.

He tried to rise to the occasion, although he felt capable of neither decency nor sensitivity at the moment. "I wasn't angry with you, Meredith. It's complicated, but it had nothing to do with the three of you hiding away in the music room. I certainly can't blame you for wanting to find a respite from this gigantic tribe you married into. I'm sorry to drag you away when you three were having such a good time. There's no need for you to apologize to me."

"Really?" Her face brightened considerably.

"Really. Now, if you'll excuse me, Mrs. Baldwin, I have some thinking to do. Good night."

"Good night, Thomas," she answered happily.

****

Thomas woke up in a very strange mood the next morning. How could he possibly have lost his temper with his family like that? The next moment, he was thinking indignantly that it was about time he put his family in their place. He was half afraid, at some moments, that his family would take him at his word and give him the shares. How in the world would he come up with the money? By Monday afternoon? Impossible. Then he was grimly planning how he was going to come up with the money, and what he was going to say to any family members who didn't sell him their shares.

The rapidly changing emotions and attitudes plagued him all through breakfast and during the long carriage ride in to the Olympus Building. He simply grunted when George said he'd be around to pick him up "at the usual time." He barely acknowledged the greetings of his employees who all had a word to say to him as he walked in.

And then—he stopped dead still as he walked through his office door and saw his desk. There in a neat pile in the middle of his desk, were his family's shares.

They did it. They took him at his word.

He sat down heavily in his chair, and spread the certificates out in front of him. He needed to have gotten angry with them earlier. He was absolutely stunned. They had respected his wishes, and given up their shares. It was now his company.

Which he now had to take care of! He had to come up with the money! Well, it wasn't the first time he'd been to the banks with his hat in his hand, begging. He should be used to it by now. Heck, he was an old hand at it.

He was aware of the stares of his employees as he headed back out the door, not having stayed long enough to even take off his hat. Naturally, he was too late to catch George, who had already turned the carriage around and headed for home. Well, it must be a nice day for a walk.

Chapter 24

It was his. Olympus Ironworks was all his. His to change, to nurture, or to destroy with bad decisions or other mistakes.

Well, actually, it belonged more to a collection of banks than it did to him, but Thomas refused to think in such unromantic terms right now.

It took until 3:00 in the afternoon to pay the visits, get the loans, and send out the money to his relatives. On the other hand, it ONLY took him until 3:00 in the afternoon. In the aftermath of his father's funeral, every man he sat down with was more generous and helpful than Thomas had ever dreamed possible.

He rested his head on the back of his chair and stared at the tin ceiling of his office. He was in so much debt. You couldn't open up a newspaper without reading over and over again about how bad things were. Companies were struggling to stay afloat. Workers were striking to keep the companies from cutting back on people and overworking the rest. And now—now! In the midst of all this, he'd gone and taken on more debt than he'd ever imagined facing in his life. One strike, and he'd be ruined.

"So, it's true," Regina's voice floated from the doorway.

How could he possibly be surprised to see her standing there? She was his guardian angel. She had a knack for knowing when to appear in his life with a twinkle in her eye and a tidbit of sage wisdom on her lips. Thomas jumped to his feet and hurried to take her wraps.

"What's true?" he asked.

"That you've gone and mortgaged your immortal soul to the Mellons, and kicked your entire family out of Olympus Iron."

Thomas raised his eyebrows. "News travels fast."

"I've told you before. Men like to gossip."

"Hear anything else good?"

"As a matter of fact, yes." Regina settled herself in the chair he offered her, and grinned at him before dropping her head to rummage in her reticule. "I found out the Liberty Bell is going to be in Pittsburgh at the end of January."

Thomas blinked uncomprehendingly a moment. "The what?"

"The Liberty Bell. You know, Philadelphia, American independence, bell that developed a crack in it almost as soon as it was out of the mold . . . . Not our best example of Yankee ingenuity, if you ask me."

"That's because it wasn't made in Pittsburgh," Thomas answered. "Now, why are you telling me about the Liberty Bell?"

"You asked me about what gossip I'd heard. It isn't all about you. And," she presented two tickets with a flourish, "you and I get to go see it. It's on its way to the New Orleans Exposition. The train is going to be stopping in several cities on the way, starting with Pittsburgh. The crowd is probably going to be something awful, but we might as well get a glimpse of it."

"Might as well. Thank you, Regina." Thomas put the two tickets in the top drawer of his desk. "So why did you choose to invite me along? Seems to me you've got other friends you might have invited . . . ."

Her smile made his toes tingle. "I can invite my business partner sometimes, you know," she answered. "Besides, it seems to have done the trick."

"What do you mean?"

"For a couple of minutes, there, you weren't thinking about the fact that you have now mortgaged your entire life to the Mellons."

****

Regina continued to provide distractions to take Thomas' mind off business from time to time. Three years of hard times were mentally exhausting. Bankers were on edge, as the list of failures stretched longer and longer. Anyone involved with the railroad, in retail, in most areas of manufacturing were tightening their belts, reducing wages, combating the strikes, and most likely doing a lot of praying.

Thomas doubted he was ever going to get a decent night's rest again. Even the ordinary necessities of life were difficult for people to afford. Housewives whose husbands were out of work hoarded their pennies carefully and opted for poorer cuts of meat. It was a grand time to own a grocery with a good reputation for sausage.

The glass industry, somehow, had escaped the blight on the rest of the country. New manufacturing processes were coming to fruition, and Regina was expanding her factory as fast as she could. Plate glass had replaced the French cylinder glass in their wintergardens, while her glassblowers and molders were turning out vials, dishware, lamp chimneys; Thomas didn't know what else. He couldn't keep up. Regina must have told him, but sometimes he merely nodded and smiled without absorbing it all.

Busy as she was, she still managed to find time to come at least once a month and coax him away from his offices. These visits usually started with the preamble, "Are you still here?" and ended with an insistent "My treat. I do need an escort, you know." Somewhere in between was an invitation likely to be either amusing, or confounding, or both. Regina possessed a restless intelligence that refused to confine itself to business any more than she could stay confined by traditional feminine pursuits. She dabbled, quietly, in politics, and he wasn't at all surprised, when he took her to a round of President Cleveland's inaugural parties, that she was rather well-known among the ranking Democrats. Amusing, considering the number of Republicans with whom she associated. She also possessed a keen curiosity for physical activities, and together they bought roller skates and explored the new craze for "rinking." That spring, they investigated the new Rover Safety Bicycles coming over from England.

This last, he assumed, was an excuse to be closer to Charles. Both men escorted her to Pittsburgh Fire Arms Company, the big retailer for sporting goods over on Fifth Avenue, and assisted in her selection. The new design was so much more reliable than the tall bicycles they'd been riding, the two men ended up investing in new Rovers as well. Depression be damned, a man still needed to break out and have fun sometimes.

Always, the specter of their relationship haunted him, and he frequently fought the urge to ask why he was providing escort, instead of her lover. He assumed it had something to do with preventing society's tongues from wagging too readily. Or maybe Charles couldn't get away from Elizabeth. Thomas never bothered to ask for permission from his wife. He simply kept his appointments and watched Meredith sulk the next day if she found out where he'd been. It was nice, in a way. If she decided to sulk, it was quiet in the house. Thomas had always had the distinct impression that Elizabeth held a great deal more power over Charles than Meredith did over him.

The first time the three of them went cycling on their new safety bicycles, Charles noted the time and they turned their wheels toward his home. He looked so hunted, Thomas felt he needed to do something for his friend. "Do you want me to come in, explain you were helping me with my new cycle?" Thomas asked.

"No, no. That won't help. But thanks." Charles gave an unhappy shrug, and left.

Thomas and Regina remounted and peddled along in silence for a moment, then Thomas commented, "I don't understand why he's so afraid of her."

"I asked him that once, myself." Regina volunteered. "He said, 'you don't understand how unpleasant she can be.'"

They rode along in silence for a moment. "Well, it's certainly no surprise that she's unpleasant. I hadn't thought about how bad it could get if she really tried."

Regina shook her head. "I wouldn't put up with it. She's as odious as she is because he lets her. If he stood up for himself, stopped letting her wipe her feet on him like a doormat, his life would be a lot less unpleasant. I don't know why, but he doesn't have the courage to fight back. Or the will. So she gets worse, and he looks more unhappy, and he'll try even harder to appease her, and she'll get more demanding . . . . It's a vicious circle."

"You don't know what it's like, living in a marriage you don't want to be in," Thomas could sympathize more easily with his friend than Regina. "It's hard to keep sane, some days. There's this person you have to live with, always under your roof, always making demands . . ." Thomas' voice trailed away. "Some days, you get tired of fighting," he finished.

"Serves you both right for not beating your respective wives with buggy whips," Regina shook her head at him.

Regina wouldn't—couldn't understand. The emotional exhaustion. The feeling of hopelessness. The days when you woke up and realized you didn't have any dreams left. That this was all there was to life: working, sleeping, escaping where and when you could from a pair of eyes that always looked at you with reproach.

"Beating wouldn't help. I'd still be married to Meredith," Thomas sighed.

"You're right. Elizabeth would be improved with sufficient beating. Meredith? Beating wouldn't make her any more intelligent. Or less selfish and vain. Sorry dear," Regina frowned at him, "you are in an even more complicated predicament. Unless you have her put in an asylum. I hear tell that's an extremely effective way of getting free of an undesirable wife."

The thought of Meredith locked away did actually make Thomas smile. "That wouldn't be much of a solution. Even if I found the perfect woman, the best I could offer her is dishonor. I'd still be married."

"At least you'd get rid of the daily fighting," Regina pointed out. Thomas couldn't tell if she were serious or not.

"What a wicked little temptress you are!" Thomas exclaimed.

The smile Regina gave him was definitely wicked. "Why, thank you."

"But I can't have Meredith locked away. It isn't decent."

Her smile shifted from positively sinful to fondly sympathetic. "And you are, above all things, the soul of decency."

"Thanks, I think." Thomas wasn't sure he liked the description. "You make me sound so boring and Puritan."

"Sorry, Sir Thomas. But if you want me to describe you as a no-account ruffian, you're going to have to try a lot harder."

Always the same story. No matter how he tried, when he was doing his best, somehow it still wasn't good enough.

****

A month later, Thomas got the chance to repay Regina's efforts at cheering him up.

The porch rocking chairs were Thomas' second-favorite place at the South Fork club. After being in a rowboat on the lake, of course. It gave him the perfect vantage point for observing the comings and goings of all the members. More than once he was an audience for the rehearsals of various melodramas, put on by the ever-larger pack of young adults who were endlessly inventive in their amusements. He even consented to be the lead villain in one of them, delighting the lot of them when he appeared for the performance with his beard shaved off and his mustache waxed into long, sinister handlebars. Meredith had been horrified enough by the change that he decided to keep the style for a while. At least until he got heartily sick of having his mustache melt in the summer heat.

Other times, the porch was blissfully quiet. Members would be walking, or napping, or boating, and the quiet was only disturbed by a mountain breeze, or the distant gleeful yells of the younger lads off swimming.

Thomas was enjoying one of those moments of pure solitude, happy in the knowledge that Meredith was spending the next fortnight with her mother on a trip to visit relatives in Cincinnati, Ohio. The entire domestic staff was as giddy as he was with her absence. To celebrate, he dismissed every last one of them over Saturday and Sunday, and left early on Friday evening for Conemaugh Lake. Since

Charles couldn't join him until later, he'd gone out fishing alone Saturday morning, and caught several bass within an hour of a rather glorious sunrise.

He'd come back in time for breakfast, declined invitations to join in a few different excursions, and deposited himself in the hammock someone had strung across the porch. He was sorry to hear the crunch of carriage wheels on the road; hopefully the new arrival would not be female, so he wouldn't be compelled to stand up. Courtesy sounded like such an inconvenience when one was stretched out and swinging gently in a hammock.

The sentiment flew out of his mind at the first words from the new arrival.

"Careful!" Regina Waring's voice groaned. "Oh, I know we're informal up here, but I do wish we had a carriage block. Ahhhhh!" She let out a cry of pain.

Thomas was on his feet immediately. "Regina? Good Lord, what happened?"

"Good day to you, Sir Thomas. Your timing is as miraculous as ever. I would seem to be in need of some rescue." Sitting with her legs dangling over the edge of the carriage, she looked at him ruefully, and lifted her skirts.

Her left foot was a huge, white bundle of bandages. "Good Lord!" he repeated, looking up into her face, which was almost as white as her foot. "What happened?"

"I went rinking last night," she answered. "They had a ladies' competition, so I entered the derby."

Thomas couldn't help but laugh. "They had a girls' race?"

Regina glared at him. "I don't see anything wrong with that. I'm sure I'll hear plenty of lecture from Charles, so don't you start."

Thomas held up his hands to protest his innocence. "I didn't say there's anything wrong with a ladies' race. I'm just sorry I missed it." He looked down at her foot. "I'm sure it was terribly dramatic, considering the outcome."

A ghost of a smile tugged at her mouth. “I wish there was a better story to go with the outcome. A young lady in front of me tripped, I couldn’t avoid her, two others behind me couldn’t avoid me, and in the end there were five of us in a very unladylike pile on the floor. One of the unfortunate ones who fell on me caught my foot as she landed on me. Doctor Oldshue happened to be there with his grandchildren. He examined me right there and told me it’s probably broken.” Her face twitched with pain as she shifted a little. “It sure hurts enough.”

“So what are you doing, coming up here with a broken foot?” Thomas asked, glad to see her, but appalled at the idea of her riding the train in this condition.

“Escaping the heat. You think it’s hot enough to want to escape the city when you’re perfectly healthy? Try breaking something.” The driver of the carriage, an awkward farm lad named Kendall, had finished dragging the carpetbags off the back of the carriage, and came around to Regina with a pair of crutches. “Thank you, Mr. Kendall. Why don’t you put those right here. Would you mind, terribly, going inside and recruiting some help getting my bags up to my room?”

Kendall nodded and disappeared up the steps and into the clubhouse. “And you, Sir Thomas,” Regina continued, “I don’t suppose I could convince you to help me down?”

Thomas thought of the stairs into the clubhouse, the stairs up to the rooms, the stairs along the wooden boardwalks. “Help you down, help you up, you don’t need a knight right now, My Lady, I think you need a horse.”

Regina laughed, but the amusement died and her face turned even whiter as he scooped her up and carried her straight from the carriage to one of the rockers on the front porch.

****

Installed on the front porch, Regina simply had to stay put and hold court. Thomas dedicated as much time as he could to dancing attendance upon her. He had a fair amount of competition; most of the "young folk" in residence moved their games to the porch, so that they could include her. Dr. Hussey brought cards. The servants kept her endlessly supplied with tea and cookies in between mealtimes.

When Charles arrived, Thomas feared he'd lose his place as her pet knight. Elizabeth immediately put an end to his fears. She seemed to be in particularly high dudgeon: every single man, woman, or child that attempted to talk to Charles got interrupted by Elizabeth, calling Charles away to carry a basket, or tend to their son, or fetch her shawl, or return her shawl to their room.

When Thomas asked whether he could be excused from their morning fishing excursion, since he was loathe to leave Regina, Elizabeth found another opening for heaping abuse on Charles' head.

"You see how considerate Mr. Baldwin is?" She gave him one of those flattering smiles that Thomas particularly disliked. "Why can't all men be so considerate?"

She didn't think Charles was being so considerate when she caught him bringing Regina a selection of books to choose from. "Hasn't she got enough people bothering her, without you adding to it?"

"It's not a bother," Regina piped up, wincing as she leaned forward to defend her lover. "He was being thoughtful. People are making such a fuss about me, I thought if I had some reading, people would stop feeling they need to keep me entertained."

"I'm sure no one's fussing over you more than you deserve," Elizabeth answered with the phoniest show of concern Thomas had ever seen. "You poor thing. It must kill you to sit there. Let us know if we can be of any help."

"Your excellent husband did help—by bringing me something to read," Regina thanked her steadily.

It was fascinating, watching the interaction between two women who must despise each other. He wondered from that exchange if Elizabeth knew about Regina and Charles. It was all the more confusing, then, when the Philander Knoxes arrived on Saturday evening. The pretty Mrs. Knox had gotten her skirts entangled on a nail of the porch rail, and Charles, being closest, had assisted her.

After Charles' moment of gallantry, Elizabeth began glaring at him silently. At first, Charles attempted to continue to interact normally with the laughing, joking crowd, but Thomas noticed he quickly stopped playing with the young folks altogether and sat quietly on the porch steps.

Eventually, Elizabeth got up from her rocking chair, and left without bidding goodnight to anyone. Thomas watched as Charles squared his shoulders, took a breath, and quietly said goodnight.

Since dusk was falling, the porch was slowly emptying. The remaining occupants were soon embarrassed into complete silence, as they all got to hear why Elizabeth had been glaring at Charles.

"So did you enjoy looking at her ankles?"

"What are you talking about?"

"Mrs. Knox. I noticed you had to be the one to go pull on her skirts."

"I was the closest, Lizzie."

"You were not—you just ran the fastest. So did you enjoy looking at her ankles? And her petticoats? See any leg while you were at it?"

"I didn't notice, Lizzie. I saw the lace of her skirt was caught on a nail that wasn't properly nailed into a board over there along the railing. I was too busy trying not to tear the lace to notice anything else."

"Sure—you hadn't noticed her at all. Just like you didn't notice anyone else around who could have helped her. You had to jump up and do it. You should have considered my feelings before making a spectacle of yourself! You know I get jealous. Lillie Knox, of all people! How could you be so thoughtless! How very funny, Mrs. Waring calling you thoughtful today. You're the most thoughtless husband any woman could have!"

"Lizzie," Charles' voice floated miserably out of the window.

"Oh, you men think that because you own the world, you can do whatever you want! Well, Robbie isn't going to grow up like you.

I tell him every day that when he grows up, I don't want him to be anything like you."

The transfixed eavesdroppers on the porch began to stir, whisper goodnight, and disappear into the darkness.

"I need to attempt some sleep. Would you please hand me my crutches, Sir Thomas?" Regina whispered to Thomas, who had been sitting on the floor beside her.

Thomas was glad to be distracted from the awful, belittling conversation that was still going on above.

"I can offer better than your crutches, My Lady." He scrambled to his feet, bent over the chair and ottoman upon which Regina had spent the entire day, and slipped his arms behind her shoulders and under her knees. "I can offer you delivery service, if I may be so ungentlemanly as to suggest it." Elizabeth's jealous words came back, and he continued with grim humor, "I promise not to notice your ankles."

Regina caught up her crutches from against the wall, and sighed against Thomas as he carried her inside. "My ankles aren't as nice as Lillie Knox's."

He couldn't help but chuckle. "I wouldn't know." He carefully mounted the steps, trying not to jostle Regina as he went. Despite his care, she whimpered a little. "I'm sorry. I'm trying to be careful."

"I know you are," she answered.

They were both silent a moment, while he carefully moved upward.

"I understand better, now," he volunteered.

"What's that?" she asked.

"Why it happened." He stopped in front of her door, uncertain what to do next. She reached out to turn the knob, and pushed open the door to her room. He stepped through the door, mindful of the bandaged foot, and deposited her gently on the bed.

"Why what happened?"

"You and him. You're his escape, aren't you?"

She smiled sadly. "I try to be. I try to show him what a woman's love is supposed to be. It's about support, not control. About working together toward a common goal, not hiding your soul in an attempt to shelter some part of yourself from destruction."

Thomas' throat closed over at her description. He wanted to know what it felt like to be loved like that.

"He's changing; he's closing in on himself," Regina continued. "He shuts down. Look at tonight. He doesn't want to fight back—I think she must make a lot of threats that involve Robbie. I suspect he's so afraid for his son, he won't do anything to defend himself." She sighed, and threw up her hands. "That boy has been a weapon since Elizabeth became with child. I feel sorriest for Robbie—he hasn't got a chance in this world. His mother will ruin him, and his father lacks the courage to stop her."

Thomas looked at Regina. "Kind of a grim prediction, isn't it?"

Regina nodded. "Oh, yes. But as Henry used to say, I'm never wrong about people. Sometimes I wish I were. But it hasn't happened yet."

Thomas looked down at her. If you're never wrong about people, when are you going to figure me out? He wondered silently. Aloud, he simply asked, "Shall I send for your maid? Is there anything else I can do for you tonight, My Lady?"

"No, Sir Thomas, you've done more than enough for me today. I'm terribly grateful to you. I don't know how I'm going to manage the rest of the fortnight without you."

"Fortnight?"

"If I'm going to have to convalesce for a while, I might as well do it away from the heat. I'm staying here for the fortnight. Doctor Oldshue thought fresh air might help me recover more quickly."

Thomas chuckled, and reached out to kiss her hand. "I'm quite sure you will make a recovery as quickly as is humanly possible, My Lady."

"You flatter me, Sir Thomas."

"Always, My Lady."

"Good night, Thomas."

"Good night, Regina."

As he pulled the door shut behind him, Thomas knew the image of her lying back in bed would be etched into his memory for a long time.

Chapter 25

As much as Thomas did not have a lot of patience for his mother's ostentatiously hypocritical grief, he did begin to develop a sense of pity, watching her mope around, full of stories of everything his father used to do for her.

She had never said a nice thing to, or about, his father while he was alive. Thomas heard the oft-repeated refrain, "Richard never does anything for me," not solely from his mother, but as a well-known mantra throughout the distaff side of his family.

Now that his father had joined Benjamin among the ranks of the sacred dead, his mother moaned for her loss, and talked to anyone who would listen about what an unselfish good provider her husband had been. "Richard always took care of that" became her favorite expression. She played up the theatrics for all she was worth—now she had a son AND a husband to glorify. No doubt if he, himself, got run over by a streetcar tomorrow, he would suddenly transform into her favorite son, her only consolation. She'd find something marvelous about him posthumously.

Thomas pitied her inability to appreciate people while they were with her. They needed to die to gain her love. If, indeed, there was any love buried among the theatrics. Perhaps there was no room in his mother's heart for anyone but his mother. That was worth pitying, too.

She had taken to visiting him at the office at least once a week, coincidentally in time for him to take her to dinner. Usually at William Lang's crowded little restaurant on Diamond Street. Not only was it considered terribly stylish, they always remembered to give her an extra pat of butter for her bread, so it was her favorite place to go.

At least the long face and plaintive sighs meant she was complaining less. Of course, she couldn't complain about his father, anymore. She seemed to be complaining less about everything else, too. She used to keep up running monologues, and all he had to do was make an occasional noise to indicate that he was still listening. Whether he was or not didn't actually matter.

Now, he could sit across from her at the table, or next to her in the carriage, and the silence hung in the air between them. It wasn't a comfortable, companionable silence—it was just empty silence. Thomas wondered what on earth he could possibly say. He felt like she expected him to say something, but he had no idea what.

He wasn't "up" on gossip about family members or neighbors, the only thing he knew about the latest fashions came from observing them on Regina Waring's delectable figure. His mother's grief seemed the opposite of Regina's: the latter's had been a very private grief, which she tried to conceal. His mother wore her grief very publicly, loudly sniffling and sighing with the trappings of her black wardrobe on display, but for all the self-pity, she wasn't in the sort of pain Regina had been in.

Still, as the only member of her immediate family, he ought to do something. Maybe, even though the circumstances were different, he ought to suggest the same cure to his mother that he'd suggested to Regina—travel. It seemed ridiculous to suggest. He couldn't imagine his mother enjoying Europe. Well—closer to home, then.

The idea hit him—South Fork! The upcoming regatta ought to prove an entertaining diversion. If he could send Meredith off to stay at the Club, why not send his mother, too? They might as well have each other for company. "Mother," he began rather tentatively. He hadn't the foggiest idea how his suggestion might be received. "Have you thought about getting out of Pittsburgh for a little while this summer? It might do you some good to get out of the heat and the smoke for a bit."

"I suppose," his mother sighed. "But where would I go? No one invites me anywhere."

"Well, it has only been eight months since Father died. Everyone respects your privacy," Thomas soothed. "Now I'm inviting you up to the Laurel Highlands for a little fresh air. The club is holding a regatta next Saturday. There will be boat races in the afternoon, and a lantern procession and fireworks in the evening. It should be quite beautiful."

"I suppose there would be no harm in watching."

It sounded like a cautious approval of his idea, so Thomas continued. "If you like, you could stay up there for a full fortnight. My membership privileges allow me to have guests for that long."

"What would I do up there?" Thomas couldn't tell from his mother's flat voice if this was a sign of interest or of protest.

"What everyone else does," Thomas actually wasn't quite sure what the ladies of the club did. He wasn't sure that any of them actually fished. "Relax. Enjoy the cool air." That ought to sound appealing, he thought, as they sat in the summer furnace that was downtown Pittsburgh. "There's acres of beautiful woods; you can walk around as little or as much as you like. If you want to take a picnic with you instead of eat at the clubhouse, we've got a fabulous chef; I'm sure he can send you with something you'd enjoy, but wouldn't be hard to carry."

"That sounds nice enough," his mother answered cautiously. "So who goes up there?"

"The Clarkes, the Hornes, the Irwins, the Rankins," Thomas wasn't really sure what families were going to be there. "Clay Frick and Andy Carnegie both have shares, but they're rarely there. I don't know why they bother keeping their memberships. And Meredith will be there, of course. She'll go up before me. You could travel with her . . ."

"No," his mother surprised him by interrupting him rather firmly.

He paused a moment, but his mother did not elaborate. "All right," he answered, "um, you can take the train with me that Friday."

He was curious about her reaction. Since his mother didn't usually withhold her opinions, he elected not to pursue the matter.

"So what do you think? Should I write the secretary to see if I can get a room for you?"

"Might as well," his mother sighed another one of her tragic sighs. "I'm not doing anything else, after all."

Well, it wasn't a vote of enthusiasm, but Thomas supposed it was a sort of victory.

****

He was less sure it was a victory when he brought his mother to the train station, to discover Regina was also waiting for the same train! Spending the trip looking at Regina would be paradise. Trying to look at Regina with his mother demanding his attention? That sounded less than idyllic.

He escorted his mother to a seat in the noisy waiting room, opposite Regina. She had propped up the mending foot along one of the hard wooden benches and leaned against a single crutch as she read The Crockery and Glass Journal, with her usual concentration. Thomas had leaned forward and was about to pluck the paper from her hand when she finally looked up and saw him. "Thomas!"

"Must be fascinating reading," he chuckled.

"Always is," she answered, letting her smile cover both Thomas and his mother. "Are you catching the Day Express, too? Fabulous!"

Their timing couldn't have been better: the announcement was made, and Thomas ushered both women through the bustle of people boarding the Day Express for Johnstown. They procured seats in the first-class car, and settled in for the ride to the Laurel Highlands.

Thomas could see Regina's foot was still troubling her a great deal. She was, however, made of stern stuff. She chatted easily with his mother about the mixed blessings of train travel. Thomas was happy to let her take over the task of trying to draw his mother out in talk. When they started discussing the latest fashions, he considered himself dismissed from any expectation of his participation in the conversation.

Maybe this wouldn't be too bad of a trip, after all, he thought. While the two women were absorbed in their conversation, neither would notice if he sat there silently, staring at Regina, drinking in the details. Even the silly tall hats that seemed to be in this year looked fetching when perched above Regina's dark hair, and she looked as curvaceous as ever in the tight bodice of her striped navy blue traveling suit. Her eyes would flick in his direction once in a while, as if to check that he was content, left out of the conversation as he was. He smiled encouragingly at her, hoping she'd understand.

She seemed to. She gaily told his mother about the anticipated events at the regatta, described the beauty of the lake, the comforts of the new clubhouse, repeated his favorable review of the chef. Before they knew it, the train was rounding the bend along the Conemaugh River and crossing the stone bridge into Johnstown.

Thomas knew that Regina was a native of Johnstown, and wondered if they were going to be deprived of her company on the rest of the trip up to South Fork. Sure enough, she sat up on the seat, checked to make sure her hat was properly secured, and reached for her crutch.

"I'm sorry to have to leave you here, but I need to check on a few things in town before I come up to the lake. Family business. I'll take the last train to South Fork this evening."

Thomas jumped up from his seat. "Let me help you off the train. Sometimes these depots have an awfully big step."

"Thank you, Sir Thomas." The train rolled to a stop, and passengers began to disembark. Thomas excused himself to his mother and saw to it that Regina made it safely down to the platform. She was still moving slowly on the one crutch, and they hadn't been on the platform long when the whistle sounded, and he was forced to reboard the train. "Are you going to be alright?" he asked her before taking his leave.

"I shall be," she answered.

"I'll send a coach for you tonight." He couldn't linger any longer; the conductors were already on board. He leapt onto the bottom step, seconds before the train started moving. He gave her a jaunty wave, then headed back for his seat, knowing his mother would be fretting.

"I thought you were leaving me stranded on this train," she observed tragically as he regained his seat.

A little more asperity and she'd be sounding like the mother he used to know. "No, Mother, I wouldn't dream of abandoning you to the mercies of the Pennsylvania Railroad. As you see, I'm here to take care of you."

"You sound like Benjamin when you say that," she sighed plaintively. "He always loved me and said such sweet things."

Nice to know his reassurances were so appreciated. He was so tired of trying. It didn't seem worth his efforts to do anything thoughtful for his mother. On the other hand, what bigger praise did she have than to compare him to Benjamin?

"Yes," was all he said aloud. "Yes, he did."

The rest of the journey up to South Fork was traveled in silence. He was glad to step out onto the train platform of the little hillside town, and have the distraction of getting bags loaded onto the carriage that would take them up to the lake.

The drive from the railroad station to the club never really needed any conversation. The road curved through the idyllic forests; mountain laurel half-hid intriguing rock formations under a green canopy, wafted by gentle summer breezes. It was slightly north of the Laurel Highlands, but the romantic name still suited the terrain. From time to time, the underbrush cleared enough to give glimpses of South Fork Creek, trickling back toward South Fork and the Little Conemaugh River. At last, the horses turned onto the road that went right over the dam itself.

It was possibly the single best view of Conemaugh Lake. The lake ended—or, more accurately, started—below them, and spread back out among the trees. Farm clearings dotted the surrounding hills. About halfway across, the cottages of the club could be seen, contentedly looking over the tops of the boathouses onto the sparkling waters. Several boats were on the lake; no doubt several of Saturday's contestants were practicing for their various races. Thomas liked watching the sailboats gliding across the water. Maybe next summer he'd talk Charles into taking some time away from fishing in one of the club's rowboats and learning how to sail.

All too soon, the dam had been crossed and the cart rolled up in front of the clubhouse. "Well, Mother," he said with his best charming smile, "welcome to my home away from home."

"About time we got here," his mother sighed. "What a long drive."

"Well, you'll get a chance to stretch your legs here," Thomas answered patiently as he handed her down from the carriage. "Let's see about getting you comfortable."

'Comfortable' would be something of a misnomer. The clubhouse was filled to capacity because of the regatta festivities, and his mother had been assigned to one of the smaller rooms without a view of the lake on the back side of the building. Her complaints and the unsuitability of the room earned the baleful stare of Mr. Boyer, the superintendent of the house and grounds.

"I'm sure you don't mean to seem ungrateful, ma'am," he answered quietly. "But the club is full of members. Since you are a guest of one of the members, we did go to some trouble to make accommodations for you . . ."

"Oh, Thomas didn't tell me I was being a burden," his mother interrupted him with a particularly tragic sigh. "If I'd known I was being a burden, I wouldn't have come."

"Then why don't you take my place in the front room, Mother," Thomas offered. "I'll sleep in the back room."

"Thank you, Mr. Baldwin," Mr. Boyer was still eyeing Eugenia Baldwin with poorly-veiled dislike. "That's very gallant of you."

Thomas shrugged. "She's my mother. Whatever makes her happy."

He didn't bother to mention that by putting his mother in his room, he could avoid having to share a room with Meredith. He'd been wondering how he was going to manage that particular situation; most years he simply avoided going up to the lake during the twelve days when Meredith was allowed to be a guest. Membership did have its privileges . . . and its limitations happened to be rather useful.

So, in making his mother happy, he'd also get to make himself happy. It was a rare accomplishment.

****

Knowing it would take quite some time for his mother to change out of her traveling dress and get settled, Thomas didn't see the need to linger upstairs. He loved the new addition to the clubhouse. It was twice as big as the original structure, and Thomas felt a lot more thought had gone into its design and construction. Despite the drastic increase in size, there was still a coziness about the building. The wide halls and staircases were well-built for the occasional horde of children running through (Thomas had to agree the banisters begged to be slid upon), and could easily accommodate any excess of fashion the female mind could dream up.

After a stroll up and down the wooden boardwalk to see the growing number of cottages being built along the lake, Thomas installed himself in one of the rockers, watching carts and carriages pull in with more members coming for the weekend.

The entire membership of the club came for the festivities. There was a cheerful excitement in the air. A pack of young adults were good-naturedly teasing each other about their upcoming races, and young Louis Clarke, the teenaged skipper of the steam-powered yacht Mountain Belle, seemed to be under perpetual assault as the organizer of the lantern regatta that preceded the fireworks.

Without thinking about it, he had established himself where he could see when Regina arrived. He really ought to consider finding some new hobbies. The afternoon seemed to slide away and before he knew it, Regina's carriage was coming along the lake. When he helped her out of the carriage, he couldn't imagine the hobby that might replace her. Her trim waist was enhanced by the bit of red piping on her navy blue suit, her dark eyes sparkled with life, her low laugh still sent shivers through him.

He realized he'd been staring at her without listening when she cocked her head a little to the side and looked at him quizzically. "I'm sorry—say that again—I was thinking about you, and not listening to you just now."

"And what were you thinking?" she asked with another one of her laughs. She couldn't possibly know what that laugh of hers did to him. "What could possibly be more interesting than listening to me babble about travel inconveniences?"

"I was thinking," he started, handing over her crutch and standing back so she could climb the porch steps, "how wonderful it is to compare the sight of you right now to the sight of you a scant four years ago. I didn't think I'd ever hear you laugh again."

He was sorry for speaking up when a shadow of grief passed over her features. But then she smiled up at him so warmly, any fear of saying the wrong thing evaporated. "I needed time to mourn, but healing was inevitable. Life is too interesting to live in quiet desperation." The corner of her mouth twitched. "Brief moments of loud, screaming desperation, certainly." The humor fell away from her face, and she looked into his eyes earnestly. "Without you, the healing process would have been much more difficult. I've thanked you before, Thomas, but I thank you again. I'm surrounded by a lot of people. But there aren't many I'm as close to as I am to you. I'm not exactly your average American girl. You understand all my quirky bluestocking ways and accept me as I am. I don't have to censor myself, or flirt with you in a blatantly insincere manner to keep you off balance. That's a little unusual."

Thomas didn't quite know what to say. Of course, the lump in his throat wasn't making it easier. "Thank you," he ventured. "No one's ever called me unusual before."

"Their misjudgment," her eyes twinkled up at him. "You're very unusual."

"There you are." Thomas couldn't remember when he'd been less happy to hear his mother's voice. The magic, intimate moment destroyed by three words, he reluctantly turned to face his mother.

"I'm here, Mother, are you settled in?"

"Thomas, you didn't tell me I was sharing a room with your wife." His mother was fairly bristling with dislike.

"This is a resort, Mother, not my private residence. One doesn't do much more than sleep in one's room, so we make do with a lot less space up here."

Before his mother opened up to respond, Regina smoothly interjected, "I need to see if my trunk made it to my room. While you're settling in, I ought to be doing the same."

His mother was seating herself in a rocker, obviously preparing to continue the argument from a sitting position. On impulse, Thomas took told of Regina's hand before she could escape and bent over to kiss it.

"Do you need me to take one of the two women off your hands?" she murmured so softly he could barely hear the words. "I have no roommate."

"No. I'll manage," he replied equally softly.

"All right, then. Good luck. Let me know if you change your mind."

He let go of her hand reluctantly, and, remembering he had his mother as an audience, forced himself not to stand watching Regina hobble into the clubhouse.

"Well, Mother, what would you have me do? You didn't want your room, you don't want my room, there aren't really going to be any other options here. Unless you want me to go knocking on cottage doors to see if the Moorheads or the Clarkes can take you in . . . ."

"No, no, I don't want to be a burden," his mother sighed.

"Then please try to relax and enjoy yourself, Mother," Thomas tried to keep the impatience out of his voice. "Why exactly do you object to Meredith's company? You didn't used to. I seem to recall you were rather insistent that I marry her . . ."

"I didn't know then that there was something—wrong with her," his mother blurted out.

"What do you mean, wrong with her?" Thomas asked. There was so much wrong with Meredith. She was stupid, she was vain, she was self-centered, tiresome, unpleasant; he could think of many things that made her "wrong" for him as a spouse, but he had no idea what his mother was objecting to.

"She's been married to you for ten years, Thomas," his mother pointed out.

Ten years! Dear God, has it been that long? Talk about living a life of quiet desperation . . .

"Yes, Mother, I guess we have," Thomas answered.

"I hadn't been married two years to your father when I presented him with your brother Benjamin," she pointed out, with the usual sigh that accompanied the names of the deceased. "Now it's been ten years. She's obviously never going to present you with any children."

Ah, so that's what's "wrong" with Meredith. No, Meredith certainly wasn't likely to be presenting him with any children. He had no intention of ever getting her pregnant.

"Not everyone has children, you know, Mother. The Warings never had any, and I wouldn't accuse Mrs. Waring of having something wrong with her."

He was a little surprised by his mother's words. "That's not the same. She's—different. Meredith's not. After you were married, I asked where the grandchildren were, and you told me it might take time. Well, ten years is plenty of time."

The idea of having children with Meredith was pretty repulsive. Imagine, a batch of blonde-haired, blue-eyed monsters with her vacuous stare. He was sure if Regina had children, she'd have a girl with her same black hair and intelligent black eyes . . .

He looked earnestly at his mother. "If God doesn't want Meredith to have any children, Mother, that's something you're going to have to accept. It's not Meredith's choice. She has spoken to me about wanting babies." Well, that much was true. "If we don't have any, we don't have any. All people are different. Try not to think that there's something wrong with Meredith." He couldn't believe he'd actually said that. It sounded appallingly close to defending her.

His mother was not mollified. "I've offered to send her to doctors. She won't go. I've given her advice; she won't listen. She's not even trying. Once she even told me it's your fault, not hers. I didn't have much to say to her after that for quite a while, believe me! The nerve, blaming you . . . ."

Thomas had no idea what to tell his mother. Meredith certainly got more than she bargained for, hadn't she? He could almost pity her. Almost. Well, at least her life was as much of a hell as his.

"Maybe it is me, Mother," he suggested wearily. "There's no point assigning blame. If it matters to you, Meredith's or my defects aside, I don't care if I don't have offspring. If you're worried about the immortality of the Baldwin name, I was thinking of leaving the money from my estate to some worthy institution of higher learning. Or I can found an entirely new school. 'The Baldwin College of Metallurgy,' I think Father would have liked that, don't you?"

"Your father would have liked grandchildren," his mother answered.

Thomas doubted that. His father had never shown much interest in his children. Why on earth would he have been interested in grandchildren? He shrugged. "That could be, Mother. A university will last longer. And benefit mankind more. The idea makes me happy. I think that would count for something." His mother was looking at the floor, a stubborn expression on her face. On a moment's inspiration, Thomas continued, "Well, even if you don't approve, Ben would have. That's enough for me."

His mother didn't say any more, but he could see from the look on her face that the matter was far from closed.

Chapter 26

"Darling, are you too busy to lend me an ear for a moment? I—well, I need to talk to you."

Thomas had been so buried in Ian MacDermott's operations report that he hadn't heard Regina rustle into his office. He looked up in surprise, pleased as he realized she'd called him "darling." But as he stood to receive her, the pleasure turned into consternation at the sight of her face.

She looked—odd. She was white, and angry and upset and afraid, but also somehow cynically amused. Nothing in her face matched the casual cheer in her voice.

"Well, of course, My Lady, when am I ever too busy for you? Sit down, please."

She was even moving oddly. She always walked with such mesmerizing grace and purpose. Except of course when she'd broken her foot last summer. Even in the throes of grieving for Henry, she had walked firmly and confidently. Now she seemed lost inside her own body as she drifted into the chair across from his desk.

Thomas studied her for a moment before he sat back down. She sat, staring, at the top of his desk, while Thomas wondered what she was seeing. After a moment's quiet, he prompted softly, "You said you needed to talk—I'm listening."

He didn't expect the first words that came out of her mouth. "I have to leave," she blurted out, looking into his face with such misery in her eyes, he hurt for her sake before the meaning of her words reached his brain.

"Leave Wintergardens?" he asked fearfully, his mind already scrambling for ways to persuade her not to desert him. How could it be Waring-Baldwin Wintergardens without the Waring, his brain was whispering urgently.

Regina frowned and shook her head. "No, no. I have to leave Pittsburgh. Pennsylvania. The whole country. I . . . ." She closed her eyes in frustration as the words failed her, and she took a breath. "I need an entire ocean between me and him . . . ." She stopped again, and looked at her hands in her lap.

Thomas had never seen her so flustered. She flushed red, then turned white again, while several emotions flickered across her face.

"Try again," Thomas suggested, getting up and moving to sit in the chair next to her. He put a finger under her chin and lifted her face until he could look into her endless black eyes. He had the most awful desire to kiss the unhappy mouth, an urge which he sternly ignored. "Where are you going, and why are you going there?"

"Elizabeth McKay is having another baby," she said bluntly, then turned her face away from him and stared out the window. "This shouldn't exactly be a surprise—they're married, after all—but he's told me they hardly have marital relations anymore—though why on earth should I believe that. He must lie to me as much as he lies to her . . ."

"Are you jealous?" Thomas asked, feeling the familiar gnawing in his own stomach that accompanied every discussion of Charles McKay.

Regina seemed surprised by the question. "Of Elizabeth having his baby? Goodness, no. I dislike her thoroughly for the misery she causes him, and the first child made her awful enough. I think it drove him into my arms. But he already has so little time for me, with a second one, there won't be anything left."

She stood up so abruptly, she nearly knocked Thomas in the nose with her shoulder. She paced the room, her arms folded protectively around herself. "I know I'm getting no more than I deserve, dallying with him in the first place. What good did I expect to come out of this?" She stopped pacing in front of the window and looked out. Thomas could swear she was turning away to hide the tears in her eyes.

Thomas cleared his throat while she swallowed hard, unsure whether he should say anything or not. Finally he asked, "So what did he say when he told you?"

She gave an odd, high-pitched laugh and turned to look at him while her hands gestured futilely. "Oh, he said he needed me, the usual nonsense. He says the same things so much, I could recite them. I already wonder if he means any of it anymore. I think we were already drifting apart, and now this."

She looked at him so mournfully, he thought his heart would break. "I'm such an idiot, Thomas," she told him, a rogue tear escaping and running over the edge of her exquisite cheekbone. "I was an idiot to have gotten into this mess in the first place, and I'm an idiot because I'm perfectly aware of the fact that it's already over. It's just a matter of time, and . . ." she gasped for breath, losing the battle against the tide of tears that started spilling more freely now, ". . . and I'm an idiot because even now, I'm so afraid of losing him."

That was his cue to stand up and offer what comfort he could. Without a word, he gathered her in his arms and gently pressed her face against his shoulder.

He could feel the anguish in her body as he held her. Even as he murmured for her to go ahead and cry, he could feel her fighting for control, instead of letting go. Then all at once she seemed to give up and the tears came in torrents.

What a complicated universe we live in, he thought as he held her. His heart ached with her pain, even as he tried not to be elated by the cause of it. If she and Charles were finished, he might have a chance. It didn't matter if he did have a chance; he wasn't free, anyway. He didn't simply want to dally with her, to find out if the skin on her belly was as soft as the skin on her cheek, to hear her sighing in his ear. He wanted to see her dark head across the dining room table every night. He wanted to sit with her in his library, discussing the household finances. He wanted to shop for her anniversary presents, dismiss the maid and help her himself with the clasp on her necklace before they went out to the theatre or a ball.

For now, he'd have to settle for being her confidante, keeping her secrets, holding her while she cried. It wasn't enough. But it was all he had.

"So," he spoke when the soft moaning sounds had subsided and her body seemed to unclench a little, "you're afraid of losing him, but you're choosing to run away, rather than fight back?"

"What sort of fighting back am I supposed to do?" her muffled voice asked from his jacket. "Whine about the fact that I never get to see him anymore?"

"Well, I suppose you could always get pregnant, too." He chuckled as she lifted her face from his chest to give him a look of pure disgust. "You're right. You'd be a terrible mother." He was rewarded by a smile that tugged irresistibly at the corners of her mouth. "So tell me, if you don't want to lose him, why are you running away?"

The shadows fell back across her eyes. "Because I can't stand the pain of staying."

****

Once again, Thomas found himself sending an unhappy Regina away, wishing with all his might that he could have the power to make her happy again. Unwilling to stand the idea of traveling merely for pleasure, Regina wrote up an extensive list of calls she intended to make, in the hopes of finding international business to add to the slightly-dipping sales of the Wintergardens. ("See, this is all my punishment for not working harder to keep sales up through this recession," she joked.) She telegraphed Andrew Carnegie, who was quick to send a response inviting her to his new castle in Scotland.

Thomas was less than thrilled to be sending her off to the Carnegie's hospitality, although his recent marriage to his patient

Louise made him less anxious than it would have if the steel magnate had still been single. Charles was much less happy about it.

"You don't want to intrude upon them; they're newlyweds!" he protested to Regina. She simply ignored his objections. After her departure, Charles was much less diplomatic in spilling out his feelings to Thomas. "I don't care if they are newly married. Andy has always liked Regina. I'm sure of it."

"Of course he likes her. Otherwise presumably he would not invite her to stay with them," Thomas pointed out mildly.

Charles was not amused. "You know what I mean. Louise is a sweet girl, and all, but honestly, she's not Regina. I can't really blame Andy if he does like Regina, how could he help himself, she's the most ravishing woman that's ever been created . . . ."

As Thomas listened to Charles sing Regina's praises, the familiar, gnawing jealousy ate holes through him. Regina's fear was entirely unfounded. Charles worshipped Regina. She was his goddess, his salvation, his escape from an unhappy marriage and business worries that never seemed to end and every other stress in Charles' life. He fretted because he never got to see enough of her. There was never much opportunity anymore. Charles even went so far as to admit he was jealous of Thomas, since the Wintergardens meant Thomas got to see Regina regularly.

"It's just business," he demurred.

"Yeah," Charles grunted. "But you get to talk to her. Listen to her. I get to listen to my wife following me around telling me everything I'm doing wrong."

At least Thomas was spared that. What few hours he actually spent at home, the library doors hid him from Meredith, so she didn't get much opportunity for criticizing.

"I'm sorry, buddy," Charles said contritely with a friendly punch on the arm. "I've made a mess of my life. That's my problem. You certainly manage not to get entangled in moral dilemmas. You're a real brick to listen to me rant like this. I wish I could do something. I feel idiotic and helpless."

"Why don't you write to her?" Thomas heard himself asking. "Tell her how you feel." Oh, so now you're an idiot too, Baldwin, he thought to himself. Why on earth are you giving him romantic advice that might help matters?

"How can I write to her? What possible pretext can I come up with to send her a letter at the Carnegies' . . ." Charles broke off and stared at Thomas for a moment. "But you can."

Thomas wasn't following. "I can what?"

"We said it a little while ago. You can talk to her. You're her business partner. If I give you a letter, will you send it from your office? No one would think anything of it, if you write to her."

Thomas shook his head. "Why can't you send her a letter? You're an old friend from Johnstown. You've spent time together both in Europe and here. You're not the only male friend of hers who will be writing to her while she's gone."

"That may be," Charles didn't look happy about that idea. "But just the same, I don't want her to have to explain my letters. She may be something of an exception, but she's still a lady." His voice turned pleading. "If she's willing to write to me through you, well, that would be more discreet."

Thomas didn't know what to say. Charles was right. A gentleman should always protect a lady's honor. He remembered the pain in Regina's voice, the pretended nonchalance in her posture as he handed her onto her railroad car. He tried to imagine if she'd be happy to hear from Charles, or angry with Thomas for disguising Charles' correspondence under his own stationery. She might be happier left alone, and given time to heal and forget the whole sordid affair.

Whom was he kidding? No matter what excuse he might find for himself, if he wanted to make Regina happy, he'd have to assist Charles in corresponding with her. At least he'd have the reflected glory of once again demonstrating his chivalrous devotion to her. Once again, he'd be her Sir Thomas.

"All right," he sighed out loud. "I'll play telegraph operator. You write your message. I'll address the envelope."

If he asks for help in composing his love letter, Thomas thought as he went to find the appropriate piece of stationery, the deal's off. I can only take so much.

****

He awaited the first letter from Regina to Charles with dread. When it actually came, and he found himself looking at a letter addressed to him lying among his correspondence, he was unsure if he was supposed to open it, or merely pass it along to Charles.

Uncertain, he propped the envelope against the inkwell while he answered his other correspondence. The scrawling handwriting burned holes into his eyes whenever he looked up. When his other letters stood in a tidy stack on his desk, he sat and stared at his name on the prim white envelope. A flash of disgust at this own squeamishness shot through him. The envelope was addressed to him, wasn't it? If he was going to play courier between lovers, they were going to have to learn to communicate with him a little better!

The penknife sliced effortlessly through the envelope. Inside was another sealed envelope with "CM" scrawled on it, and a note with "Thomas" neatly marked out in elegant, swooping scrolls. Thomas unfolded the page.

June 1887
Skibo Castle
Scotland

Hello, Sir Thomas!

Charles has asked me to write to him through you, and tells me you agreed to this proposal. I'm perfectly certain this is a horrible idea, but I'm also, as you can see, weak enough to do it.

I know you're setting aside your personal opinion on account of my possible happiness. I appreciate what a true friend you are! But I know Charles can be very persuasive. If you do not want to be stuck in the middle like this, not another envelope will darken your door (or, at least your desktop). I don't want you to be uncomfortable. Please write to me at the Carnegies', and let me know how I should proceed.

Your grateful and obedient
Regina Waring

Eventually, Thomas realized he was just sitting there, staring at her signature. What was he supposed to do? It felt like she was asking for his permission to carry on with her affair.

He had a choice. He didn't need to be involved. His mind flew back to the pier at the South Fork Hunting and Fishing Club, when she'd poured out the story with such trust in her eyes. He wanted to be her confidante. He would have gladly died a thousand deaths to be in Charles' place! So he certainly couldn't claim the moral high ground she was attributing to him.

As difficult as it would be to act as liaison in this alliance, Thomas knew he wanted to be there for her. One more page of ivory paper emerged from his desk drawer.

July, 1887
Pittsburgh, Penna.
Dearest My Lady,

Being that I am as much now as ever your True Knight, I accept the charge you bestow upon me. My opinion is of no consequence, only, as you have correctly guessed, your happiness. I am ever yours to command.

Humbly,
Thomas Baldwin

He was rather pleased with himself as he signed his name with a flourish. It sounded so dashing and romantic. He wondered if Charles was nearly as clever a writer. He hoped not.

The correspondence that sprang up afterwards was lively and interesting. Regina never sent a note to Charles through Thomas without sending letters directly addressed to Thomas, as well. The letters quickly swelled from brief notes to long missives, especially after she left the newlywed Carnegies and moved on to the Continent. Regina was a colorful writer. Both a wicked sense of humor and an almost childlike sense of wonder illuminated every page.

Sometimes she drew sketches in the margins, or even in the middle of a letter. She would sit at her breakfast table and write him descriptions of the people around her. She described the scenery everywhere she went—sunsets, full moons, night skies full of stars, blue waters and beaches both rocky or white with sand.

Despite the fact that a letter from her also meant a letter to his rival, Thomas watched for her envelopes with eager anticipation. They came with a frequency that was gratifying until Thomas got a stark reminder of the reason for their rapid appearance.

When he opened the envelope and the usual dual contents were pulled out, he found himself staring at the back of Charles' envelope.

It was unsealed.

The flap was crumpled back, exposing part of the letter. When he found himself staring at his own name, it was all over.

His heart was pounding so loudly in his ears that he could barely hear the words in his head as he read:

> *My Ownest One,*
>
> *Now, darling, you sound like you're getting jealous of our friend Thomas! Don't be silly. When I say he writes better letters than you do, I mean he tells me what he's thinking, about what's going on in his life. When I read his letters, I can feel Pittsburgh. I can taste it, smell it, even breathe it.*

I'm surprised at you: Mr. Baldwin just isn't capable of ungentlemanly conduct. He'd be shocked at your implication that he's making love to me in his letters.

Enough on that subject—speaking of making love . . . Rome cries out for your company. After those hot, screaming nights, I long for you in these cool evenings. I'm dying to brave the threat of Roman Fever, like so many lovers do, and meet you in the Coliseum on a starlit night. Or in the Forum or . . . any place. The Seven Hills are full of romantic corners—which are full of lovers. It's hard not to think of you all the time.

Yes, I'm lonely here without you—and no, I'm not coming home. I know you don't understand why a woman who has enough money to live comfortably would seek out all the "indignities," as you say, to go work in a man's world. I like it. You enjoy the power, the prestige, and the dealing. So do I. And don't you dare call me "unwomanly" again for liking it—you've seen me without my corset and combinations—so I know you know better!

I could write to you all night, but then I'd sleep too late to get this in the morning post. (Yes, I'm writing this in my nightdress, impertinent boy!)

Yours most madly,

R

Thomas' chest hurt from his heart pounding so hard. He should feel guilty for reading what wasn't meant for his eyes. (Or was it? Did she purposely leave it unsealed, when he was the subject matter?) He carefully refolded the page, tucked it back inside the envelope, straightened the crumpled flap. He wished he'd traveled abroad, so he could have some idea what it must look like, Regina sitting in some Roman villa, her dark hair spilling over her shoulders lying in contrast against her white nightdress . . .

Stop. If he kept thinking along those lines, he'd go stark raving mad. The picture persisted nonetheless, until other words came back to him and he broke into a smile.

She said he writes better letters than Charles does! The thought of Charles being jealous of him filled him with glee.

The feeling grew when he looked at the pages meant for him. Charles had a one-page note. He—he, Thomas! He looked at the six pages actually meant for him. He read her words with greedy eyes.

> *My dearest Thomas,*
>
> *Your sense of timing is impeccable, as always! Just when I'm feeling most alone and blue and utterly foreign—the post brings me a letter from you!*
>
> *I confess to you I've been most homesick of late. I fell upon your letter like a creature possessed, and read it over several times before I put it down. You have a gift with words, my friend! I can hear the barges and riverboats on the rivers, feel the soot burning my eyes, smell the blast furnaces. I can hear your wife's voice like fingernails running down slate. (You are a saint, you know. I would have drowned her by now if I were in your shoes.)*

She oozed sympathy. She described the view from her balcony, gave descriptions of the people passing on the street below, regaled him with stories about Anthra and Bit, talked business, talked nonsense.

It was a typical letter from Regina.

He broke out in a foolish grin. He leaned back in his chair, staring at the ceiling, dizzy with elation. Not only did she say he wrote better letters, but he was getting better letters than Charles was! While Charles was getting a one-page scolding, he was getting six pages of her thoughts and her affection. Six pages of her mind and her heart.

Then the phrase from Charles' letter leaped to mind—"those hot, screaming nights." Whom was he trying to fool? The warmth of her friendship seemed cool when compared against the heat of her ardor for another man.

Chapter 27

It wasn't proving to be a good year for Charles McKay.

While the financial doldrums of the past four years were lifting, and industrialists around the country breathed a hearty sigh of relief and got back to business, Charles was too busy wallowing in his unhappy personal life to care.

When Thomas congratulated Charles on his successes, they were met with little more than a smile and a shrug. It seemed odd, not to at least be pleased by the end of the struggle to meet payroll and keep the employees working, to hire instead of laying off. Although, come to think of it, Charles never had seemed as interested in his business enterprises as Thomas was in his various ventures. So the return to prosperity didn't mean as much to Charles in the first place. After all, the family business represented one more part of Charles' life of quiet desperation.

Thomas tried to bolster Charles' flagging spirits, distracting him with their favorite activities as well as with Regina's letters. He seemed to have some moderate level of success, especially when they were out fishing in the middle of Conemaugh Lake. The stories Charles would tell that night at dinner about "the one that got away" made Thomas remember the earliest days of their friendship, when Charles first impressed him as a born storyteller.

When Elizabeth went into confinement, Thomas couldn't help but notice that Charles was forced to join her. Further excursions to South Fork were, apparently, explicitly forbidden. Cycling, or even having lunch with Charles, became exceedingly rare activities. On the few occasions he did attempt to see Charles, Elizabeth was usually sending notes through one of the servants, demanding attention of some form or another.

"I swear," Charles complained on one of their attempts to have lunch at the Duquesne Club, when the waiter brought another of her endless notes, "I think she doesn't even really care about these errands—which the servants could do more easily than I could. She's doing it to find out what I'm up to."

"Being locked up all day must get pretty boring," Thomas answered tactfully. "You must be her only source of entertainment."

Charles confirmed that idea with a resigned look. "I'm sure having the servants spy on me is thoroughly entertaining."

"Do you think she knows about your — letters?"

Charles shrugged diffidently. "How could she? You get them, I read them, and give them back to you. You are destroying them, aren't you?"

"Thoroughly and enthusiastically," Thomas answered with perfect honesty.

Charles was, of course, blissfully unaware of the multiplicity of meanings in Thomas' answer. "So unless she starts sending our servants to spy on you, she couldn't know." He sighed. "She's jealous of everyone, all the time, always has been. She doesn't like anyone I spend time with. She's even taken a dislike to one of her own cousins, once I found out he's an interesting fellow, who makes family gatherings more fun. Whenever I do anything that doesn't involve paying attention to her . . . well, it becomes an unacceptable activity." He looked regretfully at the errand in his hand, and at the plate of fried mutton chops and browned potatoes that was arriving. "Send it back to the kitchen with my apologies, I guess. Sorry to desert you like this."

Once again, Thomas found himself companionless. He wondered which came first: was Elizabeth jealous because of Charles' infidelity, or did Charles' infidelity stem from a desire to find some freedom from the jealousy?

There was, of course, no way of knowing. It did seem like some kind of self-fulfilling prophesy. Why did life have to be such a tragedy? A comedy would have been so much more fun . . . .

****

Charles seemed lost, wallowing in unhappiness. When President Cleveland came to Pittsburgh that fall, Charles' Republican father absolutely forbade him from going to see him. Thomas, by contrast, got invited to go with A.W. Mellon and Daniel O'Day to set the gas wells on fire for Mrs. Cleveland. He felt a little bad when she expressed disappointment in the newspapers because she didn't get to light one of them herself. But the memory of sending the long tongue of flame shooting high up into the night sky gave him much more satisfaction than guilt.

The same was true for Charles' grumbling. "Wish I could've met Mrs. Cleveland and set wells on fire. Some guys get all the luck."

Missing the chance to revel in the spotlight during President Cleveland's visit was simply a disappointment, but the next misadventure to befall his best friend was leaning toward lifelong hardship. Elizabeth delivered a baby girl, but she was born with a cleft lip: The opening of her mouth extended all the way up to her nose.

"The doctors are going to do some surgery, but they can't tell me if she'll ever look quite normal," Charles told Thomas. "It's such a damned shame—she is awfully beautiful, otherwise."

Thomas had never known what to say to parents going on about how beautiful their babies were. He'd looked at plenty, and been forced to hold them from time to time. Most of them didn't have unpleasant facial deformities, but he'd never seen one he'd actually call "beautiful." They were all noisy, smelly things.

"She does look a lot like you," he answered aloud. That always seemed to please parents. He wondered if it was always a polite lie, since he'd never seen a baby that looked like its dams and sires, or if some people really thought they did see a resemblance. It didn't really matter—as far as Thomas had observed, the compensation for the difficulties of raising children seemed to be in the expression of vanity that went along with it.

Predictably, Charles brightened up. "She does, doesn't she? My mother says I used to look like her when I was a baby." The smile dimmed. "That is, mostly like her, except for . . . ."

"Don't dwell on that," Thomas advised him. "Just think about the parts that make you happy."

"I'll tell you what would make me happy," Charles changed the subject. "Having Regina home again. Has she written lately?"

"No," Thomas answered, a little surprised, "You haven't given me a letter to send her in a long time."

"I've been busy," Charles sounded defensive. "That doesn't mean she should desert me."

"If you're not writing to her, she may think that she's the one who's been deserted," Thomas pointed out.

"Say, whose friend are you, anyway?" Charles asked, annoyed by Thomas' devil's advocate.

"Both, of course. That gives me a privileged position slightly on the outside. I wouldn't call myself an impartial observer, but being equally partial to each of you," okay, so that was a lie. But it had to be said. "I get to draw my own conclusions."

"And what do you conclude?"

Thomas leaned back and looked at his friend. "That I'm glad I'm not in your shoes. Your life is far too complicated."

"Thanks. That helps a whole lot."

"My pleasure."

****

Charles' life got even more complicated a month later. Robert McKay died in his sleep, leaving Charles, his only son, responsible for the entire iron industry of Johnstown.

"I thought I'd get a new start with the new year, but I didn't think it would be like this," Charles complained to Thomas on their last lunch together at the Duquesne Club. Charles was selling the house and moving his family back to Johnstown. "I was hoping for an end to all the bad luck."

"All luck is double-sided," Thomas pointed out. "You've lost a parent, but you're now the richest man in Cambria County. Hopefully you'll find a way to make some good come of that."

"You're starting to sound like Regina," Charles grumbled.

"Is that bad?" Thomas asked, pleased by the comparison.

"No, I guess not," Charles answered. He slid into silence for awhile, then volunteered, "I get so busy sometimes, but I still miss her."

Thomas could certainly appreciate that sentiment. He couldn't imagine being so busy he'd forget to miss Regina. "She'll be back. She gets so excited when sales are plentiful," he chuckled. "But eventually she'll come home."

"Well, that's fine for you, you'll get to see her, but I'm moving to Johnstown, remember?"

Thomas tried to ignore the burning glee in the pit of his stomach. "You'll see her up at South Fork."

"Yeah." There was another long silence between them, then Charles commented, "I suppose that's the only time I'll get to see you, too."

"I suppose so," Thomas answered laconically.

Charles cleared his throat. "I'm going to miss you."

Thomas felt the lump creeping into his throat, too. "You'd be as good as gone, anyway, you know. I hardly saw you for a year after Robbie was born. You won't have time to take out the bicycles, even if you were in town."

Charles shrugged diffidently. "It's still nice to know you're across the river when I need a friend. A fellow couldn't find a better friend anywhere in the world. This city's been pretty good to me, but I wouldn't have enjoyed it here nearly as much if it weren't for you."

It was Thomas' turn to clear his throat. "No charge."

Thomas had hoped to be there to say goodbye when Charles left the next day, but by the time George had rolled the carriage up to the house on Ridge Avenue, the doors were locked and every last servant was gone. He had George race to the train station, but there, too, he was too late. The Day Express had left only minutes before. It seemed a fitting departure, somehow: chasing after a friend who was there for him less and less, and now not there at all . . . .

****

The loneliness of Charles' departure was eased when Regina came home, looking revived and happy, with a large selection of mythological baubles for the house, and an even larger quantity of new Wintergarden orders.

The two of them took a critical look at Waring-Baldwin Wintergardens. They had both been so busy working, neither had stopped to notice that their little joint venture was a vast enterprise. They had wintergardens all over the United States and Europe. Regina had an appointment with Montgomery Ward, with high hopes of getting wintergardens into their catalogue. With economic times booming, and good reason to expect orders to pour in, they decided a new facility was in order. Made out of iron and glass, of course.

It seemed fitting that they should join in the building boom going on all over the county. The new courthouse was nearing completion. Across the river in Allegheny, Henry Heinz, the horseradish peddler and food packer who'd gone bankrupt at least once in his career, was building a new plant. The Mellons had even supplied financing to a young maverick who was claiming the ability to commercially manufacture aluminum. In the midst of all this building, why not erect an industrial-sized wintergarden to house Waring-Baldwin Wintergardens?

Chapter 28

In order to enjoy the dwindling mild days left at the end of September, Thomas' office windows were wide open as he poured over the blueprints Regina had sent him. The idea of Waring Baldwin Wintergardens having its own building, complete with an office right next to Regina's, put Thomas in an exceptionally cheerful mood.

He hummed under his breath as he spread plans out across his desk, stopping to chuckle over notes and arrows Regina had scribbled to him in the margins. An office next to hers. His eyes unfocused, a silly grin spreading across his face. Maybe he could talk her into a single large office. With a big, oversized partner desk squarely occupying the middle of the room. It would give him that many more opportunities to look at her while they were both working. In the meantime, once she finished her current round of sales calls out west, she really ought to come home to help oversee the construction.

His mother's voice jolted him out of his reverie like cold water on a hot skillet. Reluctantly, he put aside his visions of Regina's mantle occupying a hook on the wall next to his overcoat, her glossy dark head bending over a desk a few feet from his own, the indescribable energy of her presence filling the same office as they both worked.

"Come in, Mother," he opened his office door. A disagreeable surprise met his eyes. Not only his mother, but also his wife were standing at David Smith's desk. "Mrs. Baldwin." He held the door open invitingly. "To what do I owe the combined pleasure of this visit?"

His mother seemed to be bursting with an odd excitement. "Thomas, I know you don't like to be bothered at work any more than your father did, but I was too excited to wait." She tilted her cheek toward him expectantly. Thomas kissed it with growing curiosity. His mother bustled into his office, then turned to give Meredith an affectionate look. "You should sit here, Meredith, dear, it's a much more comfortable chair."

'Meredith dear?' After the nearly-open hostilities at the Clubhouse, this was odd behavior, indeed. Thomas gave his wife a penetrating look. She dropped her eyes, blushed, and scurried past him to sit in the offered chair. His suspicions mounting, Thomas closed the door.

"Now, there's not that much time to get everything done before it's, well, it's too late," his mother gushed. "I couldn't wait to get started, so I'm taking Meredith shopping. But Thomas," his mother's voice turned half-pleading, half-censuring. "I simply cannot believe you'd be so stingy as to not give her a bigger allowance at a time like this. There's so much to buy, no man ever truly understands."

"No, Mother," Thomas agreed patiently. "I imagine no man truly does understand." He rolled up Regina's blueprints and set them—and his daydreams—aside with a mental promise to return to them as soon as he was alone again. "As far as I'm aware my wife has a fairly generous allowance, and judging by the fairly lavish gewgaws adorning her person, I'd say she seems to be managing quite tolerably."

"Oh, do be serious, Thomas! You don't expect her to get everything with just her dress money!" His mother looked shocked.

Thomas sighed. "Are fashions so radically different this year?" he asked, wondering at the vastness of feminine inventiveness in finding a multitude of ways to suspend fabric from their tiny corseted waists.

His mother faced him indignantly. "It's still nice to have something pretty, even when, well, after one stops receiving. But you can't expect her to get the furniture and new curtains and wallpaper, and other—necessaries out of that!"

This turn of conversation did not please Thomas in the least. He took great pride in the sensible grandeur of that house, and Meredith's questionable tastes already cluttered up quite a large enough portion of it. "What new furniture?" he asked as mildly as he could.

His mother looked impatiently at him. "For the—" she glanced at the door, then lowered her voice. "For the nursery, of course!"

There was a clap of thunder somewhere inside his head. Nursery. Meredith sitting there, unable to look at him, her face alternating from white to pink and back again. His wife and his mother on unexpectedly good terms. His mother, gushing with excitement at finally, finally getting the grandchild she'd been wanting all these long years.

Meredith was expecting a baby.

His mother was staring at him impatiently. He supposed he'd better say something. "I see. You're right, mother. Furniture does get expensive. I'll see what I can do. But—" he held up a finger warningly. "I'd appreciate it if you'd contain your shopping spree to the inside of the nursery. No redecorating the rest of my house."

His mother's face melted from impatient to pleased. "I'll handle everything, Thomas, but then you have been a tyrant about that house," she complained happily.

"Yes, I'm rather particular about what I allow in the front door," he answered. As he watched, Meredith changed color again. His mother did not notice.

"We won't bring home any cheap junk, Thomas. Honestly, I don't know what you're afraid of. Come, Meredith, dear," his mother dismissed his fears for the happier subject of shopping. "Let's start at Joseph Horne's over on Penn Avenue."

Thomas courteously held the door open for them as they left. His mother strode out like an Amazon going into battle, his wife scurrying behind like a nervous foot soldier.

Closing the door again, Thomas sat back in his chair and stared at the rolls of blueprints he'd set aside . . . . some lifetime ago.

****

He was staring at the scrollwork on the stone mantle in his study at home when he heard his wife's voice in the foyer, giving orders to the servants on the disbursement of the parcels she'd brought home from the afternoon's shopping. He didn't consciously decide to confront matters then and there—but of their own volition, his legs carried him to the door, his hand opened it, and his voice spoke the summons. "Mrs. Baldwin."

Meredith froze. He waited patiently while she stood, staring at him. He realized the entire household had frozen as well; absolutely everyone was waiting for his next words. Part of his brain wondered what would happen if he waited until someone else said or did something. Would everyone simply stay frozen like this? The melodrama of it all was too silly for words.

He decided to end everyone's suspense. "Mrs. Baldwin," he repeated softly, "when you are quite done creating an uproar in the hallway over your shopping trip, why don't you step into my study."

There. He'd kept his voice as bland as white rice. Meredith reddened, grew pale, dropped her eyes, slipped out of her coat and hurried across the wide hallway. He wondered what he sounded like to other people's ears.

He held the door for her to pass, then closed it gently behind himself. She stood uncertainly in the middle of the carpet, her eyes looking at everything except him. After an awkward silence, she held up a small package without actually raising her eyes to look at him. "Your mother and I got this for you while we were out shopping." Lord, how many times had he watched her, posing with her eyes downcast? He knew that if he waited long enough, eventually she'd look up. When she did, she held the package out toward him more insistently. "It's a clock. Your mother says when you were little you'd broken your father's desk clock, and he had to get a new one that looked just like this."

She was going to stand there like that until he took the package, so he went over and took it from her. "Very sentimental of my mother, I'm sure, thank you. I've been hearing all my life about how I broke the clock, and how my brother Ben never did anything like that." He put the package down on the desk, then walked around to stand behind it. As always, he felt safer with a massive barricade between himself and his spouse. He eyed her for a moment, then indicated one of the chairs.

"You might as well sit down, my dear. No doubt you are quite exhausted from spending both hours and dollars in gleeful acquisition."

Meredith obediently sat, and Thomas settled himself behind his desk. "So when were you planning on telling me that you're pregnant?"

Meredith blushed red as a poppy at the frank term, but still said nothing.

"You were planning on telling me, weren't you? Or did you simply assume I wouldn't notice, then you'd bury your progeny in the backyard, like a nun in the convent?" She gave him one of those familiar uncomprehending looks. "Never mind. Interesting that you managed to tell my mother."

Meredith smiled a small, guilty smile. "Well—it sort of did come out in conversation."

Thomas nodded calmly. "She's obviously delighted at the prospect of her first grandchild."

"Oh, yes!" Meredith gushed. "She's been after me for years, you know. She was thrilled when I told her, then she insisted that we had to come see you right away. She even gave me this locket, because she was so happy." She eagerly lifted up the chain around her neck to display a delicate gold filigree heart.

"Uh huh. So you have every intention of passing this child off as mine?"

Meredith stopped her chatter, and simply stared at him, her mouth open. Indeed, what was there to say?

Thomas continued without letting his face or voice betray any hint of malice, "Since you and I have never shared a conjugal bed in our thirteen years of marriage . . ."

"Oh, Thomas! I was afraid you wouldn't remember!" Meredith lied desperately. "Oh, you must remember. It was a couple of months ago, you came home late from the club, terribly drunk . . . ."

This ought to get entertaining. Thomas goaded her on. "I did?"

"Oh, yes. You reeked of—ah—bourbon. You made an awful racket coming upstairs. I'd gone into the hall to see if you'd hurt yourself. You were rather—attentive, even if you weren't a gentleman. You laughed and carried me off to your room—like a pirate, and . . . . had your way with me."

She finished in a breathless flutter. Thomas was dryly amused by the clumsy story. He could imagine her mental gymnastics, as she tried to think up an explanation for her condition. He abandoned his chair to go stare out the window.

"You really believe your little fantasy stories, don't you, my dear?" he asked, not unkindly. "I suppose it gets hard to separate fact from fiction after a while. You've fabricated so much for the outside world, it must be hard to keep track.

"But you need to know your audience, my dear. I haven't touched a drop of liquor since our wedding day."

Meredith obviously couldn't think of a thing to say. "Oh."

"Yes. As you so succinctly put it, 'Oh.' I realized that being married to you could easily make me an alcoholic. Then I'd be a drunkard and married to you. I saw no reason to compound my miseries. And now that we've debunked your little story, let us return to the subject at hand. You obviously intend to pass this child off as mine. Isn't the baby's father going to object?"

"No—he—I—" Meredith fell into a confused silence.

Thomas smiled at her minimal admission to a third party. "Well, if the father should turn up, he's welcome to you both. I would happily give you a divorce under any terms you'd care to name. Adultery, abandonment, wife beating, insanity, whatever would make for the biggest scandal in the newspapers. If you'd like, I could probably divorce you on the simple fact that the child's not mine, and you can spend the rest of your life with a man who has more use for you than I do."

Meredith was properly horrified. "A divorce! Thomas, no!"

Her protest answered any number of questions he might have had. "Uh-huh. It occurred to me that your lover was likely to be less wealthy than myself, and that you'd have no desire to leave your very comfortable circumstances. So, instead, you'll bring this child into the world, tell everyone it's mine, and Olympus Ironworks and my other Baldwin enterprises get an heir. No doubt the child will be an imbecile like its mother, and a constant embarrassment to me."

Anger began to swell in his breast as he turned to face her. Frightened, Meredith stood up. "I have this horrible urge to tear you limb from limb and hang your bleeding body parts from the Smithfield Bridge. I daresay society would even approve, given the circumstances. But I don't need your blood on my hands. So I urge you to retire—and quickly, if you know what's good for you!"

Without a word, Meredith ran from the room.

Was there no end to what this woman was willing to put him through? He leaned blindly against his desk. His hand brushed the package she had given him when she'd walked in, and the world seemed to turn red.

He threw the still-wrapped clock with all his might at the fireplace. The smashing, twanging crunch it made felt so good, he felt around for more objects to throw. The inkwell didn't make nearly as satisfying a sound. After he'd cleared his desk, and upended it, he found the chairs. He couldn't throw them at the door—they were too heavy—but he tried. The silver candlesticks made much better projectiles. So did most of the other knick knacks that had lived on the fireplace mantle. Since the fire was low, he stoked it with the prayer books that she used to pose with in the window seat when they'd lived on Buena Vista.

As the pages crackled and burned, he hurled the fireplace tools as far across the room as he could. There was a crashing of glass. The carpet on the floor in front of his desk ought to be burnt. She had stood upon it one too many times. He tried to drag it to the fireplace, but the heavy rug was pinned under the upended mahogany desk. He struggled with it, grunting, and then it was over. He felt worn out. He sank to his knees and put his forehead against the offending desk. "Oh, Regina, I wish you were here," he moaned. A hot wetness stung at his eyes. Preposterous—he hadn't cried since he was four years old. "A man can do anything, son—but he never cries," he could hear his father's voice saying to him.

He thumped his head repeatedly against the unyielding wood. "How—the—hell—did—I—get—here?" He asked between thumps. But he knew the answer to that. One day at a time. A stronger man would have left the city when Meredith trapped him in the music room with her breasts exposed; a cleverer man could have built an entirely new empire in California by now. A smarter man would have killed her years ago. If he didn't have enough money to keep himself out of prison, at least his sentence would most likely have been truncated because of his position. A wiser man would have found a way out of this marriage—somehow.

But not him. He was stupid, and lazy, and a coward. Too stupid to think his way out, too lazy and frightened to abandon the security of the wealth and power that came with being a Baldwin in Pittsburgh.

Well, he was paying a price for his inability to leave the comfortable and familiar behind. All the influence he imagined he carried with the outside world ended at his doorstep. Behind his own front door, he was powerless inside his own life. It seemed that, for him, this man's home was not so much his castle but his prison.

****

The ruin he had made of his office was cleaned up without a word. The following evening, when he worked up the nerve to open the heavy door, everything waited in its traditional place. The broken detritus had been carried away, the desk was back on its legs, the fireplace tools standing ready. There were plenty of scars from his destructive moment: a black smudge on the fireplace where he'd thrown his inkwell, a rag stuffed into the hole where he'd broken the window, large dings in the silver candlesticks.

When Mary showed up, balancing her dinner tray, he wondered whether she was going to say anything or not. It embarrassed him. He'd never thrown a temper tantrum before, and he wondered what his house staff thought of him.

"Good evening, Mr. Baldwin," Mary greeted him cheerfully.

"Hello, Mary." He was at a loss for words. "That smells wonderful."

"Mrs. Bishop knows how you like your brisket, sir, so she made that up for you today."

Uh huh. They were trying to be extra nice to him today. "Well, thank Mrs. Bishop for me, Mary."

"I will, sir."

Mary had retreated as far as the door when Thomas stopped her. "Mary," he called sternly.

He saw the nervous twitch to her shoulder. She turned around to face him, and he watched that imperturbable mask of hers drop into place. "Yes, Mr. Baldwin?"

"No gossip for me today? Is that because all the gossip is about me?"

He watched while she decided how to answer him. "Actually, sir, we all felt too bad for you to talk about it."

Thomas was somehow amused as well as heartened by the admission. "Oh?"

Mary shrugged her pretty shoulders. "I'm sure we would all be willing to testify for you, if you decide to divorce her for adultery."

Thomas looked at her in surprise. "Do you know who the father is?"

The brown eyes looked searchingly into his, then looked away. "I believe so, sir."

"Well, don't tell me," he answered with distaste. "I don't want to know. I don't need the pictures in my head of that woman and some gardener of mine doing indiscreet things in one of my carriages."

Mary looked amused, but said nothing.

"Go on with you," he waved her out of the room. "My brisket's getting cold, and I don't need talk of the gargoyle I'm married to spoiling my appetite."

She obediently turned and headed for the door. "Thank you, Mary," he added.

There was something sensual about the smile she threw over her shoulder as she left. "You're welcome, sir," she answered.

****

The six remaining months of Meredith's pregnancy were the worst since their engagement.

As with their wedding, Thomas found himself a bystander watching a female-dominated event. Once again, the women in his family were in a shopping frenzy—and for some unfathomable reason, he was expected to play escort.

Dressmakers, drygoods merchants, furniture stores. Thomas stood by as the women exclaimed over their intended purchases. The items had changed, but the cast of characters was still the same: his mother, her mother, Janey Mason Blyth, Elsie Thomas Morehead, Yvette Morrison Hunt.

The men's reaction was nearly identical to the wedding, too. A sympathetic pat on the shoulder following a congratulatory handshake—and that was the end of the subject.

The excitement of shopping ended when Meredith began to "show," and she went into confinement.

This began a new set of ordeals.

If all expectant women were like Meredith, it was no wonder society locked them away. He remembered how demanding Elizabeth had gotten when she was expecting; now, instead of the sort of uneasy détente they had lived with for years, she always seemed to manage her growing bulk to the front door every time he came home. Then she plied him with questions about where he'd been and what he'd been doing. Thomas now understood why Charles had made himself so scarce; if simply being home under Elizabeth's watchful eye stopped the nagging, he'd obviously been desperate to mollify her.

Thomas wasn't so easily cowed. When Meredith began to enter his traditional sanctuaries, like his office and library, he resumed his old practice of keeping the doors locked. The more she cried at him with complaints about him being out cycling, or at the Duquesne Club, or working late, while she was getting so helpless, the more rigorously he avoided being at home. He doubted she ever quite figured out the concept of cause-and-effect. She wasn't very bright in the first place, and her current state seemed to bring out an even greater degree of self-centeredness.

When her voice was washing over him, complaining about her growing bulk, or the servants, or him, he'd think about the fact that he had the right to throw her out on the street any time he felt like it. He'd daydream about it, sometimes. Unfortunately, the daydream always ended by imagining the fuss from his mother, his entire family, her entire family, and every client in every one of his businesses over the scandal that would ensue. In his own way, he was as big of coward as Charles. He, too, was caving in to social pressures.

Perhaps the most curious thing was, she seemed to forget that he wasn't the father of the baby. Since the topic of her chatter was usually herself, at first he wasn't sure of that. One Sunday, after he'd come home from taking his mother to church then having dinner with her and an assortment of aunts, uncles and cousins, she was less vague.

Joseph had barely helped him out of his overcoat and asked after his family's health, when Meredith waddled in.

"If you wanted to spend time with your family, you should be spending time with me," her voice had been getting downright shrewish of late. "After all, I'm the one about to give you a new family member."

Thomas looked at her coldly. He was so tired of her. Of having this awful home life. Of living like this. And it was only about to get worse. The usual numb feeling gave way to a hate he hadn't felt for years. "Since the baby's not mine, is it really a new family member?"

Meredith sucked in her breath and stared from him to Joseph and back again. Joseph turned and vanished, like the accomplished butler that he was.

"Now you've done it!" she whispered at him furiously. "Now all the servants are going to be gossiping—then they'll probably start gossiping with everyone else's servants, and the whole town's going to think . . ."

"You think the servants haven't already known the truth?" Thomas interrupted her. "You think the whole town hasn't already been gossiping? You wanted a baby so badly—this is the outcome."

"I didn't think it was going to be like this," she grumbled.

Thomas turned to climb the stairs. "I can sympathize with you on that score, Mrs. Baldwin. I didn't think my life was going to be like this, either."

Chapter 29

A scream ripping through the Baldwin household announced the beginning of the next chapter in the baby ordeal. By the time Thomas had stumbled out of his room and into the hallway, Mary and Mrs. Bishop had also managed to stumble down the stairs from their rooms one floor up. The three of them stood in the hallway in front of Meredith's door for a moment, staring at each other. A fresh scream breaking from the other side of the door told them with some urgency that they had to stop standing there. Both women looked expectantly at Thomas. Taking the proverbial bull by the horns, he took a deep breath, put his hand on the doorknob, turned and pushed.

Meredith lay in bed, soaked with sweat and panting. She looked back at them for a moment, miserably. Then another contraction ripped through her swollen body and she screamed again.

It had started.

Not much to do now but get on with it. Thomas turned to the cook. "Go out to the carriage house and wake up George. Send him for the midwife. After he brings the midwife, you might as well send him for my mother, and her mother."

Mary volunteered to go downstairs to get some cold wet cloths for Meredith's head. Thomas nodded and shooed her off. Feeling fairly useless and unattached to the entire proceedings, he went in and stood beside Meredith's bed. "Well, Mrs. Baldwin," he said, not unkindly, "looks like you're about to get that baby you wanted."

Meredith reached up and took his hand, which she squeezed so hard it crushed his fingers. "Don't leave me, Thomas," she begged. "Whatever you do, don't leave me."

Thomas removed his fingers from her painful grip. "Don't be silly, Meredith. A man has no place in a bedroom where a woman's giving birth." He'd always thought it was an irresponsible thing that a man wasn't present when his wife gave birth to his children. But under the circumstances, he was glad for the custom. It seemed indecent to be in the room while Meredith gave birth to some other man's child.

Out of some strange and rare sense of decency, he at least stayed and kept her company until the midwife bustled in. Then he gladly deserted his post to the expert.

His mother and Meredith's mother soon followed. Then, over the course of the morning, after dawn broke, a trickle of family members flowed through the front door, slowly filling the entire house. First the womenfolk came, one by one, then an occasional husband showed up, until by dinner, there was a full house.

Some thoughtful relatives had realized that today was going to turn into a family gathering, and several households had arrived with contributions of food and extra people to help Thomas' cook in the kitchen. By two o'clock, the house was filled with the smells of baking hams and roasting potatoes.

The parlor was full of Baldwin menfolk. Uncle Alfred and Uncle John were playing chess, while several others looked on. Small children could be heard playing both inside and outside the house. Upstairs a large collection of women were looking on and assisting Meredith in her childbirth pains. A spare woman would appear downstairs from time to time, just to report that there was no news to report yet.

Thomas wandered from room to room through his house, with a detached sense of amazement. It seemed to him that childbearing was a fairly private activity. But here was his house, crammed full. Did this happen everywhere, or was it only his crazy family that treated a private event like a family picnic?

Despite the frequent screams from upstairs, it was a fairly festive family event. Dinner was a merry affair. The cooks set up a long buffet in the dining room. Children, men, and eventually, a stray woman went through the line, filled a plate, and then people sat or stood eating wherever it happened to suit them.

But as the day wore into evening, everyone in the house realized that all was not going well upstairs. Supper was considerably less cheerful than dinner. Everyone seemed to be listening for signs of activity overhead. The women looked more worried when one would appear, and they all said less. Finally they stopped bringing reports altogether.

Eventually, many family members began to go home. Sleepy children were carted off by sleepy men. Thomas himself had fallen asleep on the settee in the parlor when his mother shook him awake. "Thomas, come with me." He could tell by her voice that something was wrong.

His mother said nothing while they climbed the stairs. They were standing outside Meredith's bedroom door before she spoke. "Thomas," his mother laid a compassionate hand on his arm. "We've lost the baby. We think we may lose Meredith as well. That's why we thought you'd better come to see her. We've sent for a doctor, but it may be too late. She had a difficult time. She's too old for a first child. Everything just went wrong." She wiped tears off her tired face, but her voice remained steady. "The midwife thinks that Meredith's going to slip away soon. I'm sorry Thomas, but you'd better say your goodbyes to her." Her voice broke, and she hurried away.

Thomas stepped into the room, and stared around a moment stupidly, still blinking the sleep from his eyes. The room had an awful bloody, musty odor. Aunt Eleanor had been sitting next to Meredith, but got up when she saw him. She put her hand on Thomas, but couldn't say anything, and left in a hurry, sobbing softly.

The midwife remained in the corner. "With your permission, I'd like to stay, in case I'm needed," she said.

"Fine," Thomas answered simply.

Meredith looked perfectly awful. As he sat down beside her, he could see how pale she was. Her sweat-soaked hair clung to her face, or straggled out over the pillow in long, wet strands. The rumpled sheets were stained with sweat, blood, and only God knew what else.

He wanted to gag at the smell, and the sight, but he pasted on his best smile and took her hand. The blue eyes he'd loathed for so many years were sunken in her face. The misery in them alleviated the emptiness he always saw there; now she was a suffering animal, and Thomas was touched by compassion.

"I lost our baby, Thomas," Meredith said. "I'm sorry. I'm so sorry Thomas. I wanted to give you a son. He was going to be smart and beautiful, and look just like you. He was going to take after you, Thomas, really he was."

Thomas stared at her a moment, feeling the compassion wither inside his chest. Did she live in a fantasy world, or was she determined to be deceitful to the bitter end? Either way, she was persistent; he had to give her that.

He toyed with the fingers of her hand for a moment. She had such small, useless hands, frequently fluttering about in nervous little gestures. Usually her hands seemed to be involved in primping, smoothing her hair, her gloves, her clothes. As he tried to imagine her doing something useful with them, his mind filled with an image of Regina's long, tapering hands. Her firm grip when he would dance with her. The elegant way she folded them in her lap when she was listening. The sympathetic touch of them on his arm.

He shook off the thought. She was always somewhere else. He should be used to her absence by now. His wife lay dying before him. At least he could pay attention to her for a few minutes at her deathbed.

"So tell me about your plans for this son of yours," he offered gently.

His query roused her. "He was going to be tall, maybe even taller than you, Thomas. When he grew up, anyway. I had plans for the most adorable sailor suits, once he grew out of skirts. I was going to cry for days when he became too big for his baby dresses anymore. But my heart was going to recover when I'd see him in his little sailor suits. With blue ribbons on them, to bring out how blue his eyes were."

"I see," Thomas answered soberly. "Practical of you to plan ahead."

"I have to be very practical. Motherhood is far more difficult than people realize," Meredith answered importantly. "But it was going to agree with me. Everyone was going to think so. People would see me with our baby, and tell me I looked like the Madonna. I have a lovely blue Merino I was going to have made up, so that when the baby was awake, people could see that his eyes were as dark blue as yours."

The monologue wore Meredith out. She stopped, closing her eyes and panting from the effort. Thomas found the washbasin on the stand behind him, and stood up to rinse one of the waiting cloths in water from the pitcher. She opened her eyes as he gently blotted her face and neck.

"Jancy always said you seemed awfully cold and distant. I set her straight. I said you were always a gentleman, that's all. Her husband isn't nearly so rich, so he isn't nearly as much of a gentleman as you are."

An ironic smile tugged at the corners of his mouth. "Is that what you told her?"

She nodded wearily. Her breathing was more ragged, the words were coming slower, and her eyelids were drooping. "Not the part about you being richer. I didn't want to hurt her feelings. We're richer than any of the other girls from my set. None of them married as well as I did. We have a nicer house than any of them."

It had been a long time since the conversation in the carriage on their wedding night, when she'd also talked about how attractive his family fortunes were to her. He wondered what she would have done if the Baldwin empire had collapsed in the Panic.

"Would you do something, Thomas?" Meredith asked groggily, the words starting to come with great difficulty.

"What, Meredith?"

"Kiss me goodnight. I'm very sleepy."

Thomas leaned over the bed and kissed her forehead.

"No, no," she protested wearily. "Kiss me."

His body gave a rebellious twitch. He ignored it sternly. He lowered his face and his lips touched hers, which were so weak, she barely kissed back.

Her eyelids fluttered open as he pulled away. "We have a good marriage, don't we, Thomas?"

"Sure," he answered. "We have a good marriage."

"At least you finally admit it, now," she answered, and closed her eyes. Her breath developed a funny, wheezing rattle. He looked at the midwife in alarm.

"If you don't want to see the end, you'd better leave now. It's almost over for her," she answered him gently.

"Would you call for her mother? And mine? I'll stay," he answered.

She left swiftly and silently, but it was over by the time she returned with the two women. Thomas stood near the bed for a frozen moment. He wanted to weep; from shock, from grief, from relief, he didn't know. The nightmare was over. The loveless marriage, the vision of a future dominated by a child that wasn't his, was over. Their mothers threw themselves on their knees beside the bed and sobbed loudly. The sound drummed painfully against his ears, and he wanted to distance himself from it. In a daze, he walked out into the hallway. It was crowded with tearful family members, all looking at him with pity.

"She's gone," he announced. "Go pay your respects."

He felt the sympathetic touches on his arms and shoulders as he passed them. He slowly stepped through the gauntlet. When he reached the center stairs, he saw Mary's face on the level below. Steadily, he descended while she waited, watching. When he reached her, she gave him a small smile of encouragement.

"Mary," he instructed softly, "you know who the father was. Assuming he's not in this house, ask George to take you to him. Tell him his child and Meredith have both died. If he'd like any memento of Meredith, find out what it is, and arrange to get it to him sometime after the funeral. And give him my condolences."

Mary nodded once, her beautiful eyes full of understanding, and she turned to follow his instructions. He was so thankful for her presence at that moment. He couldn't imagine how he'd survive if he didn't have someone around who knew the truth.

His soul felt tired. He wanted to—what? He wanted to sit on the floor, his head against Regina's knee, feeling her hands running soothingly through his hair while her deep voice caressed his ears. If he could only bury his face against her skirts, his head would stop hurting. She would put into words the things he couldn't even allow himself to put into thoughts.

His heart ached. Oh, how he needed her! A guilty thought occurred to him, which propelled his feet into his office. Gently he pulled the doors shut and locked them. It was indecent to have thought of it—no one but himself need know the timing. Only minutes after his wife's death, he was going to tell another woman that he was free.

He was halfway to his desk as that thought struck him. He stood, frozen in the middle of the room, and rolled the words around in his mind.

He was free.

His hands shook as he pulled out paper and uncapped the inkwell.

He was free.

He stared at the paper a moment, while he tried to find the words to put down on paper.

My darling, come home to me. I need you. And I am free to love you as I have wanted to for all these long years of our precious friendship.

He dipped his pen in the ink and set it to paper.

April 1889
Dear Regina,

There's been a most unexpected turn of events. Meredith has died in childbirth. The son she was attempting to deliver was also unable to survive the delivery. As you can imagine, I am struggling to find a way to survive the ordeals yet to come. I do find myself wishing you were not halfway across the country. Your insight would be of great comfort to me.

Your obedient servant,
Thomas Baldwin

****

Naturally, burying Meredith was a bigger ordeal than Thomas had anticipated. The midwife who had witnessed the tender death scene had confided to one person in his family how very gentle and loving Thomas had been at Meredith's deathbed. In two days' time, every last family member had heard the story. In four days, everyone in Pittsburgh had heard it.

Now, as Thomas stood beside the coffins of Meredith and her child, gravely accepting the condolences, he endured the popular misconception that he was brokenhearted over the death of his sainted wife. He listened to the whispered words over and over again from the well-wishers; "I know how much you loved her," "What a sweet saint your wife was!" "You don't even have the baby to comfort you!"

When Henry died, Regina had wished to get away from the respectful whispers of the other mourners. He couldn't agree more. He wanted to brush off the sympathetic pats, and shout the truth at the top of his lungs. As he shook hands with one visitor after another, he imagined the horrified stares if he answered them truthfully. "Loved her? I couldn't stand the sight of her." "The baby wasn't mine. I find that comforting, yes."

Over the years of marriage, the hate he'd felt when he married her had cooled to a resigned dislike. Now, as he acted the part of bereaved husband, the hate warmed back up. Irrationally, he hated her for dying. For forcing him into a new, loathsome charade.

During a lull in the visitation line, his eyes roamed over the room. At least he wasn't alone. Somewhere in Pittsburgh, perhaps somewhere in this room, someone else had to play a charade, too. Someone had to act as if he'd lost an acquaintance—not a lover and a child.

Thomas genuinely felt sorry for the nameless person. He truly had no wish to know his identity, but Thomas realized that someone out there had a real reason to grieve.

His face fell into bitter lines. If only that someone had taken Meredith off his hands while she was still alive!

His mother had come alongside him and put her arm around his waist. "Why don't you sit down for a while, honey? You look tired. It's hard, standing up here for so long. I'll ask Marjorie to step in for a while."

"Marjorie? Oh, right. Meredith's mother. No doubt Meredith's death would make them inseparable friends.

"Thank you, Mother, I would like to get out of this room for a little while." The look of heartbreaking pity she gave him before she rustled away to find Mrs. Burke made him feel like he was suffocating.

He suffered himself to be hugged and cried over by his mother-in-law, and then he was released from his post.

How many funerals does a person attend in one lifetime? He wandered through the house, once again full of family members. The festive chaos of a few days ago was replaced by a more muffled chaos, as adults tried to curb their offspring's play in consideration of the occasion. Wherever he went, sound died respectfully away. He endured it, and the accompanying stares and touching. Obviously he was going to have to escape the building, entirely. With excruciating slowness, he made a break for freedom through the kitchen door.

A game of tag was in progress in the yard. Thankfully, the children were too absorbed in their activity to notice his appearance on the porch. At least they didn't insist on stopping everything in order to drop their gaze and lower their voices into whispered platitudes. Thomas was tempted to join the game. He smiled grimly at the thought of the horrified expressions on people's faces if they found him running around the yard.

The smile faded. No, they'd simply look on him with pity, and say, "Look, see how badly he wanted that child? He's coming unhinged."

He turned and walked along the porch, down the steps, and out onto Highland Avenue.

How in the world did he get where he was? Fourteen years of marriage to a woman he had loathed. A family who didn't have the faintest idea who he was. Now he was burying a wife and child to whom he had no attachment, while the world looked on with pity. Everyone assumed they knew what he was thinking and feeling. He never felt or thought the way they did.

What did he have to show for his life? Lies. Lots of lies. He was wading through his life, waist deep in lies. He despised himself for the lies he was willing to live with. He deplored his lack of courage. Benjamin wouldn't have lived like this. He would have found some charming and clever way to tell people the truth. He would have run away to the territories, rather than get cornered into marriage. By now he would have started up some business of his own, and been wildly successful drilling oil, or building railroads, or something.

He thought of Charles McKay. Here was another man caught in an unhappy marriage. He'd managed to maintain his sense of humor, at least. He was willing to have conjugal relations with his unpleasant spouse, and then cheerfully had a passionate love affair on the side. Thomas shook his head. Principles. Here was poor foolish Thomas Baldwin, living high and lonely and celibate.

The sad thing was, he couldn't imagine what he might have done differently. The idea of throwing away his life, abandoning his family, Olympus Ironworks, and Pittsburgh seemed absolutely unthinkable. He couldn't imagine anything more terrifying than not having the structure of his life around him. No Baldwin name. No Olympus. No George up on his box in the carriage. In Pittsburgh, at least HE knew who he was—even if nobody else did. If he'd run away, he wouldn't have known who he was. He was that weak and cowardly.

Where else might he have avoided the mess he'd made of his life? He might have made an effort to make his marriage actually work. He tried to think of Meredith's physical features without bias. Blonde hair, empty blue eyes, little mouth pursed up in a pout. He got such an awful taste in his mouth, he spit in the rhododendron bushes nearby. No. Absolutely out of the question.

He hadn't chosen to follow Charles' example and mate with a woman he found unbearably stupid. Okay, Elizabeth wasn't stupid. Just phenomenally unpleasant. Meredith wasn't necessarily so unpleasant. But she was terribly stupid.

As for the extramarital activities? Well, there was only one woman filling his mind. For all his fantasies, he wanted so much more than a tawdry affair. Besides, he had absolutely no idea how anyone got into such relationships. A man proposed to a woman to make her his wife. Did men go through some alternative verbal contract in order to make a woman his mistress? Was there some financial arrangement, as well? Otherwise, why would women agree to such a position? He felt like a complete innocent in a terribly wicked world. He wished he had the faintest idea of how to be wicked. Everyone else seemed to be having so much more fun than he was.

He hadn't thought about how long he'd been gone until he'd climbed the hill to stare moodily down into the reservoir. He'd certainly walked a great distance! He refused to dig his watch out of his pocket. He'd return when he was good and ready. He picked up a couple of rocks, and skipped them across the water. He wished Anthracite and Bituminous were there. They would love chasing sticks and crashing into the water for a swim. They were always so cheerful and full of the joy of living. He wanted to scratch behind their ears, bury his face in their necks and cry. It didn't matter that he wasn't even sure what he wanted to cry about. They wouldn't care. They'd lick his face with canine sympathy, and tell him that they thought he'd turned out to be a perfectly fine human being. He threw sticks well.

He felt like a failure right now. Why on earth should Meredith's death make him feel like a failure? The marriage had been a failure before they had even made it to the altar. It wasn't that he'd wanted a child. He threw himself down on the clover-covered hill and stared at the serene water. Okay, so he was lonely. There were so few people in the universe with whom he could actually connect in a meaningful fashion. Meaning—maybe that was it. Somehow, he had this absurd notion that life should have meaning. So far he'd not been able to find any. Except . . . .

He had been trying hard not to think of Regina. Now the memory of the soothing coolness of her voice washed over him. What would she say if she were here with him? He could imagine the twinkle of humor in her black eyes, as she said something cynical and witty, which would drop the whole universe back into perspective. If she were here, he'd roll over and lie with his head on her lap. Maybe she'd stroke his head and murmur sympathetic and irreverent things that would make him laugh. Or maybe she'd say nothing. But she'd understand.

The image of her faded from his mind's eye, and once again he was looking at nothing more than the calm water of the reservoir. Resigned, he pushed himself off the ground and brushed the bits of greenery off his clothing. Regina was with him in spirit. He was sure of that. He could carry that knowledge with him, even if for now he had to face the world alone.

As he turned toward Highland Avenue, he paused to take in the view, as far as he could see up the street. It was going to be a long walk back. He was glad of it.

Chapter 30

Thomas waited for the afternoon train from Chicago with rapidly decreasing patience. His brain thumped out the words "Regina's—coming—home—Regina's—coming—home" as he stood watching trains moving in and out along the tracks.

It had only been a couple of months since he'd seen her. She'd been home much too rarely during Meredith's pregnancy, and he'd had to spend far too much time remembering the smile in her black eyes, instead of seeing it firsthand, while he endured Meredith's interrogations.

But this time, her homecoming wasn't like any other. She may be the same person, but he wasn't. He was free!

His vigil of anticipation was shattered by a voice at his side. "Hullo, Baldwin! Didn't you hear me yelling?" It was Charles McKay.

Thomas was speechless. What was he doing here? Antagonism swelled in his breast. This was his time—he'd spent the week since he'd received her wire waiting for this day—for the precious drive from the station, alone with her.

"McKay! What brings you to Pittsburgh?"

Charles opened his mouth, closed it again, and looked uncertain. Just then a small voice spoke up at Charles' elbow.

"Who's he, Daddy?" A small boy, about five years old, tugged insistently on his father's sleeve.

"Well, hello," Thomas heard his own surprised voice. "Does this man belong to you?"

The small boy scowled up at him. "He's my daddy," he replied, demonstrating by clinging fiercely to Charles' leg.

"I had business in town, and he wanted to come along. Then I heard—I thought he'd like to meet his Aunt Regina," Charles explained with a shrug which seemed a little bit pathetic to Thomas.

"She's not my aunt," the little boy observed sullenly.

"Robert!" his father scolded.

"Well, she's not," Robert responded, not in the least impressed by his father's admonition.

"She might turn out to be like an aunt," Thomas offered. "You know, the kind of lady who likes to give candy and presents."

The boy squirmed, but said nothing.

Thomas was eaten up with curiosity. How did Charles find out that Regina was coming back today? It didn't sound like Regina had actually written to him. So how did he know to be here?

Apparently, Charles was equally curious about him. "So, she asked you to come get her?"

He could hear the jealousy in the other man's voice! For some reason, this pleased him immensely.

"It seems to have become a tradition, my waiting for a train because of her," he replied, trying to keep a smug note out of his voice.

Charles didn't answer.

Bored, Robert slipped away from the adults and wandered out along the platform. Thomas wondered if Charles even noticed, but said nothing until the boy started throwing rocks at the porters.

"Shouldn't you look to your son?" Thomas inquired.

Surprised by the question, Charles looked down at his legs, then around their immediate vicinity. Thomas pointed down the long wooden platform. "Over there."

"Robbie!" Charles hurried after his son, who took off at a run. Eventually Charles caught the little hooligan, and carried him kicking and squirming back along the platform.

"Why don't we go inside," Thomas suggested. "At least if he runs around, he won't be in any danger of running out on the tracks."

"Oh, my son's smarter than that," answered the proud father. Thomas didn't trust himself to answer. A train whistle distracted everyone's attention.

It was a noisy, magnificent sight, watching a train pull into the station. The whistle blew again, bells clanged, pistons hissed, the air brakes squealed, and all the while the majestic black engine loomed closer and closer until it came to a stop, surrounded by clouds of black smoke and puffs of white steam. Thomas sighed in appreciation for the awesome beauty of the moment.

Charles heard him, and misread the thought behind it. "Women do take forever, don't they? Well, hopefully she won't keep us waiting for too long."

The observation and the assumption both irritated Thomas. He said nothing.

The platform came alive with bodies. Passengers disembarked, conductors, porters, teamsters, and a variety of other railroad men bustled this way and that, friends and families met people from the train. Charles put Robert on his shoulder and left Thomas at his post, in order to walk down the platform in search of Regina.

Regina spotted Thomas before he spotted her, and her smiling face was little more than arm's length away when he actually saw her.

"Hello, Sir Thomas."

The old pet name sent a warm thrill racing through his body. "Hello, My Lady." Two cold noses bumped insistently against his hands, forcing his attention away from her face, adorable under a tall straw hat with drooping ostrich plumes.

"Hullo, Anthra! Hullo, Bit! Missed me, have you?" Thomas was delighted when both black dogs crowded joyfully against him to get their ears rubbed.

"All right, that's enough!" Regina made a soft noise between her teeth, and both dogs obediently returned to sit on either side of her. But they still wagged their tails at him from where they sat at attention.

"It's a shame McKay can't train his son so well," Thomas couldn't help observing with a chuckle.

The smile dimmed a little. "You've seen him recently, then?" she asked with an unmistakable strain in her voice.

"He's here," Thomas told her, even as Charles called from behind her. "Regina!" For a bare second, Thomas caught the look of dismay which passed over her features.

A chilly, distant smile accompanied the hand she held out to Charles. "What a surprise," she said. Was Thomas imagining a drop of acid in her voice?

Anthra and Bit had turned with her, and stepped forward, not toward Charles, but toward young Robbie, who was once again clinging to his father's leg.

What erupted next was pure comedy. Robbie was obviously afraid of dogs. He stood stock-still for a moment, until Bit wagged his tail. Robbie let out a frightened yelp, and began a frantic attempt to climb his father.

"Robert!" Charles' clothes were pulled every which way as the small primate scrambled, pulled and tugged his way onto his father's back. Charles' silk hat tumbled off, and Robert now reached up to use his father's hair to pull himself higher. "Ouch! Robert, they're just a couple of very nice dogs."

"Get 'em away! Get 'em away!" the small boy cried shrilly.

Thomas and Regina stood, laughing. Both dogs were waving their tails in amusement. Charles cursed as his son pulled, hard, on his ear. "Robert, this is not funny."

"Oh, I think this is very funny," Regina remarked. She dismissed the hapless father with a turn of her shapely shoulders. "Thomas, where's George? Here come my trunks."

Thomas caught Charles' look of misery, and only shrugged at him before turning to follow Regina, the dogs, and the porters with her trunks. As soon as he'd turned his back on the comic spectacle, he let his face break into a gleeful smile. If he were a better person, he'd feel sorry for Charles. But Thomas was savoring his first victory.

She laughed with delight as they picked their way through the crowd of carriages and wagons, and she spotted George.

"Hello, George," she shook his hand while the porters loaded her trunks.

"Hello, Mrs. Waring. Welcome home," George opened the carriage door for her.

"It's good to be home, George. Thank you," she answered.

Before Thomas could help Regina into the carriage, Charles came up behind her, small Robert once again perched on his shoulders. Thomas watched the chill drop over Regina's features at Charles' hovering.

He was obviously looking for an invitation to join them. Not seeing any way around it, Thomas searched for the least inviting thing to say.

"Where's your coach, McKay?"

Charles' face lit up at the opening. "Well, actually, I'm staying at the Hotel Washington. Robbie and I had taken the streetcar here, but with all this excitement I imagine this poor fellow's awfully tired for the wait to go back . . . ."

"My dogs do travel with me," Regina pointedly glanced up at the "poor fellow," who was energetically bouncing up and down on his father's shoulders, kicking him with his heels.

"Well, that's okay, Robbie can ride with the coachman. Wouldn't you like that, Robbie? You can have fun, sitting way up high where you can see the horses."

"Horses—horses—horses—horses," Robbie chanted, bouncing and kicking his father in the chest for emphasis.

"See? I knew he'd love it. Up you go, Robbie!" And Charles handed Robert up to poor George's custody, leaving Regina and Thomas to look at each other wordlessly.

"Well?" Charles asked happily. "Shall we?"

"Your son has been deposited," Regina pointed out with that same icy chill in her voice. "My dogs need to be tended to."

Anthra and Bit were ten-year-old dogs now. Regina got into the carriage and coaxed, while Thomas stayed on the ground to help push them up the tall steps into the carriage. Charles hovered over Thomas and offered advice, as did a laughing group of teamsters observing from the wagon beside them. With their help, Bit climbed resolutely up, but after a couple of attempts, Anthra merely stood at the bottom of the carriage block and wagged her tail.

One of the onlooking teamsters took pity on the old dog.

"Here—clear out, you," he said to Thomas and Charles. "Now, don't you worry, miss," he said reassuringly to Anthra. "Ready? One, two, three!" The burly arms lifted, and in a single motion, he'd picked her up and deposited her in the coach.

"Bravo!" Regina shouted, clapping with delight. Then she dove for her pocketbook. "That was well above and beyond the call of duty. Let me . . ."

"Aw, no need, ma'am. I used to have me a dog a lot like this one, myself. Steady temper." He fondled Anthra's ears with one hand, while she gratefully licked his other.

Regina smiled and handed him something, anyway. "Then going home tonight, when you stop off on the way, drink a toast to your dog, and then one to mine. We dog lovers have to stick together."

The teamster was obviously under her spell. "Well, if you put it that way, ma'am. I will. I still miss Pete. He was a good dog."

"This is Anthracite, and this is Bituminous." She patted each black and gray head in turn. "And we all thank you."

"Well, thank you, ma'am. Good day, ma'am!" The big man touched his hat to her and moved back to join his comrades.

Charles climbed into the carriage, while Thomas called up to George, "Hotel Washington, please, George."

There was an awkward silence in the carriage. Thomas was immensely pleased that both Anthra and Bit turned to sit so they could put their heads on his knees. Charles made a half-hearted attempt to coax some attention from them, but after ignoring him for ten years, they were not about to change now.

Annoyed by the disdain of two mere animals, Charles was stung into speech.

"A fine return you make to Pittsburgh, Regina," he scolded. "You're flirting with everyone you lay eyes on."

The last two words, "except me," hung, unspoken, in the air.

"That is one of the very nice privileges of widowhood," Regina answered. "I can speak to whomever I please. No one has the right to order me otherwise." She smiled a trifle wickedly at Thomas. "It's also one of the privileges of my black reputation. I can smile at the mayor, his son, or his bootblack, and no one thinks anything of it. 'That's just Regina,' they say. 'She's always so . . . . egalitarian.'"

Charles was not willing to be put off. "And encouraging drinking? It's unprofessional. They may not be your employees, but they're somebody's. Employers should not be encouraging that sort of behavior."

"So I should shut my eyes and pretend it doesn't happen? Workingmen stop at taverns on their way home. That's how it is. I don't see the point in ignoring that."

"But you—I—it's downright unladylike," Charles protested.

Regina's eyes snapped, and her lips were parting to return a scathing remark when a petulant five-year-old voice called from the driver's box. "Daddy, I've got to go."

Regina looked out the window. They were only a couple of blocks from their hotel. "Hold on, pumpkin, we're almost there," she called out with forced sweetness.

Charles' eyes were round with horror. "No! You don't understand. We've got to stop—now! Driver—driver!"

"His name's George," Regina offered helpfully.

"Driver—George," Charles called as he opened the carriage door. "Stop—now!"

George pulled the horses to a stop, as Charles leaped from the carriage, snatched the little boy from the driver's box, and hurried him around to the alley, where Robbie watered the side of the building thoroughly.

Regina and Thomas watched the scene with their mouths open. They still had no words when Charles' face reappeared at the carriage door. "When he's got to go, well, you see how it is. We're pretty close, so we'll walk it from here."

"Goodbye, McKay," Thomas managed to say. Charles closed the carriage door, and George clicked to the horses.

Regina was literally shaking with repressed laughter. Thomas looked at her—and both of them exploded into howls of amusement.

"These are the joys of motherhood I keep hearing about?" Regina gasped.

They looked at each other a moment, then burst into spasms again. By the time they succeeded in looking at each other without laughing, they were on Fifth Avenue, within sight of the Waring chimneys.

"I hurt," Thomas sighed.

"You hurt? I think I've broken my corset strings," Regina said, her arms wrapped around her slender waist.

That casual, intimate reference made him feel shy, and thrilled him at the same time. Both feelings tied his tongue in knots. He couldn't think of a thing to say. All he could think about was the image of her corseted waist.

Fortunately, since they were both still gasping for air, talk was not required. As always, Thomas was sorry when the carriage rolled to a stop at Elysium.

Before George had the carriage door open, the coach was surrounded by a mob of people. Thomas leaped out in order to help Regina down, but the moment her feet touched the ground, she was swallowed by a happy swarm of servants, friends, neighbors, and people Thomas didn't even know.

Thomas hung back, helping Anthra and Bit make the journey back down the steps. Then he stood watching the crowd with George. He suddenly felt tired; tired of competing with so many, just to get a brief moment of Regina's attention. It would be hours before he'd be able to say anything to her again. Assuming he'd worked the knots out of his tongue by then.

Succumbing to a wave of self-disgust, Thomas turned his back on the happy noise. "Take me home, George."

"Of course, sir." It was only three words, but Thomas could hear the sympathy in George's voice.

****

The next day, Thomas presented his calling card at Regina's front door. The butler who answered the door was new; it was odd waiting in the front parlor after being treated with all the distant courtesy accorded a stranger.

"Mrs. Waring requests you join her and her guest on the porch," the butler returned with a little formal speech. "Follow me, please."

It was on the tip of his tongue to answer "I know the way" and dash past the stately gentleman. With an effort, he reigned in his impatience. She had another guest, anyway. He was still going to be foiled in his attempt to spend time alone with her.

His heart sank as he stepped onto the back porch, and Charles McKay stood up to greet him. "Baldwin, old man! What brings you out here?"

Thomas took a moment to find an answer to the jealously-asked question. "I thought I'd swing by and find out when Regina would like to go over all the Wintergarden news." He couldn't repress a swell of satisfaction at his legitimate claim on Regina. He never needed an excuse to see her. He had a constant one.

"Hello, Thomas!" Regina dropped her tatting in her lap and turned such a warm smile on him that his pulse began to race as he crossed the porch to kiss her hand. "I was hoping you'd come by," she continued. "I didn't get to thank you for bringing me home yesterday. I got inundated the second I stepped out of the carriage."

"Not to worry, My Lady," he answered gallantly. "My duties were done and I'd assumed I was dismissed. Hello, Bit. Hello, Anthra." As he took the empty chair beside Regina, two black bodies trotted over and sat devotedly before him. He scratched each head affectionately.

"Don't see how you tell them apart," Charles grumbled.

"Anthra looks like Anthra, and Bit looks like Bit," Thomas answered. "Their faces aren't the same."

"I hadn't noticed. Well," Charles stood up and took a long look at Regina. She had picked up her tatting again, and was rapidly passing the shuttle back and forth between the lace dripping from her fingers. "I guess I'll be going. I've got a woman watching my boy while he takes his nap, but if he wakes up while I'm gone, he'll be a handful."

"Better hurry, then. We understand. It's difficult, being a parent." She glanced up with an understanding smile, but then her attention returned to her lace.

"I'll see you—later," Charles raised a hand in farewell, then strode down the porch steps and around the side of the house. Regina sat quietly tatting, until they heard carriage wheels start across the cobblestones.

Regina threw down her lace with a sigh of relief. "I thought he'd never leave."

Thomas looked at her carefully. "You did seem awfully quiet. I was worried I'd chosen a bad time to arrive."

She sat forward in her chair, and earnestly squeezed his arm with her hand. "You couldn't have chosen a better time, unless it had been sooner! I nearly raced out to meet you when Alec brought me your card."

Thomas saw his opportunity to get to the bottom of the steely edge in Regina's voice, the change in her whole attitude toward Charles. "Are you and Charles fighting?"

"I wish we were! It's just that, well . . . ." She toyed with the pretty piece of lace in her lap for a moment. "The truth of the matter is, he bores me silly!" she wailed.

Thomas stared at her a moment in astonishment. "Okay," he said slowly, trying to keep the insane feeling of elation out of his voice, "let's hear it. All of it."

The words came tumbling eagerly out of her lips. "That man is a terminal, screaming bore. He never shuts up! Ask him a yes-no question, and he gives an oration on some remotely connected topic."

She paused, and Thomas asked, "So you asked him what time it was, and he told you how to build a watch."

"Not quite!" she continued indignantly. The lace fell, unnoticed, from her lap to the floor, while her voice rose in volume. "He'll tell me the history of time, the materials needed for timepieces, how to mold each part from the raw materials, and then how to assemble the finished product."

Thomas was amused by her continuation of his analogy, and wished he could ask what the actual subject matter had been. Not that she'd mind the breach of decorum, but he didn't want to sidetrack her. It couldn't possibly be as interesting as her tirade.

"At first I thought we used to talk. But then I realized—we didn't. We only had time for one topic. It used to be flattering. Now, I don't want to hear it. I don't want to hear how beautiful I am. How I own him. Or how I'm his refuge."

She shook her head in disgust. "I used to think his introspection was sensitive, and unusual. Now I wish he could take five minutes to stop talking about himself! I don't mind listening. I really don't. But listening should only be half the story. I also want to feel listened to." She covered her eyes with her hands in an amusingly melodramatic pose. "He's never listened to me. Never. What an ass I am."

Her voice had continued to get louder. Mindful of the ears of her servants, Thomas murmured, "I'm right here."

She peeked through her fingers at him for a puzzled moment before she understood his meaning. "Sorry," she murmured back. "I didn't mean to damage your hearing."

"I'm not worried about me, it's the neighbors that concern me," Thomas answered.

"Smart Alec."

Thomas returned to the topic. "So what's going to happen to your relationship now? I assume he wants to pick up where you left off?"

She grimaced. "He gave me a—thorough kiss when he arrived today, along with a wordy speech about how much he'd been wanting to deliver it, and for how long, and so forth. He was so wrapped up in making speeches, he failed to notice my lack of enthusiasm.

"You notice the trend here?" She pointed out acerbically. "It was important that he kiss me, regardless of whether or not I kiss back. It's important he talk to me, it's not required for me to talk back."

"It does appear to be a little one-sided," Thomas agreed.

"While he was sitting here prattling away, I was trying to remember what I could possibly have found attractive about him. I can't seem to remember."

"You've both had time to change," Thomas observed.

"Have we both changed?" Regina asked. "I was wondering. My feelings have, obviously. I was half-crazed with grief when we started our affair in Europe. He was exciting and distracting. It was the thrill of conquest, I suppose, after he was so unattainable when I was young. I'm not the same person I was when I was young—or when I was newly widowed."

"Maybe you've always been several people at once," Thomas offered lightly. "At different times, different parts of you come most readily to the surface."

"I hope not," Regina answered ruefully. "I hope I wasn't always a craven adulteress, waiting for the chance to come to the surface."

"So your morality is catching up with you, after all," Thomas observed, teasingly.

Regina eyed him skeptically. "Is that what it is? Morality? Or just my lack of taste? Lack of judgment? Lack of character?" She chuckled to herself, then continued with seeming irrelevance, "When I was about six years old, I stopped eating carrots. I didn't like them anymore. To this day, my mother will still go on at some length about the subject, insisting it must have been the bad influence of the children I played with. But tastes change. During this jaunt to San Francisco, I found out that I like red wine. I never used to. I've also had four years to outgrow Charles."

She rubbed her forehead. "I'd never considered him awkward before. He's so . . . . gawky. I hate the way he walks. We had tea out here before you came. I hate the way he plays with his food. He can't simply eat a scone. He has to dissect it. There were crumbs everywhere. I'd have an infestation of ants by now, if it weren't for Anthra and Bit . . ." her voice trailed off for a moment while she stared at her dogs, now sprawled happily together on a sunny spot on the porch. "I should have listened to them a long time ago. They've never cared for him."

"It's not that they disliked him," Thomas observed, feeling smug over his own privileged place in their hearts, "they're just—disinterested."

"I have to agree with them. I'm heartily disinterested. And I don't know what to do about it."

"Telling him would be a start," Thomas pointed out gently.

"If I can get a word in edgewise." She put her head against the high rattan chair back and studied the ceiling intently. "I know, I know. I have to. I've never felt like such a complete coward in my entire life."

"You may be many things, My Lady, but a coward is not on the list," he answered reassuringly.

"Oh, yes, it is," she countered. "The idea of looking him in the eye and telling him it's over fills me with dread."

"Well, if you don't tell him," he pointed out practically, "he will try to kiss you again."

She shivered and made a face. "That fills me with dread, too. You're right. I have to rise to the occasion and get it over with."

Chapter 31

The next morning was Memorial Day. Thomas had dismissed his household staff for the day, and was planning to have breakfast with his mother before taking her to the cemetery, so he was very surprised to hear a knock on the door, accompanied by the smell of coffee. He opened the door, puzzled, and stepped out of the way to let Joseph enter with a tray containing a card, the morning paper, and the aromatic coffee.

"Joseph? What in the world are you doing here? Trying to make me look bad? Some employer I make. I won't even give you Memorial Day to pay a visit to your relatives."

"Yeah, you'd mistreat all of us if you thought we'd let you get away with it," Joseph said good-naturedly while he put the tray down, then picked up the card off the tray and handed it to Thomas. "I thought you'd want this, so I figured I'd bring it up to you. Remember if I'm ten minutes late tomorrow, you owe me for today." He paused on his way out of the door. "Watch out with that coffee," he warned. "I made it, not Mrs. Bishop. So it's probably better for blacking boots than drinking."

"Thanks, Joseph. I'll consider myself forewarned." Thomas answered before he turned his attention to the note in his hand, and saw his name scrawled in Regina's handwriting.

It boded no good. He could tell by the feel of the paper in his hand. With a feeling of dread, he tore open the envelope without looking for a penknife.

Even her handwriting looked a little odd.

May 30, 1889

T—

Chas and son left early this morning. Came here to say goodbye. I'm still a coward.

(So—she hasn't told him yet, he thought.)

When you've time to spare, can you stop by? Bituminous passed away last night. Anthra and I would very much appreciate the pleasure of your company.

R

Thomas' eyes began to sting. Good ol' Bit. Poor Anthra was going to be lonely without her lifelong companion!

He looked down at the letter in his hand. Anthra wasn't the only one who was going to miss him terribly.

He dashed to the door and called loudly through the empty house. "Joseph?"

Joseph's voice floated immediately up the stairwell. "Yeah, what do you want? I'm not working anymore today, remember?"

Thomas went over to the stair rail and looked down at Joseph's upturned face. "I'll trade the entire day off tomorrow for a favor," he offered.

He felt very pleased with himself; Joseph actually looked surprised. "Must be some favor," he commented.

"It is," Thomas sighed. "Would you get a message to my mother's house, and let her know I will not be joining her for breakfast? I'll come by later to take her out to the cemetery."

Joseph whistled softly. "That is some favor," he answered.

"At least you won't have to tell her directly. Hopefully, Newland is still there. Actually, most of the staff won't leave until after my mother does."

"Yeah, probably. You Baldwins are all a bitch to work for."

"Thank you, Joseph." Thomas couldn't quite keep the laughter out of his voice.

What did people do when they didn't have a Joseph in their lives to keep things in perspective? He wondered as he went back into his room and changed into proper mourning attire. Of course, Joseph would probably shake his head with everyone else at the very idea of wearing mourning for a dog.

No, he thought as he adjusted the black armband. Joseph had more heart as well as more horse sense than most people. He'd understand.

It was raining lightly when he stepped outside. Of course. It seemed like it had been raining all spring. He grabbed his umbrella before he shut and locked the door. He paused to pick two early roses from one of the potted bushes by the front steps.

Then he realized with a start that George was waiting by the carriage block with the carriage. "George? What are you still doing here?"

"Being useful, sir. There was no point in Joe taking your message to your mother's. I can go there after I take you to Mrs. Waring's."

Thomas mock-glared at his faithful coachman. "You gentlemen are all horrible gossips."

"Yes, sir." George opened the coach door for Thomas. "Is Mrs. Waring all right, sir?"

Thomas looked down at his mourning clothes. "Yes, George. Well, in a manner of speaking. One of her dogs has died. I believe she's taking it rather hard."

"Anthra or Bit, sir?"

"Bit. Shall I deliver your condolences along with mine?"

"Certainly, sir." George latched the carriage door, climbed up to his seat, and they were off at a brisk trot.

Thomas stepped gravely from the carriage when it stopped under the shelter at Elysium's front door. "I'll be back as soon as I've delivered your message, sir," George volunteered. Thomas thanked him, and the carriage pulled away.

He could see Regina sitting forlornly in a wicker rocker on the front porch, Anthra laying at her feet in equal dejection. He was glad he'd plucked two roses from the bush; one for each lady who would miss Bit.

He stopped at the bottom of the stairs. "Good morning, ladies. May I offer the both of you my heartfelt condolences for your loss?"

Regina managed a pitiful little smile and said nothing. Then, in a rush, she abandoned the rocker, flew down the stairs, and ran sobbing into his arms.

He greedily pressed her body against his, wrapping his arms tightly around her. His eyes burned with tears. The umbrella had been knocked from his hands, the force of her flight down the stairs nearly pushed them both out into the rain. He rocked her while she cried, long and hard. He was surprised to taste salt on his own lips. He dried his eyes with the back of his hand, then caressed her head where it lay buried in his shoulder. His hand wandered tenderly over the nape of her neck, rubbed her back, then wound back around the curve of her waist.

"Go ahead and cry, sweeting," he murmured into her hair. "He was a wonderful fellow and he loved you dearly. I'll miss him, too."

She moaned something into his chest that he couldn't decipher. He leaned back a little so he could tilt her face up with his hand. "Would you care to repeat that, dear? I couldn't understand a word of it."

"I don't ever want to see any more death," she repeated with a sniffle. "I've buried a husband, his mother, my parents, now my dog," she listed while he gently wiped the tears from her cheeks. "Anthra probably won't outlive Bit by much, and I'll have to bury her, too."

"Most likely," Thomas smiled. "Unless you're planning on dying soon, your life expectancy is a lot longer than Anthra's."

"I know." Her lips trembled unhappily. "But I'm already dreading it."

Thomas chuckled and folded her back in his arms, his cheek against hers. "You'd better take one death at a time, honey," he said, his lips close to her ear. "Death is a part of life. Why do you suppose we all have a big parlor in the front of the house?"

A breath of mirth ran through Regina's body. "Silly me, I thought it was for entertaining company." She was quiet a moment, then she said in a small voice, "You just called me 'honey.'"

He buried his lips in her hair above her beautiful ear. "Mmmhmmm, I guess I did," he murmured, his mouth traveling forward until his lips were resting against her temple. "Do you object?" he asked, his breath catching in his throat.

"No," she whispered. He could feel the change in her body as she clung to him, pressing her forehead against his lips.

He'd dreamed for years about having her in his arms like this! He savored the feel of her warm skin under his lips, the wet salty taste of the tears he kissed from her eyes.

He could feel the heat of her fingers as they pressed into his back. She was pressing her entire body against his, tilting her face up toward his.

"Darling," she murmured with lips that seemed to pull at his. Ever so lovingly, he kissed her.

Her lips pressed eagerly back against his, with all the warmth and passion he'd imagined her capable of.

They jumped at the sound of carriage wheels on Fifth Street. They looked at the street, then back at each other with a tinge of embarrassment.

"This is an awfully public place for me to be making love to you," Thomas noticed the hint of a blush on her cheeks. "Can we go inside so I might continue?"

Regina smiled. "Absolutely."

Thomas reached down to find her hand and kissed the back of it, never taking his eyes from hers. They were so deep and black. He could swim lost in their depths for the rest of his life. He tucked the hand into the crook of his arm, and escorted her back up the steps.

Anthra was waiting for them, tail wagging, at the top of the stairs. "Hello, Anthra," he scratched the dark head with his free hand. "It seems to me I had something for you . . ." The roses. "Now, where . . ." he turned around, and laughed. There they were, fallen to the ground, forgotten in the throes of lovemaking.

He released Regina's hand from his elbow and kissed it again. "Be right back." Like a schoolboy, he leaped down the stairs and ran over to pick up the crumpled flowers. He took the stairs two at a time and presented them laughingly. "I'd brought these to cheer you both up."

She took them with a happy look. "I'd say you're succeeding without the flowers. Thank you." She carefully tucked one into Anthra's collar, then looked quizzically at her dress for a moment before she decided to slide the second blossom into her hair.

He watched her with admiration. The yellow rose glowed against her black hair, and went very well with the unusual gown she was wearing. It had an ivory-yellowish lace ruffle from her throat to her hem, as well as around her wrists, and seemed otherwise simple, except that her train seemed to be going all the way up to the back of her neck.

"You look like an empress, in that thing," he said approvingly.

She looked up at him with a coquettish smile. "I always did think you had marvelous taste," she said playfully.

"My taste in women, at least, has been impeccable," he answered gallantly as he opened the front door for her. "After you, My Lady."

"Thank you, Sir Thomas," she dipped in a curtsey, then sailed through the door with a royal grace befitting her name.

She waited in the hall while he closed the door. "I've greeted you in this hall and wondered what it would be like to kiss you," she confessed frankly.

"Why should you wonder? You've done it before," he pointed out, recalling their picnic oh, so long ago, and the kiss she'd given him in the carriage.

"I have? When did I do that?" she asked in wonderment.

Thomas grabbed his chest in mock horror, although he felt a stab of real hurt. "You don't remember? I've been living on that kiss for thirteen years and you don't remember? It was after our picnic on the Duquesne Heights when you listened to the whole horrible story of how I ended up married to Meredith."

"Well, it doesn't surprise me if I did. Your story broke my heart, and I felt such incredible pity for you. I felt so close to you. I'd never met a man as completely and totally honest before. You bared your soul to me without the least reservation. I was very moved."

"So moved you don't even remember kissing me," Thomas grumbled.

"That was a lot of years ago," she protested. "Can't you forgive me some lapses of memory? I'm not as young and impetuous as I was then." She stepped into the parlor doorway and looked an invitation to him. "But I'll make it up to you if you'll let me."

If he'd let her? He closed the distance with long strides, followed her into the parlor, and closed the pocket doors behind him. He caught her around the waist, and playfully waltzed her around the room a moment before pulling her close and tenderly lowering his mouth to hers.

Her lips fit perfectly against his. Her mouth was warm and sweet and soft and tasted—like no other flavor on earth. So this is what heaven tasted like!

Regina was the first to break their contact. "I need to catch my breath," she confessed with a little gasp.

Thomas chuckled, sat down on the settee, and pulled her gently to sit on his lap. He cuddled her against him, savoring the feel of her weight across his legs, the whisper of fabric tickling his face, her scent filling his nose. "You've been leaving me breathless for years, My Lady. 'Tis only fair I get the chance to do the same."

She wrapped an arm around his shoulders and playfully rubbed her nose against his. "You've left me wondering for years and years what it would be like to get behind that very proper demeanor of yours, and now you want to talk about fairness?"

He nibbled on her neck until she squealed with delight, and nearly wriggled off his lap, then he captured her around the waist and held her lips in another long, satisfying kiss.

"There, My Lady, is that improper enough to suit you?" he asked imperiously, then couldn't resist kissing her, quickly, again. "I see I've misnamed you. I shouldn't call you 'lady.' I should be calling you 'wench.'"

"Oh, poppycock," she answered archly. "Ladies and queens and scullery maids all want affection from the man they love."

"Do you love me, Regina?" he asked, tenderly and shyly, before he lost his nerve.

She smiled and nodded, looking shy herself. "I've been saying so in every letter I've written you, and I've wondered how you've interpreted it."

"As I've read and reread and reread your wonderful letters, I've thanked my lucky stars to have such a warm, wonderful and affectionate friend. But I didn't dare hope for more than that." He had to pause to nuzzle her hair and nibble gently on her earlobes.

She gasped, then laughed that low soft laugh that sent warm shivers down his arms. He'd loved her laugh since he'd first heard it, a lifetime ago, in his parents' conservatory.

"So, why didn't you dare hope for more than that?" she eventually asked.

He leaned back and looked at her in surprise. "How could I? You've been—ah—occupied with other men, until very recently. Barring that little obstacle, I also happen to be acutely aware of the fact that you've had more than a few proposals of marriage, starting the day after Henry died. I seem to recall these suitors weren't very well received by you, Madam. I haven't been eager to join the ranks of the rejected. I couldn't bear that."

Wordlessly, Regina caressed his face with her fingers. He kissed her fingertips as they passed over his lips. "Besides all that, my angel, I haven't exactly been a free man, myself."

She ran her fingers through his hair, her eyes still hungrily devouring his face. "My honorable Sir Thomas," she smiled.

"Yes, well, and speaking of honorable . . . ." he put his hands around her waist and stood her on her feet, so that he could slip off the settee and onto one knee. Kneeling at her feet, he took her hand in his, and looked up at her earnestly.

"I have dreamed of the possibility of this moment since the day I first laid eyes on you," he confessed.

"When you threw rocks at me," she teased.

"Don't interrupt," Thomas teased her back. "I'm trying to bare my soul to you, and that's hard enough as it is."

She looked earnestly into his face. "Is it? You've done it before."

"I've shown you the tip of the iceberg, is all. I've invested a great deal of myself in not saying things to you, My Lady."

"Can you say them now?" she asked with a gentle and encouraging smile.

"I'm trying," Thomas answered, unable to resist the urge to continue teasing. "But you keep talking. I can't make a pretty speech to you if you keep interrupting."

She arched an eyebrow at him. "Haven't I been telling you I've listened to enough pretty speeches?" She tossed her head indignantly, and sat down on the settee. "I also listen to plenty of pompous speechmaking windbags in order to bring home big, fat contracts."

Thomas put his chin on her knee and looked up at her. "You do more than your share of listening, don't you? Which doesn't seem right, since you have more wisdom than any other two people I know. You're the one people should be listening to. I always do."

Regina looked tenderly at him. "Yes, you do. You and Henry are the two best listeners I've ever had in my life. I'm sure it's no coincidence why I've loved the two of you more than anyone else I've ever known."

The lump rising in Thomas' throat got in the way of his saying anything more. He took her hand, turned it palm up, lifted back the lace ruffle, and pressed his lips against her warm wrist.

He delighted in the sound of her ragged sigh. He could feel her pulse pounding against his lips. Then he became aware of his own heart racing as she ran her free hand through his hair, and caressed the back of his neck. He let his lips roam over the palm of her hand, chewed along her fingers, explored each tapering fingertip with his tongue. A little moan sounded in the back of Regina's throat.

He turned her hand over and kissed the back of her hand, then wrapped his hand around hers and held it against his heart.

"Regina," he looked into her eyes and tried to remember to keep breathing. "Loving you has been the single most important thing in my life. Will you consent to marry me, so that I might do a better job of it?"

Her eyes shone as she looked back into his—then, inexplicably, a shadow passed over her face.

"I don't know if I can, Thomas." His heart stopped. He'd been so sure . . . . He stared at her in shock.

Regina touched him tenderly. "Do you realize how many rights a widow has that I'd give up if I were to marry again? I've enjoyed being able to make my own contracts."

Thomas felt desperate. "I don't want to take away any of your rights. I just want the right to love you with my whole heart and soul! You can write up a marriage contract to say whatever you'd like. But for God's sake, Regina, don't make me live without you the rest of my life!"

She leaned forward and kissed him. "What makes you think I want to live without you? I'd like nothing better than to spend the rest of my life with you."

"Then marry me," Thomas persisted. "Get your lawyers to investigate every law on the books and write the longest marriage contract ever written. Instead of combining our empires, we'll run them side by side. I don't need your property, Regina. But I desperately need you."

She looked searchingly into his face, then slowly smiled. "Combining our empires. I like the way you put that. We do work well together, don't we?"

"There are more than a few glass houses bearing witness that we're good partners," Thomas agreed softly.

"We are good partners," she smiled into his eyes.

"We were absolutely made for each other."

"I think you're right. I'll have my lawyers draw up that contract."

It took Thomas a moment to realize what she meant. "What did you say?" he asked, incredulous and elated.

"I said, 'Yes, I will marry you, Mr. Baldwin,'" she answered with a fair representation of prim maidenly reserve.

Thomas let out a whoop and, in a single movement, propelled himself off his knees, onto the couch, and folded Regina in his arms. "You will?" he laughed joyously, loving the sound of her answering laughter in his ears. "You really will?"

"Yes, you benighted boy, I will," she laughed. "I must be crazy. I swore up and down to Charles that I had no intention of ever marrying again."

The mention of Charles' name cast a pall over their giddy happiness.

"Charles. He isn't going to take this very well," Thomas commented.

"And because of my cowardice, now he'll blame you for my change in affections," Regina realized.

"Maybe it's easier this way," Thomas offered. "It'll be easier for him to understand that you've found another man, rather than trying to tell him that you've simply fallen out of love with him."

"That may be easier for his ego, but it's no easier for me to tell him," Regina snorted.

"Write him a letter and explain it to him," Thomas suggested.

Regina regretfully shook her head. "I couldn't do that. That would be . . . I don't know, wrong. I have to look him in the eye and tell him that I'm getting married and it's over."

Thomas gently squeezed her in a tighter embrace and kissed the top of her head. "We'll tell him together. He's going to feel betrayed by both of us, so we might as well face him together."

"I can't ask that of you, Thomas," Regina started to protest.

"Of course you can," Thomas answered with a smile. "I'm your fiancé."

By the time Thomas left, he had arranged to meet Regina at the train station the following morning. He rode to his mother's house on a cloud, a broad and foolish grin on his face, thinking of her clinging goodbye kisses.

Chapter 32

Thomas hardly slept that night. His brain kept him awake with memories of past dreams, added to the fresh ones he created as he lay in the dark, staring at the ceiling. His lips felt slightly chapped from all the kisses he'd given that amazing day. He savored the burning feeling, and anticipated the thought of being able to kiss her again in the morning.

The sky was barely more than gray when he abandoned his pillow and dressed for the journey. He could hear the rain falling off and on all night—now the silence seemed loud. He wished they hadn't decided to take the 8:10 Day Express. If they'd agreed on a later train, he could have had time to get to the jewelers to pick out an engagement ring for her. Ah, well. No hurry. It might be more fun to choose a wedding ring with her, rather than for her.

He wanted to giggle with glee at the idea. There was no hurry. There was all the time in the world; he had the rest of his life with her!

Joseph eyed him curiously when he showed up downstairs, early, already dressed, and asked for his breakfast to be delivered to the morning room.

"Making an early start of it, today," Joseph commented nonchalantly.

Thomas knew better than to assume any innocence on the part of his staff, but chose not to enlighten them yet. For today, at least, his engagement was his secret.

"I didn't sleep well," at least that part he could disclose honestly. "I gave up trying." He looked up at Joseph in surprise. "Wait a minute, aren't you supposed to be taking today off?"

Joseph shrugged. "Yeah, I guess you'll just have to owe me later. I was dressed and here before I remembered."

"You're a brick, Joseph."

"Don't you forget it, sir."

He paced around both the first and second floors and realized he'd have to sell the house. As much as he still admired it, and it had served him well as a refuge from both Meredith and the world, he didn't want a refuge anymore. He was tired of hiding. It was time to make a new life. It required a new house, a shared space where he and Regina could make their own memories. He liked the idea of building a home together, as well as an office. He'd build her a castle. No—a palace. They could go to Vienna on their honeymoon, and come back with the inspiration for a splendid new home, sprawling across the top of a hill . . . somewhere around here.

He continued drifting along in a happy daydream, imagining her face across from his at breakfast, her figure beside him in the carriage, as George drove him to the depot.

"Thomas? Wake up, dear, you're sleepwalking!" Regina's laughing voice filled his ears. He blinked as if he had, indeed, been sleeping. Regina was standing right in front of him, her black eyes merry and her face full of love. He wanted to kiss her right there, ignoring every one of the jostling passers-by. He contented himself with squeezing one slender gloved hand.

"I'm daydreaming, not sleepwalking," he answered honestly.

Regina's eyes sparkled wickedly. "'bout me?" she asked.

"No, about putting up a new building," he answered with as businesslike an air as he could muster.

Both black eyebrows shot up at once. "Oh?"

He laughed in triumph, and kissed her hand. "Yes, I was thinking about you, vain creature! And about building. I was thinking that we should build a house of our own in which to start our wedded bliss."

Regina smiled in delight. "Even though I'd hate to part with Elysium, I was also wondering last night if we should build some neutral territory. Or was it this morning . . . hard to say." She rolled her eyes coquettishly at him. "I didn't get much sleep last night."

"Worrying about today?" Thomas asked tenderly.

"No," she answered. "I was thinking about us."

"Is that so, my angel in . . ." he glanced down to see what color she was wearing, and got distracted with surprise. "You're wearing that on a train?"

Her dress was the sort of dark gray one always saw on women traveling by train. But the front of her dress was a riot of black embroidery, reaching completely from her neck to the floor.

She tilted her chin up proudly. "Well, I want to look pretty for my fiancée," she said.

Thomas could tell by the tone of her voice there was more to it. "And?" he prompted.

She smiled. "It's called a 'surprise dress.' I simply have to button it up," she folded the embroidery toward herself, and he realized it was entirely decorated on 2 long lapels that folded shut into a prim traveling dress with long rows of shiny black buttons, completely covering the fine needlework, "and I'm ready for the train soot."

"Ah," he smiled, only having eyes for her happy face. "Another mystery of the feminine wardrobe revealed."

Her smile changed and she lifted an eyebrow at him. "There's a whole lot of wardrobe I haven't revealed to you—yet," she murmured.

A noise escaped from Thomas, while a rush of desire left his legs feeling weak. "I hope you're planning on setting a date soon, my radiant beauty. If you're going to make statements like that, I don't think I could stand a long engagement."

Her smile softened lovingly as she looked up at him. "Next week?"

Thomas was thrilled. "Really?"

"Why not? Neither one of us needs much family around. We could even elope." Her eyes got bigger. "Maybe we should. After Johnstown let's keep going east and get married somewhere. New

York. Boston. Washington. Altoona. Wherever we feel like jumping off the train."

Thomas laughed. "We're not exactly packed for an adventure. This was supposed to be a day trip."

She smiled more wickedly than ever. "What exactly do you think you need to pack? Clothes? I don't think we'll be needing any."

Thomas pulled her into his arms and hugged her tightly. "I can see being married to you will be the biggest adventure of my life. I can't imagine a more appropriate way to start our marriage."

She buried her face against his chest for a moment. When she looked up, her eyes were bright with tears. "When Henry died and I thought my life was over, you brought me my dogs and gave me something to think about besides myself. When I started wallowing in my own self-pity and loneliness, you sent me to Europe to find myself. When I came back from Europe involved with Charles, you barely batted an eye, because all you cared about was my happiness. You've been a barrier reef against all the chaos the universe has sent me!"

"Sweetheart..." Thomas was interrupted by the announcement that the Day Express was now loading. In the chaos that followed the announcement, he pulled her behind the nearest pillar and kissed her.

"I love you," he told her, kissing her cheeks, forehead and eyes after he left her mouth alone.

"I love you, too," she whispered back, a little breathlessly. "And if we keep this up, we're going to miss our train."

He kissed her lips one more time, then, exchanging smiles, he took her elbow and they scuttled through the emptied waiting room and onto their train.

****

The familiar ride out to Johnstown had never flown by so quickly. They talked, they laughed, they watched the other passengers inside and the soggy landscape outside. People around them buzzed about the Memorial Day parades, the very wet spring weather, the high cost of a railroad ticket. A high-spirited company of actors on their way to Altoona kept up a lively flow of dialogue, turning heads frequently in their direction. It gave Thomas ample opportunities for stealing kisses from his bride-to-be.

They were both a little surprised when the conductor announced Johnstown. Thomas saw a shadow pass over Regina's face. He squeezed her hand. "Nervous?"

She looked down at their hands and nodded slightly. "Now I am," she admitted.

All thoughts of Charles left their heads when they stepped onto the railroad platform into a driving rain and viewed the chaos that was Johnstown. The city was under water!

There was a sense of patient amusement in the air. Livestock were sloshing past in small numbers, driven by adolescent children getting the family cow or horses to higher ground. There were faces in windows, and even on rooftops. Across the street from the depot, a small collection of men had gathered on a front porch, laughingly calling advice to a couple of young men trying to dislodge their mule, which seemed to be stuck in the mud.

"I should have realized Johnstown would be pretty wet," Regina groaned.

"Pretty wet!" Thomas exclaimed in disbelief. "The streets are under water!"

"That's spring in Johnstown," Regina shrugged. "When I was a child, our yard would become part of the Stony Creek almost every year. One of my sisters is still living in the house I bought for my parents up on Jackson—it was as far away as I could get them from that river." She looked around at the muddy mess and laughed ruefully. "Well, now what?" she asked.

"Do you want to go home?" Thomas suggested.

"Can we?" Regina looked shrewdly down the tracks. "This water's rising awfully fast. I imagine we've arrived on the last train that's going in or out of Johnstown for awhile."

Thomas had to agree. There didn't seem to be much course of action. He looked speculatively back at the train. "We could get back on the train and keep going. We can stop on our way home and let him know," he suggested.

Regina followed his gaze, then looked back at the rain pouring down. "I'll bet nobody's going that way, either. Let's ask. If they're not holding the trains, let's get back on and keep going. If they're holding it, let's stay here and make the best of it."

The waiting room was in as big a state of confusion as the rest of the town. Keeping tight hold of Regina's hand, Thomas eventually pushed his way through to the ticket desk.

"Is the Day Express going to be able to continue going east?" He asked a hassled-looking clerk.

"Of course," the clerk answered much more calmly than he looked. "The Pennsylvania Railroad will take care of all its passengers."

Regina gave the young man a penetrating look. "Is it continuing anytime soon?" she asked pointedly.

The clerk cleared his throat and dropped his eyes under her gaze. "Well, ma'am, a section of track up the valley has actually washed out, but we're working to fix the problem," he confessed with hasty reassurance.

Thomas and Regina exchanged looks. "Thank you," she smiled at the clerk, "that's all we needed to know."

Thomas took Regina's elbow and escorted her back outside to watch the rain pouring down.

"Well, we're stuck here," Regina sighed, then laughed. "Shall we try to get on with our intended business? The day's already off to a disastrous start. Why not make a complete wreck of it?"

"If you'd like," Thomas concurred dubiously. He peered up at the gray skies, then looked at the river flowing just off the platform. "The rain does seem to be letting up a bit, although I don't think that will matter much, if you're planning on going for a walk in this."

But Regina wasn't listening. She dashed away down the platform, out into the rain, waving. Thomas realized what she was doing. A man in a skiff was going by, laden with a jumbled assortment of boxes and bundles rescued from some wetter part of town.

"Hey," Regina called, waving to catch the boatman's attention, "could you be prevailed upon to give rides? We're trying to get to the Johnstown Iron offices."

The man in the skiff glanced back over his shoulder, Thomas presumed in the direction of the offices. "Water's higher down there," he observed, "but if that's where yinz aiming to go, I'll take yinz—soon's I get these to my cousin's house. I'll come back, if yinz want to wait."

"Deal!" Regina answered with a smile Thomas recognized from a negotiations table. "Thank you!"

The boater nodded and pulled away.

"Say—there's room for one more in that boat, isn't there?" Thomas and Regina turned at the voice. "Mr. Elder!" they exclaimed at the same time.

"Mrs. Waring? Mr. Baldwin? What are you doing here?" Besides Charles, Cyrus Elder was the only other member of the South Fork Fishing and Hunting Club who actually lived in Johnstown.

"Wishing we hadn't picked today to catch the Day Express to come up here!" Regina answered with a comic face.

"Bad timing on your part," Mr. Elder shook his head sympathetically. "I'm wishing I had left Chicago sooner. I don't know what I dread more: seeing the mess this has made of my office, or of my house!" He looked ruefully out over the water. Thomas and Regina realized they could see the Elder house from where they stood. Mrs. Elder and their daughter Nannie stood on the front porch, watching anxiously. They waved at them, and the Elder ladies responded with a wave of handkerchiefs.

"So close, but yet so far!" Regina exclaimed. "Well, certainly, if our gallant gondolier returns and doesn't mind the errands, we'll let him take you home before we attempt to go further."

Thomas noticed that Regina was not forthcoming about their errand in town. Well, how would they explain their "business" in Johnstown?

It was a long wait, but eventually the skiff bumped along the platform. "Yinz is still here, I see," the boatman remarked. "Sure yinz want to go? It's kinda wet out here for a lady."

Regina examined her dress. "I'm wet already," she pointed out. "It's too late to worry about that." She paused, and looked at Cyrus Elder. "Could we trouble you to take this gentleman across to his house first? He's just over there." She pointed at the house where the Elder women were still watching from the porch.

The boater looked across to the house and shrugged. "Sure. Yinz can all three fit on here," he offered.

Regina looked a trifle dubiously at the little boat. "Are you sure?" she asked a little uncertainly.

The chest of the boatman got a little larger. "Of course I'm sure."

Regina smiled apologetically. "Aye, Captain," she answered lightly. "You know your craft." She gathered up her damp skirts and confidently stepped off the train platform and into the skiff.

Thomas had to admire her coolness. He had a few misgivings himself about having four people in the little skiff. But since she'd committed them to this venture, he didn't see the point of fussing now. He stepped down into the boat, then turned back to give a hand to the older and stouter Mr. Elder.

The skiff sank alarmingly when all four of them were aboard. Regina gave up her seat across from the boatman to Mr. Elder, who had at first elected to hunker down awkwardly in the middle. She knelt gracefully in the small space at the front of the craft, while Thomas did the same at the back.

Finally arranged, they pushed away from the train platform that had served so handily as their dock. Almost immediately, the little boat was caught in a swiftly-moving current that pushed them sideways; and away from the Elder house.

"Ah!" Cyrus Elder let out a cry of frustration as his house got farther from view with surprising rapidity. The boatman grunted and pulled on his oars to stop the craft's momentum, but when he pointed them in the direction they wanted to go, he had trouble rowing faster than the current, and they merely traveled backwards instead of sideways.

A collection of debris floated toward them, bumping against the boat and sending it into a spin. It was a relief when they bumped rather urgently against the side of a building. The three passengers dug their fingers into the brick, and hung on with all their strength against the current. They surveyed their watery predicament.

"We need out of this current," the boatman observed.

Thomas had to agree. He watched the water for a moment, then realized that he could see calm water behind another building across the "street."

Holding onto the bricks with one hand, he tapped the boatman on the shoulder and pointed. "It looks like the current should take us pretty close to there, if we can escape behind that building."

The boater looked and nodded. "Worth a try."

On the count of three, they pushed away from the brick. The boatman quickly got them pointing forward, and he began pulling hard for the calm waters.

"We're gonna make it!" Regina cried enthusiastically.

The next sound Thomas heard was a crunch, then the sound of water rushing into his ears. He found the ground with his feet, and stood up in waist-deep water, spitting the foul-tasting stuff out of his mouth.

His companions were all emerging from the water, too. Thomas looked downstream. There were the remains of the skiff, being pushed downriver by a floating telegraph pole. They had all been so intent on their destination, no one had noticed its approach. He walked awkwardly through the mud and moving water to Regina's side.

She was pushing wet hair out of her face under a drooping hat which was, amazingly, still attached to her head. She looked up at him ruefully. "Okay," she volunteered, her voice still twinkling with her sense of humor, "I'd like to admit that this was a really bad idea."

Thomas stood protectively between her and the onslaught of the current. "So this is more adventure than even you've bargained for?"

"In a word? Yes!" She looked around to see how their companions fared. "Mr. Elder? Skipper? You both alright?"

"My dear lady, if we both survive this ordeal, I'm going to have to insist that we call each other by our given names."

"Why, thank you, Cyrus. Now, are you alright?" Regina repeated.

"Actually," the venerable town citizen cleared his throat, "I would seem to be a bit stuck in all this mud. I can't move my left foot."

"Hm. I'll see what I can do." Thomas took a deep breath and plunged down into the chilly dank water.

He blindly groped down Cyrus' leg, until his hands sunk into slimy muck. He tugged upwards on the leg, and felt the muscles straining as Cyrus tried to pull himself free. Out of air, Thomas resurfaced for a breath.

Since pulling had failed, on his second dive he started digging at the offending matter with both hands, sending it downstream and hoping more wouldn't wash in from upstream as quickly as he dug.

It took two more gulps of air, then Cyrus pulled his foot free.

When Thomas stood back up, he realized that their boatman had been standing guard upstream, making sure none of the floating debris hit the rest of them. "Let's get out of this current," he advised.

While it was only about thirty feet to the still waters, it was slow going. Cyrus Elder, being the heaviest, sank deepest into the muck, and got stuck a second time.

"I'm going to go for a horse," their boatman volunteered.

"We'll keep you company," Thomas offered while the boatman struggled more rapidly through the water.

"Nonsense," Cyrus protested. "The current's letting up, and you should get this lovely lady out of here. This water's cold."

Regina was starting to look pretty miserable. She gave a tired version of her usual smile and protested, "We can't leave you here."

"Of course you can. I'll be fine. Go. Thomas, get her out of here."

"Yes, sir!" Thomas really didn't want Regina standing in this cold, mucky water any longer, and was glad to cut the argument short by obeying. With a last "good luck" to Cyrus, he took Regina's hand, and together they struggled forward.

They were able to move a little more swiftly once they reached the shelter of the building, where the water had deposited less mud. From the far corner, Regina looked around. "This is Main Street." She frowned at the dirty canal before them, then decided, "Let's see if we can get as far as Hulbert House."

Thomas gave her hand an encouraging squeeze. "You're the native. Lead the way!"

Regina smiled and squeezed his hand in return. Behind them, they heard Cyrus Elder's voice calling out.

"Hullo, Dr. Chapman! Have you any fishing tackle?"

Heartened by their companion's unflagging sense of humor, they resumed their trudge forward with renewed vigor.

****

A lot of people seemed to think that the Hulbert House, a sturdy four-story brick building, was a good place to take refuge. The building was crawling with local families as well as out-of-town guests still in Johnstown for the Memorial Day festivities. Everyone else seemed to have arrived in a much drier condition, however. When Thomas and Regina arrived, bedraggled, cold and very wet, staff members politely refused to let them inside the building.

The front porch made a decent resting place, while they surveyed the mess and decided on a plan of attack. Listening to the other porch occupants, they learned that Johnstown Iron had closed their offices, and sent everyone home to look to their families. "You'd think Mr. Benford would be so considerate, and send us home," more than one employee sniffed.

Regina met Thomas' eyes with ironic humor. "Where do you suppose he is?" Thomas asked her.

"By now, holed up on the third floor of his house," she answered wryly. "His house is probably in the deepest part of this mess."

"It's just as well we didn't see him today," he commented.

"Not that it'll be any better, telling him while he's cleaning up after this is over."

"At least it's sort of symbolic," Thomas answered.

"I'd gladly do away with melodrama right now," she told him with a sour look. "I wanted to tell him, get it over with, and be back on a train out of here by now." She sighed impatiently. "Now we're stuck here, for goodness knows how long, and when we finally can go see him, it will be the worst possible timing. I'm wishing we hadn't bothered. We should've stayed on the Day Express."

Another refugee turned around. "I didn't mean to eavesdrop, ma'am, but are you talking about this morning's train?"

Regina smiled a trifle sheepishly. "Yes, I am."

"I hear tell they're held up at the yards in East Conemaugh. They didn't get very far. The track's washed out. So you're just as well off here, as stuck on the train." His eyes flicked over their bedraggled state. "Except for getting wet, that is."

"I hate sitting here, waiting for the water to go down." Regina shivered and looked at Thomas. "Since we're not welcome here, and Charles' house is farther away, I think we should try to get to my family's house on Jackson Street. Besides being closer, it's also on higher ground."

"All right," he answered.

Having made the decision to move, it took a while to do so. There wasn't as much traffic on the muddy water as there had been earlier; by now all the livestock were moved, and the people who wanted to find higher ground had already found it. Everyone else was no doubt sequestered in the upper floors of the homes, waiting out the boredom. It was quite some time before a homemade raft floated down Clinton Street. Two adolescent boys were propelling themselves with long pieces of wood they had undoubtedly fished out of the debris that floated by almost continuously.

"Hello!" Thomas called out to them as they came closer. "Would you consider taking on passengers?"

The younger of the two boys pointed to the frame building across the street. "We're not going far," he said.

"Can we have use of it, then?" Thomas asked hopefully.

Both boys looked at him doubtfully. Thomas dug in his pockets, and found just the thing. He held up a big, shining fifty-cent piece.

"I wouldn't want to interfere with any business you boys had planned, but I can at least compensate you for your trouble," he offered.

The boys' eyes got large. "A whole fifty cents," one of them gasped. "We could make another raft later!"

Thomas played with the upheld coin. "Do we have a deal?"

"Yeah!"

The next problem was the transfer of merchandise. Eventually, a length of rope was attached to the raft, the half-dollar exchanged hands, the boys floated to their front porch, then Thomas pulled the raft back across the street to the hotel. He and Regina established themselves on their knees on the uncomfortable lengths of log and broken telegraph poles, then waved cheerfully at the boys while they took off.

"Okay, I confess Thomas, this probably qualifies as too much adventure—even for me!" Regina declared as she freed her pole from a particularly tenacious patch of mud hidden under the water.

A soft rumble of thunder sounded in the distance, and they both groaned.

"Just what we need," Thomas observed. "More water."

"Well, I suppose thunder doesn't necessarily mean more rain," Regina answered hopefully.

It was an odd sort of thunder. It took Thomas a moment to realize why. Then it occurred to him that it was continuous, and getting louder, instead of fading away.

A strange black fog began to drift through the air. They froze, staring at each other, listening. The rumble increased like—what?

It was a cross between an oncoming train, and—and—Thomas imagined this must be what an avalanche must sound like.

Then he knew what was going on. The South Fork dam had broken!

Before he could share his insight, Regina's face changed. She stared up Clinton Street, mouth open, eyes wide with horror. She pointed, incoherent noises issuing from her throat. Thomas turned, and nearly fell off their precarious little raft.

The source of the crashing rumble was a towering wall of debris moving toward them. A misty black cloud hung in the air, occasionally obscuring the horrific sight. A writhing mass of tree roots, rooftops, planks, railroad pieces and other metal parts tumbled over and over upon itself.

The rumble had clarified into a roar of screaming and crashing as the rapidly approaching behemoth rolled toward them. They couldn't outrun it, either on or off their little craft. Regina pointed to the nearest building. The brick corners were coined, laid unevenly enough to make a decent ladder. Thomas understood without a word. They poled their way across the watery distance, desperation giving them strength and speed.

Regina looked at him as they grabbed the corner of the building. "You go first," she shouted over the noise.

Thomas didn't understand why, but this was no time to stand around arguing etiquette. He stood up on the raft, found a foothold and handhold, and clambered up the side of the building. He slowed his ascent to look down at Regina.

Gritting her teeth in determination, she was making slow progress. Looking up, she caught his eye as he waited, uncertainly, for her. "Don't wait for me! Go!" He could barely hear her over the roar.

Frustrated and helpless, he climbed up onto the roof, then lay on his stomach so that he could reach back down toward Regina. She was making better time, but he feared the wall of debris would reach the roof before she would. He scooted forward, upside down on the pitched roof, caught hold of her wrist, and managed to bodily yank her onto the roof beside him.

"Why did you have me go first?" he demanded angrily.

"No reason we should both die," she answered.

The words were no sooner out of her mouth then Thomas was absolutely certain they were both going to die. With a grinding, crunching, screaming moan, the wave hit the building.

The roof jerked free of its brick walls. Thomas and Regina clung desperately to any small fingerhold they could find, then scrambled toward the peak as the entire roof tilted and lurched. Something momentarily righted their precarious new craft as they sprawled across the peak, and they used that opportunity to rise to a crouch on all fours. Fear gripped them again as their roofraft careened swiftly toward the top of a tall frame building.

"Thomas!" Regina shrieked his name. He looked up—and saw nothing. Something large and hard hit him on the side of the head, then something else punched him in the stomach. The water was less cold than he would have guessed. The horrible grinding and crunching sounded less loudly in his ears. He felt something rough and wooden under his hands. He climbed, using both his hands and feet, blind and unsure if he was even moving upwards. His chest and throat started burning. He desperately wanted air!

Suddenly, he could breathe again. He and what seemed to be part of a barn door were floating rapidly downstream. He bounced through a lake of muddy water strewn with the remains of many a Johnstown establishment. A dead horse collided into his latest craft. It clung gruesomely to the edge for some time, then floated free when the current changed. On the far side of the river, a child on a mattress cried frantically for help. He tried to steer in the child's direction, to no avail. He was caught in a much swifter part of the current, which was pushing him upstream on a separate river from the one that had brought such destruction to Johnstown.

A blur of frightened faces flew by: people clinging to the hill that loomed over Johnstown on one side, men leaning out of miraculously standing buildings attempting to fish survivors out of the water, two nearly naked children clinging to branches of a tree. At one point, he could swear he saw a collection of small flags floating in the water. Then he found his craft becalmed, and looked around for a place to land. Nearly intact houses floated lazily by, frequently with people clinging to their rooftops or visible in upstairs windows.

He fished a longish board out of the water, thinking to use it as a paddle to propel himself toward the hill. Steep as it was, he was willing to try scaling the side rather than spend any more time floating in the perilous waters!

Unfortunately, the water wasn't ready to give him up yet. A tree caught the edge of his craft, and he found himself pulled back into the current but now heading the way he'd come.

A scream for help made him turn around. A young woman clutching a bundle to her chest was leaning out the window of a building that was crumpling as it sailed with the current. Thomas looked up and held out his arms, assuming the bundle was an infant.

"Throw me the baby, then jump!" He advised. She stared at him a moment, he didn't know whether out of fear or because she couldn't hear him over the noise. He waved for her to jump, and held out his arms again.

She tossed her bundle out the window. Thomas nearly missed it, trying to maneuver on the soaking wet and muddy surface. His fingers caught the edge. He grabbed frantically, then he was holding the bundle against his chest. The contents began to scream with fright, but he barely glanced at the baby as he put it down to help the woman. Alarmed, he realized she was still watching from the window, even though the building was breaking apart all around her.

"Jump!" He shouted, waving her toward him with both hands.

She obeyed, and not a moment too soon. Before she even reached the water, the wooden building collapsed sideways.

Thomas searched the filthy water frantically. Where was she? His breath caught with relief when a wet head resurfaced. He lay down on his stomach, held onto one end of his plank with both hands, and struggled against the current to point it in her direction.

He succeeded, and she managed to grab on and pull herself onto the relative safety of his raft.

"Gott sei Dank, Gott sei Dank," the woman sobbed, crawling over to collect the squalling bundle.

Thomas couldn't afford to pay much attention to his new-found companions. More houses and other dangerously large flotsam were coming toward them, and he realized any one of them could either dump him and his passengers back into the murky water, or crush them all to death. He stuck his plank into the water behind them, hoping he could get it to work like a rudder.

It worked!

With the first faint glimmer of optimism he could ever remember feeling, he steered toward a building that was, amazingly, still standing, and from which two men were hanging out an attic window, fishing desperate people out of the water. He fervently hoped Regina had found such a refuge.

They saw Thomas coming, and waved and shouted to him. Behind him, Thomas' passenger was praying softly in German. She was watching their approach to the building, and he knew he didn't need to give any instructions this time.

In a flash, they had approached their rescuers, she had tossed the baby into waiting arms, and was bodily lifted off the raft.

Unfortunately, Thomas was unable to affect his own escape. As soon as he'd piloted them to the building and his passengers were rescued, the current swept him farther downstream. The rescuer who had caught and handed off the baby watched in frustration as Thomas floated rapidly away. Thomas shrugged and waved as confidently as he could. He still had his rudder—he'd still figure out a way to navigate to safety.

Good Lord—and he'd better do it soon. The current was carrying him toward a mountain of debris; and this one didn't seem to be moving. Which meant he was going to crash into it, instead of the other way around.

"Stay calm, stay calm," he muttered out loud. "No point in dying now." He pushed his awkward rudder over as hard as he could, and managed to steer his craft away from the center of the debris mountain.

He breathed a sigh of relief. He was slowing down. It only lasted a moment, however, until a twisted mass of metal crashed into him, the jar nearly knocking him off his raft. But the momentary lull had given him enough time to spot a destination.

The hill that loomed over one side of Johnstown looked far too steep to scale. However, several people had taken refuge in a small level spot miraculously close to the water line.

This time, his luck held. The small group clinging to their perch on the hill shouted encouragement as he approached. Unfortunately, the current picked up speed as he got closer. He tensed to spring, ready for a crash landing.

It came with tooth-jarring force. He didn't leap from his raft as much as he was thrown from it. He clutched blindly at the hillside, feeling mud and roots under his hands and feet. He could feel many pairs of hands grabbing hold of him, then he was sprawling on flat ground.

He couldn't remember when something as simple as rocks embedded in dirt looked so beautiful. He kissed one large rock that lay close to his head, then sat up to thank his rescuers. Two big steelworkers returned the muddy hugs as unabashedly as he gave them, as did the three women and one boy who were all standing closest to him.

How far did you come?" The boy asked him.

"I'm not quite sure, I've been pushed this way and that so much," Thomas answered, feeling a bit dazed. "But I started out at the Hulbert House."

"Hulbert House!" One of his other companions on the ledge looked at him with amazement. "You're a lucky man, mister. I saw the Hulbert House collapse as soon as this—this," there was no noun for the thing that had just flattened the city, so the woman gave up and went on. "As soon as it hit, the roof got torn off and the rest disappeared underwater. I didn't think anyone could have survived. I saw the whole thing from my house across the street!"

This didn't seem possible. "You live across the street; do you happen to have two boys who were out on a raft a little while before this hit?"

As wild as the coincidence was, he was sorry he asked when shadows fell over the woman's face. "Those were my sons, yes," she answered. "They were on the other end of our roof when it split in two. I could see them being pushed the other way. Then some other things collided into us, and I couldn't watch anymore."

Thomas knew exactly what she meant by "things"—terrifying large floating lumps, made of lumber, pieces of railroad car, recognizable house parts such as doors or windows, tree limbs and dead animal parts, all bound together with barbed wire. He'd seen far too many of them in the course of his journey.

"Well, your sons were pretty darned good boatmen," he said as convincingly as he could to the distraught mother. "Their experience probably helped them." He thought of his last sight of Regina, sprawled on their rooftop, screaming his name. He managed to make it through alive. Hopefully she did too.

There was a shout, and he shook himself out of his reverie. Worrying about Regina wouldn't help her right now, but he could help his companions rescue another victim off of another roof-turned raft.

There was a steady stream of people—both living and dead—floating past. They managed to fish five more people up onto their increasingly-crowded ledge, but no one complained as they stood huddled more and more tightly together. There was some animal comfort to be derived from the close contact, as well as the simple fact that the innermost bodies had some shelter from the mercilessly pounding rain.

Soon, however, the accumulation of buildings edged upstream past their location, and they merely looked out at vast mountains and valleys of broken lumber.

The boy in their crowd was the first to spot flames as dusk settled in. "Look!" He cried out, pointing from under the shelter of the adults around him. "Something's burning!"

Thomas stared in soggy disbelief. They were all cold and soaking wet. Everything in front of them by all rights should be equally cold and waterlogged. How could anything possibly be on fire?

They all watched in dazed horror as the flames flickered eerily in the dark among the rubble. Thomas could hear a crackling hiss.

The fire spread quickly. Thomas realized that some of these piles of wood were probably soaked with fuel from railroad tanks, and engines, as well as whatever small amount of kerosene from homes and stores there might be. Plus a few broken gas lines—among the acres of debris stretching out before them, it could all go up in flames eventually!

They were far too close to the rubbish field if this all burned. "We've got to get away from here," he said out loud. "When this catches fire, we're going to get roasted alive." He looked around at the unpleasant options available. "We either have to climb this hill, or," he indicated the still-standing buildings on the far side of the debris, "we can try to get over there."

One of his companions on the ledge spotted a miraculously intact ladder among the wreckage below. "Well, if we're going anywhere, we probably need that."

"Yes, yes we will." A couple of the other men each gave Thomas an arm, and they carefully lowered him down onto the debris. He stepped gingerly across to the ladder. Everyone watched with baited breath as he struggled to free it from its home in the muck. He wrenched it loose, nearly falling over, then swung it against the hillside.

"This isn't bad," he called up encouragingly. "It's packed solid down here. It's almost like walking down Main Street."

People looked dubious at his encouragement. After a pause, the woman whose sons had given Thomas his first raft stepped forward. "Well, if my sons are anywhere, they're not on this hill." She stepped carefully onto the ladder, and started down.

One by one they scaled the ladder, then the group began picking their way across the remains of the city.

He was tired, and so wet. Not to mention cold. As Thomas and his compatriots picked their way carefully through the broken city, he cast a resentful look up at the sky. It was still pouring rain down upon them. It was slow going, traveling across the debris field. It may have been packed 'as solid as Main Street,' but it wasn't nearly as even.

The small group helped each other over walls and planks and around barbed wire-wrapped obstacles. All the while, the fire burned closer. Thomas swore he could feel its heat. He concentrated on picking his way directly away from the blaze, realizing the irony of choosing the cold and wet over the heat of a roaring fire.

The screams coming from the direction of the fire rose behind him like banshees, trying to instill abject fear into his heart. Well, they were certainly succeeding! He could feel himself shaking with fear, fatigue, and cold. He contemplated each treacherous step, one after the other. The more solidly-packed debris gave way to a marshy quagmire, and Thomas fought a rising certainty that the next step would prove to be a false one. He knew at any moment he would be swallowed by the grimy black lake around them.

It seemed like an eternity of black water and careful steps on broken wet wood. It could have been hours. It might have been a few minutes. But Thomas was startled when he realized an intact building was right in front of him, and people were calling out to them.

"You've almost made it!"

Thomas looked up. People were leaning out the windows to shout to their group. Of course—the doors would be buried, he thought dully.

Thomas watched while first the women and children were lifted into the building with a makeshift sling. Eventually it was his turn to slip it over his head and shoulders, and hang on while he was lifted.

For the second time in one night, he felt several pairs of hands reaching out to pull him in to safety. The rain was no longer pounding down on him, there was a roof over his head instead of under his hands and knees, and it seemed inclined to stay put, for a change.

"Where am I?" Thomas asked stupidly.

"Alma Hall," someone answered. The name didn't mean anything to Thomas. He nodded as if he understood. He seemed to be in some sort of office. There was no telling how many people were in there. Quite a few, he supposed. He could hear quiet rustlings, and he could feel the room was drenched in more misery than water.

He tried to see the rest of the room. He couldn't sit down with the rest of the survivors. There was no point sitting there wet and cold when there must be something he could be doing. He listened intently to every little sound. People were quiet from shock and exhaustion and murmured among themselves. In the quiet he could easily hear conversations taking place on the other end of the room. The voices carrying through the room were engaging in less than cheerful speculations about how long the building would remain standing. Most seemed to share the opinion that the building wouldn't survive the night.

"I wonder if they'll ever find my body," one person said into the darkness.

A brief silence, then someone else answered, "I don't know what sounds worse—the idea that my family might be able to find my body, or that I'll survive the night, and be able to go looking for my family's bodies."

Another person piped up, "Since none of us will be anything but bodies by morning, I suppose that makes it someone else's concern, not ours."

After that, another voice spoke staunchly, "Well, that's in God's hands, isn't it? Perhaps that's where we should be turning our minds. We should put our trust in God that He will save those of us He can, and the rest are safe in His hands."

"You're right, Reverend Beale," someone else said. """Why don't you give us a prayer?"

"Before you do," Thomas raised his voice, "Can I find out if there's a Regina Waring in here?"

His query was met with silence. "We'll pray for her, along with everyone else who's been separated from their loved ones," the reverend's voice answered after a pause. Then the reverend's voice rose in prayer, and other voices softly chimed in.

Thomas tried to listen. He couldn't find any comfort in the words. He could hear Regina's voice in his head, as clear as if she was sitting next to him, grumbling "Talk talk talk. Instead of sitting here moaning about our miseries, I've got to go do something about it."

Restless, he went over to the window to see what his rescuers were doing. Before he made it as far as the windows, he was stopped in his tracks by the soft conversation of two men conferring in low voices.

"All it would take is one darned fool trying to light a pipe, or, well—anything, and we'd go up in a flash."

Thomas looked at the speaker in the firelight from the windows. "Gas leak?"

"Don't see how there couldn't be," answered the second figure. "Every line in the city must be ruptured. At least I don't think there are any people down there, just on these three floors."

"Three floors?" Thomas' attention was riveted by those two words. "There are people in this building on other floors?"

"Yes, but . . ."

Thomas didn't wait to hear anymore. In a public building like this, there were bound to be stairs right about . . . here.

He found them, alright. It was pitch black in the stairwell. Thomas groped about, sliding his hands along the wall until his feet found a step. His hands then discovered the rail, and he began fumbling his way upwards.

He counted as he went. Ten, fourteen steps up, then a bend to the right. Another ten steps, then his feet couldn't find any more. His eyes worked hard, trying to find any light at all, but it was as dark here as on the floor below. He released the rail and groped for the wall on the opposite side of the stair. His hands slid along about a yard, until his hands found the door, then finally his fingers closed around doorknob, and he triumphantly burst into the room.

From the dim light glowing through the tall windows facing the fire outside, it looked like he'd found some cavernous meeting hall. The dark room echoed with groans of human misery. Thomas was relieved to know he was alive. Otherwise, he'd surely just opened the door to hell.

Raising his voice above the moans, the prayers, and the endless, eerie muffled cacophony of rain and screams coming from outside, Thomas asked the room, "Is there a Regina Waring in here?"

His question startled the assembly. A moment later, a rumble of "nos" answered back. Then a few other voices raised up to call out names. No one else seemed to be missing only a single family member, however, and the oppressive lists of wives, children, husbands, brothers and sisters soon silenced the hopes of the crowd.

Thomas stood, unnerved by the number of people all missing loved ones. He turned and blindly groped his way back to the stairs. Maybe on the next floor . . .

He had not gone more than four steps when he collided into someone entering the room from the stairwell.

"Hullo, who's this?" asked a voice in a body slightly shorter than his.

"My name's Baldwin," Thomas answered.

"Hullo, Baldwin, you were about to plunge down the stairs in a few more paces."

"Well, I knew I was reaching them, at any rate," Thomas answered. "I'm looking for my," he almost lied and said 'wife,' but somehow it seemed to disrespectful to all the real husbands and wives who were separated that day. "My fiancée. We got separated out there."

The voice sighed. "I think we've all been separated from somebody, Mr. Baldwin. But we can't all go stumbling around in the dark. As it is, there's plenty of reason to believe this building won't survive the night. We've set up a hall government, and we're asking people to move around as little as possible. Would you please find a place to settle down for the night? If everyone stays still, hopefully we'll all be alive to find each other in the morning."

The frantic need to know where Regina was had been growing in his chest. "I understand your concern, sir, but if you'll let me go up one more flight and ask one more time, I'll sit down in the first empty bit of floor I can find. If she's up there, there would be two people a lot less frightened and miserable in here tonight."

Out of the darkness, a sympathetic hand gripped his arm. "Go," the voice said softly. "By God, I hope by some miracle you find her up there. If you don't, there should be a guy named Walters up there. He's part of the hall government. Tell him Captain Hart told you to report for duty. You can stand by the stairs and keep everyone else from running up and down the stairs all night."

"Thank you, Captain," Thomas gripped the hand on his arm.

"Go on with you," the voice instructed gruffly.

Thomas obeyed eagerly. Through the door, twelve steps, a bend, another twelve steps, another door. Another desperate call for Regina that was answered in the negative, and a few other names got called out after Regina's name failed to produce its owner.

More softly, Thomas called out again. "I'm looking for Walters?"

"Yeah," a deep voice answered, almost behind him. "Who're you?"

"Name's Baldwin. Captain Hart told me to come up and give you a hand. Told me I can guard the door to stop other damned fools like me from running up and down the stairs looking for people."

"Good idea," Walters snorted. "You're hired."

There was not much left to do then, but stand and wait out the night. Not a soul slept. The lucky ones were only soaking wet, and shivering with cold. Others had some or all of their clothes torn off on their various harrowing journeys. The injured lay moaning in pain, not much relieved when Doctor Matthews, moaning slightly from his own two broken ribs, came through, tending to people as best he could with no supplies and no light. Children cried from fear, cold, and hunger. And always, in different languages, there was a ceaseless murmur of praying.

The last had a curious effect upon Thomas. Of all the strange and powerful emotions pouring through him, he found himself irritated by the sound of the prayers. As people murmured for comfort, forgiveness for their sins, or an end to the rain, he remembered Regina remarking that prayer was just so much whining.

For some reason, he remembered taking her to lunch at the Duquesne Club on one of her trips through Pittsburgh. When the waiter was able to procure the very last piece of brisket for him, he'd exclaimed, "There IS a God."

"Well, no, but there are nice cooks in the kitchen who will make you dinner if you pay them," Regina gave him an amused look. "You should be thanking the nice waiter, not God."

He'd always assumed she was making a point about power and privilege. Now he understood. It was about people. What Regina was driving at was that since there is no God, all we have is each other. Instead of praying for help, it is more important to ask for help from your fellow man. And to give it whenever possible.

Throughout the remainder of the long night, he tried to find anything that it made sense to pray about. Praying for the end of the night seemed silly; it would happen, pretty much on schedule. The end of the rain was less predictable, but that, too, would happen sooner or later. Thanks for being worthy of survival? Every human being in the city, dead and alive, was "worthy." Forgiveness for his sins? That got interesting. His mind ran guilty images through his head of the dam: the carriages passing each other on the road, the way the sun would sparkle invitingly on the lake as the horses trotted up to the clubhouse. He was now thoroughly soaked in that same lake water.

Belonging to the Fishing and Hunting Club was possibly the biggest sin he could imagine. But this was not a sin against God. "Thou shalt not be a member of the Fishing and Hunting Club?" This was a sin against mankind. The idea of fearing a faceless, powerful deity seemed insignificant compared to the idea of looking into the faces of the survivors once this night would end, knowing he had played a small part in inflicting this huge misery.

He wrestled with the concepts of God, and sin, and humanity, questioning his universe in ways he had never questioned it before. Regina's voice echoed in his ears at times. At others, he wished with fresh desperation to have her at his side: if not to quiet his fears with her arms and lips, she could no doubt answer the questions awakened in his soul.

As the rain ended and an eerie quiet settled over the valley, Thomas came to the conclusion that he agreed with Regina. There was no God.

A sense of huge responsibility weighed upon his heart as he listened blindly to the muffled sounds of suffering humanity. All we have is each other. After all, God didn't pull him off his raft. The steelworkers did. God didn't build a questionable dam which broke when it rained more than usual. The Fishing and Hunting Club did that.

His father would have shrugged. His mother would have sniffed. Meredith would have stared uncomprehendingly. His brother would have laughed. Thomas could do none of these.

As the darkness slowly began to melt away into a gray dawn, Thomas realized that soon he would be able to resume his search for the one person who would understand.

People began to stir as soon as it was light enough to see each other's faces. Still fearful of the stability of the building that had sheltered them through the night, Thomas and his companion, Walters, allowed people to leave in small groups.

It was comforting to be able to see faces again. Walters looked every bit the village elder that he was. Other faces were surprising. A youngish-sounding female voice close to the door belonged to an elderly woman. The thick German accent that Thomas had imagined belonging to an old bearded man turned out to fit the body of a burly young steamfitter.

They all filed past him on their way down the stairs; every last face, belonging to every voice heard in the long night. Still wet, still cold, still in various stages of undress, they went back outside to see what was left of Johnstown.

Thomas eventually joined the end of the procession. Down the stairs, twelve steps down, then a bend, then twelve more steps. A second flight down, then along the hallway to the front window where he'd been hauled into the building. Thomas crawled through, scrambled for footing on the slippery mountain of rubble—and stopped.

There was devastation in every direction. Every type of item that might possibly represent human civilization lay in broken pieces across the valley. Houses, telegraph poles, toys, ledgers, and livestock were piled in appalling mountains, all thoroughly intermixed with human corpses. The whole dismal landscape was already starting to smell. Thomas could only imagine how it must feel for the people who called this valley "home." He was only passing through, and it was the most awful thing he had ever seen in his life.

His eyes were drawn with a sickening fascination to the hands sticking up out of the wreckage. All over the place, even when the body was buried under lethal piles of books, dishes, and chamber pots, the hands were outstretched—reaching out in an appeal for help which never came.

He tried to prevent it, but the words still formed in his brain. One of those pairs of hands might belong to Regina.

Well, he had patiently waited out the long night. He had now earned the right to find her. Resolutely, he picked his way forward through the rubble.

Chapter 33

Thomas wasn't quite sure how a rescue team coalesced around him, but he found himself vaguely in charge of a crew of men, scrambling up piles of debris to free people from buried, half-intact buildings.

It was heart-stopping work. They had to rescue three of their own when a wall collapsed, bringing the piled-up debris on top of them. All three men survived, although one suffered a broken arm and had to be helped away to safety.

"Safety" was a ludicrous idea at the moment. But every living soul they liberated from their various prisons was sent toward Green Hill. It was dry ground. No need to cross any water to get there, so refugees were sent that direction. No telling what would happen to anyone after they got there, but at least it seemed like progress.

Finding people still alive in the wreckage gave each man in the group a much-needed spark of hope. They all had loved ones they desperately wanted to find. None of the children, elderly, or other men and women they rescued were related to them, but it didn't matter. While they were here saving some other man's wife, child, or parent, they silently hoped that elsewhere some man was saving their wives, children, and parents.

The harrowing work provided a useful way to control the horrible fear in the pit of Thomas' stomach. Where was Regina? He felt an awful, guilty feeling of relief every time they found a dark-haired female corpse—with an unfamiliar face.

Word circulated that at three o'clock that afternoon, every able-bodied man in town was to be at the Adam Street Schoolhouse for a town meeting. Not being from Johnstown, and, more awkwardly, being a member of the South Fork Fishing and Hunting Club, Thomas felt a little strange being there. But he dutifully answered the summons, along with every other non-injured man in town.

It was heartening, in a way, to see so many survivors in the same place. Every body in the room was alive, had full use of both arms and both legs, and was interested in rolling up his sleeves and tackling the immense problems at hand. Thomas scanned the faces in the crowd, wondering if Charles were in the room. He fought against the hope of finding Regina there, though he reasoned that if she were able-bodied, she would no doubt ignore the gender qualification and show up.

He was so intent on his search for a couple of familiar faces, he didn't see the familiar face in front of him, until he was grabbed by both arms and given a shake.

"Baldwin! Wake up, boy. It's been a long night, but we don't get to sleep, yet."

Thomas looked down into the mud-streaked face of Cyrus Elder.

"Elder!" He shouted, elated at finding anyone he knew still alive. "You're here!"

The two men hugged unabashedly. Cyrus' face betrayed the same feelings as Thomas—joy at finding a compatriot still alive. The elder man kept hold of Thomas' arm after they parted, and his face dropped into a frown.

"You get Regina to safety?"

It was Thomas' turn to frown. "We got separated. I don't even know where to begin looking for her."

Cyrus patted his arm in awkward consolation. "She's a scrapper, that girl. She'll turn up."

Horrible realization swept over Thomas. "Your wife and daughter . . . ?"

Cyrus cleared his throat and looked away. "That damned current . . . I never managed to make it home. There's nothing left of the place anymore . . ."

Thomas' throat constricted. He tried to say something, anything, but his throat clamped shut so tightly he couldn't even swallow. He settled for putting a hand on the grieving man's shoulder and squeezing.

With a general shout, the meeting came to order. It started in an oddly-organized chaos. Most people were inquiring into the whereabouts of someone named Fulton, saying he would be the best choice for a town dictator. When Fulton failed to materialize and no one could claim to have seen him, there was a gruff moment of silence for his passing.

A general clearing of throats marked the end of the moment, and the name Moxham rose from the crowd.

Thomas was surprised when, rather than a venerable town elder, a spry young man with a thick Welsh accent sprang up, thanked the assembled crowd for the honor of choosing him as their dictator, and deftly got straight to the business of defining the town's most immediate problems.

A committee for supplies, a committee for finance and a police force were created, as well as hospitals and morgues. Thomas listened for the sound of Charles' voice, as well as for a familiar feminine one, to no avail.

Thomas' heart swelled with gratitude when a registration committee was formed to take a census of every living body that could be found, as well as any dead that could possibly be identified. The room grew grimly silent as they contemplated the enormity of the task. Eventually, every last committee was formed, and Moxham called for a motion to dismiss the meeting.

In front of the school, the same men who had been working with Thomas before the meeting collected around him. "Why mess up a good team," one of them said. Thomas threw one last desperate look at the men leaving the schoolhouse. None of the dirty, tired, hungry faces belonged to Charles, and not one of them was female.

The remainder of the daylight hours passed in a blur. The sounds of the day were less horrifying than the sounds of the day before, but the sights and smells were far worse. The hands of the dead still reached out through the wreckage everywhere they turned. Less hopeful of finding live bodies anymore, they began the grim task of extricating the dead.

Thomas was glad for the ravenous hunger gnawing in his stomach—nothing was left in his body to vomit back up when they spotted an outstretched hand through the rubble, only to find it was no longer attached to a body. More bodies seemed to be intact—missing clothes, not limbs, although once again he found himself swallowing convulsively when they found another corpse that had been decapitated.

The other men showed little emotion at each new discovery. As each corpse was freed, two of the men would find some plank in the wreckage large enough to use as a stretcher and carried the latest victim back to the schoolhouse, which had become a morgue.

No doubt each man was watching each new body with the same dread Thomas felt. He searched faces, hair, clothing, even hands, afraid that at any moment he would recognize something—anything. As horrible as it was, not knowing Regina's fate, it was a relief not to find her among the dead. He hoped if he had to see her there, she would be one of the dirty but peaceful-looking ones, not one of the gruesomely mangled bodies in this nightmarish landscape. One of the men found his brother's body among the wreckage, broken, but still recognizable. They quietly loaded the body parts onto a half-shattered door while their comrade vomited. No one was surprised when the man shakily stood up and insisted on escorting the remains to the schoolhouse.

The men worked diligently, until dusk began to fall. Their hands ached with cold, their stomachs growled, and the falling darkness seemed to bring with it unnamed fears that had nothing to do with such practical matters as safety among the hazardous terrain. The fire at the stone bridge was not going to be sufficient to light up the whole valley, and the men realized it was time to stop and search for food and shelter for themselves.

They began the arduous task of finding their way toward Prospect Hill, which was closest, and where the rest of the crew knew friends. Picking their way through the rubble crammed between the surviving buildings of Main Street, Thomas began to fear they had not given themselves sufficient time to reach safety before it would be too dark to see.

A warm aroma filled their nostrils. Bean soup—it had to be! Every head lifted up, every pair of eyes searched for the source.

A makeshift ladder was propped against the side of one of the brick storefronts, and on the roof they could see a thin column of smoke.

"You don't suppose . . ." Thomas murmured.

"It looks like an invitation," answered one of the other men. "You climb up there, we'll wait for you. Wave if there's someone up there who can take you in."

Thomas climbed the first two rungs of the ladder. It seemed solid enough. He looked back at his compatriots. "What am I supposed to say?"

"That you're hungry? Try that for a start," came the reply.

Thomas climbed up, following the smoke and the tantalizing smell of bean soup.

When he looked onto the flat roof, he saw a fairly large number of people huddled together, standing or sitting, many with small bowls in their hands. In the middle, a woman stood before some sort of makeshift brick hearth. She was stirring something in a large, old-fashioned iron pot over a small fire. She looked up and spotted Thomas' face. "Another one! Well, don't stand out there, come up! My cousin Morris was clever with the ladder—but I wouldn't stand around on it if I were you."

"I saw your fire," Thomas stammered after he gained the roof. "I wanted to see if you're safe—there could be a gas leak just about anywhere in the city."

The woman approached him with a pragmatic shrug, and placed a bowl of the steaming soup into his hands. "If God meant to kill us, he would have done it by now. Since the store is still standing, and I managed to save the contents of my kitchen, God obviously meant for me to feed people, so eat."

"Thank you," Thomas lifted his bowl to her in a little salute. "It smells delicious." When she turned away, he waved to the rest of his team. They waved back, and continued making their way up the street. There was nothing else to do but sit down and obey the insistence of his hostess and his stomach.

Thomas had never tasted anything so good in his life. It was possibly the humblest fare that had ever been served to him, but he had never been so appreciative of food before. How had he ever taken it for granted all these years? As soon as he got home, he was going to send this woman a cellar full of groceries. And a ham every Christmas.

The woman leaned down to hand him a little piece of brown bread to go with the soup, and his eyes caught a small six-pointed star around her neck. Okay, it wouldn't be a ham. And it wouldn't be for Christmas. His revelation of the night before came flooding back into his mind—there is no God taking care of us. It is up to us to take care of each other. Thomas marveled at the way this Jewish woman was feeding a bunch of probably-Christians. And one newly-converted Atheist.

As he ate, he watched as his hostess worked, tirelessly stoking her little fire, stirring her pot, and disappearing down a hole in the floor which he assumed took her to the attic of her building. She'd return with her apron full of supplies, tend to her fire, tend to another refugee whose face appeared at the top of the ladder, disappear, return with more dishes.

He was finishing his food as she was dragging a larger, heavier iron pot up the stairs. He made one last swipe of the bowl with the last bit of his bread, crammed it hastily into his mouth, and leapt to his feet. He swallowed hastily as he approached his benefactress. "May I help?"

She allowed him to lug the caldron over to the makeshift brick hearth for her. "Leave it there for now," she instructed. "It's getting too dark to cook, but I'll need it in the morning."

Thomas nodded, panting a little. It was a heavy pot—he was amazed she'd gotten it as far as she had. "Is there anything else I might do for you?" he asked. "Wash the dishes, or something?"

She looked at him in surprise, and, Thomas thought he detected, with amusement. "Oy, I'm sure that's a very fine offer," she looked him over. "But considering how dirty you are I don't believe the dishes would come out any cleaner once you'd touched them."

Thomas looked down at himself in shock. He was coated in grime. There was absolutely no telling what color his suit used to be. What fabric actually showed through the mud and filth had been stained to a brownish-black. Thomas was disgusted by the color—and even more so when he realized his hands were also stained and coated brown.

He looked up sheepishly. "You may not believe this, ma'am, but I really was raised with better manners than to show up for dinner without cleaning up first."

"Such a gentleman," she answered, obviously amused. "Manners have their place, but when there's not much water to come by, washing will have to wait. That goes for dishes as well as hands—and faces."

Thomas touched his face. Well, there was two days' growth on his chin, if you could tell under the dirt. "I take it my own mother wouldn't recognize me?"

"God himself wouldn't recognize you," she answered.

Thomas smiled grimly. "No, he wouldn't," he answered with conviction. His face grew bleak. "God has a lot more important people to sort out right now. The rest of us will have to fend for ourselves."

The woman's eyes grew moist. "Yes, we will," she answered, also with conviction. Her lips folded together tightly.

Thomas touched her arm sympathetically. "You have a husband out there somewhere?" he asked gently.

"He'd gone down the street to check on the Cohens. Mr. Cohen injured his arm last week, and we thought they might need help—or they could come wait out the waters with us," she answered, her voice getting softer with each word. "I haven't seen—not one of them has made it here yet."

"I'm sorry," Thomas said, the inadequate words sticking horribly in his mouth. He cleared his throat. "Is there anything I can do?"

The woman jerked her head toward the stairs. "You can find yourself some space on the floor and try to sleep. I don't have more to offer you than a floor, but at least it's dry."

Thomas obediently walked over to the square hole in the roof. The stairs descended into the attic, lit only a little by the glow coming from the direction of the fire at the bridge. There seemed to be quite a few bodies huddled on the floor. As his eyes adjusted to the dark, he was able to find himself an unoccupied bit of floor, not far from the base of the stairs.

The entire room seemed to sigh with a quiet restlessness. He doubted a single soul would be able to sleep, despite the exhaustion. He, himself was afraid to close his eyes. Every time he did, all he could see were the dead hands, stretching upward through the piles of wood and barbed wire and mud.

"Mrs. Fineman," a voice floated down the stairs to him. "Why does it not surprise me to find you here, instead of up the hill on dry land?"

"And leave my home before I'd gotten everything to safety? We'd be starving right now, if I hadn't moved everything in the kitchen up here. I knew we were going to need it."

"Meshuggeneh. Well, I had to come and warn your husband that here's some drunks out there looting places tonight, and he should be on the lookout."

"Thank you, we'll be careful. Are you going to be all right, getting back over to your building?"

"The roof is a whole lot easier than trying to walk in the street right now," Mrs. Fineman's visitor answered.

Thomas frowned. So Mrs. Fineman didn't confess her husband's absence to her neighbor. With a building full of guests, and the access to lower floors buried, she probably wasn't in much danger from looters. Nonetheless . . . .

He climbed back up the stairs. Mrs. Fineman was scraping out the last bits of her bean soup by the light of her dying fire. "Mrs. Fineman? I couldn't help but overhear. Do you have any firearms in the house, ma'am? The least I can do to repay your hospitality is to do my duty in your husband's stead."

"What, you think we're farmers, we go hunting deer for our food?" At least she looked amused, not offended. "We're merchants. We clothe everyone in town, and we eat well. What would we need a gun for?"

"Well, tonight, to protect your merchandise from looters."

"Our merchandise is ruined. Anyone wants it, I'm sorry enough for them, they can have it."

Thomas found her fatalism hard to argue with. He'd never met a person like her before. She was a fighter, he could tell. But she certainly had a funny way of choosing her battles.

"There's also the matter of protecting your house full of people. If the looters start setting buildings on fire . . ."

"It's a brick building. If people come and want to sleep, they're welcome. If they want to kill us, we'll pull up the ladder and hit them on the head with it."

Thomas couldn't help but smile. He could picture this spirited lady, leaning over the wall, whacking at marauding hordes of looters with the ladder, shouting Yiddish curses at them all the while.

"I'll stand and keep watch, to make sure someone's up here to pull up the ladder, if it becomes necessary."

"Wake me in a few hours when you get too tired; I'll take over," one of the men sitting nearby volunteered.

"Then I'll take the next shift," another man grunted.

"All right. Though I don't think I could sleep," Thomas demurred.

"We're all afraid to sleep," Mrs. Fineman read the lot of them as effortlessly as Regina would have. "But we're all going to have to, sometime. Might as well be now, than later. I'll bring up some more mostly-dry firewood to help keep away the dark."

Thomas moved without a word to stand near the ladder, wondering if a single survivor of the past two days would ever be able to sleep again without a light burning to keep away the dark.

Chapter 34

Dark. Wet. Cold. Regina was screaming his name. He reached out to her, but she was somewhere beyond his fingertips. Why couldn't he see her? Oh—because his eyes were closed. Thomas sat up with a start. He was terribly confused for a moment—had he gone up to the servants' quarters for some reason?

The events of the past two days came rushing back to him. The death mist, bringing a horrifying wall of destruction which swallowed the city in a heartstopping roar. The determination of those who had survived and the reaching hands of those who had not.

Where the hell was he? Oh, yes. Mrs. Fineman's attic. Sometime in the darkness, he'd finally accepted the fact that his eyelids refused to stay open, and awakened one of the men. Now he was lying on the floor, still dirty, but less hungry and exhausted. And he had no idea where Regina was—or if she was even alive.

The realization propelled him to his feet. It must be well past dawn, the windows were glowing with light. The silence was deafening. No sounds of the bustling town, no voices from the exhausted townsfolk, and no rain. Thomas carefully picked his way through the maze of sleepers curled on the floor, and peeked through the curtains. The skies looked clearer than they had in days.

A woman with a shawl over her head appeared, picking doggedly through the devastation that used to be Johnstown. She had a basket on her arm, and Thomas detected a determined set to her body as she climbed over planks and through the mud. No doubt she was on her way down to resume her search for a loved one.

This meant Thomas could do the same.

He pulled out his billfold, wondering if it would be an insult to leave money to thank his hostess. Bah. She seemed far too pragmatic a soul to get insulted by good intentions. But where to put it? He realized her makeshift kitchen would probably be safest. He picked his way through the huddled bodies, then looked around the crowded little table for a place to leave the bill he was clutching in his hand. This little larder wasn't going to last long, if she was going to insist on feeding every hungry soul that clambered up her ladder for help. Thomas took another bill from his billfold. Loathe to simply leave the money in plain sight, he opened a drawer underneath the tabletop and tucked the money among a collection of dish towels. She'd find it, sooner or later.

He tiptoed back through the sleeping bodies, and climbed back up to the roof. The second man who'd volunteered to stand watch last night was sitting on the edge of the roof, arms wrapped around himself against the cold. The man looked up at him without surprise.

"Leaving?"

"Yeah," Thomas answered. "There's somebody I've got to find."

"Good luck, I hope you find her," he replied.

"Thanks," Thomas tried to swallow around the lump in his throat. "Are you going to be searching, too?"

The man shook his head. "Nah. I ain't got no family in Johnstown. I came here for the job. If anybody out there even knows what happened to us, my kin must be thinking I'm dead. Sure hope they don't worry too bad."

"Yeah," Thomas realized that, other than his house staff, no one in Pittsburgh had known he'd left town. He wondered how on earth he'd be able to let his family know he was alive.

That is, like the man said, if anyone even knew anything was amiss in the first place. Thomas climbed resolutely down the ladder into the mire.

How could anyone in the outside world even know what had happened? The remains of telegraph poles and railroad tracks were strewn about the floor of the Conemaugh valley, tangled with barbed wire, draped with horse carcasses, rammed through houses, and crammed by the acre, burning, against the stone bridge. The stone bridge stopped the deluge, so people downriver might have no idea that their upriver neighbors were even in trouble.

Ridiculous. More than a few trains didn't get through. People in both directions must have an idea that something was amiss.

Lost in thought, Thomas trudged around a half-buried railroad car, and stopped in astonishment. There, on a section of what Thomas thought must be part of the Baltimore & Ohio line, a train was sitting smugly on a section of cleared tracks.

He shook his head in amazement. The railroads must have employed big crews, all night long, to get through. Somebody had obviously known.

Mesmerized by the sight, he turned his feet in the direction of the first sign of unscathed civilization he'd seen in some time. As soon as he got home, he decided, he was buying more stock in the railroads.

Early as it was, there was a substantial crowd of people when he approached the B&O engine. The train stood in the island of Johnstown buildings that had miraculously survived the destruction. Piles of debris were everywhere, as were hungry flood survivors, many walking away from the station clutching small bundles of food. Thomas anxiously searched the dirty faces, looking for a pair of familiar black eyes.

He did find one familiar face. Elizabeth McKay's features were smeared with grime like everyone else's, yet unlike the haunted faces of Johnstonians that were touched by tragedy and miserable suffering, her habitual petulant temperament still shone through. She looked merely annoyed and inconvenienced by the entire catastrophe.

"Mrs. McKay? It's Thomas Baldwin. I'm so glad to see you! Does that mean your children and husband made it through?"

Elizabeth McKay looked up at him with the same awful fawning expression she'd always used on him. "Oh, Mr. Baldwin!

What on earth are you doing here? You must have come with the relief trains, you always were the most generous man I've ever known."

"No, actually, I was in town when that . . ." there were no simple words to describe that Olympian-sized horror, the rolling, crashing, groaning, screaming wall of destruction. "When the contents of our own lake came tumbling down for a visit."

His words had a surprising effect on her. Her eyes narrowed cagily, and she gripped his arm almost menacingly. "Don't talk about it that way," she hissed, looking around her as if afraid they'd been overheard. "Everyone knows the dam broke, but we don't need to say it out loud."

There was honest fear in her face. Thomas gathered she was thinking of the culpability of the club members. The town of Johnstown would still be standing, if they hadn't made their own private lake up there at the Fishing and Hunting Club. He'd never known a thing about the dam itself. It was originally part of the canal system. The man who'd refurbished the dam, stocked the lake with fish, and started the club had died a few years ago. But he'd never questioned its safety.

It obviously hadn't been safe. Was the entire membership guilty of criminal negligence, resulting in this horrible loss of life, this unimaginable destruction?

He wrapped his hand around hers where she still gripped his arm. "I'm sorry, Mrs. McKay, you're right. Not very astute of me." He attempted to smile. It felt like a grimace stretching across his face. "Is your house one of the lucky few to make it?"

"I wouldn't call it lucky," she sighed plaintively, reminding Thomas of Meredith when she'd put on a show for his benefit. "The entire first floor is absolutely buried in mud. We'd pulled up the carpets, thank goodness, but the wallpaper is going to be entirely ruined. It's going to take me forever to get things right . . ."

Thomas tuned out her voice as she continued her litany of small woes, while the world around them was laboring under much bigger ones. His mother, Meredith, Elizabeth McKay—how was it women like this kept coming into his life? Was he supposed to believe that women were naturally self-centered? Was this all that society raised women to be? Or was he somehow a magnet for women who could be annoyed by inconveniences, completely insensitive to others' tragedies?

He needed to find Regina. She was the lodestone for all his faith in the universe, the proof that for every bad, there was a good, that women were capable of so much more than pettiness. She had to be alive, somewhere. He needed her. Never in his life had he needed her as much as he needed her now.

"Well, at least you're alive to be standing here, telling the tale," he curtailed her list of inconveniences. "You didn't tell me; were Charles and your children with you when this all started?"

"My husband must be dead," she answered flatly. "You'd think he would have managed to get home by now if he were alive."

Thomas frowned down at her in concern. "Where was he when the—flood—came?"

"Well, he wasn't home with his wife and children," she answered sharply, then turned her uncomfortably flattering smile on him. "You wouldn't have deserted poor dear Meredith to a second floor of your house in order to go help your riffraff employees, would you, Mr. Baldwin?"

Thomas didn't know what to say for a moment, then decided he didn't have the mental energy to be diplomatic. "Yes, yes actually I would have done exactly the same thing. I guess that's why we're friends. We both believe in helping people."

Elizabeth either didn't recognize his insult or was well bred enough not to respond to it. "Oh, you men," she sighed.

Thomas had been fearing Charles' death since his failure to appear at the town meeting the day before. "I'm sorry to hear about your loss." Unless of course Charles was merely taking advantage of the disorder to have a few days away from this creature. He could see Elizabeth insisting Charles stay home with her, rather than allowing him to rescue people trapped in the wreckage. "He's been my best friend for years, and I'm going to miss him. Are you really sure he's dead? Have you been to the registration office? The morgues?"

"I don't see why I should," she answered indifferently. "The house is still standing. It's the only one left around the park. It's not like he couldn't see it."

Thomas looked down at her gravely. "So you haven't registered yourself or your children? No one knows you're alive, either?"

"It's easy to find ME," she pointed out loftily. "The house IS still standing," she repeated.

"True," Thomas acknowledged. "Safer at home than out here." There was really no point in asking, but on the other hand, it would be foolish not to . . . . "So you haven't seen anyone else, dead or alive? I'm trying to find Regina Waring."

A look of frank dislike settled on Elizabeth's features. "So that was her," she mumbled.

Thomas' heart skipped a beat. "You've seen her?"

Another disinterested shrug from his companion. "I don't know. I was in the attic with the children, praying, while people were sweeping past the dormer windows. There was all this screaming, and I wished Charles were home. Then there was a loud thump, and I could see a woman was holding onto the window. She was dirty, and she was only wearing her—well, her dress was gone, but I thought it was Mrs. Waring. I stared at her for a second, since I couldn't think of why she of all people would be in Johnstown. Then there was this great smashing sound, and she was gone. There was blood on the window for a while, but the rain washed it away."

Thomas looked at her, sternly swallowing down the bile that was rising in his throat. She could have saved her. It didn't matter to him right then whether the woman had been Regina, or any other hapless victim of the thundering horror. Elizabeth's inactivity probably meant the difference between someone's life and death. "So why didn't you open the window and help some of those people?" he asked.

"I did. I prayed for them," she answered archly. "And if it was Mrs. Waring, well, far be it from me to speak ill of the dead, but good riddance," she answered, her own voice tinged by a telltale sharp edge. "Charles thought so highly of her, but I'll never understand why," she sniffed. "She was so—common. Her father was a bookkeeper, for heaven's sake."

Thomas had to leave. Now, before he said too much. "Well, Mrs. McKay," he reached up habitually to touch his hat in farewell, but of course it had been days since it had sat upon his head. "Good luck to you. I hope you get the mud off your floors and wallpaper."

His desertion changed her manner as if by magic. The dreadful fawning expression came back into her eyes, and she clutched his arm again, this time by way of entreaty. "Oh, Mr. Baldwin, where are you going? What on earth am I going to do, all by myself with two small children? Why don't you come back and help me?"

The anger that washed through Thomas was surprisingly powerful. He gently removed her grasping hand. "Go home and pray for help," he advised her through clenched teeth. "Pray for me, if you will. But most people in town need my help far more than you do."

He turned and walked away from her. He wasn't even sure where he was going, as long as it was away from her.

Regina was alive. She had to be. After all, he was the one who had been swept under by the torrent, not her. She was no doubt doing the exact same thing he was, helping people, looking for him. He himself had not registered his name among the survivors, perhaps she had, and was wandering from morgue to morgue looking for his body. If Elizabeth McKay was right, she'd at least survived for some significant length of time.

What was it Cyrus Elder had said? She's a scrapper. Well, she was. He simply had to find her.

He knew they were setting up a post office at Adams and Main, where the living could register their names. Since he'd spent the day before scouring the city for survivors and hauling corpses, he had, in a funny way, learned his way around the devastated town better than he'd known the intact one. When he made it to the corner where the office was supposed to be, all the buildings were still closed. Funny to think that even in this state of anarchy, they had already established business hours. He looked around at the surviving buildings, wondering if any of them were harboring his fiancée safely behind closed doors. He dearly hoped so. He turned his feet toward the Adams Street schoolhouse. He realized as he approached the sturdy brick building that had become the morgue, for all the times he had been here already, he had not really gone inside. Maybe this wasn't necessary. He was so certain that she was alive. But he would still have to accept the possibility that she might not be. Better to know than to wonder . . . .

Thomas felt surprisingly queasy as he looked at the bodies lined up outside the door. The corpses hadn't bothered him this much yesterday. Maybe that was because yesterday, he was simply delivering the bodies of strangers here for others to find. Now he was peering into their faces trying to find Regina among them.

The dead, like the living around them, came in all ages and sizes. Old men were laid next to young women, next to very small children. Old women, young men, and youngsters Thomas would still describe as children were wandering among the rows of corpses both inside and outside the schoolhouse, searching the bodies with the same mixture of fear and hope that Thomas imagined must be mingled on his own face.

A tall, thin teenaged lad was walking forlornly between the rows. There was something poignant in the young man's face. He seemed both very young and very aged—no doubt by his experiences in the last two days. "Looking for your folks?" Thomas asked the young man gently.

"Yep," the young-old boy answered, his eyes roaming tiredly over the vast expanse of unidentified bodies. "I saw our house crushed like an eggshell right before my eyes," he answered honestly, without the least bit of self-pity in his voice. He was simply telling the facts. "My parents were inside. I don't know how they could have survived the house collapsing. But I can't find them anywhere among the dead." He shook his head in a sort of daze. "It's a miracle I survived, maybe they have, too."

Thomas nodded. "I'm amazed I'm among the living. My fiancée saw me swept off the roof we were on; if she's alive she must be thinking I'm dead."

"There was a lady at the stone bridge last night, who was looking for her husband even though she was afraid he was dead," the boy volunteered comfortingly. "Most other ladies were crying or praying, and we sent them away once we rescued them before the fire could get to them. This one, she was climbing over the piles with us, helping us rescue other people. We said she didn't have to help, but she said she wasn't going to sit and pray when her Thomas was in trouble, and she could be doing something."

A jolt of lightning struck through Thomas' heart. Regina! "What—what did this lady look like?"

Thomas' eager question made the young-old eyes regard him with interest. "Very dirty. Short." Thomas' heart sank. Regina was the tallest woman he knew. The fellow continued with a feeble attempt at a grin, "I guess all girls are short, compared to me. I don't know how to describe her. We were too busy trying to get people away from the fire. She was pretty strong, for a lady. And she was a lady, too, I think, not a farm woman or someone more used to hard work. She had an interesting voice. It was sort of low, and she had a way of telling you to do something, and you'd find yourself doing it." Thomas spirits soared. It had to be her! "I think she was a blonde, but it's hard to say, she was as dirty as the rest of us."

His heart plummeted. "Her name," Thomas' throat could barely let out enough air to release the words. "Did she tell you her name?"

His companion shook his head. "I'm sorry. I don't know. I never saw her in my parents' store, I assume she was some railroad passenger. Are you Thomas?"

Thomas nodded, then blinked to clear vision that had become terribly watery. "If you ever see your lady again, if her name's Regina, would you tell her that her Thomas is alive, and looking for her?"

"I will," promised the younger man, his voice also sounding suspiciously watery. "And if you run across a man or woman with a German accent, and their name is Heiser, would you tell them the same about their son Victor?"

Thomas held out his hand. "I can do that," he promised in return.

The two of them shook on it, then each resumed his separate search. Victor continued to pace through the rows of bodies, while Thomas looked around to see who was in charge of the makeshift morgue. He seemed to recall it was the same reverend who had been leading the prayers at Alma Hall, but he couldn't remember the man's name.

He found a smaller room off the larger one, where two men were busily doing something—Thomas was trying very hard not to see what—to one of the endless number of corpses that was going to require burial. "Excuse me," he interjected. "But how would I find out if a fortyish dark-haired woman had been brought here for internment?"

"With a whole lot of good luck," one of them said. "We've been trying to keep some records, but we don't have much of anything to keep records on. If you find any sort of paper, we'd be obliged if you could bring us some." He jerked his head toward the door. "What we've got is right by you, if you want to look."

Thomas had not noticed the makeshift table next to the door—it was simply a few pieces of flotsam stacked up, with some loose scraps of paper on top. Thomas half-reluctantly, half-eagerly read the rudimentary records: "Unknown. Male. Wearing red flannel underwear. Unknown. Female child. Light blonde hair. About five years. Unknown. Female. Initials MRJ on silver watch." Thomas read the somewhat vague descriptions with horror. It would be impossible to find anyone with so little to go on!

He determinedly read through every scrap on the table. There were four "unknown females" that could have been anyone. Then again, at least there were only four.

With a renewed feeling of futility, he left the morgue.

Chapter 35

When the post office opened, Thomas left his name, and the names of Elizabeth McKay and her two children, at the registration office. Regina's name was not there. Then of course, any number of people hadn't been there yet.

Broken as it was, the town was springing to life. Besides the residents of Johnstown, relief workers were pouring in: railroad workers, doctors, undertakers, newspapermen, people from neighboring towns bringing supplies of all sorts, even politicians began arriving. The influx of new faces made it that much harder to try to find one particular person.

Thomas haunted the still-standing buildings along Main Street, the new temporary hospital, the crews who were stringing a rope bridge across the Conemaugh. A train from Pittsburgh was on the far side, and he made the precarious journey over the still angry, swollen waters to carry the much-needed relief supplies back over the river. It gave him the chance to send a message back to Pittsburgh with an obliging brakeman; and make sure there were no black-eyed women trapped on the far side of the raging waters.

After gratefully accepting some lunch from the relief trains and carrying several bundles over the rope bridge, he picked his way through the people hovering around the still-burning fire at the stone bridge, in hopes that perhaps Victor's plucky but nameless lady continued to search. He learned from the anxious spectators that several new morgues had been established all over the valley.

Since he'd been everywhere that the living had congregated, it was time to try again among the dead.

He spotted Cyrus Elder coming out of the morgue that had been set up in Kernville. Thomas almost hadn't recognized him. He looked haggard, with dark circles under his eyes, and the characteristic cheer gone out of his face. His family, his house with all its worldly possessions were destroyed, as was his hometown. He had been put in charge of the Finance Committee, which no doubt brought plenty of new troubles.

Thomas picked up his pace to catch up to the older man. "Cyrus," he acknowledged. "You find them yet?"

"Thomas." The older man sighed. "No. I've been everywhere. My wife and daughter are dead, and so far I don't even have the cold comfort of locating their bodies." His voice rose in pitch, trembling suspiciously. "Did you find Regina's remains over at the railroad depot?"

Thomas' knees wobbled. The Pennsylvania Railroad Depot was one of the new morgues that had been set up that day. "I haven't been there yet—is she . . ."

"I'm sorry, son," Cyrus' voice was getting thinner and thinner. "I'm pretty sure it was her. Her face was not," he cleared his throat, "in good shape, she must've been hit by something big, but I think it was her. I left her name with the morticians, and told them you would probably come by and verify my identification."

Thomas felt dizzy. No, oh, no. It couldn't be her. Victor thought he had seen her, alive . . . .

He vaguely felt Cyrus put his arms around him, barely heard the other man break down into sobs. He realized his own face was wet, his eyes were stinging.

He had no idea how long they'd stood there, both of them feeling too weak to let go.

They finally parted, and looked at each other without embarrassment. "I need to go see," Thomas said simply.

"She was one amazing lady. I'm sorry, Thomas."

"Thank you, Cyrus."

As he made his way toward the depot the fatigue of the last two days seemed to settle upon him. He hadn't noticed until now how much he hurt. Every inch of him ached with injury or from his unaccustomed labors. Carrying the weight of all his fears, he resolutely trudged onward.

****

The Pennsylvania Railroad Depot was swarming with people. Besides being a morgue, it was also a relief station. Neighbors from other towns were sending supplies for distribution, or were coming themselves to help the blighted city. Everyone seemed to congregate at the station as they sought aid or the local undertakers, hospital, or cemeteries.

The morgue part of the station was as busy as the rest. It took Thomas a long time to attract the attention of someone who knew what was going on. A system, of sorts, was falling into place: the undertakers were busy in the back of the station, while the less knowledgeable in mortuary science were closer to the door recording descriptions of the bodies that continued to arrive.

A harried man with graying hair helped Thomas find Cyrus' identification of Regina. "Waring. Waring. Yeah. They took her to the back a little while ago."

Thomas anxiously asked to be taken "back." He needed to see her for himself one last time.

"I've got a family member here for Waring."

The undertaker didn't even look up from the body he was bending over. "Waring—which one's that?"

Thomas cleared his throat. "A woman in her forties, long black hair, black eyes."

"We finished with her an hour ago, I'd guess. They must have her at the cemetery by now." The man looked up at Thomas sympathetically. "I don't know that you'll want to—well, her face was pretty badly smashed up. Mr. Elder was pretty sure it must be her."

Thomas felt a growing panic inside. "I don't care. I want to see for myself."

The man nodded, and looked back down at his work. "They've probably taken her up to Prospect Hill."

Thomas asked where the coffins were staged when they left the room. They pointed—but Thomas didn't see where. He had just caught sight of the body that was lying on the mortician's table.

It was Charles.

He stood, transfixed, staring into his best friend's face. It was smiling, peaceful, and, thank goodness, intact.

"I'm sorry," the undertaker broke into his reverie gently. "Can you identify this man?"

"Charles McKay," Thomas answered automatically. "My best friend."

He heard the man scramble for a pencil. "Can you tell me his age and occupation?"

Thomas looked at the man. "You're not from around here, are you?"

"Philadelphia. Since we have family here, I thought I should come help."

Thomas nodded. "He's a few years older than me—I think he's in his early forties. He's an iron manufacturer—he owned the iron works here."

"You wouldn't know if he's got any family still here?"

"His wife and children are still alive. I guess I'll have to go tell them." Thomas heard his own voice, but he felt like he wasn't connected to it.

"Thank you, sir. We're pretty busy, but I guess we can let you have a moment, if you'd like . . . ."

"Thank you, but no. You do what you have to do." He swallowed hard. "Which way did you say the coffins are?"

The undertaker pointed, he murmured his thanks, and hurried out behind the railroad station.

Empty coffins were everywhere. Thoughtful donors must have sent a shipment in, or else some very enterprising locals had been extremely busy. Perhaps both.

He didn't know how long he stood staring around him. He came to himself when four men calmly walked past him to the window of the mortician's room. Charles' body was passed through the window. The four men slid it through the window with practiced efficiency, then lowered it gently into an empty coffin waiting beside the window.

Thomas turned his head and hurried away. He didn't want to see anymore.

Thomas approached a lad, who was busily pounding bent nails straight, no doubt for fastening coffin lids. "Excuse me," Thomas had to repeat himself twice, the boy was so immersed in his task. He pointed at the stack of coffins, lidded and awaiting their trip to a cemetery. "Where do these go from here?"

The boy nodded with his head. "They've been carrying them that way," he said. "Once they're clear of all this, someone's got a team that's hauling them up Prospect Hill."

There was no sign at the moment of any of the pall bearers. "Will someone be back soon?"

The lad shrugged. "Should be. They keep comin'." To illustrate the point, two men went past, carrying an empty coffin.

Thomas paced alongside the stacks of waiting coffins, his eyes scanning the hills for returning pall bearers. He had to talk to them. He'd help them carry one of the coffins, and see if he could get a ride with the driver up to this cemetery. He only hoped he didn't have to beg someone at the graveyard to unbury her.

It had only been minutes since he'd stepped outside of the railroad station morgue. But it already felt like hours. He started to sweat. He had to find her. Had to.

He looked at the stacks of coffins, waiting to make the journey over the ruins and up the hill. There were an awful lot of them. What if . . .

He realized that there were marks scrawled on the coffin lids. He walked around where he could read better. "Unknown man." He looked over at the top coffin of the next stack. "Mrs. Mary Harris." More urgently, he moved to the next. "Agnes Baker." He quickly read through all the names on the top of the stacks, and wondered how on earth he was going to read the names buried under other coffins.

He was so absorbed in reading names he didn't even see the returning pall bearers. A short, stocky man in a striped shirt tapped him on the shoulder as he was trying to figure out how to slide the top coffin over, hopefully enough to see the writing underneath.

"Have some care for the dead, mister," the stocky man admonished him in tones that brooked no argument. "What are you doing?"

Thomas was too frantic to care. "You've got to help me," he begged. "The undertaker thought he put my—my wife in one of these about an hour ago. He told me to look up on Prospect Hill, but what if she's still here . . . . I've got to see for myself."

Three other men joined the first at that point. All of them stood around Thomas, staring at him for a moment. "If you can help me find her, I'd be happy to help you haul these over the hill."

Two of the men wordlessly slid the top coffin off the first stack. Another man said gruffly, "It would be nice if someone knew where his family was, for certain."

Coffin after coffin was lifted, or slid over, to reveal another penciled name. There were far too many unknowns—but the bodies needed to be buried, identified or not. Entire families had been wiped out, in some cases. There were plenty of strangers in town—there might not be anyone *to* identify the body.

They were almost through the entire wall of waiting coffins, when the men lifted a child-sized coffin off the top of a stack, and there, in pencil, were the words. "Regina Waring." Thomas stared at them. No. Oh, no. Finding her coffin had been his only thought. He hadn't realized how terrible it would be once he actually found it.

"Mr. Waring." Thomas didn't realize at first they were talking to him. Oh, of course. He'd said she was his wife, and her name was on the coffin . . . . "Mr. Waring?"

"I'm sorry, yes?" Thomas blinked hard and looked at the pall bearer who was offering him the lad's hammer.

"Do you want to—or would you like me to? It looks like there's only four nails in it . . ."

"You do it," Thomas choked out. "Please."

It only took the man a few skillful tugs to pull the four nails halfway out of the coffin lid. Another man got on the other side, then the two of them looked at Thomas. "Ready?" They asked him.

Thomas nodded.

The men lifted the coffin lid, and carried it away from the box. Thomas took a deep breath, and looked inside.

The hair was black, flowing loose in tresses to her waist. The mortician was right. Her face had been hit with something heavy, or rapidly-moving. It wasn't recognizable. At least she'd probably died instantly. Her hands were free of jewelry, and Thomas regretted deeply that he hadn't at least been able to give her an engagement ring. She ought to at least have had that.

He stared at the woman's body, with a shock of realization. It wasn't her. It wasn't Regina.

The corpse in front of him was wearing striped stockings, frilly drawers, a locket on a chain that had miraculously not been torn from her neck when her skirt had been torn from her body. She was also wearing a green and beige plaid bodice with a lace collar and cuffs—which were remarkably clean. She was not wearing Regina's clever "Surprise Dress."

It wasn't her.

Thomas wept with relief. "It's not her."

One of the men put a comforting grip on his shoulder. "That's right. Remember what she was like before. She must've been a looker."

Thomas shook off the gruff but friendly comforting hand. "No—it's not her. That's not my wife's dress. She was wearing a gray travel dress, not that. This isn't her."

Everyone dropped their eyes, looking decently away from the now-nameless lady. The two men who had taken off the lid carefully replaced it. "Dreadfully sorry, ma'am," Thomas murmured, but loud enough for the other four men to hear. "We never would have dreamed of disturbing you, but I thought you were someone else. Rest in peace."

"Amen," another one of the men murmured when Thomas finished his apology.

The man with the hammer replaced the nails in the lid, while another one found a stub of a pencil, and scratched out Regina's name. Another "Unknown" joined the ranks of Unknowns waiting in their boxes along the railroad platform.

Thomas turned away. It wasn't her. He knew Regina must be alive. He just knew it. Somewhere in this wreck of a town. Maybe Victor's "lady" was her. Maybe not—Thomas was a pretty common name. She was a native of Johnstown—maybe somebody here would only know her by her maiden name. He didn't even know what her maiden name was.

He'd find her. Somewhere, somehow, he'd find her. Alive *or* dead. If he didn't find her today, well, then, he'd find her tomorrow. Or the day after. But he wasn't leaving Johnstown until he did. Resolutely, he squared his shoulders and turned to resume the search.

Finis

About the Author

Jeanette Watts couldn't help but notice that all romances seemed to be set in the American West or the South. A staunch Yankee girl, she asked what is unromantic about the North or the East? After living for four years in Pittsburgh, and falling deeply in love with southwestern Pennsylvania, she found it the perfect location for a love story.

Besides writing, she is also a dance instructor, an inveterate seamstress, the artistic director for several dance companies, an actress, and a history buff. Wealth and Privilege took her 10 years to write, because she felt the research needed to be thorough. Everything from big events and famous people to little details like dog breeds and women's fashions have been carefully researched.